SHIPMASTER

Serafino Ciccolanti, a young ship's officer with a strong inferiority complex and a genius for making enemies, suddenly finds himself Acting Captain of the liner *San Roque*. In the midst of a hurricane, he is forced to battle with both the elements and a hostile ship's company. Among those caught in the violence of the storm are a group of emigrants to Australia who spear-head a mutiny, a predatory female, a British submarine commander, and the ship's second officer, who allows his loath-ing of Ciccolanti to smother his nautical judgment.

In this merciless pitting of people against people and people against the sea, Gwyn Griffin unfolds a powerful tale of a young man caught between the demands of cap-taincy and the shoals of human frailty.

by the same author

THE OCCUPYING POWER
BY THE NORTH GATE
SONS OF GOD

GWYN GRIFFIN

Shipmaster

Collins
FONTANA BOOKS

First published 1961
First issued in Fontana Books 1963
Second Impression, February 1964

The publishers are grateful to Sir George Rostrevor Hamilton and Messrs William Heinemann, Ltd., for permission to reproduce the poem " Ship Master" from " Collected Poems and Epigrams "

Printed in Great Britain
Collins Clear-Type Press
London and Glasgow

Ship Master

Lean ship, what pilot he
Harries thus mad
The long, moon-molten, iron sea ?

One who in equal great
Derision had
Iniquitous birth, unbending fate ;

And having still a mind
For ghostly wars
With his peer, the ocean-mastering wind,

Writes now with tottering mast
Among fixed stars
His own proud future's proud forecast.

G. ROSTREVOR HAMILTON

I

All the time he was shaving he worried about the cost of the dinner. You could hardly feed eight people, even if three of them were children, for less than eight hundred lire each. Over four thousand—twice as much as he had saved on his epaulettes—and then there would be the wine. He wondered briefly whether he might get a two-litre bottle filled at the corner shop beyond the cobbler's and take it along with them, then saw in his mind's eye the faces of the waiters and the other diners at the Four Swords Restaurant, and knew he could not. At that moment he came as near to anger as the long tiring day, the foolish improvidence of his family, worry about the future and the nagging pain in his foot could bring him. In the gilt-framed mirror the gold-flecked brown eyes narrowed slightly and lost their usual mildness, the long mouth hardened, accentuating the almost adolescent gauntness of a face which still bore, at twenty-six, an odd look of weary childhood. Four thousand was out of the question—the figure would be closer to eight if they all had their way. And they might have lived reasonably well for nearly a week on that.

If he had been quick—if, for instance, he'd said that he was having a farewell dinner with D'Angelis—that eight thousand could have been saved. And once again his mind started to juggle wearily with figures it knew too well—the rent of the four rooms in the Vicolo Re Galantuomo, the cost of electricity, gas, the family's food. They were not managing well enough, they would have to do much better in the future. Why did Vittoria's pension always seem to disappear without trace? And Salvatore—why couldn't he contribute more? Another thousand a week would still leave him a thousand for pocket-money. Then there were Silvio—surely an intelligent, sturdy twelve-year-old could get some sort of part-time out-of-school job? But Silvio was too intelligent, too sturdy, that was half the trouble, he thought grimly as he wiped Salvatore's borrowed razor on a damp and sticky towel.

The heat this evening! It seemed to strike at him from the white-washed walls, to press down on his shoulders from the low curves of the vaulted ceiling. They needed an electric fan—fifteen or sixteen thousand lire at the least; perhaps after this voyage he could afford one, only then, of course, it would be winter and an electric fire would be more useful. Winter meant fuel bills; last year. . . . Sighing abruptly, he turned and found that Simone had his clean white shirt on the floor and was fingering the epaulettes. "Give that here!" But the child took no notice of him and, leaning down, he gently released the grasp of the small hands and looked around for some substitute plaything. There was only the cardboard box with the Cellophane panel which had contained the bottle of liqueur he had bought for Vittoria two days ago. He thrust it into his brother's hands, and as he did so the door opened and there they all were under the yellow electric light in the passage, laughing, chattering, spilling over into the cobbled alley beyond, excited at the prospect of a meal outside this room, pleased with themselves and this moment in which they lived, never thinking of to-morrow.

Salvatore, a narrow-hipped, lanky eighteen-year-old in black jeans and a vivid green shirt, his beaky, vulpine face alight with sly amusement as he teased Mamma, red-faced, fat and chuckling, in her inevitable black. Rachele, sallow, dark-eyed, her usually tragic expression changed to one of mild content as she heaved her heavy, drooling baby higher in her thin arms. Chiara, spotless and polished, her dark hair in prim pigtails, her grubby cotton frock changed for a gleaming white party dress of starched muslin and bows, nothing but her sharp, glittering black eyes to betray her as the yelling little virago of the alleys she was by day. Aunt Vittoria, in an ancient costume of faded puce, swaying gently on her spindly legs, grinning and purring like a cat watching a milk-bowl descend from a table, while beyond her Silvio, square and tough, his brown face no more than half washed, thrust his grubby hands arrogantly into the pockets of his over-tight denim shorts. Neapolitans, all of them—for years past, and now, presumably, for ever. The younger ones had never known anything except this huge, sprawling city, and it was doubtful if Mamma would really go back to Certaldo even if the chance ever presented itself. And yet to him the small, quiet town far away in the north—Boccaccio's town, with its old castle on the hill—had always been home. Naples—never! He feared and hated it.

"Serafino, *carissimo*!" Mamma pushed past Salvatore into the hot little room and seized him by the shoulders. "Ah—you are ready, then." She eyed the second-hand epaulettes with deep pleasure. "Three bars! A chief officer already, at twenty-six! You will be a captain before you are thirty."

"And then you can take us all to live in a palace on Vomero," added Salvatore from the doorway with the nonchalant mockery under which he hid the mixture of envy and affection he felt for his eldest brother. "No." Chiara fiddled primly with her necklace of pink glass beads. "I would prefer a house on the Via Foria because——"

"The Piazza Municipio, down by the docks," grunted Silvio, automatically at variance with his sister.

"If we are going to move," Rachele whined, "why not the sea? Bathing and paddling would be good for Sandro. Positano—or perhaps Amalfi."

"We're not going to move." For a moment Serafino eyed them bleakly, a small thin figure, in his starched white drill, erect despite his crippled foot. Not one of them had so much as mentioned Certaldo. "Anyway, no one gets money to buy houses, let alone palaces, in the Flotta Soto, except Don Ildefonso."

But they were not listening to him—they never did. They were pushing out into the Vic' Re Galantuomo now, laughing and shouting as if they were a whole bus-load of trippers on an excursion. And following them into the hot narrow alley, with Simone's small sticky hand confidently grasping his thumb, Serafino felt his exasperation fade and dwindle imperceptibly into a weary, amused fatalistic affection for this happy, raucous family, stupidly feckless, unthinkingly, innocently selfish, who depended upon him and took everything he could give them—everything he had—and waited expectantly for more like a lot of eager nestlings with gaping beaks.

The walls of the old houses, their cracked and grimy stucco peeling leprously in the heat, steepled up on either side of the Alley of the Gentleman King and seemed to lean out over it—not threateningly, but with a benign, dirty affection. At eye-level they were covered with advertisement posters: "*Ferro China,*" "*Birra Peroni,*" Fernet Branca's eagle on its sunset globe, Energol's black, red-tongued snakes; then, next to the door of Dr. Gallifuoco (*Emerroidi e Varici*), a line of five identical placards advertising the military academy of Modena. Serafino glanced up at them with fascinated revulsion. From each a dark, broad-shouldered, blue-uniformed youth with a slyly prurient Neapolitan grin jeered down, hand on sword-hilt, thinking of indecencies. Then, out of the corner of his eye, he noticed something odd about the child holding his hand, and turned abruptly. Simone's head had suddenly become elongated, faceless and square; the cardboard box with the Cellophane panel had become a spaceman's helmet and the child was grimacing through it at a slatternly chicken which, tethered by a length of string to Dr. Gallifuoco's door, was eating cold spaghetti from a scrap of green newspaper on the flagstones. "You can't come out with that thing on your head." He tried to remove it, but Simone pulled hard down with both hands and, as usual, he gave up the struggle with a shrug.

At the end of the alley, set back under its heavy porch, the side door of the Church of Christ Crucified was a great black mouth in the decaying wall. As his family passed it, Serafino saw them move swiftly into the dark entrance and then, one at a time, stand on tiptoe, reach up a hand to touch something, and as quickly emerge. He knew what they were doing and the corners of his mouth turned down. Neapolitan superstition: magic playing almost visibly like soft lightning around wooden crosses, wax images of the Madonna, dusty relics of saints in glass cases; the quick genuflection at a certain spot in the street opposite an almost obliterated picture, the low, garbled mutter and the furtively crossed fingers. It had always been like that in the city—but not with him; not since his tenth year when God had betrayed him and the whole gilded, coloured world of saints and angels had collapsed into a heap of tarnished rubble at his feet.

Yet as he too came abreast of the dark doorway he felt an unusual compulsion to look in. High up, its head and wrenched, agonised arms almost lost in the dusk and cobwebby grime of the porch roof, a great wooden crucifix loomed against the wall. Its feet alone were just within reach, and the pitted old wall below them was covered with little wax hands and arms, small tarnished metal hearts and holy pictures, mostly bearing the legend "*Per grazia ricevuta.*" God fixed to a dingy wall at the corner of a dirty alley, consoled for an eternity of pain by little gifts of coloured postcards and cheap tin decorations. And gazing up, staring into blackness, trying to make out the sad, dusky features far above him, Serafino felt a sudden pity, sorrowful and oddly personal, as if the tortured wooden figure had been some friend of his whom he had known long ago. Slowly he raised his arm, lifted himself on the ball of his left foot and touched the wooden toes, worn and polished by countless fingertips. Then he was outside, blinking in the bright, neon-flashing lights of the Via Cirillo, with Simone, a squat, mad little figure becowled in his cardboard box, trotting beside him.

The Four Swords Restaurant was on the corner of the Via Alessandrio Poerio. It had promoted itself from being a *trattoria* some twelve months ago by the simple expedients of adding a few gilt-framed mirrors to its walls, half a dozen potted palms to its floor, and putting up its prices. Salvatore had a friend who was a part-time waiter there, but this evening, when two tables had been put together for the family on the pavement beside the main doorway, it was explained that Oreste was not on duty. Salvatore was downcast, Oreste would have seen that they all got larger portions than the other diners, thus reflecting credit on his friend. It was credit Salvadore could well do with before telling his elder brother that he had paid the first instalment on a motor-scooter. He glanced, sidelong and smiling, at Serafino sitting thin, silent, his brown eyes a little morose, his lips compressed, at the head of the table. For six years now Serafino had been the head of the family, and for most of those years the source of at least three-quarters of its income. Yet somehow—it was one of the strangest things about him—the long effort to earn and save, the weight of such early responsibility on those narrow shoulders, did not appear to have aged him or changed him at all. To-night, wearing his chief officer's epaulettes, he seemed to his younger brother to look no older than when he had first gone to sea as an apprentice. There had always, surely, lain upon him that air of patient, over-burdened childhood. The broad-browed, triangular face, the slightly hollow cheeks, the wide, stubborn mouth above the small chin—they had been the same since early boyhood; and his arms, deeply bronzed below the shirt-sleeves, had the slender bones and the smooth skin, dusted with fine gold hairs, of adolescence.

Of course, as Serafino himself never forgot, he had in some ways been lucky. Ten years ago, in 1949, their father had been alive and there had still been some money in the family: not much—and with the war but four years past times were brutally hard—but enough to pay a premium to a small shipping company, to send Serafino to sea in the scanty remains of Italy's mercantile marine, with a reasonably complete outfit of uniforms and equipment and even a very small amount of pocket-money. Yes, Serafino had been lucky, much luckier than the rest of them; and now—a chief officer. Emboldened, Salvatore said, "By the way, I'm getting a Lambretta."

Serafino stopped drinking the fish soup which was nowhere near as good as they got at home—full of bones and rubbery rings of cuttlefish—and stared at his brother. "Did Mamma say you could?"

Salvatore shrugged, his narrow face sulky and a little defiant in the flicker of the pink-and-green neon swords above the restaurant's door. "It's my money."

"What you get of it. And it's only a temporary job you've got. You might be out of work again any day. Haven't you sense?"

"It'll last round till Christmas, at any rate. I know, because——"

"And what then, eh?" Serafino, who because of the family's total dependence upon him, lived in a chronic state of nervous fear for his own job, could never understand his younger brother's happy-go-lucky attitude towards employment. "Winter's a fine time to get thrown into the street—even if you can go home on a Lambretta!"

"If——" Salvatore pushed a spoon idly about among the fish bones on his plate—"if I'd had some proper training I might have been in a job where I could get a scooter—get a car if I wanted." His voice was low and he had even managed to contrive a hint of tears. The result was as he had expected; Serafino sighed quickly, smiled, and put out a hand under the table, touching his knee. "All right then, you can have your scooter. I'll send you something to help when we get to Sydney. I can get an advance there."

And that was the end of any hope that Salvatore would contribute another thousand a week to the family's expenses. But it was natural that a boy of eighteen should want a motor-scooter; probably some of his friends had them and he felt left out. Besides, it would help to get him out of this baking, stinking city sometimes. For a moment Serafino had a vision of Salvatore, with Silvio behind him, driving out through the green country of the Campania among the vineyards under the summer sky. But he knew that it was much more likely that Salvatore only wanted the scooter to *far figura*—to show off. He would zoom and stutter round the city's myriad squares and alleys, revving the engine shatteringly on corners, swaying, skidding, weaving in and out of the traffic, playing the new, dangerous game of *caccia la macchina* with a gang of other boys similarly mounted. Still, if it gave him pleasure that was what really counted; there had not been much of that for any of them since Papa died and they came to live in the Vic' Re Galantuomo. And even though they were really a Tuscan family, they had all, except himself, adopted Naples and Neapolitan ways and the Neapolitan philosophy that luxuries came before necessities and to-morrow could look after itself.

He heard Salvatore's voice, a little subdued and self-exculpatory. "I mean you *are* a chief officer now, after all."

"Yes, yes," chimed in Aunt Vittoria, dragging herself from a prolonged study of the menu and slopping wine liberally into her glass. "Of course he is! Chief Officer! Yes, and soon it will be Captain. Captain Ciccolanti! Ah, how proud your poor father would have been!" They were all looking at him now, beaming with admiring pleasure in the coloured neon light. From the corner of his eye he saw that people at neighbouring tables were smiling too. Even the waiter, moving round with plates of *fettuccine alla marinara,* was cocking an eye at him, grinning, hoping for a tip worthy of a master mariner.

"Listen." He glanced round the table, trying to collect their attention which had automatically reverted to the food. It was ridiculous; they had *fettuccine* practically every day at home, and yet there was Vittoria twining the long tomato-covered noodles on to her fork and thrusting them ravenously into her nearly toothless mouth as if they were a delicacy which she saw only one or twice a year. "Look—I'm *not* a chief officer yet! I've tried to explain that at least twice already. I'm not even on probation as a chief officer—not even on trial, do you understand?"

"But——" began Salvatore.

"Listen, can't you, for God's sake! I'm still second officer to D'Angelis on *San Ramòn.* That's my position and that's the pay I'm drawing—eighty thousand a month, just like always. What's happened is that last night Parodi, *San Roque's* chief officer, told his captain that he was leaving—at once. He'd got another job as second on—on an Italian ship."

Salvatore raised his dark eyebrows. "You mean he threw in a job as chief officer to take a job as second somewhere else? Without notice or anything?"

"He's got some influence somewhere—an uncle, I think.

He'll get much more pay, of course—steaming under the Italian flag; and leave and conditions are standardised—not like with us. Well, *San Roque's* got her new boats so she leaves to-night, and someone's got to go there. They were short of a deck officer before Parodi left, in any case. Their second officer, Bressan, has only been with the line three months, so they told D'Angelis I'd have to go—temporarily. There's no question of its being permanent; they didn't even send for me to the office until after midday. Even then they didn't seem sure."

Mamma, who had been listening with a frown of concentration on her round red face, said: "But if you do well why should they not make it permanent? They need a chief officer for this ship, do they not? This Parodi is not returning, after all."

Serafino glanced across at her briefly. "It's not likely. Don Ildefonso wants his chief officers to come from other lines—like his captains. Besides, he's old; he doesn't really approve of young officers at the top."

"This Don Ildefonso—he disapproves too much. I wish sometimes, *caro mio,* that you were with another line."

Serafino smiled, a wide, shy smile, affectionate yet holding no hint of amusement, demanding no reciprocation. With the coloured neon lights glinting on his short-clipped pale-brown hair, he looked suddenly very young. "I've been with the Flotta Soto almost three years—nearly half the time it's been going. I don't know if I'd want to leave, even if I could." He frowned. "I suppose I would, though—if I could get on to an Italian ship. But there's no chance of that as things are—particularly after the *San Raphael* affair."

They were all on the next course now, except Simone sitting on Serafino's right and muddling his *fettuccine* about in the greasy tomato sauce, idling, making puddles among the serpentine yellow strands. Serafino glanced at his watch—nearly eight-fifteen. He should be on board in another hour—less, if possible. He wondered distractedly how to hurry the meal forward. "Come on, Simone. Eat up!"

"I've had enough."

Mamma looked across threateningly from her attack on a tough veal steak. "Eat it up, Simone! At once!"

Simone's small face darkened. All four brothers were apt at times to display a certain angry stubbornness—a Tuscan rather than a Neapolitan trait—but it was most apparent in the two youngest. "I want some meat! I've had enough pasta!" And as if to emphasise his last words he brought his spoon down hard into his plate. A shower of thin, oily tomato sauce spurted out across the table in all directions, spattering everyone. "Simone!" And then the family were on their feet, flourishing napkins, shouting apologies to the waiter and, because they were Italians, choking with laughter and berating Simone with a theatrical exuberance of mock fury.

Serafino alone sat still. The front of his shirt was spotted and mottled with yellow stains. He should be reporting on board *San Roque* in less than an hour and there was neither time to change nor anything to change into—his three other white shirts were still unpacked on the ship. Inside him a spring, which all day had been wound more and more tightly, broke at last. His narrow shoulders sagged hopelessly, he slumped back in his chair, his face empty of expression, one lax hand motionless on the wet tablecloth stained by Salvatore's overturned glass. Why should he go on trying? Everything was against him and always had been. A malicious fate moved before him along the path of life, strewing it with thorns and broken glass, arranging traps and pitfalls at every turning. No one helped him; obstacles of every sort were placed in his way; more and more was demanded of him both by his family and his employer. Because he had worked hard and uncomplainingly in the Flotta Soto for three years, Don Ildefonso was making him take a more responsible job without any additional pay. And because of this his family rejoiced at the thought of spending still more of his meagre wages and wasting them on motor-scooters and meals in restaurants, where they laughed only, when his one clean uniform was ruined. No, they were merely disregarding him; they were laughing at Simone, who, pleased yet slightly embarrassed at making himself the centre of attention, had put on his cardboard helmet and surveyed the confusion he had wrought in safe anonymity through the tinted Cellophane.

Mamma and Aunt Vittoria noticed the state of Serafino's shirt simultaneously. They flung themselves upon him with cries and cluckings, brandishing napkins and water jugs. He submitted apathetically. His shirt was ruined: they could not make it any worse.

The progress of the meal, slowed already, was drawn out still further by the arrival on the other side of the street of a great American Ford bearing Venezuelan number plates. The re-seated family regarded it with the open, admiring envy of true Neapolitans for all things flashy, large and opulent, and made guess after improbable guess at its cost, mileage per litre and owner's income. And of course it made Salvatore return to his perennial demand that they should all emigrate to South America. It was no use telling him of the true state of the continent; of the soaring prices, the economic and political instability and the squalor of the hideously overcrowded cities: the car on the other side of the road came from South America and was a shining symbol of the wealth and status he so passionately desired. He had to accept his elder brother's statements, for Serafino had been on the Naples-Venezuela run for the last three years and had been in La Guayra as recently as seven weeks ago, but he did so with a sulky resentment that did not disguise his disbelief.

The couple from the car, middle-aged and prosperous, came over to the restaurant, sat at a nearby table and ordered coffee; with them was an American soldier in his pale, stiffly starched summer uniform. He was young and only a private, but his pay, while stationed in Italy, would be several thousand lire a day. Next year Salvatore would be drafted for his eighteen months' military service; he would receive one hundred and fourteen lire a day—not enough to buy a packet of even the cheapest cigarettes. The American and Italian soldiers throughout the country were said to be comrades-in-arms defending a common ideal, a common belief in democracy and freedom—but it was not always easy to remember this when Italian soldiers walked behind Americans in order to pick up the butts which their comrades threw into the gutter.

The sight of the soldier, reminding Salvatore of his approaching ordeal, made him still more sulky, but then he remembered that he was going to have his scooter and the meal ended on a more cheerful note. Serafino paid the bill quickly—as he had feared it came to just over eight thousand lire—with his wallet on his knees below the table so that no one should see how little it contained, and then they were jostling down the wide, crowded street towards the tram terminus on the Piazza Garibaldi.

Flashing neon lights, blazing shop windows, the shattering roar of motor traffic, three-quarters of which was made up of open two-stroke engines, unbaffled, unmuted, meeting in a whirlpool of exhaust gases about the wilted formal flower-beds surrounding the great statue; political slogans slashed in white and red across the dirty walls—"*Libertàs,*" "*Trieste e l'Istria sono Italiane!*"—and always the twisted sickle and hammer of the communists, indistinguishable at a distance from the old German swastika. And on this hot August night the Piazza was even more densely crowded than at midday. There was not a table free at any of the cafés, where the older men sat with open coats, the younger with open shirts, before their tiny coffee cups and the accompanying glasses of water. It was, like all crowds in southern Italy, predominantly male, though here and there the bright dress of a woman tourist or a girl whose family tolerated progressive ideas, gleamed under the glittering lights. Soldiers in pale khaki drill, sailors of half a dozen nationalities in more or less identical white, wandered slowly down the table-cluttered pavements looking for women, beer, or merely somewhere to sit, while, out of range of the brighter street lights, gangs of boys in striped T-shirts and blue jeans—the international uniform of mid-twentieth-century youth—laughed and jeered and scuffled in small tight-knit groups against the towering advertisement hoardings. Carabinieri sauntering in pairs—one to read and one to write as the old saying was—kept an eye on the military and the blue-jeaned gangs while among them all, flitting bat-like under the high swan-necked lamps, priests and nuns moved quickly, unsmilingly through the crowd upon their own mysterious, purposeful errands.

So at last, in a few minutes now, he would be free again—or at least in brief transit from the servitude of his family to the servitude of his employer. And now that it was time to make the change he felt strangely reluctant. Ever since *San Ramòn* had come in for her re-fit a month ago he had been at the beck and call of the family in the Vicolo Re Galantuomo. There had been the arrears of rent to straighten out with the landlord and the haggling and threats necessary to make him replace the stove. There had been the abortive attempt to find a better job for Salvatore; the interview with the doctor who had pronounced Rachele's Sandro to be an incurable defective; the interminable confusion of Vittoria's pension; the question of school for Simone; the business of Chiara and the convent outing, and the affair of the bicycle Silvio was accused of stealing. Day after day the attempt to hurry through his work, the increasingly embarrassing requests to Captain D'Angelis for extra time off, the tram from the Darsena Armando Diaz up the Corso and the quick walk down the Via Cirillo—and then the round of listening to complains, explanations, arguments and requests in an atmosphere of heat and flies and cooking food.

But now that he was really going, even though it was back to the sea that he loved, it seemed somehow different—not like that at all. To-morrow there would be no "*Buon' giorno, Signor Ciccolanti*" from the old beggar at the corner of the Vic' Re Galantuomo, no half genial, half contemptuous wave from the communist cobbler at No. 2, no mildly condescending nod from Dr. Gallifuoco feeding his chicken with scraps of his breakfast outside No. 10—most of all, no glad welcome from Mamma as he came to his own home. For it was his home, hate it at times as he did, until the day of the fading promise, long made to himself—the day they should all return to Certaldo.

They scurried across the roadway among the wheels of the hooting, stuttering cars and scooters and collected, a little breathlessly, under the ragged palm trees beside the entrance to the underground, Gabinetto di Pagamento, whose foul breath hung, a fetid miasma, above the short ventilators poking through the littered flower-beds. Then, on the thin-legged hoardings edging the nearest pavement, he saw it again—the poster advertising the military academy at Modena which had leered down at him from the walls of the Vic' Re Galantuomo. And perhaps because his tiredness, the heat of the night, and the confused emotions of parting from his difficult family had induced a feeling of slight unreality, detached and a little hollow, the figure on the poster took on a new and wider significance. The blue uniform with its shako—a cheap imitation of a West Point cadet's—was surely some shoddy, ill-fitting affair run up hurriedly by a cut-price manufacturer, the sword was of tin, the gold braid of tarnished tinsel, there were only five lire in the trouser pocket—and the whole outfit was paid for by America as part of a doubtful, and therefore cheap, insurance policy. And the face above the uniform collar, the face wearing that sly, jeering, unconfident grin, seemed to say it knew all that—knew it perfectly well—was not fooled for a moment. For the second time that evening Serafino felt a stab of sorrowful pity for an image which, strangely, seemed to know him and be known to him.

He shuddered slightly, glad once more that he was getting

out to-night—getting away to the clean, ordered life of the wide sea-ways. In a month's time he'd be in Sydney, walking up George Street in the cool spring sunlight. There were recruiting posters there too, of course—he remembered them from the time he had first visited the city years ago—but they were plain and uninspired rather than ghoulishly sardonic. "Join the Forces and Keep Australia Strong," they suggested, mildly and without much hope, at street corners. But the Australians, who, despite their endemic drunkenness and outrageous national conceit, were practical enough in most matters, did not join the Forces—they were far too busy making easy money and living their old rackety lives —and no one bribed them to.

"Yes, of course I'll write, Mamma—like always. From Port Said, then Aden—and Colombo, too. And you—don't forget——" But they were all round him now, the women kissing him, the boys patting his shoulder, trying to take his hand. "I'll be back in October . . . Silvio, you behave while I'm away—see?" He pushed his hand affectionately through the boy's short stiff hair. "And Aunt Vittoria: if there's more difficulty about the pension—there shouldn't be, but if there is—you can write to me at the agent's office in Sydney. Salvatore——" He turned to find his brother seemingly engaged in conversation with an adolescent Alpini staggering under a huge suitcase, and an old hook-nosed lady in black whose ancient dachshund was sniffing among the wilted flowers at the base of the statue. Chiara said, "The soldier asked that old woman where the station was." She giggled, her bright eyes snapping. "He must be a fool—it's right in front of him across the square! But she just stared at him as if—as if he had said something nasty. So Salvatore——"

A screech from Rachele cut her short. "The tram! Your tram, Serafino, *caro*—here it comes!"

And here it came, glaring with light, groaning slowly to a grinding halt. "Well, then——" He embraced Mamma again, quickly, before she began to cry, hearing, as on how many previous occasions, her tearful, "*Carissimo,* come back safe and soon. *Gesù te guarde!*"

He was on the step of the tram, jostled by a group of large German youths in scanty hiking-clothes and hung about with bulging rucksacks and guitars. "*Addio!* Till October!"

And then the bell clanging, the conductor's hand, polite but firm, pulling him into the doorway.

Turning, he caught a last sight of the little group of people to whom he belonged and who belonged to him smiling, and waving under the golden glow of the tall lamps, while high up, looming blackly against the soft blue of the southern night, the gigantic statue of the Liberator, poncho-draped, head sunk on chest, hands clasped on sabre-hilt, brooded over them.

2

" Guiseppe Garibaldi." Reading the simple inscription on the great plinth, Countess Zapescu sniffed contemptuously and reflected that if Karoly had been here he would have spat—spat quickly, delicately, with an expression of extreme distaste, and then touched his lips with his handkerchief.

She would not do that: it would be unladylike, and besides, the *carabinieri* might see her. Meanwhile, however, Brown should make his puddle in the flower-bed at the base of the statue, right under the nose of the Liberator—bandit, adventurer, scoundrel!—and if anyone thought that the spot had been chosen at random he would be quite wrong. " *Vite, vite Brown! Mais tout de suite—et d'un seul coup, je t'en prie!*" She spoke loudly in French lest any passerby should mistake her for an Italian—like that stupid boy in his ridiculous hat with the eagle feather. Way to the station, indeed! He was plainly a peasant's son from some village in the north, probably a traitor from lands filched from the Empire in 1918. If that showy, vulgar youth in the green shirt had not butted in she would have sent him off up the Corso with enough instructions to keep him wandering about half the night, or until he fell dead over that absurd suitcase. She gave a sharp cackle of laughter at the thought, and Brown, having done what he should, wandered out of the flower-bed, wagging his tail. " *Enfin! Bon petit chien!*"

And now, since the shipping company was too mean to give them a meal on board before sailing, they would go and find somewhere to eat; there was bound to be some cheap place down one of those side streets off the Corso. She would have to carry Brown across the road. Creakingly, she bent and gathered the old dachshund into her arms; then, taking no notice of the traffic, she lurched out into the square. Brakes screamed, tyres whined and grated on the stones, a three-wheeled delivery van mounted the kerb at a perilous angle, while from all sides Italian voices volleyed abuse.

She smiled grimly under her huge beak of a nose and scurried quickly across and into a side street.

Towards the far end, on the corner of a darker, narrower alley, a dim, blistered sign over an open archway mumbled "*Bottigliere*" in almost illegible lettering. The old woman put Brown down on the cobbles, brushed a few brown hairs from her ancient black coat and skirt, and entered a low, vaulted cave, hacked apparently from a solid block of masonry. A few small tables, rows of dusty bottles, some great wine casks piled in the shadows, and a kerosene stove below a shelf of battered saucepans. There was no other custom and she went to a table at the back, under the inevitable dusty plaque of the Virgin, and raised her thick dark eyebrows at the young girl beside the stove. "Do you speak French?"

"I am sorry, no, signora."

"German, then?"

"I am sorry——"

"Ah, well, we must manage as best we can."

"The signora speaks very good Italian."

"Ha? No, no—not good. Not good at all. Now what have you to eat here?"

The girl put a small square of greasy cardboard on the wooden-topped table. Yes, as the Countess had thought, it was cheap—well, cheapish, for nothing was really cheap to-day. The soup would be best, and the pasta—meat was so expensive. But Brown naturally liked meat, though he was used to many other foods, poor old thing. If she had a chop she could give Brown the bone. She called to the girl and demanded to see all the chops in the establishment. It was plainly an unpopular request, and when three ragged, pallid pieces of meat were reluctantly produced on a cracked plate, she could well understand why. None the less, she chose the biggest, taking care that it had a reasonable bone, and sat back waiting while the girl lit the stove and started to cook.

Her last meal in Europe. Sixty-nine years were finishing to-night in Naples and it seemed so like dying, this feeling of things slipping away for the last time. People said that just before one died one's past life came back to one in vivid pictures like a cinema film, and in this last hour on its soil, Europe tugged at her desperately with memories. Memories of good times, memories of others that had not been so good but which, gilded with the retrospective light of far sunsets, seemed milder, less important.

Slumping unseeingly, unsightly, in the dirty little eating-house, an old woman now, ugly and very poor, she escaped to times that to her seemed as close as yesterday, when she had been none of those things. Klagenfurt at the beginning of the century and her father's tall house, smelling always of furniture polish, cigar-smoke and hothouse flowers. Fräulein Mohrbutter giving them piano lessons in the dark music-room, and through the heavily draped portière, the sight of rain splashing on to the glass walls of the conservatory and trickling down the long narrow panes behind the palms; the melancholy of the uncertain piano notes in the still house and the softness of the summer rain.

The relations, by blood and by marriage: Uncle Stefan, the Herr Hofrat as the servants respectfully called him, with his odd light laugh and quick black eyes; Uncle Otto, burly, dour, standing in the gas-lit hall, snow on the shoulders of his military cloak and on the top of his schapska; Aunt Sophie; Great-aunt Ermengilda—ghosts from the far distant past turning faces bearded, whiskered, framed in ringlets, asking accusingly, "Bella—what are you doing? Where are you going?"

Vienna in the winter of 1907: dances, the balls, meals in restaurants to the music of gipsy bands, the gilt-wheeled carriages of the Imperial family in the snowy streets and the men taking off their hats and the women curtseying from the pavements. Full gilt wheels for the Emperor and his immediate family; three-quarters gilt for the Archdukes and the Blood Imperial; and so on down to the minor cousins who, because Habsburg blood also ran in their veins, were allowed a quarter of the spokes gilded—and it was said that the Court circle referred to such carriages as "shabbies."

Looking up, the Countess scowled at a flyblown oleograph above the dirty stove—the Bersaglieri charging at Porta Pia. Soldiers, indeed! And she thought of Karoly in his blue-and-gold hussar's uniform. His face had been a little too broad for true aristocracy; those wide cheekbones had shown his Slavic blood, for though the Zapescus had been settled in Hungary for more than two centuries, they came originally from Roumania.

It had not been what to-day was known vulgarly as a "love-match." Papa and old Count Constantin had arranged it between them. But both she and Karoly had concurred contentedly enough in all the correct and long-drawn-out manœuvres of courtship, and when at last their elders had judged the time to be respectably right—when Karoly had come in with a huge bunch of roses, placed them in her lap with his quaint little bow, and said, "Bella dearest, will you marry me?"—they had both burst into peals of laughter and rushed outside into the frosty air and thrown snowballs at each other like small children.

The birth of Franz and five years of such happiness and pleasure before the war came, and Karoly, with a certain grim enjoyment, led his cavalry regiment through the mountains towards Trent with the firm intention of regaining the lost Italian provinces. She had never seen him again.

An era ended—not only for her but for Europe. The sun which had set in 1914 rose again four years later on a new age—a cold, bleak windy dawn. The Dual Monarchy, defeated, broke in two, and the Empire was taken apart like pieces of a jigsaw-puzzle and given away. Bitterly she saw Karoly's death proved vain. Far from the restoration of the lost provinces for which he had fought, a large section of Austrian territory was seized by triumphant Italy. Practically everyone was poor, many were ill and most were hungry. Filled with a melancholy restlessness, she had moved continually—accompanied always by one of a succession of small dogs, each of whom was christened with an English name as had been the custom in her youth—from place to place during the years in which Franz was growing up. Paris—Dresden—Zurich—Brussels—London for some months, but it was too wet—The Hague for a year, but it was too dull. Italy—she would not go there at all.

They were back in Vienna in the 'thirties, and Franz, an aimless, sullen, colourless young man suffering from headaches and chills, became involved with the Nazis in the Greater Germany movement—not deeply involved, for he was incapable of sustained enthusiasm, but he attended a few parades and once made a rather stupid speech in a tavern. He lived at home, unmarried, unsmiling, never very well. Had she done enough for him? Really loved him? No, she feared not. Her only son—almost her only living relation by then—yet she could never *know* him. He was not of the past, nor, it seemed, of the present—and it was unthinkable that he was the future. He lived in a limbo world of his own. Very quiet, hollow, like an empty, still, grey day in one of those short, undecided periods of the year that are neither of one season nor the next.

Then the new war. She was old now; she shrugged, staying

at home. Franz, wearing his brown uniform more often, stayed at home too. And soon it was rationing again, and no fuel, and ragged clothes and hungry faces in the streets. Fear, growing steadily greater, pervading the city like a colourless gas; and the autumn winds sighed, "*Die Russen kommen*"—and the winter winds screamed it.

She was cooking something in the kitchen that grey afternoon and Brown—no, Picture, Brown's mother—was watching her and sniffling hopefully when Franz came in, silently as usual. "Mutti—Mutti, you must leave here." He had stood cracking the knuckles of his cold, bony hands in the chill gloom of the basement kitchen. "You must get away to Switzerland. I have arranged it and you must leave to-night."

She had turned, looking closely at him. "And you, Franz? You are coming too?"

"No."

"But——" She was sure, then, that she had seen a gleam of horror in those pale-grey eyes—a flash like lightning over a dark, still sea.

"They would not let me. I—I have to stay."

They had said other things but she could not remember them—did not, perhaps, want to. He had seemed, after that first silent glare of terror, only morose and bored. On the way to the station he had complained fretfully of a cold coming on. Her last sight of him as the train steamed out had been of a thin man, prematurely aged, feeling disconsolately for something that he had lost in the pockets of his overcoat.

The Russians had found him taking his perpetual aspirin tablets in the bathroom—they thought it was poison and forced him to disgorge them, before leading him away to a limbo of their own making from which he had never returned.

So then she was quite alone and really poor. Paris, and a succession of cheap pensions and small furnished rooms, and bits of paper on which one worked out complicated sums in small change and made difficult decisions about a quarter of a kilo of sausages and whether to get one's shoes repaired. Picture died, but there was Brown then, golden, long-eared, happy and excited at life, loving his old mistress, jumping on to her bed in the early mornings and rousing her with sharp little barks, making a pleasant subject for conversation with strangers in the streets. "What a pretty little thing! How old is he, madame?" "He's two—aren't you, Brown? And I had his mother and grandmother as well, you know." But he was not so popular with landladies, of course. "You understand, Countess, it is not yourself, but the little dog . . ." Frau Willich had said almost tearfully, on the balcony of her pretty little chalet out at Saint-Germain. And, " Either the dog goes or you both do," had growled grim, grey Mlle. de la Bouheyre in her tall house of the Place Gambetta. So—on to somewhere else, and on again.

And the years had passed, and there were good times when one walked with Brown in the parks in bright summer, and rather dull, unpleasant times when one sat with him in one's lap before a small gas-fire in winter. She had always assumed that, somehow, there would be just enough money to last her lifetime, but slowly and unwillingly she had been forced to realise that this was a delusion. Then, last winter, she had met the old German prince again in the Halles. He had been, she remembered, sitting at a common bench drinking onion soup, bowed, hollow-cheeked and grey, over his bowl. " Ah, Madame!" He had risen, smiling shyly, raising his old-fashioned Homburg, obviously searching his memory for her name.

" Prince—how delightful to see you! So you have left Basle?"

" Yes—yes, I have."

And looking down, she had seen the string-bag of vegetables at his worn shoes and had guessed at once that the guest-house where they had first been introduced years before had become too costly for him.

They had met often after that, generally, as if by tacit appointment, at a certain spot in the Parc Rousseau, and after a short stroll for Brown's benefit, they parted at the gates with an almost old-world ceremony of bows and handshakes—two elderly people in shabby clothes getting in the way of the crowd.

Then, one cold, still day in very early spring, the Prince had casually mentioned the name of Dorothea von Reichenbach. The Countess was overjoyed: Dorothea had been one of her dearest friends. " But of course! She was a bridesmaid at my wedding. She was only a child then—twelve or thirteen. How pretty she looked that day! Dear Dorothea! Where is she now?"

She was, the prince understood, in Australia—in Melbourne.

" Mel——?"

" Melbourne, Countess. It is a large city, I believe. One of the two largest in that country."

"What an outlandish place to live! But Dorothea was always eccentric. I remember once—you know how her uncle, old Max, used to drink?—she took three white cats and dyed one pink and one green and one bright blue . . ."

Yet later she had written to Dorothea and received a prompt and delighted answer. Throughout the clear days of spring and the glowing days of that hot, brilliant June they had sent their letters round the great curve of the globe, and by mid-July the Countess found herself looking for a cheap passage to Melbourne, where, it appeared, Dorothea would be overjoyed to share her apartment in St. Kilda with her old friend. She was shortly intending to open a small flower shop and Bella would be welcome to assist her. They could perhaps run it as partners in business. . . .

It was, of course, a little ridiculous to start work for the first time at sixty-nine, just when everyone else had left off, but so many things were necessary in these peculiar days that one hardly found it surprising. At any rate, she and Brown would eat well and, sharing Dorothea's flat, she would have company. She had accepted the situation with an excited complacency, as if a stroke of luck, still somewhat nebulous but long-expected, had arrived at last.

Yet now, on this last night upon its soil, Europe tugged at her with old memories—tugged so strongly that she felt bemused and unreal and torn with contrary and warring emotions. Time had such curious stretches, such depths this evening, and always at the back of her mind the voices—Karoly's? Franz's?—warned on and on, telling her that she was making a grave mistake. She refused to listen, almost angrily demanding their silence. They had done with life; by what right did they clamour to her who still lived? Let them leave her alone to have her last few years of peace with her old dog and her old friend far away across the world. In any case, the arrangements were all made, she had somehow scraped together the money for her passage and paid it—there was no going back now.

3

The evening was full of memories: staring down unseeingly over the myriad sparkling lights of the city and port which stretched out below the terraced restaurant high up on Vomero, Roger Lannfranc recalled his last visit to Naples less than three years ago with a flotilla from Malta. It had been a courtesy visit, a naval occasion; flags, bands, the flat banging of saluting cannon, glittering medals on white summer uniforms. . . . *Sting-ray* had moved slowly into the harbour, her big diesels throbbing silently, her crew ranged at attention on the fore- and after-casing, a petty officer up in the prow behind her jack, her jumping-wire bright with fluttering bunting. And he, her captain, standing on the bridge in the conning-tower with his officers ranged behind him, his right hand rigid at his cap peak acknowledging the dipping tricolours of the Italian ships, the thudding gun salutes. . . .

"*Roger!* Wake up, for goodness' sake! How many more times——?"

"What——?"

"Do you want any coffee? The man has asked you twice already."

"Oh—yes, I suppose so." With a quick frown of irritation on his handsome, florid face, Roger glanced from his wife to the smiling waiter at his elbow. "Yes, coffee. And two cognacs. You'd like one, Bron?"

"Well, yes, I suppose so. If you don't think it will hurt the sprog."

"Won't do it any harm. It's probably got submariner's ruin in its veins—if it has veins at this stage." Roger smiled briefly and then slumped back into his chair, while his face, heavy-jowled and sullen, became vacant of all expression.

From the other side of the small table Bronwen watched him with growing irritation. A small, dark-haired young woman whose clear, precise voice and expensively severe clothes lent her an air of decision and formidability, she was becoming bored and annoyed by her husband's increasingly frequent habit of sombre abstraction. Roger was only bodily in Naples, in spirit she guessed that he was back at Portsmouth, in Fort Blockhouse, either reliving the past or inventing a might-have-been future. Roger had been out of the Navy for over twelve months—one among scores of officers prematurely but compulsorily retired in the sweeping naval cuts and economies of the past three years—but ever since the failure of his first civilian job, his habit of day-dreaming himself back into the Service had become worse. At any time of the day when he was not actually doing something—and as he had been unemployed for the last six months that really meant all day—his mind seemed automatically to slip through time and space to Dolphin, the great Portsmouth submarine base, or perhaps more often to the control room of H.M.S. *Sting-ray,* his last command. He would sit in a chair, relaxed, smoking, gazing unseeingly out of a window, only returning to the present with an irritable effort. "Yes, yes, Bronwen, I heard you. I *was* listening."

But listening with much less than half his attention—in the same way as he put much less than half his energy into the business of starting once more to earn a living. Sometimes Bronwen believed that he consciously adopted a negative attitude towards the future and his duties as a husband and a prospective father, in some queer way believing that thus he was revenging himself upon society for the injustice it had done him—unconsciously of, or more probably indifferent to, the harmful effects upon himself and his wife.

Plenty of other officers had been prematurely retired from the Service—some of them almost certainly more able than Roger—and had managed without too much difficulty to adjust themselves to civilian life. Perhaps they had not been as devoted to the Navy as Roger—or perhaps they had not *enjoyed* it so much. It had been difficult for Bronwen to judge her husband's ability as a naval officer, for the most important duty of a service wife was the adoption of a blindly, fanatically unswerving devotion to her husband's professional career. In the closed circle, the great club of the Service, a wife might discuss every personal shortcoming of her husband with his colleagues' wives; might commiserate with them on the extravagance, drinking habits, or even the infidelity of theirs—but to mention the technical blunder which had disorganised a naval occasion, damaged a piece of expensive equipment, or grounded a submarine on a Gosport mudbank, was to invite complete and everlasting ostracism.

Though Roger's career had not been free of professional errors, few officers could have radiated a more personal air of naval brilliance than he. Short, stocky, square-shouldered, with a heavy bulldog jaw and surprisingly bright grey eyes, he looked every inch the submarine commander of popular fiction. Incisive, good-humoured in a genially bawdy way, his cap worn always at a cocksure Beatty angle, he epitomised that image of itself, as mirrored in the public mind, which gives the British Navy such a naïvely narcissistic pleasure in every glowing aspect of its own romance. Yet perhaps it was this very ability to symbolise in his own person the popular conception of the Submarine Service that had been Roger's undoing. An indulgence in somewhat gaudy histrionics should not have resulted in his removal from a service with such a long tradition of the best sort of melodrama, but perhaps Roger's stagier mannerisms—his slow-motion salute from the conning-tower against a white ensign or a red sunset, his fervent double handclasp and his slow-spreading grin full of boyish camaraderie—had at length become infuriating to his colleagues or intolerable to his superiors. At any rate, the axe had fallen, and to his own shocked fury and his wife's hurt surprise, Roger Lannfranc and the Royal Navy had parted company.

Bronwen had recovered much more rapidly than her husband. After all, there were compensations. The Navy had been generous: there was a pension for life and a not unreasonable gratuity. The pension was not enough to live on, nor was the gratuity sufficient capital to finance a business, but both ensured that the road back to civilian life would be comparatively easy. Roger was only thirty-three and there was plenty of time to look around for a satisfactory job. Secretly, in those first days, Bronwen was not displeased at what had happened. She was a young woman (no one, somehow, had ever thought of Bronwen as a girl, nor did she ever think of herself as one) who possessed a peculiarly strong ambition towards wealth—the well-ordered, unostentatious, rather heavy richness of English wealth—and the life of a junior naval officer's wife had often bored and irked her. The gay mock-poverty, the *gamin* readiness to make do with under-furnished flats and cottages, the parties where everyone wore jeans and submarine sweaters and sat on the floor drinking beer and gin out of teacups—these all grated on her more sophisticated tastes. Now all that was finished, and instead she saw a future of decorous affluence. A house of her own in which she could give proper dinner-parties and use the cherished wedding presents of glass and silver which were so wasted in naval lodgings, a good car, holidays on the Continent, and Roger in a responsible executive job—Roger as a successful businessman.

There had not been much difficulty to start with—probably Roger was still a little numbed by his abrupt removal from the world of his own romance. He had let Bronwen find him a job as assistant personnel manager in a boot and shoe factory. The Lannfrancs had moved to Northampton, Bronwen had unpacked the china and glass, and Roger, looking oddly out of place in a business suit, had gone off to demonstrate his single qualification of man-management.

But it was man in his naval rather than his industrial capacity whom Roger knew how to manage, and this was brought home to him after the first week. "Your whole attitude is *wrong*, Lannfranc," his immediate superior wailed, a wizened little man who handled the factory personnel in a manner which suggested that they were dynamite bombs. "I fear the—er—what is it?—the habit of command is *ingrained* in you."

"Of course it is," Roger agreed a little crossly. "What do you suppose I was doing in the Navy?"

"Yes, yes. But you can't command *here*."

"I don't."

"But you *talk* as if you do. You behave as if our people were lucky not to be keel-hauled or put in irons. It won't do, Lannfranc—it won't do at all. Cannot you moderate your naval manner somewhat?"

But he could not. He tried, and the result appeared as a dreadful sort of condescension. He started calling the workers by their Christian names, and it sounded as though he were patronising a rabble of stable-boys and scullery-maids. Within two months he was sent for by the managing director and gently asked to find a position for which he was more suited.

It was a terrible blow to Bronwen: it shook to their foundations her confident expectations of continually increasing wealth and success. She did not openly blame her husband, but her implied criticism was sufficient to start a bitter little quarrel from which Roger emerged red-faced, sulky and silent, and wishing more fervently than ever that he was back in the Navy—back in the control-room of *Stingray* with a crew who expected him to command them and no one at hand to criticise how he did it.

But he was not. He was a short, angry, red-faced young man out of a job in a flat in Northampton. He had long been accustomed to the actor's peculiar ability to view himself from without—from a position about six feet from where he stood and a height some fifteen inches above his own. How often he had watched himself with that curious inward vision as he gripped the two handles of the periscope, the cold sea-light from far above reflected down the multiple mirrors to glint eerily from his eyeballs. . . . "Stand by to surface . . . Down periscope! . . . Blow Two, Four and Six. . . ."

And now there was nothing but this angry, sulky figure standing in a small room in the grey light of a winter afternoon—ineffective, unwanted, futile and valueless. It was a sudden agony of the spirit greater than any physical pain he had ever, even in his most sombre moments, conceived of experiencing. It changed him more in five minutes than the most severe illness of many months' duration could have done. From that day he retreated behind a defensive structure of his own making, returning during many of his waking hours to the Navy which had rejected him. He no longer considered the future, but dreamed of the past, sometimes changing it a little, sometimes adding to it, reviewing in a long, never-ending cinematographic serial the story of Lieut.-Commander Lannfranc, R.N., both as it had been and as it should have continued to be.

Living in two worlds, the real and the imaginary, Roger was unable to make anything of either. His daydreams left him with an ever-increasing sense of frustrated irritation that effectually prevented him from holding down for more than three weeks the second job—that of assistant sales manager in a small electrical manufacturing firm—which he had reluctantly found under strong pressure from his wife.

The months went by. Money was spent, but none earned. Then, as if things were not already difficult enough, Bronwen announced with a distracted fury that she thought she was pregnant. It was the height of one of the hottest English summers on record and they were back in London in what was termed a " flatette "—one large room and a kitchen-bathroom leading off it. Bronwen took and did all that could be taken and done to prevent the appearance of another unwanted Lannfranc, but to no avail. She might, perhaps, have found someone to put the matter right—London was full of little basement surgeries where immigrant Asian doctors specialised in " gynaecology "—but she had a prudish and fearful attitude towards such places: they were not made use of in the circles in which she had hoped to move. Instead, worried, ill and angry, she turned one exhaustingly hot evening upon her husband.

"I *wouldn't* mind having a baby if only there was some prospect of being able to feed and clothe the little wretch! If only you weren't such a bloody failure! If only you'd get a job and stick to it. . ." And then there had come that short, diffident ring on the door bell, and Roger, his face darkly suffused with rage, had crossed into the cupboard of a hall and jerked open the door. Bronwen heard him grunt "Well?" and then another voice in which a brisk geniality did not entirely conceal an undertone of impatient weariness, "Good evening, sir. I wonder if I can interest you in some rather neat little—Christ, it's Roger!"

She heard no more, for at that point the sitting-room door slammed shut in a sudden puff of dusty breeze from the open window, but five minutes later she heard the outer door close and then Roger was back, coming in quickly, silently, almost stealthily, as if he were hiding from someone. Looking questioningly up at him, Bronwen saw the fear and anger in his dark, hot face. "Who——?"

"Miles Abbot—you knew him when he was Number One to Roy Gander in *Sea-hare*. He's been out two years. He was selling things. I don't know what—some sort of kitchen gadget, I think. I asked him in, but he was too busy. He said he'd got a lot more to do before he finished up this evening." Roger's voice was fast and hard, and his eyes flickered round the room as if he was searching for a way out of a trap. "He asked what I had been doing and I told him. He—he said I'd probably end up selling things too! My God, he's a dreary bastard now—you'd never believe: servile and shabby and dismal. He said there wasn't anything else for people like us except what he's doing."

"But that's not true—there *must* be other things!"

Roger had turned on her ferociously. "Must there, eh? I don't think so! If there are, I can't find them—and what's more, I'm not going to go on looking!" His eyes were narrowed, sweat stood in shining pinpoints on his forehead. "Listen—we're getting out. We're getting to hell out of London—out of England—just as fast as we can bloody well make it—see? I'm not waiting here till *that* happens to me!"

Bronwen, sensing his shocked nervous panic, caught the infection, too, for like him she came from a position and class which regarded the door-to-door salesman as the ultimate end in failure and degradation—a creature of grey streets and mean eating-houses, a whining voice and a shabby case of samples. Roger—no, it was impossible: that could not happen to him. But it might if they stayed here. "Yes, yes, we'll do that. We'll get right away, Roger. Somewhere where things are different."

And standing there in that high-ceilinged London room which was somehow dim and depressing even in the sunniest summer weather, they both felt a wild sense of irrational relief. The last year with its disappointments and disillusions, with, above all, its desolating drabness, was to be thrust into the past—rejected, forgotten. They would begin again somewhere else.

Now, suddenly, Roger came to life. He acted with as much speed and decision as even the most ardent admirer of the British Navy could have expected. Australia was as far away as it was reasonably possible to get from London, from Miles Abbot's shabby little suitcase and the threat that it implied. There were no liners leaving for Australia within the next week, but it appeared that one had recently left—a small ship bound for Sydney and which could be boarded at Naples where she was putting in to collect further passengers—the Panamanian liner *San Roque.*

II

She lay under the arc-lights of the Stazione Marittima, the Blue Peter drooping at her mast, the great red-and-blue starred flag of Panama hanging in heavy folds at her stern—a seven-thousand-ton, twin-screw turbine steamer with smart, sharp lines and a knifelike stem raked almost to a clipped prow. From the height of her single broad funnel with its great red " S " to her carmine boot-topping she was painted a showy, staring white, which shone so brilliantly under the high port lights that she seemed almost phospherescent—a confectioner's model of glittering white icing sugar made for a wedding-cake. On the beautiful slender curve of her racy prow the name *San Roque* was painted in scarlet forward-slanting letters, as if the letters themselves were eager to drive a cutting path through the sea. A handsome ship, certainly, if a little on the small side for the Australian run.

Limping a little as he always did when he was tired, pushing through the thick crowd which jostled along the quay, Serafino edged out between a group of policemen at the foot of the gangway and went quickly up to it to the embarkation deck. Two seamen shuffled to the slow, undecided attention of the mercantile marine, and Petelli, the *Capitan d'armi,* a square, brawny man with a face like an angry, weather-beaten brick, saluted perfunctorily. " *Buona sera, Signor—Signor——?*"

" Ciccolanti."

"Signor Ciccolanti. Welcome on board, signore."

Serafino smiled and nodded, the big gold badge on his high-peaked white cap glittering in the strong electric light, and the two sailors grinned with hopeful approbation.

"Where's the captain? *Ponte comando?*"

"*Ponte comando—si, signore.*"

But when he had climbed to the bridge he found only an apprentice, a dark, slender, olive-skinned boy, wearing the gold anchors of a cadet on his black epaulettes, who turned from tidying the chart table, a little startled at the sight of a strange officer. "Oh——"

"All right, all right. Where's the captain?"

"In his cabin, signore—with Don Ildefonso."

"Oh—I see." Serafino bit his lower lip. It was bad enough to have to meet his new, and by repute most formidable, captain for the first time, without having the owner present at the meeting. Besides, like all the other officers of the Flotta Soto, he was frightened of Don Ildefonso. He loked at the boy at the table, noting the sallow skin, the thick mop of unbrushed black hair. A southerner, obviously. "Who are you?"

"Luigi Pavanoli, signore—*allievo.*"

Serafino smiled, remembering his own cadet days. Probably the boy was almost as scared of him as he himself was of the owner. "How many cadets do we carry?"

"Only me this trip."

"I see. I'm acting Chief for this voyage. You know that?"

"Yes." The cadet nodded gravely. "You're Signor Ciccolanti from *San Ramòn.*"

"That's right. Well, let Signor Bressan know I'm aboard when he comes up."

"*Senz' altro, signore.*"

Outside the captain's cabin Serafino paused, licking his lips nervously. It was ridiculous, really, to be so frightened of Don Ildefonso, for the owner must be contented with his work or this new position would not have been entrusted to him. He took a quick breath, knocked, heard a clipped voice call "*Entrate!*" and, taking off his cap, he opened the door and went in.

Two elderly men sat beside the big, paper-littered desk in the soft light of a shaded lamp. One was squat, heavy-bellied, with huge, sagging shoulders and the face of a haughty, discontented bull. The other, wearing the four bars of a captain, was smaller and wiry, with a colourless lined face, high

Kalmuck cheekbones, a tight mouth and narrow light-blue eyes.

Serafino bowed quickly to the latter. "Ciccolanti, *Signor Capitano,* reporting on board."

Without getting up, the captain held out a pale, hard hand and smiled. Serafino, feeling more than ever a schoolboy in front of two masters, came forward and took it. "Good. I am glad to have you, Signor Ciccolanti. I am afraid it was rather sudden for you, this move—yes?"

Before Serafino could reply, Don Ildefonso growled, "He has to go where he's sent, sudden or not. He is too young for this position—far too young. Twenty-six, isn't it, Ciccolanti?"

"*Si, signore.*"

"Far too young. But that's the best I can do for you, Pavel."

Serafino stood, his hand still held in the captain's steely grasp, uncomfortably aware of his stained shirt, while both his employer and his new superior gazed at him appraisingly, wondering how much value he would be to them, whether he was worth his wages—the eighty thousand lire a month which kept the family in the Vic' Re Galantuomo. From the corner of his eye he caught a movement in the shadows outside the lamp's rays and, turning his head, saw another young man, in officer's white but without epaulettes, lounging on a bulkhead seat. Don Ildefonso said, as if the introduction bored him, "My son's sailing with you this trip. Gil, this is Signor Ciccolanti."

The youth smiled briefly, and Serafino suddenly felt that he had seen him somewhere before—probably in the offices of the line, where he must often go. He smiled in return, grateful for the presence of someone who was also young—even the notorious Gil Sotomayor—to lend him some slight sense of companionship in the heavy atmosphere of age and power that emanated from the owner and his senior captain.

"Well, sit down, Ciccolanti. There are one or two remarks I want to make and Captain Onestinghel won't mind you hearing them."

Serafino glanced quickly at his watch remembering that he was a Chief Officer now and that there were a dozen different things which . . . But Onestinghel's light, accented voice said, "Don't worry—Bressan's got it in hand for the present." And he sat down carefully at a polite distance from the two old men.

But Don Ildefonso was in no hurry; he took a crocodile-skin cigar-case from the pocket of his bulky white dinner-jacket and, after frowning moodily at the contents, offered it to Onestinghel. Serafino, watching respectfully as the expensive cigars were clipped with Don Ildefonso's gold cutter and lit with the captain's gold lighter, felt neither envy nor jealousy, though cutter or lighter could have kept the family in the Vic' Re Galuntuomo for nearly a month—only admiration. He had the full measure of Italian deference towards riches and success; and in this case it was hardly misplaced, for both men, particularly Don Ildefonso, had risen entirely by their own efforts.

Everyone in the fleet knew the outlines, and some even knew the details, of Ildefonso Sotomayor's life. Enlisting at seventeen as a gunner in the Spanish Army (he was still occasionally known by his old nickname "*El Artillero*"), he had served in Morocco for several years before deciding that after all the sea was his vocation. He had deserted on a ship bound for Norway, and after that it had been years of seafaring on every sort of ship that sailed the high seas—trawlers, tankers, coastal tramps, passenger liners, he had known them all and worked them along every seaway of the world. During the Spanish Civil War he had run the blockade for the Government forces, fore-seen the outcome of the struggle, changed sides, and, because of his knowledge of the habits of the other blockade runners, had been of considerable service to the victorious Insurgents. They had rewarded him by cancelling his ancient proscription for desertion and giving him the rank of commander in the Spanish Navy.

But once more his dislike of any sort of military discipline had caused him to leave the service—though this time in a more regular way and with a handsome gratuity, and, buying an old coaster, he had joined in the then highly profitable business of shipping refugee Jews illegally into Palestine.

The risks of this occupation were extreme: ships intercepted by the British naval patrols were sunk or confiscated and their crews imprisoned. But the rewards were in proportion, for the refugees, fleeing from the certain death of Hitler's Europe, would pay anything even for standing room in the filthy hold of any craft, however unseaworthy, bound for Palestine. Packed to the gunwales with shivering, fearful humanity, packed, in some cases, until a bare twelve inches of freeboard showed above the water-line, the grimy old coasters and tramps would chug out hopefully from Greek or

Yugoslavian shores across the broad calm lake of the summer Mediterranean, and, if fortunate, would slide quietly, lights extinguished, into some deserted cove on a moonless night, to send their cargoes, weeping with joy and relief, scuttering up the sand. If they were fortunate.

But slowly the risk became too great, the chances of getting through too slender, until the odds were set against success. It was then that Captain Sotomayor came to the conclusion that there was no need to take his cargoes all the way to Palestine—half way, still out of reach of the British Navy, was far enough. A larger crew of big men with guns and clubs, tear-gas bombs for the holds, and powerful fire hoses were all that was needed to dump a cargo in mid-ocean. . . . Or so it was rumoured among the officers and seamen of the Flotta Soto, who, after all, owed their livelihoods to the fact that in some way or another—and who cared how?—their employer had made enough money to found his own small shipping line six years ago. .

Shipping migrants. War-torn, fear-wracked, broken Europe was full of people who longed to find a new life in a new continent, to start again in some land in which they fondly hoped that their chances of a livelihood and a little happiness for themselves, and more especially for their children, would not take second place to the fulfilment of the personal ambitions of elderly politicians, the pandering to the hurt pride of outdated royalty, or the contentment of some generalissimo's overweening vanity. Ildefonso Sotomayor was well aware of the emotions which induced this unprecedented desire of mid-twentieth-century European man to cut his losses and start afresh, for he had often felt them, and acted upon them, himself. Yet unlike these modern fugitives, he had never allowed circumstances to overwhelm him. He had fought his way doggedly, brutally, but victoriously, through all the complications, turmoils and dangers of the last thirty years. That was why he was the owner of a fleet of three ships, with more to come as fast as he could buy them. He scorned the migrants who filled his pockets, for they were doing something he had never done—they were running away. Because they were running away he realised that they were more interested in getting to their destination quickly than in what manner they got there. Because they were running away it stood to reason that they had failed somehow—and in most cases that meant financially—in their own countries, and were therefore poor and concerned more with the cost of their passages than with the comfort of them. Don Ildefonso, a man of practically no formal education, was in many ways a psychologist of a high order.

So he bought small, fast ships with large, cheap, tourist-class accommodation: great multi-bunked dormitories for both sexes, with the absolute minimum of lounge and deck space—and a very small first-class section to add the necessary tone to the Line. And if European Boards of Trade and European mercantile regulations looked askance at such practices and were apt to demand certificates of seaworthiness and to make rules about overcrowding and life-saving appliances and general safety, then all such unpleasantnesses could be evaded and avoided by sending the ships to sea under the flag of Panama. The Panamanian flags flown by the little ships of the Flotta Soto were very large indeed—they would have looked quite big enough on liners of over twenty thousand tons—and a picture, more or less up to date, of the current President of the Republic hung behind every purser's counter.

For a time, too, collection boxes for various international lifeboat funds had stood ostentatiously on these counters—to the considerable amusement of Captain Onestinghel, who was a Russian and therefore a cynic, but they had recently been removed. It was about lifeboats that Don Ildefonso was now speaking in a resentful growl.

" . . . What happened to *San Raphael* in Freemantle. The fine itself is not important—it is the prestige of the Line that matters. So you have these new boats, the best boats that can be bought, modern, hand-propelled screw boats recommended by every maritime safety board in Europe." He frowned, his huge grizzled eyebrows drawing together, his mouth turned down. "I suppose your views on these boats are the same as mine, eh, Pavel?"

Onestinghel was shaking silently with inward laughter. "If one decided—do not ask me why—to abandon the ship in a flat calm, one could, of course, launch boats. And if, at the same time, all one's passengers were exceptionally healthy young male athletes who had been trained as galley-slaves—why then, my dear Don Ildefonso, I imagine one might find some use for these new creations. They are, after all, only slightly more ridiculous than the older lifeboats. Why lifeboats are not abandoned and Carley floats used for all mercantile ships—as they are in the world's navies—has long passed my comprehension."

"Of course, of course. It is the psychology of the passengers, though, that must be taken into consideration. So long as they see plenty of boats they feel safe. For that purpose our boats were perfectly satisfactory. If, however, the Australian port authority chooses to staff itself with landsmen who know no more of water than they have learned in a hired canoe on a lake in a city park and who therefore have the mentality of passengers. . . ." Don Ildefonso lifted his huge shoulders in a disgusted shrug. "Well, they have the last word of course; it is of no use to defy authority unless one is quite certain of winning. I have apologised deeply and explained that it was a most regrettable oversight which shall never be allowed to recur. You will, of course, see that these new boats are in perfect condition and that the crew's drill is fast and accurate by the time you reach Australian waters."

Onestinghel nodded and refilled the two pot-bellied brandy goblets on the desk between them. Don Ildefonso sipped from his and continued, moodily, "Another thing. It has up till now been the practice for officers to eat in their own mess. I want this changed. It is a British custom for deck officers and first-class passengers to eat together. It will do no harm, now that all our ships are switched to the Australian run, if this practice is followed in the Flotta Soto."

Onestinghel's thin mouth twitched. "Certainly, if you wish it. Fortunately at least two of my officers speak most adequate English so that conversation at meals should not present an insuperable problem—for the English, of course, can never speak any language save their own." He turned to Serafino and, speaking in English asked: "Mister Ciccolanti, do you know this language?"

Serafino smiled unhappily. "Some—some several words is all."

Accusingly Don Ildefonso lifted his bull-like head. "But did you not learn it at school?"

"I—I learn, yes. But is long time. And there is no practice. On the Venezuela voy—voy—*viaggi,* I speak Spanish. For this——"

Relapsing into Italian, Don Ildefonso growled, "All officers—but most certainly chief officers—should speak at least competent English to-day."

"I——"

"No, I do not want excuses. My son here is younger than you, yet he speaks good English. You must learn to speak it properly—you are still quite young enough to learn." He paused. " And for God's sake wear a clean shirt at meals in the first-class saloon. You're supposed to be an officer on a smart passenger ship—not a deck-hand on a coal barge!"

Serafino, his face a dull red, nodded humbly. " *Si, signore.*" He clasped his hands together to disguise their trembling, and Onestinghel glanced at him sympathetically and turned to the owner. " I am delighted to hear that Don Gil speaks English so well. It may be most useful. The purser——"

Don Ildefonso looked up quickly, as if reminded of something. " Ah, yes, Semprebon. Yes. . . ." He paused a moment. " Ciccolanti can go now, if you do not wish to give him any instructions, Pavel."

" No, no. Bressan has it in hand for the present."

Serafino, getting quickly to his feet, saw Gil Sotomayor smiling slightly, but whether with sympathy or derision it was impossible to guess. He paused for a moment—surely Don Ildefonso would wish to say some word of farewell or encouragement?—but the two old men disregarded him as if he had ceased to exist, so he bowed, muttered, " *Buona sera, signori,*" and backed quickly out of the cabin.

2

So that was Naples—that glittering roaring city behind the glare of the docks. Heat, dirt, filthy smells; an unattractive place with the colour drained from its grey volcanic stones by the fierce sunlight of day, and the sticky heat only heightened, like the intolerable noise, by the fall of darkness. Pacing slowly along the boat deck beside his sister, Colonel Chelgrove was glad he had not gone ashore and secretly resolved to go ashore at no other port of call until they reached Sydney. If Paula wanted to make any shore excursions, though this was unlikely except at places with Imperial associations like Aden and Colombo, she must go alone or find somebody else to accompany her. " See Naples and die," he commented with mild sarcasm. " I'm sure it would be very easy to pick up something deadly enough here—diphtheria or T.B. or some horrible skin disease."

Paula gave her invariable harsh, sharp bark of laughter. " What rot you talk, Perry! Just because you're too damned lazy to go ashore. . . ."

The Colonel shook his head, as if someone had splashed him with water. " No, no. I really think there is a danger of infection in a place like this." His voice was patiently plaintive. " And, anyway, there's nothing to see."

" Nothing *you* want to see, you mean. And nothing I want to either, as it happens, or we would have gone ashore. Anyhow, I'm not particularly interested in these Continental places. Father wasn't, either. Do you remember how he used to laugh at the Baverstocks for going off every year to Antibes or Rapallo or somewhere?"

" Yes, yes, indeed."

" Do you? I doubt it." Paula pursed her lips sardonically. " You always *say* you remember Father so well. . . . Anyway, it was his view that good families with background and traditions of place didn't rush off to the Continent every year like a lot of gaping townees trailing guide books and cameras. 'I feel poor Baverstock shows a certain lack of breeding by all this gallivanting in France and Italy,' he used to say. 'It only demonstrates how little he and his family think of this country and how little they are tied to it.' Of course, Father *was* tied—the Hunt and the Bench and the Rural Council."

The Colonel flinched slightly. " Yes, of course he was. Well, *I've* never been one for travelling, Paula—you can't say I have. Only where the Army sent me. You can't count that, I mean."

" Nobody said you were." Reaching the after-end of the boat-deck, Paula Chelgrove turned abruptly on her heel and, with her brother lagging slightly behind her, began to retrace her steps. A tall, spare figure with the hard, reddish, weather-beaten complexion of the upper-middle-class English countrywoman, and cold grey eyes above a long bony nose—the Chelgrove nose of which she was so proud—it was difficult, noting her vigorous walk, hearing her hard, clipped voice, to realise that she was in her mid-sixties rather than ten years younger. Now she halted suddenly and lowered her voice to a brusque hiss. " Look—over there! That wouldn't be her, would it?"

" Who? Where?"

" That woman over there—very fat and wearing those ridiculous glasses. She's just come up. Would that be your friend's wife?"

" Malcolm-Bruce's wife?" The Colonel glanced quickly in the direction his sister indicated and then shook his head.

"No, no. Malcolm-Bruce's wife is much smaller—quite small and thin. Yes, very thin. Besides, he'd be with her." He sighed. "I fear they won't be getting on here, after all."

"I thought you asked the purser."

"I—well, I meant to. I forgot."

Paula gave a disgusted sigh. "Well, of course you won't know when they're getting on unless you ask the purser, will you? Ever since you saw their names on the passenger list you've been saying you'll ask him. I suppose you just couldn't be bothered to take the trouble. You hoped I would do it. Well, I'm not going to!" Her voice took on a deeper, angrier note. "Now do try to pull yourself together, Perry. There'll be a lot to see to when we get to New Zealand, and you can't expect me to do every damned thing. You're well enough now, after all—or so Dr. Gregory said. And——"

"Oh, yes, I'm really quite well—quite well. Only I still get tired rather easily, you know."

They were back at the after-end of the boat-deck, and he stood for a moment gripping the rail and looking down at the small square of the swimming-pool on the deck below. He seemed lost in some grey speculation upon which the multiple noises of the docks, the groan and rattle of winches, the impatient hooting of tugs, the high harsh cries of stevedores, beat unheeded like waves against a sheer cliff face of flat rock. A tall, stooped man in his early sixties whose protuberant eyes of faded blue, long nose, white moustache and runaway chin lent him something of the White Knight's look of ineffectual sadness, he stood resting one foot on the lowest rail, frowning in thought—or what appeared to be thought. At last he sighed and turned almost briskly to his sister, emanating an air of unnatural, over-firm decision. "Paula, I think—I'm sure—it's time I was in bed."

3

"*Signor Romano per cortesia a vestibulo!*" shouted the amplifiers urgently along the open decks—across the brightly lit lounges upholstered in plastic imitation leather, in the jazzed-up glass and chromium of the first-class bar, and through the long, narrow red-carpeted corridors. "*Signor Romano per cortesia a vestibolo!*"

Time was running out and the ship's business must be completed with all its multitudes of papers to be signed and forms filled in, stamped, dated, punched. *San Roque* was about to leave her home port, for despite her Panamanian flag, she bore the word "NAPOLI" below the name on her stern, and to drive her way across half the world. She would use thousands of gallons of fuel and pay harbour dues in half a dozen different ports before she reached Sydney. Her passengers and crew would consume tons of food, crates of beer and spirits, carton after carton of cigarettes before the voyage was done. And everything must be stringently accounted for—every gallon of fuel, every side of beef, every bottle of olives for the first-class bar.

"*Attenzione! Attenzione, per favore! I signori passeggieri Ricciotti e Valpatena con i loro passaporti. . . .*" Passengers and their documents: a few, a tiny minority of seasoned travellers, with the correct papers ready displayed for the quick scrutiny, the thud of the rubber stamp, earning a brief smile of thanks from the purser and his harassed staff; the vast majority a flustered herd of sheep, bewildered and distracted by the noise and newness of their unaccustomed surroundings, needing to be told everything twice at least, rummaging for mislaid identity forms, tickets, permits, receipts, while children cried and tugged at restraining hands, luggage piled up, blocking corridors and companionways, and tempers became strained and frayed in the heat.

"No, no. Your cabin is number two hundred and fifteen—two-one-five—on 'B' deck. That is the deck above this—you go up those stairs. Yes. . . . Excuse me one moment, please. . . . Meal tickets? First or second sitting? From the chief dining-room steward in Number One saloon. Aft—that is towards the stern of the ship from here—a steward will show you. Ettore! This lady wishes to go. . . ."

And the amplifiers once more drowning speech with their insistent, despairing demand: "*Signor Romano per cortesia a vestibolo!*"

"No, sir, the baggage room will not be open until ten o'clock to-morrow morning. . . . You say——? No, no—quite impossible, I'm afraid. . . . Excuse me one moment. . . . Malpiero, this gentleman's ticket seems to be incorrect. He says that in the office this morning . . . One moment *please*! The first-class bar? Two up and farther forward. Yes, towards the front of the ship. One of the mess-boys will . . ."

"Not until after we sail. . . ."

"As soon as we are at sea. . . ."

" To-morrow morning. . . ."
" Excuse me one moment, please. . . ."
" Signor Romano per cortesia a vestibolo!"

4

Don Ildefonso Sotomayor had not squandered money unnecessarily on the tourist-class accommodation. The long, low dormitories deep below the water-line had been fitted up from war surplus material discarded from reconverted troopships and sold for next to nothing. Set after set of chromium-painted, three-tiered iron bunks filled every inch of available floor space, leaving only narrow rat-runs of footway between them. Every bunk was made up with rough sheets and a folded brown army blanket embroidered with a large red " S." At one end of each dormitory was a multiple washroom, shared with the dormitory beyond, and here and there big litter-bins were clamped to the bolt-studded iron walls. No attempt had been made to mitigate in any way the indecent lack of privacy. Bare electric bulbs behind wire protectors glared above and at all sides of the stacked bunks, filling the crowded rooms throughout indistinguishable night and day with a hard white light, in which each man must perform every action under the scrutiny of his fellows. Even so, the Flotta Soto was giving its tourist-class passengers a bargain. It was shifting them out of Europe—right across the world—and for a journey of some four weeks was providing them with three fairly substantial meals a day at rather less than three-quarters of the price charged by any other line.

Armando Lodigianni slid past a group of partly-dressed men leaning beside an open dormitory doorway, and started to worm his way along one of the narrow, baggage-cluttered alleys between the high tiers of bunks. Two men, seated on opposite beds, were playing cards on a checker-board balanced across their knees. Armando waited patiently for a few moments, but they disregarded him as if he did not exist. Presently he muttered "*Permesso*——" and one of the men looked up, raising his sandy eyebrows. " Whatsay?"

" 'E wants to get by. S'nother of 'em."

" F—ing 'ell!" grunted the second man irritably and lifted the board on to the bed beside him. " Come on then, sonny —'op to it!"

Armando murmured "*Grazie*" and slid quickly past, a small, compact figure in his dark-blue workman's shirt and trousers. These were English passengers, migrants embarked at Southampton, and there were a lot of them. Yet they were so unlike any of the English he had seen occasionally in his native Naples that he would not have recognised them as being from the same country. He eyed them now, quickly, furtively, and with fear, as he alternately waited, apologised and slipped past with muttered thanks. They were mostly small men of a physique which appeared at once poor yet strong—fleshless, bony, powerful, but somehow deformed, as if they were a species a little apart from ordinary mankind, constructed on a pattern slightly yet distinctly different. But it was in their faces that this queer dissimilarity, this subtle deviation from the rest of the human race, seemed most marked. It was not merely that they were ugly, though Armando could not recall ever having seen such ugly faces before, but that they were so badly made—noses, jaws, brows, all appeared accentuated to a crude, shiny knobbliness at the expense of the eyes and mouths, which by comparison seemed too small. It was as if an incompetent and malignant sculptor had set himself to caricature humanity in a set of uncouth masks. Armando knew that these men were poor—otherwise, like himself, they would not be here. Yet it puzzled him, not realising that he was looking on the human product of the oldest industrial nation, that they should be so unsightly.

He came at last to the tier of bunks beside a bulkhead where his elder cousin Niccolo had left the luggage. Niccolo was there, sitting on the lowest bunk, smoking and morosely staring down at the iron floor. Armando slid quickly down beside him. "Where's Emilio? Hasn't he come back yet?"

Niccolo shook his dark head, still staring down at his feet in their worn canvas shoes. "Not yet. He had to fix up about our meal times. I expect there are a lot of people waiting."

Armando sensed his cousin's misery. Niccolo did not want to leave Italy and had done everything he could to prevent his brother's plan of selling the garage-workshop and emigrating to New South Wales. But he could do nothing against facts, against less money coming in each week, bills mounting, creditors pressing.

A voice—a deep indignant voice, suddenly said, "'Ere!" and the two young Italians looked up to see one of the English migrants, an enormous man in a collarless shirt and creased grey flannel trousers stretched across a bulging belly, a man with a round red ball of a face in which all the features were grotesquely small, staring down at them angrily. "'Ere—I say! Whicher you two put yer things on this 'ere bunk?" The Englishman reached up easily to the top bunk of the tier and, pulling down Armando's suitcase and the rucksack he used when camping with the *Giovantù Esploratori*, dumped them on the floor with a look of extreme disgust. "You f—ing lot come aboard 'ere an' start leavin' your f—ing kit around on other blokes' bunks—thinks you own the whole f—ing outfit, doncher?"

Niccolo got to his feet, a nervous, tentative smile on his narrow, sallow face. Trying to remember the few words of English he had occasionally used in the garage, he said, "*Signore—scusi*. But this bed. Is for you? You sleep?"

"Now, laddie—now. I don't sleep on it. Since you ask —an' what f—ing business it is of yours I *don't* know—since you ask, I don't sleep on it. Sleep on t'other side. Since you ask I'll tell yer: I keeps my stuff on it—see?"

A small man with a mass of crinkly red hair receding from his forehead swaggered across, tapped Niccolo on the chest with mock geniality, and attempted to translate the big man's remarks into simpler, slower English. "What 'e says is—'e wants that bunk 'isself. Got it, chum?"

Niccolo smiled, fearful yet persistent. "But not for sleep?"

"You *'ave* got it! Good for you!" The small Englishman crowed with laughter and turned to some of his friends who were watching him with dour amusement from neighbouring bunks "See? 'E can understand English when *I* says it. Can't understand ol' Ron's English—no offence, Ron, chum, no offence—but 'e can understand mine. Can't you, matey?"

Niccolo swallowed. "I understand—yes."

"F—ing Eyetie," grunted big Ron briefly.

"But for my—my *cugino*——" Niccolo nodded towards Armando—"he too has need for bed."

"'Ow yes. Yes, 'course 'e 'as. Got to kip too. An' a very nice bit of kip 'e'd make for some as likes it that way. 'Course, not that *I* would, mind. But——"

"You got a nasty dirty mind, Ted Condron!" called out a voice in a shrill falsetto imitation of a woman's. "What you need's a wife to keep you in order."

Condron crowed exultantly. "What—get married? Me? Not bleeding likely, chum! Now! It's a dirty duck what always paddles in the same puddle—that what *I* says!" There was an answering burst of laughter from his friends, and Niccolo said patiently, "But—where——?"

Condron, suddenly conciliatory, patted his shoulder. "Over there, chum, over there in the corner. There's a place there."

5

And now the ship's agents, the emigration officials, customs officers and police of the port authority were taking their leave at the head of the gangway leading from the crowded vestibule amidships to the quay. Smiling, bowing, shaking hands with the tall, aristocratic, grey-haired purser. "Cavaliere, good-bye—and a most prosperous voyage? Good-bye, good-bye!"

White papers thrust into black brief-cases, ties adjusted, foreheads wiped. The overloud chatter and laughter of farewell. "Signor Malestroit, we're leaving now—yes, yes, at once. . . . And again many thanks for your kindness. . . . That letter, if you will be so good as to remember? The office in O'Connell Street. Yes, Signor Bressan knows about it."

Tunics pulled down, white gloves thrust into belts, hands raised to shiny cap-peaks. "*Signori,* we leave. . . . *Buon viaggio—addio!*" Scraps of urgent, last-minute conversations: "Of course Rodolfo knows that quite well, but . . ." "Yes, yes, I assure you it shall be taken care of. Signor Malpiero will understand. . . ." "Cavaliere, good-bye—and once more a thousand thanks! . . ." "Well, then *ciao,* Aldo. Have a good time in Sydney. I envy you, my boy, I do indeed! . . ." "Good-bye, gentlemen! A most prosperous voyage to you! Cavaliere, *addio!*"

Petelli and his sailors slamming the iron half-doors shut, the rumble of the descending gangway and the heightened roar of the dockside crowd. Streamers—hundreds of thin paper ribbons, red, blue, yellow, violet, green—curving upwards in parabolas from the quay, downwards from the decks, a cataract of fluttering rainbows under the arc-lights. The excited shouting of the crowd cut through by the quick, high hooting of a tug, and then all noise drowned by the deep organ-boom of *San Roque* saying her own farewell. Three blasts of increasing length roaring out from the circular louvres high up in the front of the funnel and echoing over the decks, over the sprawling, glittering city like the bellow of some huge sea animal challenging its own element.

As the last gusty roar faded, *San Roque* moved slowly from her berth under the power of the straining tugs. The line of oily black water widened between her gleaming white hull and the stone quay, the coloured streamers snapped and fluttered down, the cries of the crowd lengthened into echoing calls and whistles, and suddenly the ship's amplifiers flooded out music— " *Addio a Napoli* "—the tune to which she always left and entered port.

Surrounded by his deck officers on the open port wing of the bridge, Captain Onestinghel frowned and his mouth turned down at the corners in distaste. He disliked this new, vulgar innovation of liners using signature tunes as if they were popular dance bands rather than ocean-going ships—and if Don Ildefonso wished this custom to be followed in the Flotta Soto, could not *San Roque,* the pride of the fleet, have had something a little less trite than this loud, gay Neapolitan song? "Pavanoli! Phone down and have the amplifier volume modified—lowered considerably."

" *Subito, Signor Capitano!*"

The bronze horses on the seaward façade of the Statione Marittima slid past and the cries of the quayside crowd began to fade. " *Addio, mia bella Napoli,*" remarked the captain without any emphasis and to nobody in particular. He glanced at his new chief officer standing beside him and gazing back towards the lit city where the terraced lights of Vomero crept up the hill. "Are you a Neapolitan, Ciccolanti?"

"Me?" Serafino did not take his eyes from the glittering panorama slowly receding behind them, but an odd shy smile flickered over his face. "*No, Signor Capitano.* I—I live there, but I am not a Neapolitan."

6

Roger Lannfranc stood on the deck beside his wife, watching the docks slide slowly past. So had they slid past as *Stingray* moved out of Portsmouth harbour fourteen months ago, while he, her captain, stood on the bridge giving his short, terse, exact orders. This was the first time he had stood on a moving ship since those so recent days which were yet so far off, so unattainable except in dreams. But now, with a deck once more beneath his feet, it was difficult to realise that he was not back in the Navy. A sailor hurried past, and Roger felt the muscles in his right arm begin to contract in readiness to return the salute that did not come. The gilt buttons on his blue naval blazer glittered in the passing harbour lights, but now there were no gold rings on his sleeves. Glancing up, he saw a cluster of officers on the bridge—black epaulettes on white shirts, gold cap-straps, the uniform of sea command—and he was filled with such a passionate, burning envy that it was almost a physical pain to watch them.

7

" Guest of honour," murmured Vera Crambatch as she stood, her bulky figure almost filling the narrow doorway between the two connecting cabins she had taken on "A" deck. She glanced with a deep and restful satisfaction at the piled cases in the second cabin, the boxes and parcels which contained the more precious and valuable of the countless things she had purchased during her tour of Europe. In six weeks' time she would be unpacking them and displaying them in her big South Island home. And then—then at last everything, the troubles, humiliations. annoyances and endless expense of the past four months, would be more than made up to her. There would be the Welcome Home lunch from the Guild, of course, and certainly another from the Ladies' Bowling Club. The Parents and Citizens Association too, even though she and Mrs. Doubleday were no longer on speaking terms, would surely have to do something to mark the occasion. Then there would be the tea in the Mayor's parlour—and she would undoubtedly be asked to open the Red Cross fête in December. . . . " Guest of honour," she murmured again, wondering whether Victor would bestir himself sufficiently to make sure that her return was properly mentioned in the local paper. Perhaps—surely—it would be somewhere on the front page. " President of Ladies' Guild Returns from Extensive Holiday Abroad. To-day Mrs. Vera Crambatch, the well-known President of the Dunedin Ladies' Arts Guild and sister of Dr. Victor Pease, has returned from a long and most interesting visit to Europe. . . ."

She frowned, her eyes narrowing behind her decorated spectacles; her tour of Europe had proved less a holiday than a penance, and Europe itself not so much interesting as interested—not in herself, of course, it had made that painfully, contemptuously, obvious—but in her money. Cynical and grasping, it had singled her out at once as a gullible victim, a novice even as a tourist, a fat, rich, elderly provincial widow from far New Zealand, visiting Europe for the first time in her life. To the countless hoteliers, guides, travel agencies and couriers she knew now that she had appeared merely as someone to be harried, brazenly overcharged, cheated, stolen from—she had lost two handbags, a full suitcase and innumerable smaller things—and then pushed on, flustered, dazed and unavailingly protesting, through the great milking machine of Continental tourism. Looking back over the past four months, she saw no grand and sweeping vista of innumerable soaring cathedrals, craggy castles and sun-washed southern palaces, but only a kaleidoscopic jumble of extended palms, of thumbs and forefingers insinuatingly rubbed together, folded bills on plates and trays, and suave, sardonically expectant faces.

All Europe, it seemed, had conspired to snub, ignore and rob her—and she was not used to being snubbed, ignored or robbed. Back home no one would have dared to treat her so—back in Dunedin, with Crambatch's Emporium taking up nearly a whole block in the centre of the city and poor Leslie's long mayoral record (he had laid more foundation stones than any previous mayor of Dunedin) and two Crambatch names on the '39-'45 war memorial and another on the '14-'18 one.

She had waited so long for this trip, and year by year as it had been continually postponed—first by the big merger in 1938 which had lifted Leslie from mild affluence to riches, then by the war, and afterwards by Leslie's years as mayor, his unsuccessful attempt to stand for Parliament, the start of his long illness—Europe had become increasingly necessary to her; Europe, which all her friends had seen and which they continually discussed, while she sat humiliatingly silent; Europe, the continent every New Zealander longed to visit, if only as a matter of status.

And now it was over and she was immensely glad that this was so. She had even managed to reduce her visit by nearly six weeks though it had meant cancelling her booking on a large English liner and taking passage on this small foreign ship instead. Now there was only the voyage home, and that, surely, she would enjoy. She remembered vividly the outward trip on the big P. & O. liner, when filled with excited anticipation, she had plunged headlong into every social aspect of shipboard life. She had joined the Sports Committee, won the Single Ladies' shuffleboard competition, helped to organise the children's fancy-dress dance and to raffle a bottle of champagne on the captain's birthday, and had actually been voted the Ship's Most Popular Passenger. And those shipboard meals! Perhaps it had been the air, perhaps the new surroundings, but how well she had eaten! She hoped most sincerely that the food on this ship would be as good. It should be, for she had to admit that, though she had come to hate almost everything European with a smouldering, embittered resentment, she had found that the legends of *hautecuisine,* of Continental cookery, were largely true. Some of the meals she had eaten in the capital cities —and, indeed, in several of the smaller towns—had been magnificent, from the vast smörgasbrods of Sweden to the piled Arab couscous still served in southern Sicily.

She sighed with reviving pleasure, remembering the haggis of Edinburgh, the fried baby octopi of Athens, and the superb cheeses of Normandy. She had been, she had seen, she had eaten. And soon—Guest of honour. Dunedin, with the praise, the compliments, the admiration which awaited her, seemed comfortably close. Then suddenly music blared with irreverent loudness from an amplifier somewhere outside her cabin. Mrs. Crambatch frowned resentfully; it was not right to play a tune like that at the present time; there was about such music a touch of the cynical frivolity which she had found so disquieting in many Europeans. Why could they not have played "*Ave Maria*" instead?

8

In a smaller cabin on "B" deck Brown lifted his muzzle at the sudden music and barked loudly. Without a moment's hesitation Countess Zapescu took her old fur coat from a hook on the door and flung it over him. It was the only thing to do when Brown started to bark; otherwise he would go on and on, the short, sharp yelps rising to higher and more hysterical notes every second. But if one enveloped him at once in something thick and heavy, a blanket or a coat, he stopped immediately and lay down. "There, there, Brown. Quiet now, that's a good boy—or you'll be taken back to that kennel." And that, of course, was where he was meant to be—in the small iron kennel right aft on the stern of " C " deck. That was where the young boy with the gold anchors on his black epaulettes had taken them both when they came aboard. But of course, as soon as he had gone away she had whipped Brown out of the little kennel, humped his old blanket at the back in order to give the appearance of a dark, dormant lump in the corner, and smuggled him to her cabin, concealed, as always in such eventualities, under her fur coat. And now, somehow or other, she would keep him here. There would probably be complaints, demands and talk about regulations and so forth, but she would use all the weapons at her disposal, the rusty weapons of the poor and old —lies, rudeness, tears—and in the end she would win. For Brown was all she had; there was nothing else, after sixty-nine years in the world, that she could call her own. The coloured harbour lights passed before the open scuttle, throwing gleams of red, green and gold into the cabin. She slid one hand under the fur coat and touched Brown's cold, damp nose, and he sniffed slightly and licked her fingers.

9

Down in the big dormitories on " C " deck the ship's signature tune, loud, gay, nostalgic, was having a bad effect on the British migrants. It was a foreign sort of music, and because it was foreign it mocked them with an assertion that the world was large and existed in its own right outside the boundaries of their limited knowledge. It drew from them that response peculiar to the fathomless insularity of the British industrial classes—an incoherent, resentful anger. They stared, some furtively, some arrogantly, but all with open dislike at the newcomers, the bronzed, olive-skinned strangers in their foreign clothes, who had come among them that evening. Ted Condron got out his banjo amid general approval. "That's right, Ted!" they called. "Give us a proper tune, like." But though he tried " Blaydon Races " and " Knees Up, Mother Brown," he could not drown the foreign song. At last, with an angry grin, he put down the banjo and lifted a raucous shout of "Are we down-hearted?" And a roar of most uninternational working-class solidarity answered "No!"

And now *San Roque* was nearly past the long arm of the Molo San Vincenzo and turning out towards the Gulf. The tugs, *Camaldoli* and *St. Elmo,* hooted their quick farewells, and the liner's deeper note boomed its reply. Far down in the engine room the turbines began their deep, throbbing hum, and the decks vibrated gently to the churn and thrash of the twin screws.

White, and flashing with row after row of lights, with the great red " S " on her funnel floodlit from below, *San Roque* moved out, gathering way, into the Gulf, while the music lilting from her amplifiers carried across the dark water. And at the stern rail of " C " deck, leaning out over the foaming wake, Armando looked back at the great sparkling city in which he had been born and lived all of his sixteen years, and watched the long vista of lights widening and expanding along the curving coast with every revolution of the ship's screws far beneath his feet. " *Addio, mia bella Napoli—addio, addio*."

III

" There is no fresh milk this morning?"

" No, Cavaliere—not really fresh. Of course, if you wish——"

" No, no. It has to be completely fresh—otherwise it is no use. All right, you can go." Cavaliere Semprebon heaved his long legs wearily out of his bunk and sat for a moment on its side, slumped, head hanging. It had been another wretchedly bad night; heartburn—though he had scrupulously observed his diet at dinner—had racked him all through the small hours. It was the worry that did it; the lying awake and thinking, going over conversations held in the office at Naples and drifting back to remarks, chance words overheard from time to time among colleagues and then away down dark corridors of speculation and fear. There could be no doubt any longer about Don Ildefonso's dissatisfaction, and every one knew what Don Ildefonso's dissatisfaction spelled—dismissal. And that would mean—no, it was best not to think of what that would mean. Yet one could not help, during the long hours of darkness, but think of it. The throbbing hum of the deep-buried turbines beat out " Dismissal . . . Dismissal . . . Dismissal. . . . No job. . . . No job. . . ." And one tossed and turned and the pain burnt acidly below one's breast-bone like a smouldering fire. It was difficult not to envy the deck officers their long watches on the bridge.

He groaned and yawned, rubbing his long fingers over his face, feeling the lines and wrinkles, the hollowness of the cheeks above the short, neatly trimmed beard, which, with his high-arched Roman nose and wavy grey hair lent him, he believed, the appearance of a diplomat of the old aristocratic sort. His gold wrist-watch told him that it was nearly half-past eight—he must hurry. Malpiero would be behind the counter in the vestibule with young Pavanoli helping him, but still—the purser should be there to supervise. There were bound to be a few complaints from passengers to be dealt with, and Malpiero's English was terrible and his training as a restaurant head-waiter had left him with a bottomless contempt for customers' complaints which he was not always able to hide. Malpiero was not the right sort of man for the post of assistant purser; he had not that air of calm dignity, or unruffled urbanity, which did so much to set passengers at their ease and to enhance the tone of a Line. He was good at figures, of course—really most efficient; one could not complain. The Naples office approved of him, for it was regrettably true that Don Ildefonso appeared to set a higher value on efficiency at figures than on the well-mannered enhancement of the tone of his fleet. If it had not been for Onestinghel . . . Onestinghel was a queer creature certainly, and one could never tell whether he was being serious or the reverse, but at least he was a gentleman, and though he had not actually said so, one felt that he appreciated the company of another gentleman on his ship.

Yes, the captain had never been anything but pleasant to him, reflected Cavaliere Semprebon as he got out his razor and his expensive English shaving soap in its wooden bowl. It was not a particularly bright ray of comfort, because Onestinghel, except on Sundays, was habitually pleasant to everybody—and in any case he would be completely overridden by the owner in any matter of appointments or dismissals; but it was something, at any rate, a small gleam in the gloomy prospect of the future.

He put in his teeth and tried his smile in the mirror—his special first-class smile, for he had another for the tourists

—and felt despair settle over him like a cowl of lead. Fifty-two, and the mirror told him that he looked every day of it, particularly at this early hour of the morning with the bright Mediterranean summer sunlight flooding in through the open scuttle. Nearly twenty-five years at sea, on and off, and twice torpedoed in the war—and it had taken twelve years and all Mafalda's cousin's influence at the Ministry to get any recognition of his services to Italy. A Cavaliere Repubblicano they called it now. Ridiculous! He wrinkled his arched nose disdainfully. If only they still had the King perhaps—certainly—the title would mean a lot more than it did to-day.

If only . . . And dressing slowly, carefully, bending only very gently in order not to bring back the heartburn, Cavaliere Semprebon let his mind wander into a long daydream in which he led the life of a Roman gentleman of leisure, suave and dignified. Some culture—not too much; an attractive mistress—not too young, who would share with him a table for two at Alfredo's and an evening's sedate dancing at the Cabala. A life in which he could exercise to the full his good taste in clothes, his talent for pleasant little conversations and small, pleasing gestures: a bunch of red roses delivered with a conspiratorial little secret joke neatly written on a gilt-edged card; a box of early quail sent by special messenger with an invitation to the opera. . . .

But as he sprinkled a little German eau-de-Cologne on a silk handkerchief and carefully fitted a black Russian cigarette into his long amber holder, the dream faded. He could manage such a life for a week or two when on holiday, and it gave him infinite pleasure to do so, but as a permanency it was financially far beyond his reach. And if—if he lost his present job there would be nothing for it but to retire to the little house poor Mafalda had left him in the Campania—only a cottage really, with its two acres of stony, rather second-rate vineyard which never did well and was always late in production because of the cold spring winds from the Apennines. One would be very little better than a peasant then; in fact, old Bonamati who owned more and better land nearby was unashamedly a peasant, a heavy, unshaven man in blue cotton trousers, smelling of mule dung. The Cavaliere shuddered slightly, picked up his cap and left the cabin.

It was nearly nine o'clock; he had been longer over dressing that he had thought. He hurried down to the vestibule, passing the English Air Force priest bound for Aden—a small, red-headed man with a bristling moustache belied by his sad, diffident manner: " Good morning, Mr.—er—good morning;" a quick, apologetic smile, for as purser he prided himself on remembering the first-class passengers' names. And now here came the old Colonel—well, he was not old really, of course, only about ten years older than himself the purser supposed. "Good morning, Colonel Chelgrove. I trust you slept a good night?"

"Oh—er—good morning, Purser. Yes—yes, thank you."

"It is a beautiful day."

"Yes, indeed."

"You will be able to parade the boat deck and recline in the sun. I envy you. For myself, duty keeps me in my office."

" Ah, yes, of course."

" Yet I hope to take a short rest before luncheon. Perhaps you and your nice sister would then join me for an apéritif in the bar?"

"Thank you. Yes, we'd like to. Most kind."

"Excellent. But I must not keep you from breakfasting. Au revoir, Colonel, until later."

In the wide vestibule amidships with its sham oak panelling and concealed lighting he found Malpiero engaged in an altercation with a small, red-nosed man whose thin brown hair, oiled flatly to his narrow head, added a touch of rat-like anger to his air of sullen hang-dog exasperation. As he came up Semprebon caught the words ". . . Well, if it 'appens again I'll *'ave* to take notice. I'll sue—if it 'appens again. . . ."

Malpiero, his pallid face expressionless, turned his cold dark eyes to his superior and spoke rapidly in Italian. "Cavaliere, I think this is a matter for you. This tourist passenger, Signor Ampel, has three children—boys. They have been in trouble several times already since we left Southampton. They go continually into places forbidden to passengers—the crew's quarters, the lifeboats, the kitchens. To-day they have broken into the paint store. They took a four-litre can of green paint and poured it into the swimming-pool—to colour the water, this man says." He shot the dejected Mr. Ampel a look of contemptuous dislike. " Petelli found them doing it. He told them to stop. They did not—they laughed. One boy threw some green paint over his shoes. Petelli—understandably, I think—hit him across the backside with a piece of rope. His father now complains."

"I see." Frowning slightly, Semprebon took the long cigarette-holder from his mouth and blew a small puff of smoke across the counter. He looked down from his great height, and with a calculated mixture of sternness and quizzical humour, at the sullen little Englishman. He had had experience of this type before—the English worker, ugly-tempered, dogmatic, bitterly resentful of everything outside his own constricted vision of life. One had to handle such a person with great care, and even then the results were seldom satisfactory.

"Well, well. I am told your boys have been mischieving with the ship's things; going where they should not and now insulting the Master-at-Arms." He paused and Ampel lowered his eyes sullenly and shuffled his feet. "I dessay they may 'ave bin larkin' around a bit. Kids is kids, an' always will be. No real 'arm done, anyway. An' there's no——"

The Purser lifted his hand. "One minute, one minute. No harm is done, you say? I think that you are mistaken. A four-litre can of paint has been stolen by these boys. It has been thrown into the swimming-pool. The pool must now be emptied and most carefully cleaned. That means that some sailors must be taken from more important work to do this. That is harmful to the running of the ship—most harmful."

Stubbornly, the Englishman said, "Don't call that no reason to 'it them—with a dirty great piece of rope. Might 'ave injured them. Knocked an eye out or something."

"No, no. I think not. And they threw this paint at the Master-at-Arms."

"Only 'is shoes. An' e's a grown man an' they're kids. My wife an' me, we got a right good mind to sue."

Semprebon sighed deeply. "My fellow, my fellow! You are quite wrong. You have no legal position at all."

"'Ow d'you mean? 'Course we 'ave."

"No. The Captain is in total charge of the passengers as well as the crew."

"We've paid our fare—leastways the Government did."

"Doubtless. Also you have agreed, by taking your ticket, to obey the rules of the Line. Did you read your ticket—on both sides?"

"Now. But . . ."

The Purser smiled with weary satisfaction. "Ah, I thought not! Now let me advise that you go away and read it. You will see that you have agreed to obey these rules. You will see that the Captain can put you ashore if you do not do so. Yes, yes, I assure you. Your children—you must see that they also obey the rules. It is, after all for their own good. If they go into dangerous places they may get hurt. Good. Now you understand?" He glanced at his watch. "Now I have, I fear, no more time. Good morning, Mr. Ampel."

"You see, Malpiero," he said a minute later when Ampel had left the vestibule, sullen defiance plain in his stamping walk, "that is the way. Remember always that in such cases they have *never* read their tickets. You are always quite safe to assume that—unless you are dealing with a lawyer. And lawyers, of course, do not travel in the tourist class."

Malpiero nodded, but his cold, reptilian face remained expressionless. He was not impressed and saw no reason to pretend to be; he knew, better than anyone else, what they were saying about Semprebon in the office at Naples. "Yes, Cavaliere. Now, here I have to-day's first-class menu from the chief steward. You will want to see it." He handed a typed sheet to his superior. "I have translated it, of course."

Semprebon frowned at the menu thoughtfully. "Ah, yes—yes. We do not say 'Roasted Hen,' Malpiero. 'Roast Chicken' is correct English."

"I will change it."

"Yes. But I think perhaps it would be better to have it boiled. Let us say 'Boiled Chicken,' then. And what in the name of God is this? 'Fish Cooked at the Furnace Grating!' My good Malpiero, is this some private recipe of your own? Some dish they eat at Easter in your part of the world—Calabria, is it not?"

Completely disregarding Semprebon's bantering tone, Malpiero said briefly, "Grilled fish—that is how the dictionary translates it."

"So? Well, then, the dictionary and I do not agree. But what sort of fish?"

"Hake."

The Cavaliere wrinkled his long nose. "I think we will have that steamed in milk. Grilled fish is most indigestible. You will alter it on the menu to 'Poached Turbot.' I should not have to tell you these things, Malpiero, you have worked in a restaurant. And see always that the words 'Fresh Bread and Country Butter' are added at the bottom of the card—it helps to fill it up." He returned the typed sheet to his assistant and glanced briefly through the open doorway of the office. "Where's that boy?"

"Pavanoli is on the bridge."

"Why? I told him to report to you at eight-thirty—there's a great deal of typing to do."

Malpiero shrugged. "I understand we are to be deprived of his services in future. The bridge telephoned for him at a quarter to nine. I informed them that it was customary for him to do two hours' work here every morning. I was told that this would no longer be the case."

Cavaliere Semprebon's long, aristocratic face flushed slowly. He took the amber cigarette-holder from his lips and his mouth hardened. So they were to lose Pavanoli, were they? He'd see about that! He looked at Malpiero and knew exactly what the Assistant Purser was thinking. If they lost the cadet in the mornings a lot of work would have to be redivided and he himself would have to do more. It would be necessary for Malpiero to do the typing, and he would have to take back some of the duties he had delegated to his subordinate. There would be less time for casual chats with the first-class passengers; no time for a pre-luncheon apéritif; a shorter afternoon siesta. "And who told you this, may I ask?"

"The Chief Officer."

"This new man? This—this Signor Ciccolanti?"

"Yes."

"And you told him that the arrangement had been sanctioned by Signor Parodi? That it was quite customary and in order?"

"No, Cavaliere. I told him that I would report the matter to you."

Semprebon nodded angrily. "Yes. Yes, you did rightly. Very well, very well, then! I will deal with it." He picked up the telephone and snapped, "Give me the bridge—at once!"

Ten feet behind him in the small ship's exchange the operator plugged in a connector. There was a buzz, and then Semprebon heard Pavanoli's voice: "*Ponte comando!*"

"I want to speak to the Chief Officer."

"Who is it?" A note of gay impudence sounded in the boy's voice.

"You know perfectly well who it is—the *Commissario*. Hurry up!"

"*Si, signore.*"

A pause. Then a voice—a peculiar voice, deep and hard, rather slow—said, "Chief Officer here."

"Ah—Signor—er—Ciccolanti, is it not?" Semprebon's tone was one of haughty condescension. "I am sorry to trouble you but I am anxious to know why Pavanoli has not reported for duty at the *vestibulo* as he has been ordered."

There was a long pause during which Semprebon neatly ejected the gold-banded end of his cigarette from the long holder into an ashtray. Then the voice from the bridge said slowly, "Pavanoli is a deck officer."

"Indeed? He is not—as far as I am aware—an officer at all, yet."

"He is training to be a deck officer."

"He is—excuse me—a cadet, an apprentice. It is his duty to learn all sides of the ship's routine. For two hours in the morning he learns from me personally the duties of the Purser's Department. It will be most useful to him later."

"In what way?" asked the voice unexpectedly.

"Well——" Caught off his guard, Cavaliere Semprebon rattled his cigarette-holder up and down on the counter rapidly. "In many ways it will be of great help to him—very great help."

"It will not assist him to pass his navigational examinations. He is here to be trained for those."

"He is here,"—burst out the Purser—"to make himself useful when and where he can—and to learn his work as well! That is how it was when I was a boy. Of course it may have been quite different when you got your training, Signor Ciccolanti. Standards have changed a lot in these past years—as is very evident to those with greater experience."

Stubbornly, slowly, the voice repeated, "Pavanoli is learning to be a deck officer. He belongs entirely to the *Ponte comando* and has no more to do with the *vestibulo* than he has to do with the engine-room. I am sorry if it inconveniences you to lose him, but he should not have been working on purser's duties in the first place."

"Ah, so! Indeed? In the first place, you say. You do not know, perhaps, that Signor Parodi was in *complete agreement* with this arrangement 'in the first place'?"

"That does not concern me."

"Does it not, Signor Ciccolanti? Perhaps you may realise by what I have said that Signor Parodi's agreement undoubtedly means the personal agreement of Captain Onestinghel?"

"I have spoken to the Captain. He told me that it was entirely a matter for the Chief Officer. I cannot agree to continue to allow Pavanoli to spend any of the time in which he should be learning my profession in learning yours. Is there anything more you wish to ask me, *Signor Commissario*?"

From the corner of his eye Semprebon saw Mrs. Crambatch approaching from the other side of the vestibule, the soft, concealed lighting gleaming on her costume jewellery and on the gold-and-ivory crucifix round her neck. He did not wish Malpiero to deal with whatever it was that she wanted. Mastering himself with an effort, stilling a trembling hand on the counter, he said venomously, "That is all. For the present that is quite enough. Mr.—er—Chief Officer." And replacing the receiver with careful nonchalance, he turned to the counter with a forced smile—his first-class one, but a little strained at the edges. "Ah, Mrs. Crambatch, is it not? Good morning to you, madam. In what way, I wonder, can I serve you at present?"

2

High up, far above the multiple decks, in the full brightness of the white, many-windowed, sun-flooded bridge, Serafino put down the telephone. He turned to where Pavanoli stood watching him with joyful admiration. "Well, that's that. From now on you have no more to do with the Purser's office."

"*Mille grazie, signore!*"

"No, no." Serafino flicked over a couple of pages of the navigating log. "He had no right to keep you down there." He sighed quickly, already blaming himself for what he had done. He could get on perfectly well without Pavanoli—did not need him in the least, in fact, whereas the Purser probably did, for Don Ildefonso saved money by short-staffing in every department and particularly in the *vestibulo*. This Cavaliere Semprebon would have a just grievance against him now; he had made an important enemy and gained a very unimportant friend. But he had not demanded Pavanoli's release from his hated duties in the vestibule office in order to make either friends or enemies, but because the boy was being cheated. His parents had paid the Flotta Soto to teach him the duties of the bridge and the deck, and though it was part of the contract that he must also work, it was understood that it should be work for which he was being trained. Two hours a day in the Purser's office were two hours wasted, two hours which would have to be made good at some other time by extra study. The older officers would not see it like that, for in their own distant, almost forgotten boyhoods training methods had been altogether harsher and more oppressive—unendurably so, if one believed them, which Serafino did not. He had enjoyed his own days as an apprentice, and they were still close enough behind him to induce a strong fellow-feeling towards other cadets.

Taking a ball point pen from his shirt pocket, he scribbled some figures on the back of a radio form and handed it to Pavanoli.

"Look—Luigi, isn't it? What do they call you—Gino?"

"*Si, signore.*"

"Right. Well, see if you can work this out. *San Raphael* passed through the Canal last night. She radios that she left Port Said at eight forty-five this morning. Assuming her course and speed are what I've written here, I want you to tell me at what time we'll pass her—you can assume our speed as constant. When you've done that you'd better plot her position at the time when we shall clear Port Tewfik, assuming five hours at berth in Port Said and the usual twelve hours in the Canal."

He smiled briefly and moved away to the other end of the bridge, passing the quartermaster at the wheel, checking the course on the big gyro compass, noting with the automatic immediacy of ten years at sea that the slow swell was dying down under a light breeze from the south-east. Far below him *San Roque's* graceful prow cut smoothly through a sea of cobalt blue and, flanking the ship on either side, the fast, dark shapes of dolphins flickered in swaying curves. Slowly a calm contentment filled him, a sensation he had not felt since *San Ramòn* docked for her refit a month ago. Naples—the Vic' Re Galantuomo—seemed infinitely far away in time as well as space. He wondered with an interest curiously impassive and detached what the different members of his family were doing now in that baking, sprawling city, and whether they thought of him. If only he could take them all on a voyage like this, show them for a little his own life of the bright sea and sky and the sun-filled bridge. If only . . .

There came the sound of feet on the starboard bridge ladder and Malestroit, the Third Officer, strode in, grinning. He was a short, stocky Belgian, two years younger than Serafino, with thick, straw-coloured hair and a nose as snub as a hog's. "Well, well, well—how's everything here? All secure? Not in sinking condition, yet?"

Serafino smiled; he liked the happy, ugly young Third Officer far more than his superior, the pale, fat, shy Bressan with his light, oddly inflected voice and ambiguous manner.

"No, she's still afloat."

"God is good. Yet to-day I have been an instrument of His will. Really, I think I shall become a *dévot*—like the Captain. Listen—I will tell you. For no reason whatever I decided half an hour ago to descend to the tank top." Malestroit's square, heavily-muscled body was shaking with suppressed laughter, his face scarlet. "I had—this I must make quite plain—no reason whatever for doing so. None at all, you understand. In fact, I was really on my way aft to see Petelli about a practice swing-out of some of these so glamorous new lifeboats with which we have been provided, when a small voice within me whispered, 'Berthold Malestroit, descend thou to the tank top.' So I did. And there I found friend Rock, complete with short-handled sledge and a large cold chisel. I said, '*Bonjour, mon jeune ami*—and what is it now?' He said—you understand English?—*'I'm gonna sink this f—ing boat, mister.'*" Malestroit burst into a roar of laughter. "Yes, but truly! Just like that! So I said, 'Do you not like our ship, then?' And——"

"Who is Rock?"

"Rock? Who is Rock? Ah, but of course you have not yet had time to make Rock's acquaintance. But you will—yes, undoubtedly." Grinning, Malestroit turned to the cadet who had ceased working on his two problems and was leaning over the chart table, shaking with laughter. "Gino knows him, don't you, Gino? Come then, *mon p'tit*, tell the Chief Officer who Rock is."

"R-Rock," stammered Pavanoli with difficulty, "is the brother of Dirk, who——"

But Malestroit took up the explanation himself. "Who is the brother of Burt. Yes—Rock, Dirk and Burt, named, one understands after their mother's favourite film actors. Their other name is Ampel, and they are the children of

British migrants bound for Sydney. Poor Sydney! Little do its citizens know what we are bringing them! That bridge of theirs of which they are so proud will not last long after the Ampel children land." He shook his blond head in awed wonder. "But they are fiends, my friend! Absolute devils incarnate! They destroy everything they touch. And they are ubiquitous, they are everywhere. Also, I fear they are immortal—indestructible. Listen: I will tell you. . . . Two days out of Sot'ampton one of them climbed up the port hydrocrane. Another—he must have watched it done in port, for they are wickedly quick at picking things up—started it. So it began to lift. The brother at the top fell off—right down to the deck—bam!" Malestroit slapped a fist into his open palm. "Over seven metres on to iron plating. I saw it. 'My God!' I thought, 'here is one less migrant for Australia.' I ran down and the child lay flat on the deck. His brother stood looking at him without any great concern. One—I think it must have been Burt—said, '*'E's 'ad 'is chips, ain't 'e, mister?*' But no! As I bent down the child arose, rubbed its head, blew its nose—with its fingers and upon the deck, they always do it thus—and kicked me on the leg!"

"And to-day," broke in Pavanoli happily, "they threw paint over the *Capitan d'armi*."

"So?"

"*Si signore*. He caught one of them with a rope's end—made him screech like a whole roost of chickens with a fox among them!"

Malestroit slapped his thigh delightedly. "Ah, the brave Petelli! But they will be revenged, I think. To use their own ugly argot, I think Petelli will receive his chips."

"That is not all. Listen——"

But Serafino cut short a further account of the Ampel children's outrages. "Gino, have you done those two navigating problems?"

"Not yet."

"Then please do so. I did not rescue you from the *vestibulo* in order that you might waste your time gossiping about the passengers." He turned to Malestroit. "What does the Captain think of all this?"

The Third Officer shrugged, looked sideways at the helmsman and lowered his voice. "I don't know. No one ever really knows what the Captain thinks of anything."

"But if these little savages damage the ship?"

"He was asked that by Bressan. He said he thought that they were more likely to damage themselves. He said—I was there too: 'Bressan, there is an English proverb which suggests that if one presents a person with a sufficient quantity of rope he will, in due time, hang himself. If these regrettable children are given sufficient freedom it seems to me almost certain that they will break their necks or fall overboard or electrocute themselves.'" Malestroit shook his head dubiously. "They have not done so yet—nor do I think they will." Then, as if remembering something of greater importance, he swung round to Pavanoli. "Gino—have you got a full white uniform? A white coat?"

"No. Why? It is not necessary."

"No, no. I have not, either. And—you?" Malestroit was uncertain as yet how to address Serafino. It had been different with the last chief officer, a much older man and confined in his rank; with him it had always been a respectful "Signor Parodi." But this Ciccolanti from *San Ramòn* was much his own age and only acting Chief. He could perhaps have called him by his unadorned surname, but, like most people of his age and time, he disliked that mode of address; it was outdated and somehow slightly ridiculous when used between young people of the same status. He compromised with "you."

"I have only got blues."

"Good! Then it will be all right. You know the new order that we must eat in the first-class saloon? Well, the *Commissario* says that we must wear full white uniform—coat, tie, collar-badges and so forth—but I have none. Neither has Bressan. So it seems that none of us deck officers have got it—excellent! It appears from what Semprebon says that we will therefore be able to stay in our mess with the engineers. Semprebon will have *all* the first-class passengers to himself—just what he wants."

3

The first-class saloon was aft on "A" deck, and at eight o'clock that evening it presented a spectacle of smart if slightly vulgar luxury. The buffet at the forward bulkhead glittered with polished chromium and starched white cloth; there were large sprays of artificial flowers—an unseasonable mixture of yellow wax tulips and papery red roses—on every table, and the menu cards were garnished with scarlet and white silk bows and had "*Buon' appetito!*" printed genially across them in silver lettering.

The saloon itself was not large, and though it was decorated in a flashily pseudo-modern manner with walls of rose-tinted mirrors etched with swooping, stylized seagulls, it was entirely dominated by a large, dark oil-painting of Don Ildefonso above the buffet. The owner had sat for his portrait in Spanish naval uniform, but he was not a man whose personality could be effectively disguised by fine clothes and "*El Artillero*" frowned across the room, his strong, tough face and huge shoulders creating the immediate impression of a pirate masquerading for his own sinister purposes in the uniform of the law.

As the musical notes of the xylophone, struck by one of the mess-boys, died away down the corridors of "A" deck, the passengers began to trickle in and were met by Cavaliere Semprebon near the doorway. The Purser, tall, urbane and immaculate in his white uniform with the broad scarlet-and-gold bands glistening on his epaulettes and the tiny pale-green and red rosette of a Cavaliere Rebubblicano in his buttonhole, greeted them in turn as they entered the saloon: a cheerful word for the men, the first-class smile and a slight bow for the women. "Good evening Mrs. van Staedtler—Professor van Staedtler. The places to-night have been somewhat rearranged, as you will see. I have placed you and your husband at the Captain's table. Madame, if you will be so good—there, yes, beside the Captain's chair. He will be here quite soon. . . . Ah, Wing-Commander Catchpole! To-night I have placed you here beside myself—I have taken the liberty . . . And Miss—Miss McKenrick is it not? And how did you find the swimming-pool? Malpiero—show this lady to her place. Signor Malpiero is my assistant; he sits at your table. Signor Malpiero—Miss McKenrick . . . Countess, a very good evening to you! And how is the little dog? I have rearranged the places. You are now at the Captain's table. Yes, there if you will be so good . . . Ah, Commander and Mrs. Lannfranc—you are this evening at the doctor's table. You have met Dr. Gavanian, our ship's doctor? No? You will find him most interesting; he has spent so many years at sea, seen so many strange places and . . . Excuse me . . . Mrs. Crambatch, my dear lady—good evening! I have to-night altered the seating. You . . ."

Waiters moved solicitously in and out with napkins, rearranging the silver, pulling back chairs, handing menus. Captain Onestinghel appeared suddenly in his place, smiling thinly, bowing quickly to right and left, three rows of variegated medal ribbons glowing on his white uniform. Following him, sulky and flushed, was a dark-haired young man, square-shouldersd and bearing a close family resemblance to the big portrait above the buffet. Catching sight of him, Semprebon leapt forward. "Ah, Don Gil—good evening! I have placed you here at the Captain's table beside Mrs. Crambatch. Mrs. Crambatch, allow me to present Don Gil Sotomayor. And——"

"Cavaliere." The Captain's voice possessed a peculiarly penetrating quality even when, as usual, he spoke softly.

"Yes, Captain?"

"Where are the other officers?"

"The other——? Oh, yes. Yes. They had not correct uniforms. They understood that full uniform was necessary and as they had not got it they assumed that it was not necessary for them to dine here."

"Then they assumed wrongly," remarked the Captain mildly enough as he unfolded his napkin. "Full uniform is, of course, most desirable and they will have to purchase it when we get to Port Said, but lack of it at present is no excuse for disregarding my orders. Please inform the ones who are not on duty that they are to dine here."

"Very well, Captain. You mean from to-morrow?"

"I mean now."

"We are not, apparently, among the favoured few," remarked Paula Chelgrove to her brother as she turned her cold grey gaze slowly about the room. "Though that old Dutch couple and that down-in-the-mouth R.A.F. chaplain seem to be."

Colonel Chelgrove looked up from a close scrutiny of a wax tulip with the nervous start he always gave when his sister addressed him. "Yes—yes. Actually, I saw the Purser about it—about seating arrangements. I told him we'd like to share a table with the Malcolm-Bruces. I suppose he thought we'd rather have them to ourselves."

"But now we know they're not getting on till Colombo! I can't see why that's a reason for putting us at a small table while that old Dutch couple sit at the Captain's." Paula's long, lined face bore a slight flush on the cheekbones, her mannishly cropped grey head began to shake slightly and her back became rigid. These, as her brother knew, were signs of anger, and his own head cowered between his shoulders which rounded in a nervous hump as he leant over the menu. "Poached Turbot—bound to be frozen. H'm, well—well, actually he *did* ask me—the Purser did—if we'd like to be at the Captain's table. I—I said on the whole—no. You see, when the Malcolm-Bruces *do* come——"

"It wasn't anything to do with the Malcolm-Bruces!" Paula's voice was loud and cold and the twitching off her head increased. "It was because you felt someone might know about you, wasn't it?"

"No, no. Nothing at all like . . ."

"Wasn't it?" Paula's cold, grey eyes—Chelgrove eyes—bored into him.

"I tell you——"

"Now, listen to me, Perry! I'm not going to stand any more of that attitude. We discussed it all when you were in bed. You've got nothing to hide or be ashamed of. Since the court was obviously prejudiced in advance, and as all the main witnesses were obviously lying to save their own reputations at your expense—but we've been into all that, dozens of times. If you're going to become—become worried by a set of foreigners now, how on earth do you think you'll manage in New Zealand? And another thing: we have a right to be at the Captain's table. There's nobody else on board who *is* anybody."

Colonel Chelgrove refused to look up from the menu, the silk bow of which he was studying intently. His sister's words seemed to have shrunk him still further, and no one glancing at him as he crouched beside her could have guessed that he was over six feet in height; he looked quite a small man. "Oh, well," he mumbled unhappily at last, "the R.A.F. padre's getting off at Aden. And that old black-haired woman's a countess, after all."

Paula gave a snort of contemptuous laughter. "A foreign countess—yes, I've seen her. She looks as if she was the proprietor of a third-rate knocking shop!"

The Colonel flinched. Really, Paula got worse and worse. During the two occasions he had seen her early in the war she had never used expressions like that—even though she had taken to the Army like a duck to water. It was only in the last few years that she had started to play the old soldier in this wretchedly embarrassing way. "My dear, a foreign countess may come from a——"

"Certainly not from a family as good as ours! You can be quite certain of that. And you meekly let her take——"

This was too much. "Not meekly, Paula! I am *not* meek!"

"Well, if you're not you soon will be. You're beginning to get like that awful Major Arlesford who was secretary of the Bosingworth Golf Club. He embezzled their funds but he somehow got off, and afterwards he used to slink about the village, raising his hat every time he saw anyone and smiling and bowing like an old beggar. You can go back to the Purser to-morrow and tell him that we must have seats at the Captain's table—until Colombo, at any rate."

"My good Paula, of course I can't! Don't you see that they're all filled? Do have some consideration!"

She laughed bitterly. "I wonder if I haven't had too much consideration already, sometimes. When I consider how I've backed you up through everything! You've never thought of *my* feelings—all I've had to put up with. The talk in the village——"

"Rallstead is a very small place and its views are quite unimportant. I should have thought that by this time, Paula, and after all you've seen, you would have ceased to worry about parish pump gossip." And that, of course, had been a mistake. Now he was going to have the family thrown in his face again. He quickly started to drink the soup which a steward had placed before him and to concentrate his mind on the wax tulips again.

". . . is the whole essence of the best English families. Each to his own home. . . ." Oh, God, thought the Colonel, she'll start quoting Kipling in a minute. He was quite right. ". . . God gave each man a place to love.' . . . And our place has always been Rallstead. It's no use trying to think it doesn't matter. You remember Father's little poem he was so proud of? 'Paul Edward Chelgrove is my name and England is my nation. Rallstead is my dwelling-place and Christ is my salvation.' . . . poor Father! What he would have thought of all this——"

"All what, Paula?" asked the Colonel, exasperation mingling oddly with self-pity in his voice.

"This run—this leaving Rallstead and going off to a foreign land."

"New Zealand is *not* a foreign land. Of all the Empire it is the most English. You chose it yourself, and it's most unfair to talk as if we were going to live among a lot of

Spaniards or Greeks. Dr. Gregory suggested the Canaries or Rhodes, but I told him that such places were quite out of the question. We didn't speak the languages, and anyway he ought to have known us better than to suppose that we'd go and live side by side with a lot of foreigners. But New Zealand——"

He stopped suddenly and loked up, surprised. Two young men had come to the table and slipped quietly, wordlessly, into two empty chairs. They were both ship's officers, one of them a boy in his teens, wearing not over-clean, white, open-necked shirts and white trousers, and they were both scarlet-faced and furiously embarrassed.

Paula looked from one to the other with coldly questioning surprise, as if waiting for some explanation or apology—but none appeared to be forthcoming. "Well—er—good evening," she said pointedly at last. "*Buona sera,*" one of them replied in a mumble, hardly moving his lips. A waiter removed the artificial flowers which were now in the way and placed soup plates before the newcomers, who began to eat rapidly and silently.

Colonel Chelgrove glanced at his sister, raised his eyebrows and shrugged slightly. His expression said "Foreigners!" "What was I saying? . . . Yes. New Zealand is a totally different thing altogether. It's very possible, I imagine, that the Malcolm-Bruces will be going there to—and they're a very old Scottish family, very old indeed. There's nothing in the least odd or unusual in persons such as ourselves and the Malcolm-Bruces going to settle in New Zealand. It's really only as if we were moving from one part of England to another."

He had been speaking in a still lower voice than usual now that they were not alone, hoping to calm Paula a little. He had grown acustomed to these spasms of bitter chagrin which possessed his sister at increasingly frequent intervals, though he still dreaded them—fearing always that one day she would say publicly what he believed to be in her mind. These moods came upon her, he knew well, when she thought longingly of Rallstead—or rather, the position she had occupied in the vilage. Miss Chelgrove, the owner of Rallstead Manor, the Honorary Secretary of the Rallmouth Foxhounds, the President of the local Red Cross Association, the driving force of the Women's Institute, sitting on committee after committee, *getting things done*; ex-Commandant Chelgrove of the A.T.S. canvassing for the local Tory candidate with a ruthless mixture of parochial blackmail and bribery. And then . . . But it had been her fault more than his and she had only herself to blame. If she hadn't pressed and pressed him to demand a retrial, exhorted him again and again to "clear the family name publicly," they would not be on this foreign ship sailing far across the world, leaving Rallstead for ever. If only she had let him alone . . . But of course she never had and, with the curse of insensate family pride resting upon her like some black incubus, she never would.

He sighed despondently and leant back in his chair while the next course was placed before him. It was boiled chicken, and the sight of it seemed to enrage the elder of the two officers, a thin young man with an odd, triangular face beneath thick, fawn-blond hair. He turned over the wing of chicken on his plate with a vicious prod of his fork and suddenly said in grating, broken English, "Boil! Always boil meat!" He turned to the Colonel, who noticed that his thin hands were trembling with rage. "Look—always it is so! The Purser make all food for him. Boil, boil—always boil!" His deep voice was bitter with malice. "Look—it is because he has bad stomach! To eat like other peoples he can not! But none must to know this. So always it is boil, boil, boil!"

The two Chelgroves stared at him in wordless astonishment. Then Paula let out a harsh bark of incredulous laughter which caused the rest of the diners in the saloon to look curiously in their direction. The gaunt young face of the officer who had spoken paled with a stricken fury, his eyes narrowed. He drew in a long breath and appeared to be struggling to say something more, when suddenly there was a uniformed sailor standing before the table who bowed and spoke quickly in Italian. The Colonel heard the words "Signor Bressan" and "*Ponte comando*," and then the officer jerked to his feet, nodded brusquely and left the saloon.

Pausing at the foot of the bridge ladder, Serafino tried to control his breathing—tried to steady himself. He was astonished at his own rage, amazed that he could feel such fury, ashamed and somehow a little exultant, as if in the full flood of his tearing emotion he had grown in moral stature. How dare Semprebon treat him like that! First to trick him and the others into failing to appear in the dining-room as instructed, then to send for them in the most insulting manner possible—"The Captain requests me to demand that you come immediately to dinner in the first-class saloon as previously ordered. Semprebon. Cav."—so that none of them had time to change into clean clothes. And then, when they had trooped unhappily into the saloon like errant schoolboys, to find Semprebon sitting opposite the Captain while he himself was relegated to a small table with the cadet. It was too much! And as he had passed the Captain's table Semprebon had broken off his conversation with a fat foreign woman and lifted his head with a small, irritated frown, as if at the annoying intrusion of some inferior!

Remembering that look, his cooling rage kindled once more. He was Chief Officer, second in command of *San Roque* and everything about her and all that pertained to her. He was a trained seaman holding a Master's certificate, while Semprebon, despite the ridiculous airs he gave himself, was only a sort of mixture between a hotel manager and a pay-roll clerk.

He would complain. He would complain to-morrow to the Captain—vehemently and at length. He would see Semprebon put in his proper place. Yet inwardly he knew well enough that he would not. This odd, never-before-felt rage which filled him this evening would not last, and to-morrow all the old fears and worries that it had temporarily vanished would flood back—and then he would not dare to complain. He had only been on the ship twenty-four hours, whereas Semprebon had been on it more than a year. And the *Commissario* was old—and age called to age nearly as much as youth to youth. Captain Onestinghel might very well prefer to back an older man against someone still in his twenties.

He shook his head, breathed deeply the cool, dark sea-breeze, and started to climb the ladder, feeling empty and a little sick. That old English woman had laughed at him—because he could not speak her language properly. What had he said? About Semprebon and the ship's food—what Malestroit had told him. And it was true, too.

Scowling, he entered the dimly lit bridge. Bressan was sitting at the chart table and his face, illuminated from below by the bluish chart lamp, looked more that ever like a corpse's—pouchy, heavy-lidded, waxen, the soft, drooping mouth hanging slightly open, the almost bald head sparsely clotted with thin tufts of hair which looked like decaying wool. He turned at the sound of steps and looked up. " Oh—I did not wish to disturb you. I told Ruggiero to bring back your answer."

Serafino nodded brusquely. " I know. But I wanted to leave."

" I see." Bressan's soft voice held no inquiry; he nodded gently, expressionlessly, and Serafino wondered for a second whether Bressan had known that the other officers—those who were not on watch—would be sent for. He beckoned him into the small office behind the chart table; it was little more than a cupboard for storing signal-flags and old maps, and was used by the officers mainly as a place to talk out of earshot of the helmsman and the bridge telegraphist. He said coldly, " I'd better tell you that we *have* got to eat with the passengers, after all—uniforms or not. That—that *figlio di putana* sent for us!"

" The Captain?"

" Semprebon."

" I see."

And Serafino guessed at once that before another day was out the Purser of the *Turbo/nave San Roque* would be informed that the ship's Chief Officer had referred to him as the son of a whore.

IV

Port Said, hot, dusty, shabbily gay, perpetually welcoming everyone in the world with a sticky handshake, a fervent gold-toothed grin and a breath of garlic; Port Said, the most Levantine of all the ports of the Levant, a greedy, garish, cosmopolitan old whore, back again in business, battered but complacent, after the sudden savage attack of a couple of armed thugs.

San Roque, her spotless white paint glistening in the vivid morning sunlight, lay surrounded by the inevitable jostling bumboats at her berth beside the quay, almost directly opposite the Simon Arzt store. In the crowded vestibule the Purser and Malpiero, assisted by three taciturn Egyptian immigration officials, were exchanging landing-cards for passports. It was a cumbersome arrangement, necessitating the checking of several lists and causing considerable delay. It was also unpopular with most of the passengers, who, whether or not they had travelled before, were imbued with the twentieth-century respect for the sacred nature of their passports and gave them up reluctantly and only on repeated assurances that they would be returned later.

Countess Zapescu in particular was being difficult. She knew something of the lot of the stateless person in modern society, and her French Passport was to her as precious as life itself. She stood at the table, a bulky fur coat clasped clumsily in both arms, arguing vehemently. "But, messieurs, I wish only to walk on the shore. I do not intend to remain here; merely, you understand, to promenade the waterfront within view of the ship. For this I do not think it is necessary to give you my passport. No, no—it is quite out of the question!"

Cavaliere Semprebon sighed with weary irritation. "Madame, I assure you——"

"Come on, come on!" The tourist passengers were queuing impatiently in the heat. "Come on, lady—there's others wants to go ashore too! Cor—look at 'er coat! What's the ol' tart want with a fur coat in this 'eat? I ask you! A fur coat!"

"P'raps she's goin' to play bears with Nasser."

"Goin' to flog it, more like. You c'n get pounds for them things from the Gippos. Buy anythin', they will. Our young Bob, what done 'is National Service out 'ere before the bust-up, tol' me . . ."

The ship's doctor edged carefully through the crowded vestibule with two large suitcase. "Excuse—excuse, please!" He was a short, fat Armenian who took the opportunity for a quick visit to his home in Cairo whenever the ship passed through the Canal. The tourist passengers let him pass reluctantly. "Wonder what *'e's* goin' to flog? Got arf the ship's bleedin' stores in them cases, most like."

But the doctor only smiled widely and waved from the top of the gang-ladder to Cavaliere Semprebon, who responded with his usual dignified inclination of the head, half bow and half nod, before turning back to the other passengers. "Miss McKenrick—thank you, madam. Give half to the sailor at the foot of the ladder and bring the other half with you when you return. . . . Miss Chelgrove—yours. Thank you. Yes, at the gangway. . . . Mr. Condron. Yes. Mr. Hogben. . . . Mr. Ampel *and* family. . . ." The Purser glanced with apprehensive distaste at the three ugly, pallid, bullet-headed boys of ten or twelve years old, who, hands thrust deeply into the pockets of their tight jeans, stared back at him with the animal malignance, the secret, implacable hostility of the industrial slums. "Fart-arsin' ol' toff!" muttered one, and the others grunted their corroboration. The Cavaliere's arched nose lifted still higher and with one glance he relegated the Ampel family to the cesspit from which they had undoubtedly originated, but it was with a slightly heightened colour, a sharper note in his usually suave voice, that he turned to the next in line. *Nearly twenty-five years at sea. . . .* " Signor Polin—for yourself, wife and children. We sail at noon " . . . *and twice torpedoed in the war* . . . " Signor Valpatena and wife. Yes, please, at the foot of the ladder." . . . *And not at all well, really. The doctor had said* . . . " Wing-Commander Catchpole—yours, sir." . . . *And still to be doing this—still to be dealing with creatures like the Ampels* . . . " Yes, yes, we sail at noon."

2

In his cabin in the officers' quarters forward on " A " deck Guido Bressan glanced at his watch, frowned and put down his book. Ten-thirty—Gino was fifteen minutes late already. That meant that they would only have half an hour to buy the white uniforms necessitated by the owner's new orders. It was quite usual for Gino to be late on these occasions, the time when he agreed to go ashore with the Second Officer, and Bressan was accustomed to waiting for him. He would sit reading one of the highly coloured adventure stories in which he delighted—stories designed more for the tastes of schoolboys than for men of thirty-two—listening half-consciously for Gino's light step in the corridor, the quick rattle of his knuckles on the door. But fifteen minutes—a whole quarter of an hour. . . . In the rigid timetable of shipboard life that was too long a delay for even the most unpunctual young officer. Unless, of course, something had held him up, delayed him in some unforeseen way. It was hardly likely that the Purser or his staff would try to usurp his services after the attitude the new Chief Officer had taken over the matter two days ago, but it might be worth ringing Malpiero, all the same, for the Assistant Purser always seemed to know where everyone was to be found and what he was doing. Bressan lifted the white telephone beside the bunk and was put through immediately. " *Vestibulo?*"

" Yes. Assistant Purser speaking."

" Ah, Malpiero. Bressan here. Can you tell me if young Pavanoli is anywhere around your part?"

" Pavanoli is ashore."

"Ashore?"

"Yes. He and the Chief Officer left the ship together about twenty minutes ago. I heard the Chief Officer tell Petelli that he would be back before eleven, so I imagine Pavanoli will be back by then, too."

"I see. Thank you." Bressan's soft voice seemed to fade on the last words, but his face, as he put down the telephone, was as devoid of expression as ever, round, flabby, sallow, the drooping eyelids, the always slightly open, drooping mouth below the bulbous nose. He caught sight of himself in the mirror over the washstand and closed his mouth, but the effect was not much better—he merely looked prim instead of stupid.

So it had happened again—as it had happened so often before. He took infinite pains and care trying to make a friend, never demanding, never effusive, always there to help or advise, ready to fall in with any plan—and then someone else would come along, someone more forceful, better-looking, more—more like other people, and he was abandoned at once, cast off without a thought.

It had always been the same ever since the boyhood to which he often looked back so wistfully. An only child, the son of elderly, well-to-do parents, his poor health had for long prevented him from going to school or mixing with other children on equal terms, and it had not been until he was nearly fifteen that he had been considered strong enough to take part in the normal activities of his own age. How he had longed throughout those dreary, shut-in years to have a friend, a single friend who would be to him all that his lonely heart could desire—brother, comrade, lover—a compendium of human relationships, intense, glorious, holy and quite impossible. But at his release it was too late. He was too shy, too diffident, too delicate in his feelings for the loud ebullience of boyhood; he remained alone and apart.

Yet he was not entirely discouraged; he knew it would be different when he went to sea. For despite considerable opposition from his parents who wished him to enter the family business, he had long determined to be a sailor—an officer of the merchant service rather than the Navy, for the Italian Fleet had singularly failed to cover itself with glory during the nineteen-forties and presented an unattractive appearance to a romantically-minded boy in his teens. All the stories Guido Bressan had read during the slow years of his childhood had lauded the seafaring profession above all others as that in which men and boys came closest to knowing the warm, happy ties of the devoted friendship for which he so longed. And during his time as a cadet he had not been entirely disappointed. If he was ugly and not as strong as the other boys in the apprentices' quarters, at least he was unassuming and helpful when it was within his power to help. Also, he had a certain dry wit which, oddly enhanced and pointed by his soft, slow voice, earned him, if not popularity, at least the amused respect of his fellows.

Yet still, as the busy months turned into years and he became more and more acquainted with the profession of master mariner, the perfect friend, the unique relationship that he sought, continued to elude him. It was not that he was particularly hard to please, desiring only some unlikely combination of perfections; there were dozens of other boys possessing few exceptional attractions save for the ordinary charm of Latin youth among whom he might easily have found the companion he sought had any of them shown any sign of reciprocating his feelings—but they never did. For youth naturally takes people at their face value, and Guido Bressan's physical appearance was unattractive, his gestures slow and clumsy, his voice as soft and low as a nun's. They laughed at him—not unkindly for they were southerners—but treated him always as someone set slightly apart from themselves, somehow different.

In the end Bressan had tacitly accepted this valuation of himself, but moving out into adult life as a qualified ship's officer, he still retained a deep, nostalgic affection for the youthful dreams which he had never realised. Perhaps because of this, he retained, even into his thirty-second year, certain characteristics normally associated with teen-age youth; a shyness in approach, a diffidence of manner, an evasive obliquity in his behaviour which often caused him to be disliked and distrusted among his colleagues. He was, in part at least, aware of this, but made no effort to remedy it. Outside his work—and he was a competent enough deck officer—he had no particular desire for the company of the other adult officers, for somehow he never felt at ease with them—and they bored him, too, with their talk of their wives or their amorous adventures, their salaries or their deeds during the war. It was still towards the cadets that he looked for companionship, finding an odd spiritual affinity with them which seemed to increase rather than lessen as the years went by. Their shyness, the natural hesitancy and diffidence which they would soon outgrow, resembled his own more permanent inhibitions. The freshness and happy expectancy of their outlook matched in him the streak of romanticism which the years had not dulled and which he kept alive with his adolescent adventure books. Most of all their innocence pleased him, the surprisingly well-armoured innocence of mid-twentieth century youth, knowledgeable, gravely derisive, sardonic. And on the whole they liked him to intercede for them when they got into trouble, coming to his cabin and borrowing his books—even going ashore with him occasionally, though they generally preferred to be without adult supervision at these times.

Only once, when for a short time he had worked on an English merchantman, had there been any complaint. The Captain had sent for him, and after a good deal of embarrassed circumlocution, had told him that he must only speak to the apprentices in the course of duty, in order, he had said, staring fixedly out of the port-hole, to avoid giving the wrong impression. Bressan, once he had understood what the Captain was implying, had been so deeply hurt and shocked that he had been almost incapable of anger. To be even furtively accused of harbouring such ideas!

Yet if the cadets liked him it was only in an idle, happy-go-lucky way—never with the awed hero-worship they might bestow upon some other officer who approximated more closely to their idea of the prototype of their profession. Bressan could not, by any stretch of imagination, see himself inspiring that, nor could he compete with it. But was it possible that this new man—Ciccolanti—could have aroused such a feeling in young Gino? Of all the cadets he had known, Gino Pavanoli came closest to Bressan's ideal. Handsome in his sallow, southern way, with his olive skin and dark eyes and thick, unruly hair, he was also, like the Second Officer, an only child and possessed all the gentle, smiling courtesy of an upbringing on which there had never been any noisy bickering or rough, quarrelsome behaviour. Also, he was alone, the only apprentice on *San Roque* and —at least until Naples—Bressan had not had to compete for his attention with anyone else, for Malestroit, though far closer to the cadet in age, was still savouring the pleasure of not being one himself and treated Gino with an offhand geniality as if to prove it. No, there had been no one to take Gino from him until this Ciccolanti came aboard.

Though Bressan had too humble an opinion of himself to be

professionally ambitious, he had hoped, when Parodi gave his abrupt notice of resignation from the Line, to be promoted Acting Chief Officer at least for the voyage to Sydney, and it had come as a disappointment when Captain Onestinghel had told him that another second officer from a smaller ship was to have the job. If Ciccolanti had been older than himself in years as well as in service to the Line, Bressan would not have minded, but the new Chief Officer was six years his junior and looked even younger—looked almost a contemporary of Gino's, in fact. Perhaps that explained his attraction for the cadet—and of course he had helped the boy to escape from old Semprebon, a thing Parodi should have done but never had because he and Semprebon had been close friends.

Well, there was nothing to be done about it now except to hope that Ciccolanti left *San Roque* at the end of the voyage. He probably would, for Don Ildefonso's preference for elderly and fully experienced men as his senior officers was well known. Then some middle-aged man like Parodi would be appointed, Gino's silly infatuation would cease, and he would be back again in this cabin, borrowing books, gossiping happily about the passengers and their doings, and making plans for shore excursions at the next port of call.

Bresan sighed and picked up his cap. He would go ashore now, alone, come back alone, and for the next two months he would have no bright-eyed young friend to fill the emptiness of his sad heart. It had happened often before, it would probably happen often again—until at last, one day, there would be no one at all any more.

3

By half-past eleven most of the passengers who had gone ashore had come trailing back, hot, dusty and clasping wooden camels, handbags of coloured goat's-hide, or specimens of that deplorable art so beloved by the Egyptians—the inlaying of cedar wood with ivory and mother-of-pearl.

The sun stood high in the pale sky, glaring down upon the dirty jade-green waters of the harbour, radiating heat from the stonework of the quays, and emptying the waterfront of all but the persistent hawkers, the strolling policemen and the various port officials in their military-looking khaki uniforms.

From the foot of the long gang-ladder Petelli shouted up, "How many more to come?" and at the top Pavonoli repeated the question to the Purser.

Cavaliere Semprebon, leaning against the counter, his long cigarette-holder clamped between his teeth, affected not to hear. Since the cadet had sided so openly with the new chief officer, the Cavaliere had refused to have anything more to do with him. He had told him so yesterday. "Very well, young man," he had said coldly, "if you do not wish to acquire instruction from me, that is your affair. When I was your age I would have been delighted and properly grateful if an officer in another department had offered to teach me some of the duties of that section of the ship's management. But things were different in those days, of course. In those days we worked hard and liked it. We respected our superiors and were industrious and polite. To-day, I know, it is different. I know, too, that cadets cannot entirely be blamed for the change in standards. When inexperienced, ill-bred young men still in their twenties—people of no family and no background, sons of tradesmen or small shopkeepers, doubtless, if not of actual beggars—when such people can suddenly rise overnight to become senior officers, what can one expect? Boys must follow someone's example. Still, I should have thought that when it was a question of working with a gentleman or someone who so very obviously is not one . . . However, have it your own way." He had shrugged and turned away—admittedly rather more quickly than dignity warranted because Pavanoli's dark eyes were gleaming with derisive laughter and it would not do to let the little fool be openly insolent.

This morning it was Malpiero who answered, leaning across a somnolent Egyptian police official and neatly flicking over the stacked passports still to be returned. "Eighteen still out."

"They'd better hurry, then. We're leaving at noon."

Malpiero looked up sharply. "You mean twelve-thirty, surely? Noon was what we told the passengers."

"No, we really *are* leaving at twelve." Pavanoli stared into the vestibule through the big black sun-glasses in which, like most Italian deck officers, he clamped himself almost permanently during the summer.

Malpiero raised his eyebrows. "But we always get the passengers aboard half an hour early. Otherwise they would always be——"

"I know. But this time it was a mistake. It was not done like that on *San Ramòn,* it seems, and——"

"The Chief Officer is responsible, then?"

Pavanoli nodded unhappily, and Cavaliere Semprebon took his cigarette-holder from his mouth, blew a wavering smoke ring, and, addressing the ceiling, said, "If one makes new friends, however undesirable, it would surely be wiser to assist them occasionally with a little timely information."

"I did tell him, but it was too late. He'd already made the announcement."

No one answered him and Gino turned back to the small railed-in platform from which the long flight of wooden steps descended the ship's side. A family of Italian migrants wandered out of a side street and, crossing the quay, came slowly aboard up the swaying ladder. One, two, three, four, five—the Polins. Gino greeted them with a happy grin; that meant only thirteen still ashore. He glanced at the big watch on his wrist and the grin faded. It was a quarter to twelve. Thirteen people must appear in fifteen minutes, or else . . . It was not as if *San Roque* was in an ordinary port—Naples, or Aden or Fremantle—where a delay of ten or twenty minutes, if not longer, could be borne with reasonable equanimity. So exact and punctual were the arrangements for the Canal convoys at Port Said that a lag of five minutes could hold up a group of six or seven ships, or more probably, result in a missed convoy, with consequent heavy extra expenditure for the Line. A delay here could not be tolerated.

Two more passengers: women. Their pale, flowered dresses, annihilated by that fierce Mediterranean sunlight which is the enemy of all half-tones and pastel shades, proclaimed them to be English. That left eleven.

There was a long wait and Gino felt the palms of his hands grow sticky with a dampness that was not all due to the heat. Ten to twelve. A ship's hooter blasted a long note somewhere off the starboard quarter—the first ships of the convoy were starting to weigh anchor. The three Egyptian officials rose to go, shook hands quickly, unsmilingly, with Malpiero and descended the swaying ladder, leaving only a single police constable at its foot beside Petelli.

Seven minutes to twelve. Thank God, here were some passengers! The Ampel family, all of them wearing tarboushes, even the blowzy mother. They trailed slowly up the steps, and Gino noticed that each of the three children carried a short riding-crop of imitation plaited leather. He guessed what these contained and shook his head wonderingly; were the parents, then, quite mad? His guess was confirmed when the first boy, on reaching the top of the steps, whipped a long thin steel dagger from its disguised sheath, and with a snarling grin presented it at the cadet's stomach. Pushing it aside, Gino whispered, "You go to make like this at the Purser—yes?" and hustled the three of them quickly into the vestibule.

More passengers. Perhaps they would just make it on time, after all. The Venerucci family and two middle-aged British migrants. Four more minutes; *San Roque's* foghorn blasted out its deep warning, and as the noise faded, dying away in the still, burning air, Gino found the Chief Officer standing beside him. "They're not all aboard yet." It was a flat statement rather than a question. Below the inevitable dark glasses, Ciccolanti's face wore its customary expression of weary, stubborn patience.

"There are still three to come, signore."

"No—here are two." And, glancing quickly down the steps, Gino saw two young Sicilians swing on to the ladder, grinning placatingly at Petelli's angry comment on their lateness. They were tall, heavily-built youths going out to work as cane-cutters in the North Queensland sugar-fields, and they knew that they would be able to make more money in a single season than the *Capitan d'armi* earned in three years.

Suddenly the ship vibrated to the metallic, rattling roar of the rising anchor chains in the hawse-pipes, and once more the boom of the foghorn blasted out its impatience. The vestibule was beginning to fill with its usual throng of passengers wanting information, wanting to change their cabins or their money, or merely coming to watch the ascent of the ladder and the hurry and bustle round the head of the gangway which heralded the ship's departure.

"Well——" Gino heard the Chief Officer draw a quick sighing breath, saw him glance at his watch, compare it with the clock set above the Purser's counter and shrug—"we leave, then. If this passenger cannot be on time we cannot hold the ship for him."

Malpiero, picking up the last passport, said, "It is Mrs. Crmabatch." The name meant nothing to Serafino, and even Gino, who was clever at remembering passengers' names, was not sure of this one—but it galvanised the Purser into immediate protest. "Mrs. Crambatch! No, no, we cannot leave without her!"

"Why not?" asked Serafino briefly. He took off his sunglasses, closed them, and put them in his shirt pocket, staring a dry challenge at Semprebon.

"Why not? Because, Signor Ciccolanti, she is our most important—our wealthiest and most important—passenger! She has taken not one but two——" Semprebon held up two fingers and shook them dramatically—"I repeat *two* first-class cabins! She is therefore paying double fare."

The urgency in his voice, the indignant gesticulations of his long cigarette-holder, drew the attention of the strolling, lounging passengers. They ceased talking among themselves and stood listening, forming an interested, if somewhat mystified, audience.

Serafino said slowly, coldly, "That is no reason for her to delay the ship."

"Is it not? Wealth, my dear sir, has its privileges. This lady, as I happen to know, is only travelling on a ship of the Flotta Soto because she cut short her tour of Europe and was thus unable to take up her later booking on a large English liner. It should surely be obvious, even to somebody quite young and inexperienced and knowing nothing whatever of my department, that she should receive special consideration, so that she may speak well of the Line to her friends in New Zealand—many of whom, doubtless, are also of great wealth."

Twelve: the hands of the vestibule clock lay one upon the other, pointing imperiously upwards. Serafino stood alone in the middle of the big room, the eyes of everyone upon him. The decision was now his. For a long moment he stood, his face cold and stiff, struggling to make up his mind. What the Purser had said was of considerable importance. If this wretched woman was abandoned in Port Said, she would certainly complain bitterly to Naples; she was in the wrong, of course, but that would not stop her complaining. And she was rich. Like most Italians, Serafino considered that money always meant power. If this woman was wealthy she would be powerful. Naples, at any rate, would see it that way and act accordingly. And yet to miss the convoy would be worse—Naples would never forgive that. They would expect him to do both—to wait for this woman and also to get *San Roque* into her place in the line of ships now forming up—because it would be more convenient for them if he did both. But one could not do the impossible—even for Don Ildefonso. If only the Captain would . . . But he knew quite well that Captain Onestinghel would not. For a captain's lofty position could be considered, if he so wished it, to place him above such small decisions; they were for his Chief Officer, while he himself reigned, a benevolent or frowning deity, above the turmoil. In a case of fire, or shipwreck, or mutiny, Captain Onestinghel would take over personal control of *San Roque*—but for little else.

There was a quick flurry among the passengers crowding near the top of the gang-ladder, and Serafino saw Gino elbowed aside by a large, sweating Egyptian official of the Canal Authority who stared angrily round the vestibule, caught sight of the Purser and brandished a file of papers clipped to a board. "Chief Officer! Chief Officer, what for are you waiting? Do you not——?"

Semprebon took the cigarette-holder from his mouth and pointed it silently at Serafino, with the air of a medieval witch-hunter indicating his victim. And now there was nothing for it. "*Va bene*—we leave at once." Serafino strode over to the gangway and the Egyptian turned grumblingly and jolted down the steps.

"All right, Petelli!" The Master at Arms saluted briefly and shouted to the sailors far above him. They heaved on the ropes and the ladder started its rattling, swaying ascent.

"There she is!" said Gino suddenly, and as he spoke a taxi slowed to a halt on the quay and Mrs. Crambatch, fat and flushed, her thick red arms full of parcels, scrambled awkwardly out. "Wait! Wait a minute!" She lifted her hot, florid face towards the two white-uniformed officers high up on the little platform jutting from the ship's side.

Sighing loudly with angry despair, Serafino slammed his hands down on his narrow hips. "All right, Petelli—*lower* the ladder!" And a minute later Mrs. Crambatch, assisted solicitously by Gino, was on board.

"Petelli!" Once more the ropes squealed in their falls and the ladder began to rise, when Mrs. Crambatch, catching sight of it and recovering a little of her breath at the same time, thrust the pile of boxes she was carrying into Gino's arms and turned to Serafino. "No! No, wait! In that car—a lot of other things—more than I could—carry. I must go back. Or—no! . . . You must send a—sailor."

And now at last he rounded on her, his voice hard and taut. She might easily have been the cause of his dismissal and so toppled to ruin the unsteady economy of the family in the Vic' Re Galantuomo. "Listen, signora! It is beyond of the time of departure! You have made so we wait for you! You delay the ship! Now we go—*subito!* No more wait one second!"

Trembling slightly, his mouth a grim line, he turned from her, while she, purpling at the affront, her eyes glittering behind her decorated spectacles, gasped for breath. But she had seen the determination in his face, and realising the incipient loss of the quantities of Egyptian knick-knacks still in the car, she called urgently to Semprebon. "Purser! Purser, you must help me. Can't you make this young man, whoever he is, wait a moment? Look!" Still panting, she pointed to Gino who stood, his arms full of brightly coloured boxes of Turkish Delight, beside her. "It wouldn't take this boy a minute to run down and——"

"Yes, yes, madam. I agree entirely." The Cavaliere had sauntered up, an assumed look of polite concern upon his aristocratically bearded face. Now, turning to Serafino, speaking in English and loudly enough for all to hear, he said persuasively, "Mister Ciccolanti, I realise that we are about to depart, but if you would spare two minutes to send Pavanoli——"

Suddenly there was a diversion round the head of the gang-ladder and Roger Lannfranc, grinning, his arms full of parcels, pushed into the group around Mrs. Crambatch. "Here you are; these are yours, aren't they?"

"Yes—yes! But how very kind! How——"

"I told them to hold on a moment—while all the natter was going on up here." He chuckled contentedly. "I've been in the Navy, you see, and I suppose I've got so used to having my orders obeyed by sailors . . . Anyway, your driver had brought all these to the foot of the ladder." He turned, still grinning, to Serafino and patted him on the shoulder. "Sorry to interfere, old boy—but it seemed silly to waste time jabbering away up here when it didn't take a second to nip down and get the things. I've told Petelli he can ship the ladder now." Everyone was laughing; Semprebon contemptuously, Mrs. Crambatch with spiteful triumph, the lounging passengers with ironic amusement or derision; even Gino was grinning stupidly, his arms still full of Turkish Delight.

Serafino breathed deeply, his brown eyes glaring into the amused grey ones of the stocky, florid Englishman almost on a level with his own. There was only a couple of inches difference in their heights.

"*Mille grazie, signore!* You would perhaps like to command all the ship—yes? It is bad that we have no cannons for you to——"

"Torpedoes, old boy. I was a submariner."

Serafino ignored him with an effort and turned to the cadet. "Gino, put down those things at once! You are training to be a deck officer, not a mess-boy. Go to the *Ponte Comando,* give the Pilot my compliments and tell him I will be with him immediately." He turned and strode rapidly from the vestibule, his narrow back flat and rigid against the renewed laughter that broke out behind him.

V

All through the long afternoon *San Roque* moved slowly down the Canal in the calm wake of a Greek tanker bound for the Persian Gulf. A breeze of incandescent heat blew gently from the pale, empty expanse of the Sinai desert and lapped the ship in its dry, fiery breath, raising the temperature of all the exposed metal surfaces to a degree at which they could no longer be touched. The small swimming-pool was so crowded with passengers from the tourist class that someone, probably Ted Condron, had chalked "Standing Room Only" on the blackboard used for indicating the hours of the pool's use by adults and children, while someone else had added "Except for Wops."

The original dislike of the British migrants for the Italians embarking at Naples had increased with the growing heat as *San Roque* drove steadily southwards. Due, in the first place, to an instinctive fear of all things foreign, the dislike was heightened by the rising temperature, the dilated brightness of the tropical day, and the uneasy feeling that England with its cold rain and obscuring mists was small and far away—and getting smaller and farther away with every turn of the ship's screws. The heat and the vivid brightness, welcomed in the first Mediterranean days with joyful wonder, were becoming overpowering now, unnatural and somehow ominous.

"Aren't we never goin' to 'ave no thunderstorm?" Gladys Ampel had complained, gazing disgustedly up at the brassy sky and fanning her flushed face with a paper handkerchief. "It can't go on an' on like this, surely!"

And the Third Officer, Malestroit, who had been passing at the time, had grinned and said, "Here—no. Here it does not thunder. And soon it will become—oh, very, very much hotter."

"Oh, no!"

"But yes—I assure you!"

It annoyed the British that the Italians did not seem to notice the heat or the glare; they lounged in it all day, chattered, slept, ate heavily and slept again, without apparent concern or discomfort. "Always lived like pigs so they don't notice no difference now," Ron Hogben said disgustedly. 'Ah—but they're in with the crew; *they're* all right," someone else had said darkly.

The fact that the Italians were easily able to make their wants known to the crew, and still more easily able to get them supplied, was another source of constant exasperation. "My 'usband asked for oice. 'Oice!' 'e said, plain as plain. 'Bring me some oice for the kids—see?' An' this feller gives 'is stupid grin an' says, 'No oice—no oice.' Nex' minute we sees them Eyetie kids—Ricci-somethin' or other—an' every little bastard's suckin' a dirty great lump of oice the size of your 'ead! So I says to Mrs. Throsby, 'Just look at that,' I says. 'That's not right,' I says. An' I goes an' finds this feller what tol' me there was no oice an' I takes on of these Eyetie kids along with me—see? An' I says, 'What you mean, tellin' me an' my 'usband there's no oice? What the flamin' 'ell d'you think this is?' An' . . ."

The Italians themselves were reluctant to adopt the same hostile attitude. They were poor, and believed that all poor people had too much in common to quarrel over anything save the most urgent problems of living. Under the present circumstances there seemed to them to be nothing to quarrel about at all. The weather was fine, the sea calm, the food reasonably plentiful and no worse than that to which they were used; and better than all these reasons for contentment, there was no work to be done; for nearly four glorious weeks they could be as totally, as restfully, idle as never before.

Besides, they were going to Australia, a country owned by these British, who would enter it with the full freedom of their own home, while they themselves must accept the status of not particularly welcome guests and long years of second-class citizenship with all its slights and disadvantages. It would be unwise to quarrel with these people who were kith and kin of the Australians among whom they would be living. It was easier, as well as more prudent, to affect not to understand the more pointed remarks of their fellow-passengers and to keep out of their way as much as possible.

It was with the intention of avoiding the British in general, and in particular the huge foundry-worker Hogben who had taken a violent and unreasonable dislike to him, that Armando Lodigianni had made his way on to the after-end of "C" deck. It was a part of the ship which was roped off and bore a notice stating that it was out of bounds to passengers. Sometimes members of the crew or an off-duty mess-boy would climb up the ladder from the service deck below and sit smoking on one of the iron deck-heads or leaning against the great wooden pen which contained the stern hawsers, but if they saw Armando they only grinned and nodded amicably, knowing him to be young and poor like themselves and asking nothing but to be allowed to sit quietly in the shade.

Armando had found a small space between one of the deck winches and the kennel which was supposed to house the old dachshund Brown, but seldom did. Here he sat, hands clasped round bare brown knees, blinking at the glaring plain of white sand which stretched out limitlessly beyond the slowly passing bank of the Canal. They had been at sea nearly a week now and it would be nearly another three before they dropped anchor in Sydney Harbour. And after that . . . But his two cousins would decide what happened after that; the responsibility would not be his. Probably there would be a lot of hard work, but after all, that was why they were going to this distant land. He had heard it said that an Italian workman in Australia could earn three times as much as an Australian because for the Italian it was natural to work three times as hard. It was also said that this fact was the reason for the unpopularity of Italian migrants in the country. It seemed an odd reason, for presumably there was nothing to stop the Australians from working equally hard, or harder if they wished. Unless, of course, they were like these English, always boasting and drinking and explaining that the reason *they* were going to Australia was to do considerably less work than they had done in England—which, by their own account, seemed to be extremely little anyway. Their talk too, or the small amount of it which Armando could partly comprehend, centred generally upon aspects of industrial trouble, endless grumbling monologues about strikes, lock-outs, overtime and Union rules, confused rigmaroles of whining self-pity and shifty defiance.

Last night Hogben had stretched out a huge hand and caught hold of Armando's belt as he passed. "Come 'ere, Armander. I wants to ask yer a question." Grunting, he had swung up to a sitting position on his bunk and drawn Armando up against the vast knees of his dirty flannel trousers. "What I want to know is—what you goin' to do in Aussie when we gets there?"

"What I do in Australia?"

"That's what I said."

"Work, of course."

"What sort o' work?"

Armando had shrugged. "What is possible I find."

"Ain't you got no trade then, eh?"

"I am *macchinista* for *officina*—garage."

"Are you now?" Hogben's small eyes crinkled suspiciously in his huge red face. "A qualified fitter, eh? 'Ow old are you?"

"Sixteen year."

Hogben had given a grunting snort of anger and triumph and raised his voice. "Listen to this! Kid says 'e's a qualified fitter—says 'e's a qualified fitter an' *admits* 'e's only sixteen! Ah, I knows! I knows what you're after! You're goin' to steal a trade off of some bloke. You'll do *anything*, won't yer? You just said so!"

"Yes."

The answer seemed to enrage Hogben. His face had flushed still more fiery and his hand tightened convulsively on Armando's belt. "Ah! Ah, 'e admits it—see! One minute 'e says 'e's a qualified fitter—which *I* says is a bleedin' lie 'cos 'e *says* 'e's only sixteen an' prob'ly 'e don't know a big end from 'is own end—an' nex' minute the dirty little scab turns round an' says 'e'll do anythin'! Ah, I've 'eard about these dagoes! Come out to Aussie as kids—'Yes, sir, no, sir, very good, sir—kiss-your-arse-sir!'—an' nex' thing anyone knows they got a job. Workin' for nex' to nothin', of course, an' livin' on the smell off of an oily rag. Then they doubles up gets *another* job as well—do it in their off-time, see? Oh, no, they won't join no union, oh, no! Not if they can bleedin' well 'elp it, they won't! An' then they saves their money—don't think of spendin' it an' 'elpin' other blokes to live, oh, no! An' then they buys a business an' works it eight days a week an' takes on others like themselves to work for 'em. Before you know what's 'it you, they got a bloody great firm!"

Growls of angry agreement had come from other bunks, and someone had grunted, "Stinkin' dago blacklegs!"

But Hogben had not been listening. He had worked himself up into a rage and his face was contracted into an orb of crimson hate, his tiny hot eyes narrowed and glinting with spite. Through clenched teeth he said thickly, "Well, it's not goin' to be like that, Armander—not this time it aint. We got wise to your little tricks at last, see?"

Armando had swallowed, his eyes widening with fear. "I do nothing—I do not understand. What . . ." He had tried to pull himself away but Hogben held him tightly. "You stay still till I finished with you, Armander, see? Or you'll tear them pretty white knickers, won't yer? An' that'd be a real shime, that would——" he had thrust his face forward aggressively—"'cos you looks so nice in them, don't yer? Just the things for 'angin' round a public convenience in, ain't they? An' that's just about your mark, I reckon! That's a trade you can't steal off of another bloke, at any rate! Ah, get to hell out of it—you make me wanter throw up!"

He had given Armando a savage push which had hurled him against the sharp corner of a bunk, bruising his back so painfully that, badly frightened already, he had started to cry and limped quickly to his own bunk and lain there sniffing, until Hogben had lurched out in search of more beer at the tourist bar.

Che bestia! If only Emilio or Niccolo had been there things would have been different, but they had been, as usual, sitting by themselves up on deck, smoking and endlessly discussing their plans and prospects for Australia, and when he had told them they had sighed, nodded and said he must just keep out of Hogben's way—they didn't want any trouble if it could possibly be avoided.

Armando's eyes narrowed to the glare of the sun on the pale sand of the passing desert, his mind drifted back in a vague, disconnected reverie over the past year: the job in his cousins' garage on the Via Gianturco, the trouble over the radio, Emilio's face of anger and fear, and his own answering fear. One became involved too easily—years ago it might have been different—Napoli. . . .

Half an hour later Second Officer Bressan, rising from peering into the empty kennel, found the boy asleep beside it and prodded him gently with the toe of one white shoe. Armando awoke, saw an officer above him, and would have scrambled to his feet had not Bressan waved him back. " No, no. Don't disturb yourself. I only wanted to know where the dog is."

" Signore, I don't know. It wasn't here when I came."

" When was that?"

But Armando had no watch. " I'm not sure. About an hour ago, perhaps. I shouldn't really be here, I suppose." He saw that he was not going to get into any trouble and his confidence increased. " It's the only place to be quiet."

Bressan nodded, privately resolving to rebuke Gino sharply over Brown's absence from the kennel; it would at least be a mild revenge for this morning's betrayal. " Yes, but it doesn't matter unless the *Capitano d'armi* finds you—and he can only tell you to go away."

" *Grazie, signore.*"

" *Niente, niente.*" Bressan sighed gently, wiped his hot, damp face with a handkerchief and glanced down with a mildly compassionate interest at the boy beside the kennel. How typical he was of the young worker from the south—from Campania, from Calabria, from Sicily. The too-easily-smiling, rounded face below the thick, springy black hair; the strong shoulders, deep chest and smooth, heavily-muscled legs—a powerful, apparently sturdy little animal, bred for heavy agricultural work. But that dark glowing skin, that appearance of blooming health, was so often a short-lived illusion. An inadequate diet of bread, pasta and odd bits of fish, a childhood in which an almost Oriental lack of hygiene must be accepted and survived—these laid up future penalties which would appear all too soon. Once in Australia there would be a period of long and heavy work for this boy, probably under another Italian who would exploit him shamefully. Then, with money carefully saved, would come the purchase of a business or a share in one. And in, say, fifteen or twenty years, a fat, partly bald, ill-tempered little man, purse-proud, grasping, suspicious and venal, would be exploiting other newly arrived young Italians, with a cynicism and brutality which he would justify with the remark that things had been worse in his own day.

If only, thought Bressan despairingly, if only it didn't have to happen like that. If only youth could stay handsome and happy and innocent! To-day this boy was a triumphant example of what Italy could produce from next to nothing; in twenty years he would be a disgrace. Once more he wiped his face and sighed. "Well—how are you liking the trip?"

Armando flashed his usual piano-key grin. "Very much, signore. It is like a lot of Sundays, one after the other."

Bressan smiled. "Yes, I suppose so. Are they feeding you well?"

"Oh, yes. We have meat all the time."

The Second Officer thought of the tough, stringy beef—third-grade oxen slaughtered after years of work and purchased in some shrewd commission deal by one of Don Ildefonso's financial hatchetmen—which turned up day after day on the tourist-class menu as "Cooked Bull" if Malpiero had his way, or "Old English Country-style Roast Beef with Horseradishes sauce and mustards" if Semprebon corrected it in time. He said, "I'm glad *you* approve, at any rate. The British migrants have been complaining to the Purser, I understand." He gigled softly.

"Oh, yes. They say that it is bad for their stomachs. And they are always wanting a great deal of potatoes—boiled potatoes—and cake. I think in England they must live entirely on potatoes and cake—and beer." Armando grinned. "Cike," he said, mimicking the English migrants, "we wants more cike!"

"Cake," corrected Bressan automatically, but Armando shook his head politely. "*Permesso, signore*—no. Cike—like that. They always say it thus."

"That is only because—" Bressan broke off with a shrug. "Well, it doesn't matter. It will be 'Cike' when you get to Australia anyway, so you might as well learn it like that. Are you learning English, then?"

"I try. I already know a little, of course, from school." He shrugged. "But it is not easy," he finished lamely, aware that he was blushing slightly under his heavy tan.

"No." Bressan took out a packet of cigarettes, lit one himself and threw one to the boy, who caught it expertly between his fingers. "But perhaps one of the British will help you?"

Armando shook his head decidedly. "No. They hate us, I think." He glanced thoughtfully at the cigarette he was holding. "You know, signore, what my cousin Emilio told me about the British? How during the war when the American and English troops were in Naples the children were all asking for cigarettes—you know, '*Sigaretta, signore! Sigaretta!*' And the Americans gave them cigarettes and said '*Goddam, get the hell outa here!*' but the English said '*Yes, yes—sigarette*' and got them to come close and seized their hand and—so!" Armando made as if to grind out his burning cigarette in the palm of his left hand. "But I didn't really believe him." He paused. "I do now, though."

Bressan's pallid, moon-round face clouded; he said firmly, "I do not think that at all a likely story. All soldiers are good to children—it is their nature. Something bad happens once in a way, perhaps, and then it becomes exaggerated out of all proportion." He made a small, unhappy gesture with one hand and sighed, filled with a momentary sad awareness of the briefness of life and the darkness of men's hearts. "Well, perhaps I can teach you a little English. I've taught others."

Armando looked pleased and a little startled. "*Grazie, signore*. I should be very grateful, but—do you have the time?"

"Oh, yes—generally." As if remembering something, Bressan glanced at his watch. "But I have none now. I will let you know when I can manage a lesson." He smiled and was about to move away, when Armando said urgently, "Signore—one thing. You have been to Australia before?"

"Yes, several times."

"Are they like these English on board??"

Bressan, reading fear in the dark eyes that looked up at him and sensing the demand for reassurance, hesitated a long moment. "No," he said carefully at last, "they are not like this lot—most of them are not, at any rate." He paused, frowning. "It is like this. In Italy—in Europe—everywhere, there are failures. Persons who, because of vice or weakness or stupidity, cannot live sensibly and work properly like everyone else. In Europe they sink—become beggars and are despised. In Australia they do not sink so much as float, like a sort of dirty scum. They are not ashamed and they are not despised. They are tolerated and given money. There are a lot of them and most of them are old. I think they are treated in this way because long ago they were soldiers and the Australians venerate soldiers. You will meet them, and I will tell you that compared to them these English migrants are good and friendly people. But these paid beggars—the Australians have many names for them which I will tell you later—are only the surface. Underneath the Australians are not like that." He paused again, wanting to reassure the boy, wanting somehow to praise the Australians and yet not to raise useless hopes. "Well, anyway, you must try to like the Australians, even if it is not easy at first. For it is their country, as they will continually remind you, and there is no reason why they should try to like you." He smiled sadly, seeing Armando's obvious disappointment. "Well, I must be going."

2

The first-class passengers were subjected to no such strains and stresses and, with the exception of Flora McKenrick, they were more or less indifferent to the presence of the tourist-class migrants on *San Roque*. And even her interest only centred round the ship's small swimming-pool. The tourists and their children practically monopolised it, and the latter—well, they were the most unhygienic-looking bunch of kids she had ever seen, and as a schoolmistress of considerable experience she had seen a lot.

On the boat deck after lunch she mentioned the matter to the Purser, who was always so attentive and helpful. "Mr. Semprebon, are the first-class passengers never allowed the pool to themselves? I should have thought that some arrangement of different hours for different classes could be managed. As it is, the only time when I can get a swim is at dawn. The rest of the time it's just a screaming mass of children—and you know, I think that they are probably dirty in the water."

"Yes, yes. I agree most fully. I have no doubt at all that you are right. But—well, it is, in fact, the Chief Officer's responsibility. The deck——"

"Then he ought to do something about it. Someone ought to tell him."

The Purser had smiled, lifting his hands in mock despair. "My dear lady! No one can tell the Chief Officer anything. He is—how does one say?—impenetrable of all suggestion."

"It's that boy with a limp, isn't it?"

And Cavaliere Semprebon had burst into laughter. "Oh! Oh, ha, ha, ha! Yes, my dear Miss McKenrick, as you say, it is indeed that boy with a limp!" Chuckling, he had fitted a black cigarette into his holder and glanced round the boat deck. "Confidentially I will tell you something, though I ought not to, perhaps. He is very young, this Chief Officer, and he is only here because our—our correct Chief Officer left the ship with suddenness at Naples. We must have someone, and this young man only was available. Confidentially I will tell you that he is being very difficult and silly, but——" And again he had laughed and gestured with amused resignation.

But Flora McKenrick was only concerned with the swimming-pool. "Well, then, would it be all right for me to bathe in the evening—after six?"

"But the crew bathe then."

"Only a few of them."

"Yes, yes. The mess-boys, I think. Proper sailors, of course, do not like water. Did you know that?"

Stubbornly she said, "Does it matter if I bathe when they do?" And the Purser had glanced at her with amused but slightly shocked surprise. "My dear Miss McKenrick! Really, I do not think——"

She had coloured under his obvious disapproval. "I suppose I had better ask the Chief Officer?"

"Yes, yes, certainly that would be best."

But on second thoughts she had decided not to ask the Chief Officer. She had watched him, later that afternoon, strolling with the Captain on the forward end of the boat deck under the bridge, a section cordoned off with chains and the notice "*Riservato al Comando,*" and had decided at once that he would refuse. There was about that short, thin figure with the high-peaked white cap set cockily aslant on its head, a touch of bitter austerity which reminded her strongly of Kevin Turner, the small cripple in her senior class at Gyana. For most of the twenty years of her professional career she had been in charge of mixed classes, as was inevitable in the schools of the tiny townships—mere hamlets by European standards—of the Australian countryside, and her understanding of men was entirely based on the behaviour and attitudes of the boys in her charge. Kevin's behaviour had been coldly grim, defensive and resentful. It had been the simplest exercise in applied psychology to realise that this attitude was the result of his smallness and his lame leg. The same defects in the Chief Officer's body would almost certainly result in a similar frame of mind: like Kevin, he would refuse most requests on principle, and particularly requests to do something which he could not—

swim or play games. And if he did refuse and later saw her near the pool in the evenings, he might become suspicious; then she would be unable to watch Agostino and his friends diving and leaping in the water like pale-brown dolphins. She had given a brief sigh, almost a grunt, and turned away.

Evening was falling as *San Roque* slid gently between the two halves of the swing bridge at El Ferdan. Four miles away the trees of Ismailia lay, a dark patch, on the curving bank of the Canal, and the desert on each side was a glowing rose and gold under a sky of softly deepening blue. Of all the many sights to be seen on the long voyage, this short period of evening while the ship passed slowly, silently, through the sunset desert was the most beautiful.

But to Flora McKenrick, sitting in her cabin on "B" deck, it was a period of steadily mounting tension and anxiety. Agostino was off duty at six-thirty—or so he said. He had promised he would come to her cabin then—but would he? She swallowed with difficulty, thinking of Agostino, his wide shoulders, his strongly-muscled forearms, his broad grin and mop of dark hair. But he had proved unexpectedly—not prudish, really, but—laughingly hesitant. He liked to talk to her, liked to air his few words of English, and tell her about his home and this *fidanzata* of his of whom he was so fond. He liked her obvious admiration and her brief comments on his prowess in the swimming-pool, but beyond that . . . All this talk about the magnificence of Latins as lovers was ridiculously untrue, she told herself dourly; all they wanted was chatter and compliments. Still—they probably came round in the end, and that was more than could be said of the Australians. She thought briefly and with cold despair of Gyana—small, tin-roofed, the peppermint trees along the dusty main street, the old hotel, its façade ornate with Victorian balconies of rusty ironwork, the new white wooden school with its big windows and sunblinds, the red brick church; Gyana, where if a boy was seen talking to a girl more than once he was forced to marry her, where everyone knew the life-history of everyone else, and the life-history of his parents and grandparents into the bargain. Gyana, where God, in a black frock-coat and black gloves, leaned out of his parlour window in Heaven and ruled through His regents—the half-dozen grim matriarchs of the Church Committee. To Gyana she was returning—alone and with the thousand pounds she had won in the Queensland Lottery nearly all gone. She had escaped for a little, and now

slowly worked himself up into an ugly, smouldering rage. He had tried to blackmail her and she had laughed at him; she was quite prepared to go on paying him—but not for nothing. He had turned suddenly and hit her—they were leading the ponies down a narrow track—knocking her down among the stones and whins, and then run off up the heather-covered slope, disappearing into the falling mist—and she had never seen him again.

And with that one episode she had been forced throughout the remainder of her trip to remain content. For she had at last located some McKenrick cousins, had stayed with them and been passed to friends and friends of friends. Later she had travelled in France and Germany, but in closed groups under the management of a courier. Somehow, neither the time nor the opportunities to further her desire had presented themselves in any way as to be other than dangerously vulnerable. There had been nothing—until she boarded *San Roque* and, coming into her cabin, found Agostino polishing the brasswork round the port hole, whistling some Italian tune, pausing, head on one side, to admire his work.

Talkative and cheerful, he had been totally unlike the grimy youth on the Scottish hillside and her own approach had been far slower and more careful. She had tried to moderate her gruffness, tried to treat him not as a mere object of her physical desire but as a nineteen-year-old human being. It had been intensely boring, listening to his half incomprehensible chatter about his home, his parents, his *fidanzata* whom he hoped to marry next year if he could afford to do so and who sounded both vain and silly, but in the end she had managed to make him understand that she would like to help him with some money—she had hinted at ten pounds—if he cared to accept it. She was not certain, even now, whether he had fully understood her. She glanced at her watch—nearly six-thirty. She would soon know.

3

San Roque swung slowly round the curve of the Canal, past the little bathing beach of Ismailia with its high diving-boards and painted beehive huts, and entered the buoyed channel of Lake Timsah. Sunset flared and died along the western horizon, and night swept in across the cooling desert. The

Egyptian pilot on the bridge spoke to Bressan, and the great electric lamp on the ship's prow flashed its guiding beam across the still, dusky water. In a small compartment behind the vestibule the steward who had been pressed into the Purser's service to replace Pavanoli changed the records on the radiogram and amplifiers all over the ship poured out the unaccustomed music of the Second Empire's "*Partant pour La Syrie.*" The records had been bought hurriedly as a job lot, none of them was under ten years old, and as the steward whose job it was to operate the radiogram was musically illiterate, the concerts given to the passengers of *San Roque* were of an eccentrically miscellaneous nature. This evening they had already been given the 1812 *Overture,* the "Nuns' Chorus" from *Casanova,* the inevitable "*Addio, mia bella Napoli,*" and a thunderous rendering of the "*Horst Wessel Lied.*"

In the first-class bar Colonel Chelgrove sipped a mild whisky and soda and nodded sleepily to Wing-Commander Catchpole, the R.A.F. chaplain bound for Aden, who was complaining in a mousish monotone about the soaring prices of accommodation and their effects on his flock. ". . . ou little community reasonably happy and contented as it should be. Now there's a Flight Sergeant I know, a *good* man, with twenty-five years' service, living in one small hotel room with his wife and two children and paying one hundred and twenty pounds a month. That's at Tawahi. And at Crater there's a young Pilot Officer, a really *nice* lad, living in two windowless rooms with his family of three in a smelly Arab hotel. And I personally know of four families, all *excellent* people. . . ."

At the bar itself the duty steward, Agostino, was handing over to his friend, Ettore. "These are all who have been here for the last half-hour. The heretic military priest drinks Coca-Cola with rum. He complains if you forget the ice. The old Englishman has whisky. I have filled up the John Haig bottle; if it gets empty, take it into the scullery and fill it with what you'll find in the tin basin on the side of the sink. Oh, and you can add a little water, as well. . . . Later there will be the Lannfranc couple—pink gin—and the rich New Zealand woman. She will talk all the time about the friends she had on an English liner but she won't drink much until Semprebon comes. Then it will be sweet sherry for her and Campari for him. He pretends to pay—signs the chits and gives them to you. You just tear them up under the counter."

"But"—Ettore's small, sallow, monkey face looked doubtful—"how do we make it up? I mean——"

"Any way you can. You want to keep your job, don't you? Overcharge the old Englishman, if possible. But for God's sake don't try it on the priest, he's up to everything. Well—okay?"

Ettore nodded, grinning. "Okay, Tino. Are you going to *her*?"

Agostino nodded, clicking his tongue against the roof of his mouth, and smiled a shade nervously. "I'm late already."

"Waiting won't do her any harm. How much is she going to give you?"

"I think she said ten pounds."

"*Ma ché!*" Ettore's eyes widened and he nodded his appreciation. "About seventeen thousand lire—that's a fine big lot of money!"

"And I'm a fine big boy—well worth it!" Agostino slapped his friend on the shoulder and left the bar. Then he popped his head back again. "Oh, I forgot. If Professor van Staedtler asks for whisky and soda he means tonic water, so don't use the siphon—otherwise he won't take it. And you can water that bottle of sherry for the New Zealand woman—she won't notice."

On his way to the "B" deck cabins Agostino reflected a little unhappily on what he was about to do. It was all very well to joke about it with the other mess-boys and to become a source of ribald envy to them, but they did not have to go through with it and he did. He hoped suddenly that the big, hard-faced woman with the ugly voice and the unpronounceable name would not, in the end, want what he had thought she did. After all, she spoke only a little broken tourist-Italian, and his own English was confined to hardly more than a dozen short phrases. It was quite possible that he had misunderstood her. Perhaps all she really wanted was companionship because she was lonely; a little fumbling and kissing in the darkened cabin—no more. She would give him a cigarette and a glass of Strega (since Naples all the first-class passengers seemed to have bottles of Strega in their cabins), and sit with him on the bunk and stroke his knee or hold his hand while he told her, in so far as he was able, more about his parents' home at Livorno and about

Giselda. At the thought of Giselda he frowned unhappily, and his big, unintelligent brown eyes widened in distress. But it was for her that he was doing this, really. They needed money to get married and seventeen thousand lire was a lot of money—more than a month's pay—for, like the rest of the mess-boys or apprentice stewards as they were supposed to be called, he received the lowest wages of any of the lowly paid employees of the Flotta Soto.

Seventeen thousand lire—ten English pounds. Would she really pay that just to talk to him and stroke his hand? His common sense told him at once that she would not. He shrugged, catching a glimpse of himself in a passing mirror, noting quickly that his thick black hair was neatly combed, his open-necked white shirt clean and stiff from the iron. Well . . . For a moment he hesitated outside the cabin door, then knocked and heard a quick, gruff voice say " *Entrate!*"

4

Entering the bar twenty minutes later for a cold beer before changing, Roger Lannfranc found it deserted except for the Third Officer and the cadet who were sitting at one end of the counter rolling dice. He strolled over and joined them. "Hallo. Throwing for the next round?"

"For the first round," Maelstroit corrected, without looking up from the dice he had just clattered on to the polished counter. "We are a most abstemious couple."

Roger laughed. " I'm afraid I can't lay claim to abstemiousness myself." He paused. " We used to do that all the time in the Navy. I'll take a hand too, if it's all the same to you."

Malestroit gathered the dice and, throwing them back into the leather cup, pushed it over to Roger. "To us it is all one. For we are permitted by the gracious kindness of our employer—whom God preserve—to buy from this bar our drink at the price of its cost alone. You however, monsieur, must pay as on the tariff."

Roger laughed. " Never mind. I dare say I can stand it." The feel of the dice cup in his hand, the muffled rattle as he shook it, brought back the old days with such poignant clarity that for a second he almost imagined himself back in the small, bunk-lined ward-room of *Sting-ray,* almost heard the mock anger in the slow, drawling voice of Ricky May, his Number One. " Roger, you're cheating! You're doing something nasty with the dice! Oh, you vile old sailorman!"

"Come on, dice," he said, and threw.

"No good, monsieur. I commiserate deeply." Malestroit shook his head. That, therefore, will be two Camparis, I think."

Ettore came grinning out of the scullery and served Roger with beer and the two officers with Campari-soda. "We drink this," Malestroit explained, noting Roger's glance of amused disgust at the fizzing crimson glasses, "because it is not an apéritif of alcohol. So we do not get drunk and drown ourselves—and you, too, of course. Are you not impressed deeply with our temperance?"

Roger smiled a little irritably. Sitting here beside the two white-uniformed officers, watching the warm, star-filled tropical night beyond the wide-open windows of the bar and the lights of the shipping anchored in the lakes, sliding slowly past, it was possible to forget the future and to feel a part of this shipboard life. To feel as if, wandering lost over miles of desolate country, he had crossed a ridge and come suddenly into—not his own home, that was too much to expect—yet the home of some colleagues whose ways of life, unlike those of the strangest among whom he had been so long benighted, were his own, known and dear. He would have liked to sit in a companionable silence, allowing this new and probably short-lived content to seep into him, to feel it like an almost physical warmth in his veins, expanding him into the role he had so reluctantly laid down: Lieut-Commander Lannfranc, R.N.

But Malestroit's ornate English, sardonic and self-satisfied, jarred his mood, reminding him that, whatever his own feelings might be, to these others he was merely a first-class passenger, someone to be treated with friendly condescension—not even a colleague, let alone a superior. He said, "If you mean do I find it impressive that you drink that stuff—yes, I do."

"Good." Malestroit's smoke-grey eyes glinted. "And you like to-day's journey?"

"Very pleasant," said Roger shortly.

"Less so three years ago. I was on one ship at Port Said when the attack came. Another three-four hours and we should have been in the middle—in these lakes and caught like a trap!" He drew the fingers of one hand together in a grasping motion. "By God, my friend, your country so nearly started the next war that day! My captain said to me—it was not on this ship, you understand; it was before

I joined this fleet—' Malestroit, you speak so good English that I think you understand these people. Tell me, then, are they mad that they do this? Do they mean to destroy us all?' So I am very pleased that he should speak thus to me, you understand, for I am then but a cadet—like our little Gino here——" Malestroit flicked Gino affectionately on the cheek—" and I think carefully for a little and say, ' No, my captain, I do not think they are mad. I think their rulers make a very big error. The English are clever; much too clever to want to start again a war. But clever people often make bad mistakes.' And I was, of course, right." He grinned at the Chief Officer, who had just come in and was ordering a Campari from Ettore. " I have just told our English friend that——"

But Roger interrupted him, an admirably feigned air of weary good humour masking his true feeling of sharp annoyance at the introduction of a subject in such bad taste. "You're not, old boy, I'm afraid. You're not a bit right; couldn't be wronger, in fact. The whole thing's very complicated and it's rather foolish to discuss it at present because so much has not yet come to light. One thing, I think is fairly generally agreed, and that is that the Anglo-French action was completely justified. Now if you were to say that the Americans made a mistake in their attitude over the matter—then you would be talking sense. But to say the English made one—well, I'm afraid the only answer to that is—balls!"

" At Suez??" Serafino held his glass up to the light. " Ettore, you are not keeping these glasses clean. What England does at Port Said is right? You think to destruct the town, kill thousand of peoples, and to—to *sbarrare* this Canal is good?" His deep voice was bitter. Britain's thwarted exercise in vindictive duplicity three years ago had thrown the Italian shipping lines into doubt and confusion just when he had been attempting to join one or other of them. They had refused to take on new officers and he had been forced instead to sail under Don Ildefonso's Panamanian flag. " I think not."

Malestroit grinned widely, his grey eyes gleaming. "Yes, yes. The Chief Officer is correct. You English, you like to hurt other people—always it has been so. Then you say, ' Oh, no, it was their fault—not ours!' "

" Oh, God, give me patience!" Roger shook his head in wearily contemptuous exasperation. " For Christ's sake don't be so bloody childish! If you'd only taken the trouble to read the newspapers at the time——"

"Which newspapers? The English?"

"*Any* responsible newspapers. You'd at least have seen that we prevented a third war. And——"

"You prevented! *Pour l'amour de Dieu!*" Malestroit and the Chief Officer looked at each other and shook their heads wonderingly. Gino laughed and put down his drink. "And if Egypt send ships to bomb England to prevent war—then how you like, eh? Then you think it is right? No, no, you think it is very wrong!"

Roger gave him the look he reserved for impertinent midshipmen, a quelling cold, unbelieving stare, "as if the cat had belched" as a friend put it. But it had no effect, the silly little sprog merely grinned. In a tone of voice as icy as his glance Roger said slowly, "And that, if I may say so, is about the most bloody silly remark I've heard in years. Egypt attack England? To start with, they wouldn't dare——"

But at this the three officers broke into delighted laughter. Flushing deep crimson, Roger glared a them furiously. Three young officers, one a mere kid, laughing at *him*. Laughing openly in the ward-room—the bar—at a naval officer of his seniority and experience! Of course they were only a collection of dim-wit foreigners and it was only that somehow, earlier on—until Number One had come in—he'd felt as if—as if in a way he was among colleagues again—sea officers. What had happened was Number One's fault of course, butting in like that. Stupid, lame little bastard. Obviously violently anti-British and still furious over that business this morning at the gangway when he'd made such a bloody silly exhibition of himself. Someone had said that he'd only just been promoted to his present position, and, remembering this, Roger looked at the tarnished epaulettes on the narrow shoulders with a sneer. Trying to pretend he'd been wearing them for years; everyone knew that old Navy trick! He finished his beer and rose. "I'm afraid none of you knows very much about the Suez affair," he said dryly. "And as it was no business of yours in any case, I don't think your opinions are of much value. If Italy had been engaged I've no doubt everything would have gone very much better. We've all been so used to the spectacular successes of Italian military operations, have we not? Well, I must go and get ready for dinner."

5

Controlling his harsh breathing, Agostino gently closed the door of the mess-boys' dormitory behind him without switching on the light. The hot, stuffy smell of overcrowded humanity enveloped him, with the darkness, in a sense of grateful security. He moved, with an instinctive sense of direction born of long practice, round the tall pier of bunks on the left, turned right where the lockers ended, pulled off his shoes and climbed quickly into his place above Ettore's empty bunk. It was intensely hot down here far below the water-line on "E" deck, but he was damply cold with sweat and shivering with nervous distress, his jaw muscles trembling, his legs weak and boneless. Nothing like the last hour had ever happened to him before, and his mind was still caught up in a queer nightmare of fear, shame and revulsion.

He had hardly had time to say "*Buon' sera, signora*" before she had started on him. There had been no question of cigarettes or glasses of Strega or talk about home and Giselda. Instead, she had pushed five notes into his hand. "Here's half the money, Tino. We'll see about the rest later. I've got something else for you, too." And she had handed him a pair of expensive satin bathing-trunks, patterned like leopard skin. "They're much better than your own. They should be, too, seeing what they cost me this morning."

He had the average Italian's naïve delight in bright clothes. "A thousand thanks, signora! They are wonderful! I have never seen——"

"Well, stop talking, for God's sake, and try them on."

He had looked up, surprised. "What—here? Now?"

"Yes—I want to see." And as he had hesitated, smiling uneasily, "Come on, Tino. Get your clothes off."

It had been worse later. She had ordered him about as if—as if he was a schoolboy being taught some horrible shameful lesson. "Do this. Do that. No idiot, I don't mean that way!" She had not the slightest use for endearments or the milder sort of love-play. "Stop talking, Tino!" He shuddered, making the iron bunk rattle beneath him. It had been like the mating of some animal—brutal, blatant, ugly. And when he made mistakes or failed in instant compliance, she had given a grunting curse and slapped him or pinched him with vicious twists of her strong fingers. Under such treatment it had been next to impossible even to pretend to reciprocate her savage passion, and the more he had failed her, the more angry she had become. At last she had pushed him away. "All right, all right, that'll do! Now go and wash—you're sweating like a pig!" And later, grinning that queer, hard grin: "Well, do you think you've earned the other five pounds, Tino? I'm not sure, myself. Still, you'd better have it. Probably you'll do better next time."

"Signora . . ." But she had pushed him out of the cabin. "You talk too much, Tino."

He had been about to tell her that there would never be a next time—never, never again. He slid his hand into the pocket of his trousers and touched the hard edges of the folded notes. Ten pounds. He felt like crying, darkly aware that something important had been lost to-night, some part of life would never be the same for him again. Instead, he sighed explosively and someone in another bunk turned over angrily and grunted, "Less noise there, for God's sake!"

VI

"As you say, we managed to take our place in the convoy—but only just in time. That is not the way I like my ship to leave Port Said."

"*Signor Capitano*——"

"You realise what the consequences would have been had we missed our convoy?"

"*Si, signore.*"

"You know, too, upon whose shoulders the ultimate blame would have rested—mine. As master I am responsible for everything to do with this vessel. I, and I alone. You know that well enough."

"*Signor Capitano,* I thought——"

"You thought! My dear young man, chief officers are not supposed just to *think* things: they are supposed to make certain. What if we had missed that convoy as we so nearly—so *very* nearly did?"

"*Signore*——" Serafino's thin shoulders lifted in a small despairing shrug. It was true that they had nearly missed the convoy yesterday morning and that the Captain had every right to be angry. Nothing had been said at the time, but Serafino had sensed the Captain's extreme displeasure the moment he entered the bridge. He had guessed that an unpleasant interview was in store for him once they were through the Canal, and he had been quite right.

Now Captain Onestinghel knocked the ash from his cigar and leant back behind the big desk in his day cabin. "But—as you have said—we did *not* miss the convoy, and therefore I would not, normally, have brought this matter up." Though the whirring brass fans set in angles between the walls and the ceiling did practically nothing to dispel the moisture-laden heat of mid-morning in the Red Sea, the Captain was not sweating; the colourless skin of his high-cheeked, Slavic face had the cold, dry, dead look of an embalmed corpse. "But there was something else. I understand that you had—h'm—words with a female passenger: this Mrs. Crambatch."

Serafino nodded glumly. "Yes. It was her fault that the ship was delayed."

Onestinghel shook his head. "No, it was yours. Had you followed our practice of announcing our time of departure to be half an hour before it actually falls due this woman would have been in plenty of time. But I understand that *San Ramòn* does not follow this method?"

"*No, signore.*"

"H'm. Possibly Captain D'Angelis will find it useful to do so now that his ship is on this run and must catch the Canal convoys." Onestinghel rocked back in his chair, his narrow, pale-blue eyes fixed expressionlessly upon Serafino's gaunt, unhappy face. D'Angelis's Second Officer. Very odd. One would have thought that D'Angelis, with his ebullience, his buoyant Latin gaiety, would have had a crew as carefree and lighthearted as himself. "Is it true," he asked with sudden curiosity, "that Captain D'Angelis used to sing over *San Ramòn's* amplifiers?"

"Yes, signore." The young man before him did not smile. "Sometimes he did, when we were on the Venezuelan run."

"What did he sing?"

"Oh, Italian and Spanish songs. '*Santa Lucia,*' '*La Spagnola,*' '*Celito Lindo*'—songs like those. The passengers liked it. His voice was very good.

"I see. H'm, most versatile. I knew a master once who was a very expert conjuror. He spent nearly all his time in his cabin practising tricks. Even on the bridge he would practise—removing eggs from the quartermaster's ears, producing pigeons from the telegraph. Most adept. In due course his lack of interest in seamanship resulted in a collision between his ship and another. Much damage was done—several persons killed. He lost his job in consequence and then went on the stage. He made a great deal of money, I believe—far more than he had been earning as a ship-master."

Serafino swallowed, his face a dark red. Humbly he said, "But I cannot even do that, or sing."

Onestinghel's head jerked up and he stared at his Chief Officer for a long, astonished moment. Then he began to laugh silently. "My dear boy! You are quite, quite wrong! I was not suggesting for one moment that you should leave the sea. Oh youth, youth! Why is it so delightful in retrospect and yet so distressing at the time? Yes indeed, Don Ildefonso was right: you are very young. When you come here you make me feel I should offer you chocolate rather than cigarettes. No, no, but seriously—and we must not be too serious, for seriousness is perhaps your trouble—you are a good seaman. I tell you so and I have much experience behind me. Now you are worried because of this little slip on your part. It is not important. It was quite natural, under the circumstances, that you should lose your temper a little with this woman, though it would, of course, have been more satisfactory had you been able to control it. I bring the matter up only in order to suggest that you refrain from such diversions in future. No, no. What is important is that you have taken a liner—not a big one, certainly, but still a passenger liner—from Naples to the Red Sea with as much skill as Signor Parodi would have shown. I know that it is largely routine—that is why I do not interfere—but still, at your age that is something of an accomplishment. Now—are you happier?"

"*Grazie, signore*——" Serafino smiled shyly—"much happier."

"Excellent!" Again the Captain carefully knocked the ash from his cigar, bending forward as he did so to hide a smile. Really, these Italians! How they made him want to laugh! A scene from the distant past, a scrap of conversation, suddenly returned to him with all the vivid vision of old age. The bottom steps of the Admiralty at St. Petersburg, its gold spire lifting a glittering, tapering finger up into the summer sky; Alexis Obledinov, back from the Imperial Embassy at Rome, hitching his sabre round in order to lean upon it. "My dear Pavel Constantinovitch, how I envy their king! They are the most delightfully satisfactory people to rule over that you can imagine. They really love their masters—but truly! *Baciare le mani* and all the rest of it. And they are not fools, either—like our own intolerable animals—but a most intelligent lot. They are too easily elated and distressed, but only like children—tears and then laughter. Yes, indeed, like a lot of very charming children!" That had been nearly half a century ago but it was just as true to-day.

The Captain eyed his young Chief Officer with amusement but without envy. Things seemed so difficult when one was young and taking on life in a hand-to-hand struggle. One imagined the world was an immensely complicated affair, but it was not true: the complications lay within oneself, and only the passing of the years sorted them slowly out. Old people were relatively simple and easy to understand; it was the young who were a mass of intricate contradictions and complexities.

"You were on the Venezuelan run for nearly three years, were you not, Ciccolanti?"

"*Si, signore,* but I have made this voyage before that—several times. Just after the war when I was a cadet on a cargo ship."

Onestinghel nodded thoughtfully. "I see. There is, of course, a difference between carrying cargo and passengers and——" he glanced up carefully—"between carrying Italian migrants to South America and British ones to Australia."

Serafino nodded silently, and the Captain continued: "It is in some ways a pity that Don Ildefonso should have given this order about eating and mixing with the passengers just as you were taking over Signor Parodi's position. I fully understand that you have quite enough to do on *San Roque* without attempting polite conversation with strangers in a foreign language."

"If people are saying——"

"People are not saying anything—as far as I know," lied Captain Onestinghel smoothly. "But what *I* was about to say is that an officer of a passenger ship has social duties as well as nautical ones. The bigger the liner, the larger and more important become the social duties of its officers. On the *Colombo, Colombo,* for instance, the Chief Officer would of necessity be a man of great worldly sophistication and address, able to converse at ease not only with Italian dukes and Spanish grandees, but with American statesmen—and English generals." He paused and there was a long silence. Then Serafino said sullenly, "I do not like the English."

This threw Captain Onestinghel into a further bout of silent laughter. Recovering himself, he said, "My dear young man! Really now, do you imagine that anyone else does? Of course not! No one likes the English, though I believe that at one time the Portuguese were thought to do so. Yet the English must travel like other people. We must put up with them—and you Italians are better than anyone else at doing that."

"I can hardly speak their language at all."

"You probably speak it much better than they will ever be able to speak yours," Onestinghel smiled.

> "Your Roman-Saxon-Danish-Norman-English,
> From this amphibious, ill-born mob began
> That vain, ill-natured thing an Englishman.

Can you understand that?"

"Only one or two words."

"H'm. It is a very uncomplimentary and unfortunately a very true, remark about the English, written nearly three centuries ago by one of their own countrymen—a sensible and clever man named Defoe. They put him in the pillory, and really one is hardly surprised: I doubt if Defoe was, either." The Captain paused, smiling. "Yes, it is not, perhaps, easy to get on with the English, particularly when one is young—for they dislike youth, or not very well born—for they have a great respect for birth. In their eyes the only remedy for these defects is a period of time at one of their public schools—institutions which are largely responsible for the arrogance and bad manners which make the English so unpopular outside their own country. As you have not been to one of these places, I fear you are doomed to remain an outcast in their eyes for ever. Not that it need worry you overmuch since it is the lot of the vast majority of mankind." Onestinghel stared musingly down at his hands on the desk before him. "They are a most peculiar race, the English. Very few people really understand them and I do not think that you ever will, for no Latin can really comprehend their odd mixture of malevolence and mysticism—their malevolence towards other peoples and the mysticism with which they regard their own institutions. Did you know, for instance, that the English Constitution is an unwritten one, Ciccolanti?"

"But—how do they know what it is, then?"

"How indeed? In fact, of course, the vast majority of them do not. Instead, the lower classes put their faith in a powerful system of trade unions, which they have elavated to a semi-sacred and quite impregnable position, while the upper classes worship the reigning sovereign, whom they venerate as the guardian of their wealth and privilege." He shook his head. "A strange people, Ciccolanti. Other nations, finding it almost impossible to comprehend them, often fall into the error of believing that the English character must therefore be one of profound depth. They are quite wrong, for it is, of all character, the most exceptionally shallow." He pulled himself upright in his chair. "But come, this is not what I wished to say to you. I am anxious that you should try to get on better with the first-class passengers—and this largely for your own sake, for you will not achieve a high position in the passenger service if you do not attempt to cultivate at least a few of the social graces. To-morrow evening I am going to give a cocktail-party. All the first-class passengers will be invited and it will therefore be possible to hold it in the bar—for I do not particularly wish an invasion of this cabin. You will be present. If it is your watch at the time you will arrange for one of the others to stand it for you. You understand?"

"*Si, Signor Capitano.*"

"Very well, then. That is all."

Serafino brought his heels together, bowed and turned away. As he reached the door the Captain called, "Oh—Signor Ciccolanti!"

"Signore?"

"One thing more: don't worry so much!"

2

The next day was Sunday. Early in the morning Malpiero, the Assistant Purser, was sitting at his table behind the counter in the vestibule, typing out the list of "Daily Activities." This was a recent innovation of Cavaliere Semprebon's, designed, by informing the passengers of the various entertainments available to them during the day, to enhance the tone of the Line. Like the ship's menus, it was ingeniously compiled on the *multum in parvo* principle. Thus the erratic gramophone recitals became "Concert of Classical & Light Music, 11 a.m.—12 noon," while "Open air Swimming & Diving," indicated that the pool could be used as usual, and

" Library hours, 5 p.m.—6 p.m." informed such passengers as might be interested that in the evening a mess-boy would preside over some fifteen tattered paperbacks at a folding table on the promenade deck.

Nor could the Purser restrain himself from delivering small hints on correct behaviour when he felt, as he generally did, that many of the tourist passengers stood sadly in need of them. " It is requested to be realised that the evening meal is the formal meal of the day. Please assist to make this so by wearing similar apparel to which you would expect to wear at home—namely, socks, shoes, long trousers and shirt. For your compliance we thank you."

To-day Malpiero typed: " A Service of Religious Worship will be conducted in the 1st class saloon by Wing Commander Reverend Maurice Catchpole R.A.F. 11 a.m.—11.45 a.m. All persons are very welcomed." Mr. Catchpole did not care for holding services while returning from leave—he considered that his holiday did not really end until *San Roque* reached Aden; but the Purser, who felt that any sort of religious service was in good taste, had kept on offering " full facilities " in such a pointed way that in the end the chaplain had been forced reluctantly to agree.

Captain Onestinghel, an atheist for the first fifty years of his life, was now an ardent Roman Catholic and entertained the strongest prejudices against all other forms of Christianity. He did not like the thought of heretical practices taking place on his ship, and had been quite sharp with Semprebon over the matter. However, since it had been arranged he could do nothing save give his permission—but with bad grace and considerable annoyance, as was obvious from his face this morning when he strode into the vestibule.

Malpiero leapt to his feet and bowed. " *Buon' giorno, Signor Capitano!*"

The Captain nodded briefly and glanced round the vestibule. He was on his Sunday morning tour of the ship, attended deferentially by his Chief Officer and Master at Arms, and, unexpectedly and much less deferentially, by Gil Sotomayor. Malpiero, glancing at the anxious faces of the two sailors, was devoutly thankful that his own presence was not required. Every member of *San Roque's* company held Sunday in some dread. Onestinghel was by no means a harsh captain; he treated his subordinates with an amused and kindly politeness which generally endeared him to them—except on Sundays. On Sundays he inspected the ship thoroughly from bridge to engine-room, and as the tour proceeded farther and deeper into the ship's interior, a change seemed to come over the Captain. The geniality of his normal manner evaporated, and left a dry, stern, silent man and one curiously tense and nervous. In this state he would snap and snarl at any minor infringement of ship's regulations which his pale, slanting, Slavic eyes could detect. By the time he reached the engine-room he was invariably in a grim tight-lipped anger. Not that Mynheer Joost Aafjes, the Dutch chief engineer, or his men needed to worry overmuch; their department was of too technical a nature for the Captain to be able to comment upon it one way or the other. Indeed, he was generally quite silent in the engine-room and merely glanced into the fire-room, where the great oil-furnaces roared softly behind their ovenlike doors, each with a small spy hole of mica gleaming scarlet from the flames within. This was the nadir of the tour. Then the process went into reverse and the farther the captain climbed towards the deck and the sun, the better became his temper, until, once more upon the bridge, he was restored, as far as Sunday would permit, to his usual good humour.

No one on *San Roque* guessed that Captain Onestinghel himself dreaded Sundays. But he had to inspect the ship: it was his duty to visit every part of it, even the engine-room where he could do nothing, and the fire-room. He was in a particularly bad mood to-day because Gil Sotomayor had asked if he could come and there had been no way to refuse the request, though the Captain had made every effort to do so.

"You'll be very bored and hot. It's only a dull process of ship's routine and it takes me right down to the engine-room, you know."

"I shall like that, Don Pablo." Gil spoke Spanish to the Captain, who, like so many of his exiled compatriots, had achieved a cosmopolitan fluency in half a dozen different languages.

"My dear boy, I did not know that you were interested in engines, but surely you can spend as much time in the engine-room as you like without accompanying me. Aafjes would be only too delighted. . . ."

"But I should like to see the ship properly. I still cannot find my way about easily. With you it would be different."

"Yes, yes, perhaps. But you would have to get up early—

much earlier than you usually do. It really hardly seems worth it."

"Oh, yes, I think it is."

"Oh, very well, then—if you're so set on it." What more could one say if, as appeared obvious, the boy couldn't take a hint when he was not wanted? The question of Gil Sotomayor was a difficult one and Onestinghel was doing his best to cope with it. He was sorry for the boy, though he could not approve of him. The fault was largely Don Ildefonso's, of course, as the owner had himself grudgingly half admitted. It was the usual story of the self-made rich man's son. The father desiring to give his child far more, in youth, than he had himself been given and inevitably falling into the error of giving him far more than was good for him: fast cars, speedboats, an allowance as big as a captain's salary. And worse still, a toleration of—even, it seemed, a fatuous admiration for—the prodigal and reckless behaviour which was the natural result of such easy lavishness. The crash, when it came as it was bound to do, was unpleasantly spectacular because it included a dead girl of sixteen who, it was later found, had been introduced to Gil by a woman who combined that occupation with blackmail and drug traffic. It was never seriously claimed that Gil had murdered the girl, but it was suggested in certain quarters that he had been partly responsible for her death.

To Don Ildefonso a single death was not a very serious matter, but the Italian police did not see it in that light. They investigated, and, despite frantic bribes from his father, Gil's recent behaviour was brought to light and publicised. The Sotomayors were rich foreigners, Spaniards living in Italy, suitable targets for underpaid, overworked Italian journalists. They seized on the chance with malicious avidity, and Gil, who had often seen his photograph in society magazines, now found it in the popular press above significantly worded discussions of the more unpleasant aspects of the scandal—the seduction of minors under the influence of drugs, and offences of a like nature. Though he only appeared as a witness when the case came up, this did not prevent the court from making several harsh comments on his behaviour, and on his father's blindly doting liberality which was the cause of it. Furiously, Don Ildefonso started a round of libel actions, and then turned his attention to his son. He had already taken away all the cash and the cars and the speedboats, and now he threatened to send Gil to sea as an ordinary deckhand on one of his ships. As Gil had guessed, this was an idle threat, for Don Ildefonso had his full share of Spanish pride backed up by an *arriviste* social snobbery, yet for some time he had thought that the best he could hope for would be a pair of cadet's epaulettes and a position at the beck and call of every deck officer who wanted an unimportant job done.

Fortunately for himself he had no head for figures, could never have mastered the principles of navigation, and his father, realising this, decided to send him to Sydney to learn the business side of shipping migrants at his agents' office. None the less, it was an extremely sullen and unhappy youth who found himself handed over to his father's old friend and senior captain on board the *San Roque* in Naples Harbour.

Captain Onestinghel was a bachelor and had a horror of family life. His own had finished abruptly in 1918 with the murder of his parents, the gruesome execution of his two brothers, and the disappearance of most of his other relatives, while his own experiences had been such as to blunt effectively any shock he might otherwise have felt. One life ended abruptly in blackness and a new one, without any ties or background, began. He was perfectly contented by himself. Parental relationships he considered particularly obnoxious—full of emotional strains and embarrassments which drove otherwise sane and clever people into ridiculously stupid behaviour and made them objects of derision and scorn, like his unfortunate friend Don Ildefonso. It was therefore with resignation rather than surprise that he received the owner's directions for the transportation of his son to Sydney. Gil was to travel neither as a passenger nor as one of the crew, but as " a member of the firm "—whatever that meant. He was to have no special duties on board, but was to " make himself useful and be kept busy." He was naturally to be considered the social equal of the officers, but was not to be given alcohol or allowed off the ship before it reached Sydney " My poor friend," the Captain thought, nodding commiseratingly as Don Ildefonso gave these instructions. " That you, who know mankind so well, should be guilty of such folly! What your son needs is a defined position with a little responsibility. He should come to me as a supernumerary second officer or an assistant purser; this business of something and nothing hedged round with restrictions will only make a bad job worse. Ah, well, thank God that I am not a father! Possibly I too might have become equally aberrated!"

Yet, a week out of Naples, the captain's prophecy of trouble from Gil had not been realised. It was true that he had refused to work in any way, but he had made quite polite excuses for this; either he had a headache or he could not manage figures or he was unable to type. He seemed only to want to be left alone, and spent all day shut up in his cabin in the Captain's quarters, a suite of four comfortable rooms directly beneath the bridge. The only complaint he had made was when he was told he was to have his meals at the Captain's table in the first-class saloon. Onestinghel attempted to reassure him. "My dear boy, you can be quite certain that none of the passengers will know about—about this troublesome affair of yours. It was not reported anywhere except in Italy, and mainly locally at that. Anyway, they are British and almost certainly don't speak Italian—let alone read it."

"The officers know about it."

Onestinghel had looked surprised. "The officers? Yes, I suppose so. But really—in any case, with the exception of the Cavaliere, they are all young themselves; doubtless they feel both sympathetic and not a little envious." But as soon as he had spoken the words he had known they were not true. They would have been true enough in St. Petersburg of half a century ago, among the gilded youth of the Semenovsky Guards and the Corps of Pages, but they did not apply to the more sombre youth of to-day, and particularly not to hard-working young men of the middle class. No, with the possible exception of Semprebon not one of his officers would feel sympathetic towards Gil and none would feel envious. And Gil knew this: he had been keeping out of the way not of the passengers but of the officers. How interesting! And how lucky that Don Ildefonso had not done as he himself would have done—made Gil a supernumerary officer. That, he saw now, would have been disastrous. "Well, I think, however, that we can arrange this matter to your satisfaction." And he had given instructions that no officer other than Semprebon should sit at his table.

It seemed, however, that Gil was beginning to take some slight interest in *San Roque,* or so his request to join the Sunday tour of inspection suggested. This morning he followed in the Captain's wake, unintentionally causing considerable inconvenience. He was the owner's only son, and whatever the Chief Officer or the Master at Arms might think of him personally, they were unable to overcome their feelings of deference for the power and wealth he represented. Every time the party turned a corner or passed through a bulkhead door after Captain Onestinghel, there was a fussy edging to the side to let Gil pass second. This was particularly irritating to the Captain, who, on turning to address Ciccolanti or Petelli, invariably found himself confronting Gil. His Sunday temper grew shorter and he tapped his leg rapidly with the leather-covered cane, a relic of his cavalry days, which he always carried on inspections.

He found a cigarette end in the scuppers. " Petelli, when you lose your job—as you undoubtedly will before this voyage is out unless you pay more attention to the cleanliness of the ship—you will not even qualify as a street scavenger in Naples." Right aft on the fantail of " C " deck, one of the sections of the heavy wooden pen in which the great stern cables were coiled was lying on the deck. " Signor Ciccolanti, has it ever occurred to you that it is a wise precaution to go round the ship and make certain that everything is in its place *before* my tour? Or perhaps you don't care? Perhaps you feel that it really doesn't matter if the decks look like the backyard of a bankrupt ship chandler's establishment? Perhaps, even, you think I like to see them thus?"

" Signore——" stammered Serafino, scarlet-faced. This was indeed a different Onestinghel from the one who had spoken to him so kindly yesterday in the big cabin. His fears for his job, his wages, the money which kept the family in the Vic' Re Galantuomo, began to return with renewed force. " Signore——"

They were right over the screws and the vibration caused the Captain's face to appear as if it was trembling with rage. " Well——? Don't just stand there saying ' Signore ' like a mendicant organ-grinder begging in the gutter! *Why* is the front of the cable pen unbolted?"

Petelli bowed and said, " *Permesso, Signor Capitano.* It is those children—those British children. Twice already I have caught them down here. They get into the pen to hide—it is a game of theirs."

" Are they there now?"

" Signore——?"

" Go and look."

Petelli peered gravely into the open pen. " *No, signore.* They are not here."

" It is your job to keep them out of places in which they

have no right to be. You've used a rope's end once—go on using it! You, Ciccolanti—put that pen front back in its proper place and make it fast."

Serafino bent and tugged the great wooden section upright. It was well over eight feet across and very heavy, and he wondered how on earth the Ampel children had got it unbolted. Petelli sprang to help him until the Captain called him back. "No, let Signor Ciccolanti do it himself. It may teach him to be more careful over the appearance of the decks in future."

Down into "D" deck. The kitchens were scrupulously clean, but they found a mouse in the flour store. "Petelli, where is the ship's cat?"

"I think it left us at Naples, signore. It was about to have kittens."

"Inform the cooks that they are to buy two more at Sydney out of their own money. And they must be tom-cats."

On 'E" deck the Captain flung open the door of the mess-boys' dormitory and strode in. In the middle of the room Agostino, wearing his new leopardskin bathing-trunks, was performing a hand-stand and trying to watch himself in the mirror. The Captain caught him a sharp crack across the behind with his cane and he scrambled to his feet. "And who in the name of Almighty God and all His holy saints do you imagine you are—Tarzan of the Apes?"

Crimson with embarrassment and his recent inverted position, Agostino rubbed his smarting buttocks. "*Signore Capitano,* I—I'm off duty."

"He is one of the mess-boys, *Signor Capitano,*" supplied Serafino quickly, though the Captain knew this perfectly well.

"Have you been in the swimming-pool?"

"No, signore. It is forbidden at this hour."

"Then why are you wearing nothing but these ridiculous tights? If you are practising for the role of a street acrobat I can inform you that you are starting far too late in life."

Agostino nodded dumbly, and the Captain turned to his chief officer. "Signor Ciccolanti, this ship is not a travelling circus and I will not have members of my crew dressing as if it were. Also, if the service staff wish to preen themselves in a semi-naked condition before mirrors, they will not do it on Sunday mornings. Take that boy's absurd costume away and do not give it back until the termination of the voyage.

Not *now*, idiot!" For Agostino, reduced to a condition of dazed bewilderment, was starting to take off his cherished trunks. "Later!"

At the top of the catwalk which led down in a spidery maze of steel ladders to the engine-room they were met by the second engineer, Zocco—a Sicilian so small as to be almost a dwarf. Captain Onestinghel stared over his head, affecting not to notice him and looking for Aafjes. Zocco, fumbling nervously with a piece of string, bowed and shuffled at his feet. Without looking at him, the Captain asked coldly, "Where is the *Direttore di macchina*?"

"*Signor Capitano, scusi.* Signor Aafjes is a little unwell this morning. I am standing his watch. He requests me to present his compliments and his apologies."

"So. And what is this illness which incapacitates Signor Aafjes from his normal duties?"

Zocco twined his piece of string tightly round his knuckles. Both he and the Captain knew perfectly well that the Chief Engineer was suffering from his usual Sunday morning hangover and had not felt able to face up to the inspection. "Well?"

"Signore——"

"For God's sake stop playing with that bit of string! You can make the necessary preparations to hang yourself later. Now, answer my question!"

"S-signore," muttered Zocco desperately, his black eyes popping, "I—I think he must have consumed something that disagreed with him."

"So do I," remarked the Captain coldly, and, leaving the second engineer crimson with distress at his own maladroitness, he descended the intricate web ladder with an astonishing agility for his seventy years and strode off between the giant humps of the twin turbines, the great hillocks of dingy white, composed of layer after layer of casing and insulation within whose guarded depths steam, heated to unimaginable temperatures and expanding explosively through a series of revolving fans, drove *San Roque* on her way across the world.

This was the shortest part of the tour. The Captain, disregarding the three or four figures in grimy overalls who straightened themselves meticulously at his approach, walked to the fire-room door, glanced in and turned back. As he did so, his eyes met Gil Sotomayor's. The young Spaniard was looking at him—how? Curiously? Knowingly? It suddenly flashed through the Captain's mind that this might have been the reason for Gil's anxiety to join the inspecting party. But how——? Of course—the boy's father! If Don Ildefonso Sotomayor had been prepared to give his son every material thing he asked for would he not also impart all his confidences? If he had done so in this respect, it was very unpleasant. The Captain's face tightened into a hard, cold mask, his pale, narrow eyes narrowed still farther, became splinters of arctic ice, and his thin lips compressed to a scarline in his pallid face. One's past was one's past—dead and over and done with. Besides, there were certain things he himself knew about Don Ildefonso. . . . As the inspecting party mounted from deck to deck on the return journey, it was noticed that the Captain's temper did not improve in its wonted manner but remained uncompromisingly bleak.

It was still in this state when they emerged into the vestibule and heard a shrill, furious, female voice issuing from a small group near the counter. "Ah, dear God! And you think I believe you? You think for one moment I accept as true the word of an *Italian*? Ah, I know you! I know you have always hated him—well do I know it. It is no use making up lies to me! All Italians are born liars. But I shall go to law. I shall punish you! You will lose your position and become, doubtless, a bootblack! You will not laugh then—oh no! Not when you are in rags and starving and——"

"And what is supposed to be going on here?" demanded the Captain, his high, hard voice rasping with un-Italian aspirates.

The group broke apart to reveal at its centre Countess Zapescu, clutching a shivering silver dog in her arms, and Gino Pavanoli, his shirt and trousers liberally covered with aluminium paint.

"What is going on ? Dear God, I will tell you what is going on, Captain! Yes, indeed I will tell you! This miserable little Italian boy officer of yours——"

Onestinghel lifted a hand. "Please, Countess, one moment! I wish to hear from Pavanoli."

"*Signor Capitano*——" Gino was on the verge of tears; one hand was bleeding badly and the left side of his sallow face bore the red imprint of the Countess's fingers—"I found this lady's dog running down the *Ponte d'Imbarcazione* from the direction of the starboard hydrocrane. I caught it and brought it back to her, and it his me and she says it is my doing and——"

"Why is it in this condition?"

"Signore, they had been painting the hydrocranes. The *Capitan d'armi* had given orders——"

"*Si, Signor Capitano,*" corroborated Petelli. "I gave orders that the hydrocranes were to be repainted yesterday."

Onestinghel nodded. "Well—go on, boy."

"The sailors must have left a can of paint beside the hydrocrane, and those British children——"

"Ah——" the Captain drew in his breath—"I see!"

"Do not believe him, Captain," snarled the Countess, furiously. "British peoples would not do this. He has always hated my dog because I would not let him lock it up!"

Onestinghel turned on her at once. "I do believe him, however. It is an utterly preposterous suggestion that one of my officers should have done this! And if your dog had remained locked in the kennel—as it most certainly will in future—this would not have happened. Ciccolanti, see that this dog is cleaned and then locked in the *canile*. Pavanoli, you are to keep the keys yourself and I warn you that there will be trouble if I find this animal in unauthorised places in the future. Now go and change your clothes and get Tomei to see to your hand. And as for you, Madame, I really must request you to exercise considerably more care in future in the manner in which you address the ship's officers, or the law which you are so fond of invoking may be brought to bear upon yourself with unpleasant consequences!"

One way and another it had been a most distressing Sunday morning.

VII

The middle of the Red Sea in August was not the best place to hold a cocktail-party, particularly when the ship in which it took place was not air-conditioned. Captain Onestinghel realised this, but he himself was almost impervious to heat and humidity and at seventy he felt he was too old to have to worry about other people's discomfort. Moreover, he wished to get the affair finished and out of the way early in the voyage. A captain's cocktail-party was the one piece of entertainment which had hitherto been obligatory on ships of the Flotta Soto, for in general Don Ildefonso's policy had always been one of quick transport and cheap fares without any unnecessary extras to swell costs. However, he was prepared to sanction a single cocktail-party for the first-class passengers, for which on each voyage the ship's captain received an allowance of ten pounds.

Captain Onestinghel, unlike the Purser, who was able to produce his special pride—two dozen gold-edged glasses engraved with the monogram of the Line, detested these cocktail-parties. He had to invite every adult first-class passenger, and he invariably found that he had nothing in common with any of them; often he disliked one or more of them intensely. Yet he always made a point of spending at least twelve pounds on his party, even though the allowance was quite adequate in itself, for he had an Oriental horror of meanness and any form of illiberality or skimping.

This evening he stood, a small island of coolness in his well-fitting white uniform ornamented with his Cross of St. George and his three rows of medal ribbons, smiling thinly, making polite comments to his guests in his quick, precise English, and watching with an irritated amusement the way in which the majority of them carefully avoided approaching his Chief Officer.

Ciccolanti stood by himself near one of the two potted palms which had been brought up from the vestibule for the occasion. He was wearing a ready-made white uniform which did not fit him too well, his tie was badly knotted, and the big gold " S "s on his lapels were as tarnished as the pair of chief officer's epaulettes he wore on his shoulders; Onestinghel guessed correctly that they were second-hand and the only ones he had. In one hand he gripped a glass of sherry in a manner which suggested he was guarding it against sudden theft, and his broad-browed face bore an expression of glum, resentful embarrassment. He was staring out of the window at the calm opalescent evening sea and enviously, doubtless—at the long low shapes of three tankers making their way back to Suez, heavily laden from the Persian Gulf. He looked as out of place at the party as a child from a poorly endowed orphanage.

Onestinghel expected his officers to mingle with his other guests; both Cavaliere Semprebon and Bressan were doing so, and Aafjes had, of course, got into conversation with the old Dutch couple bound for Colombo. Even Dr. Gavalian, whose perennially unhappy relations with his young wife in Cairo were rumoured to have reached some sort of crisis, was listening gloomily to the Air Force chaplain's tale of woe. The Chief Officer should follow these examples. Onestinghel walked over to him. " Come, come, Ciccolanti; you do not appear to be enjoying yourself. Or do you find those tankers of more interest than this party?"

Serafino glanced up unsmilingly; he had not forgiven the Captain for instructing him to supervise the cleaning of the dog; whichever way you looked at it, it was hardly a task suited to a chief officer— Petelli should have done it. "I have a friend on that nearest one, *Stanvac Stronghold*."

"Ah, so? An American?"

" Yes, the third officer. At least he was third when I met him last, but——" Serafino shrugged—" their promotion is incredibly quick by our standards."

" That is true. Yet I doubt if a great many American passenger ships have chief officers of twenty-six." The Captain smiled. " You envy your friend? For myself, I do not. I would not care for this plodding up and down the Red Sea all the year round in a never-ending stench of crude oil. But now I suggest that you come and talk to someone other than myself, of whom, after all, you see so much." The Captain glanced round at his assembled guests and became aware for the first time that his party was not going well: people seemed to be trying to avoid one another rather than to mix. Aafjes would of course try to keep as far away from his host as possible, for he doubtless feared a sardonically solicitous inquiry after his health; and as for young Pavanoli it was obvious why he was keeping at the farthest end of the room from that painted old harridan of a countess. But still, a little more circulation of the other guests would be desirable. The Captain saw that one of them, the big Australian woman, was holding an empty glass and, turning to a hovering steward, he said sharply, " That lady over there! Go and give her a drink at once. What do you think you are here for?"

"*S-subito, signore.*" Agostino shot a glance of startled despair at his surprised Captain and, blushing a fiery crimson, went reluctantly across to Flora McKenrick, who, in an unbecoming dress of jade green, was standing by herself near an open window. " Signora——"

She grinned at him. " I've been wondering when you'd think of bringing me a drink, Tino. The Captain had to send you, didn't he?"

" I—no—I make to come. I——" stammered Agostino painfully. He dared not look at her; he kept his eyes on his tray.

"You didn't enjoy yourself the other evening, did you? That's the trouble, isn't it?"

"No. I——"

"You don't have to pretend. I don't particularly care if you didn't. You got paid, after all."

Agostino swallowed dumbly and the tray shook and shivered in his hands. Flora McKenrick gave a quick snort of laughter. "We get to Aden to-morrow and I know you're off duty in the evening. Come to my cabin at six. I'm going to get you some of those Japanese silk pyjamas—I'm getting some for myself as well, if they've got my size. We'll try them on together."

Crash went Agostino's tray, and there was a startled pause in the meagre conversation of the guests in which only the Purser's voice, saying, ". . . it is, of course, the Chief Officer's responsibility, but . . ." sounded clearly through the room.

"It is not, however," remarked the Captain mildly, "the Chief Officer's responsibility to control the behaviour of the stewards. Please, Cavaliere, try to let me have ones of a slightly less clumsy nature for these parties in future."

Uneasily, unwillingly, like a reluctant motor-cycle engine on a cold morning, the talk started up again. Ends of conversation were groped for, retrieved and resumed. ". . . The very *best* sort of people—all eight of them in what is really little more than a mud hut, and paying well over a hundred pounds a month, if not . . ." ". . . And he is, one admits, old and his teeth need attention—they make his breath smell most distressingly. And this man, what did he say to me? 'Madame, I am a pharmacist, a qualified apothecary. It is neither my duty nor my desire to cure elderly dachshunds of halitosis.' Like that! . . ."

". . . Real Parma ham with thick cream. Only it should, I was told, have been cooked with white truffles and they don't have truffles in July. I was really quite cross. I said, 'Haven't you heard of deep-freezing machines?' Why, back in Dunedin we can get anything, absolutely anything, all the year round. Oh, yes, we could teach Europe a thing or two, believe me! The last thing poor Leslie did—that was my husband—was to have infra-red cooking ovens installed in the Emporium kitchens. *And* he got small household ones specially designed for the middle-income group. They sold like hot cakes, too. Our Dunedin housewives are said to be among the most go-ahead in the world. 'Crambatch's Quick Cooker Cuts Costs'—it was all over the town . . ."

Mrs. Crambatch broke off to help herself to a couple of canapés from a dish proffered by Ettore. The small monkey-faced Calabrian bowed and grinned happily; he had a bet of two hundred lire with Renzo, the third mess-boy present, that the fat New Zealand woman would eat more than ten canapés, and she had already eaten six; she liked best the ones with the tomato and prawn mixture, and he had been furtively removing these from the other dishes and putting them on to a special one for her. Renzo said that this was cheating and a fiercely whispered quarrel was in progress whenever they met on their circle of the guests.

Mrs. Crambatch, perhaps alone among those present, was really enjoying herself. She liked parties of this sort, and who could be a more attractively aristocratic host than Captain Onestinghel? Now she was deep in conversation with the young English couple, the Lannfrancs. Ever since Commander Lannfranc (of course she called him " Roger " now) had come so nobly to her assistance at Port Said, she had spent an increasing amount of time with both of them. Roger's wife, Bronwen, was charming—not in the least stiff and conceited like so many young Englishwomen she had met during her tour of Britain, but deeply, sincerely, interested in New Zealand, Dunedin and Crambatch's Emporium. She was a serious and rather solemn girl, but then, poor thing, she had recently had such bad luck, she and her husband, over the abrupt curtailment of Roger's career. It seemed shocking that the British Navy should treat people like Roger and his wife so shabbily. England—as she had said indignantly—did not deserve to have people like the Lannfrancs if it behaved like that to them. Of course it was a great pity that they were going to Australia; they would be much more appreciated in New Zealand. Privately Mrs. Crambatch had determined to induce them to change their minds and their ship at Sydney, but with such nice people one had to be very careful. She was, she considered, being the soul of tact.

To-night, at the first proper party to be given since *San Roque* left Naples, being waited on so solicitously by that funny little steward and after four glasses of sweet sherry, she felt gay and at peace with the world. So much so that when the young cadet, looking very smart in his white uniform. came round with a large silver cigarette-box, she patted him on the arm. " And how are you this evening, you bad boy? I know a thing or two about you, you know!"

She turned to Roger and Bronwen. " Yes, I've heard that this young man's been very naughty to the poor Cavaliere. Shall I tell?"

Gino smiled unhappily and tried to move away, but Mrs. Crambatch had him firmly by the arm. "The Cavaliere wanted to teach him all sorts of things that would be useful to him when he's grown up, but he refused. He wanted to be on the bridge all the time." She shook her head with mock severity. " Now that was rather naughty, wasn't it? Rather naughty and ungrateful?"

Gino wriggled in her grasp, the short hair on the back of his head prickling with embarrassment. He was furious with Semprebon for discussing him with a passenger, particularly with this garrulous painted old bag of fat. This evening she had scented herself until she smelt like a perfume manufactory; his nose wrinkled in disgust. Semprebon scented himself, too; he wondered briefly whether it would act as shark repellent if either of them fell over the side, and hoped sincerely that it would not.

Roger said with malicious geniality, " Well, I don't know what the Purser wanted to teach him, but he could do with some instruction in *Realpolitik*. He thinks Egypt ought to send ships to bombard British ports, or something. He's a great one on Britain's Suez sins, an absolute fire-eater. Aren't you, Gino?"

Mrs. Crambatch shook her head until her opal-edged spectacles corruscated like miniature clusters of moons. "It's very wrong for young people to talk loosely about war. I've always said so. We older people, we know all about it." She looked sternly at Gino. " Now when Commander Lannfranc talks about war, he knows what he's saying and it would never be something irresponsible or dangerous, you can take it from me. Commander Lannfranc was captain of a British submarine—did you know that? Now that's something, isn't it? Something to be proud of! He's a *real* hero, if you like!"

But this was a little too much, even for Roger. He cut in quickly, " Not in the war. Later, much later. During the war——"

" During the war," echoed a cold, brusque voice, and Paula Chelgrove joined the group, reluctantly accompanied by the Chief Officer. Serafino had been handed over to her a few minutes before by Captain Onestinghel in a further unsuccessful attempt to get his guests to circulate properly. She had realised that neither of her usual conversational gambits, "Do you hunt?" and "What sort of dog do you keep?" would be any use with this common-looking young foreigner, and they had stared at each other wordlessly until hearing the words "during the war"—a phrase which never failed to rouse her deepest interest—she had turned thankfully to join the Lannfrancs. "I've always meant to ask you, Commander: did you know my cousin, David Chelgrove? He was a submarine commander in 'forty-two."

Roger's face lit up. "Yes, of course! That is, I met him once or twice. He was very much senior to me, of course, and a lot older. His boat was lost on patrol about two months after he got her, I remember. Of course, in those days 'T' boats weren't——"

Mrs. Crambatch, remembering the names on the Dunedin war memorial and determined not to fall below Miss Chelgrove in patriotic reminiscence, said, "I lost two nephews in the war. They were both in the R.N.Z.A.F.—you know our boys wore the same uniforms as the R.A.F., that nice grey-blue. Albert and Edward their names were. It was a dreadful blow—two of them, I mean. I doted on those boys, never having had any children of my own. They were to have been Leslie's heirs—after me, of course."

Bronwen, speaking for the first time, said sympathetically, "How dreadful for you. Were they the only nephews you had?"

"Yes, dear, the only ones. You can imagine what it meant to me! Albert—he was the clever one—left a beautiful little poem about how, if he died in battle no one was to weep for him because he died happy, knowing he was defending Freedom. It had a Latin name—now let me think—ah, yes! It was called *Dulce et decorum est pro patria mori*; at least, I *think* so; I don't know Latin myself. Anyway, Leslie had it engraved on a little stone monument and erected in the garden. Ah, war! It's a dreadful thing. I hope our boys to-day—*all* boys to-day——" she glanced reproachfully at Gino—"will never have to go through that again. I—oh, thank you, steward!" She broke off to take another canapé from the dish proffered by Ettore, and Roger, looking up from lighting a cigarette, saw a quick glance flash out from the cadet to the Chief Officer. It was a fleeting schoolboy grimace of amused contempt—contempt for all of them and what they had been saying, contempt for their presence on this ship and for their status as privileged live cargo to be taken for a stated number of miles across the world and dumped on shore again; the contempt of the sailor for the landsman.

"Yes, I agree." He turned to Serafino. "Were *you* in the war? No, of course not—you couldn't have been, could you? You were far too young. Though his words were harmless enough, his voice was contemptuously, deliberately, insulting.

Serafino eyed him bleakly. "In the war? You say correct —I was too young. But still in the war. How you think I get this?" He tapped his right leg. "Bomb. English bomb. In—in nineteen hundred forty-three. I am at school and the planes come. Two bombs are on the school. I am for hours lying in the stones with one great iron across my leg." He spoke with a cold matter-of-factness, but the memory of that agonising time, the fiery waves of pain alternating with periods of sick semi-consciousness, the screams and wailing from the shattered ruins, narrowed his eyes and thinned his mouth, revealing the bitterness behind his words. "Yes. The doctor want to cut off my foot in order to release. It is half off, he say, and is better that way. But my father say no. I was ten years, then. For me that was the war."

There was an embarrassed silence. Then Roger gave a short, angry laugh. "Little Nell just isn't in it, is she?"

Then the Captain's light voice cut in with dry amusement: "Ah these doctors! 'Fly, fly before the face of a physician!' as an old admiral I once knew used to adjure his staff when in his cups. Poor man. He fell into their hands at last—quite accidentally with a broken ankle. They cut off his supply of spirits and he was soon dead. They kill us all in the end." He smiled, glancing surreptitiously across the room to where Dr. Gavanian, his face dark with gloom, was morosely filling himself with whisky behind a potted palm.

Mrs. Crambatch brindled at once. "Well, really, Captain! I'm sure that in N.Z. at least, we don't look on it like that at all! In N.Z. a doctor is—is the most respected man in the community. After all, he is a healer! My brother, Dr. Victor Pease, is probably Dunedin's most revered citizen —now that Leslie has entered into his eternal reward, of course."

But Captain Onestinghel was not easily abashed. "Ah, so? I too had a brother who became a doctor; a worthy soul in many ways, if a trifle slow mentally, like so many of his kind. I remember that it was said of him that he saved the lives of a great many of his patients by generally arriving too late to do anything." He smiled blandly and took a glass from Agostino, who, fortunately appearing with a tray of various drinks, gave the hostile little group a chance to break up. Mrs. Crambatch, holding the two Lannfrancs firmly by the arms, turned the conversation southwards to New Zealand, while Miss Chelgrove, towering over the unhappy Gino, started putting him through a catechism of the games he had played at school. For the second time that evening the Captain found himself with Ciccolanti on his hands. "Well now," he said resignedly, "let us see. Ah—Colonel Chelgrove! Have you met my Chief Officer yet? But of course! You sit at the same table, do you not?"

The Colonel bowed slightly and smiled mildly down from his six feet two inches at Serafino. "Yes, we've sometimes seen each other at meals. As a matter of fact, I didn't realise *you* were the chief officer. I thought it was that fellow over there." He inclined his head in the direction of Bressan, who was giggling over his glass at once of the mess-boys.

"But——"

"No, no." Onestinghel lightly touched the epaulette on Serafino's left shoulder. "Three bars, you see, Colonel. You will note that Signor Bressan wears only two."

"Of course. Stupid of me. But then I've always been a soldier, and the Services are notoriously bad at recognising one another's insignia. Doubtless it's the same everywhere." He smiled quizzically. "I wonder, for instance, Captain, if you could tell me the rank badges of a British colonel?"

"I think I should be right in saying one crown and two stars, should I not? I too have been a soldier in my time, you see."

The Colonel looked surprised. "Indeed? How interesting. May I ask in what branch of the service?"

"Cavalry," said Onestinghel briefly.

"Really?" The Colonel was becoming more and more impressed. "Light or heavy?"

"Particularly light, I imagine. I commanded a squadron of cossacks in the army of Kolchak." Onestinghel's hard mouth thinned to a line. "And you, Colonel? What branch were you?"

"I? Oh, I was infantry myself. Queen's Rifles, actually."

" So? They were, I think, engaged in Burma at one stage of the last war."

" Yes. Yes, that's correct." The Colonel drained his glass and exchanged it for a full one proffered by Agostino, who was passing to and fro with extreme diligence, hoping thereby to make up in some measure for his earlier mishap. " Yes, the regiment is often engaged abroad—in the tropics. Yes. You see, we are in a rather difficult position when it comes to fighting a European war against the Germans, because ever since Waterloo, when the Queen's Rifles and a regiment of Von Bulow's corps fought side by side—that is to say, they *would* have fought side by side if they hadn't marched together in the wrong direction and arrived too late for the battle—ever since then we've had a Prussian prince as our colonel-in-chief. It's hereditary—goes from father to son. So naturally it's most embarrassing if we have to fight the Huns. You follow me, Captain? In the fourteen-eighteen war, when our Royal family was still more closely linked with the Boches than it is to-day, we were sent to garrison the Bahamas. I spent the whole war there myself. Delightful place—and the fishing was quite superb. In this last show there were other enemies besides the Germans, of course. As a matter of fact, I had resigned myself to spending the war in the Bahamas again. I'd actually bought a lot of extra kit for the place, too—and some most expensive fishing tackle." He paused, smiling sadly. " But it was not to be, I'm afraid. Since the end of the war the Regiment have tried to take up the old traditional ties again. They tried to get our colonel-in-chief over for a most important anniversary recently, but he couldn't come. He's a terribly rich old fellow, a great landowner: the Prince of Sebelin-Rukenthal, quite a——"

" And that," remarked Countess Zapescu, appearing suddenly like a jack-in-the-box between the Colonel and the Captain, " is one big lie!"

" I beg your pardon!" Colonel Chelgrove jumped convulsively (the tone, if not the voice, had sounded so like his sister's) and spilt his gin on to the carpet. He goggled at her in astonishment. " How——? I mean—what?"

The Countess's beady black eyes snapped. " You saying he is so rich. But no! He is, oh—vairy, vairy poor! I am for him an oldt frient—I know. For him I am most fondt. To me last year one day he say, ' My goodt Countess, I have to-day one invitation from one English regiment of which I am colonel to make to visit them.' Andt he say, 'But to go I cannot.' 'Why so?' 'Because, my dear friendt, I have not the money for the passage. Also my clothes are no longer correct wearing for a nobleman and my military ornaments have long been away from me. So I cannot go.' Yes. So I think, monsieur, that this so fine English regiment do better to sendt to the Prince, their colonel, some gift to assist. It is not excellent to make boast of a great nobleman of most ancient family andt allow that he starve!"

Colonel Chelgrove stared at her glassily. Like most English Army officers over forty, his mind only moved at the speed of a paralysed tortoise, and this gave Onestinghel time to fill the pause before it could grow too painful. With staccato tact he said, "So much has changed since the war. It is too difficult to expect that one should keep up with such constant alterations—one cannot. I myself have lost touch with many friends who doubtless are suffering extreme poverty. I would help if I knew how, but I do not. It is most sad, most regrettable. No one, however, is to blame. Come. Colonel, let me introduce you to my chief engineer. He is a man who has seen a great deal of the Far East and——"

But the Colonel was not to meet Aafjes that evening. Even as the Captain started to lead him away, there came a sudden screech of pain, a clatter, and a fearful crash of breaking crockery. Renzo had caught Ettore furtively removing the last prawn canapés from one of his own dishes and piling them on to a small plate for Mrs. Crambatch. There had been a hissing, whispered argument, a quiet, panting struggle, a sharp kick and a jabbing elbow—and then both mess-boys were on the floor among the broken pieces of the ship's best china and the splintered remains of all the Purser's gold-edged glasses.

VIII

Next morning *San Roque* lay off Steamer Point with the early sun glistening on her wet, newly washed decks. She shared fore and aft moorings—two great iron buoys like inverted mushrooms—with the tanker *British Sovereignty* and the Russian freighter *Ivan Setchenov,* the near presence of the latter being a source of extreme displeasure to Captain Onestinghel. He stared at her in grim silence for several minutes and then turned to Serafino standing beside him. "What do you think of her, Ciccolanti?"

"Fast—but very little cargo space, I should say. She must be most uneconomical to operate as a freighter——" Serafino grinned sardonically—"but I suppose that doesn't matter as she's really an *incrociatore*." For of course the Russian ship was convertible; her lines, her raking prow and long, low, rounded stern were so obviously those of a light cruiser that nothing could disguise them, and she lay among the other shipping off the Point like a pike among a shoal of fat carp. All she needed was her guns.

Onestinghel gave a brief grunt of assent. "A month at the most in Cronstadt, and then . . . I wonder if they still use the *palka*. I suppose so." He smiled grimly. "I should perhaps send Petelli over with my compliments and a request to borrow it—then there would be three of Cavaliere Semprebon's mess-boys who would not be able to sit down before we reached Sydney. I——" He turned suddenly at the sound of an unaccustomed step on the bridge behind him to see Colonel Chelgrove, in an ancient tropical suit and a yellowed Panama hat, blinking in the glare of light from the great bridge windows.

"Ah—ah, good morning, Captain."

"Good morning." Onestinghel's voice was cold. The bridge was out of bounds to all passengers and he himself had seen more than enough of the first-class ones last night.

"I'm sorry to intrude. Yes—well, actually it was my sister's suggestion." The Colonel took out a very ancient silk handkerchief full of moth holes and, removing his hat, wiped his high, bald forehead. "I'm sure you aren't to blame. I told my sister so, but——"

"To blame for what, Colonel?"

"—But she would insist that it must be put right. After all, she——"

"Put *what* right, please?"

"She said we were in a British port, after all. I said I was sure that you personally had not meant——"

Captain Onestinghel's brows puckered in angry exasperation and then cleared in sudden understanding. "Oh, yes, I see. I regret it as much as you do, my dear sir. Unfortunately we have no option."

It was the Colonel's turn to look surprised. "No option? I don't think I understand——"

"There were no other moorings available. We are, in any case, only here until noon."

"But——"

"I assure you that it is much more painful for me to be moored alongside a Soviet ship than it can possibly be for anyone else on board."

Colonel Chelgrove shook his head rapidly. "No, no, no, it's not the moorings. I don't know anything about that."

"Then what——?"

"The flag, my dear sir, the flag. You're flying the Union Jack upside down."

2

The sun rose higher over the great cindery mountains behind the town, the harbour became a glaring bowl of pale-green water under a sky drained of all colour by the intense heat. Complaining, fretful and sweating profusely, the passengers disembarked in large wooden motor-launches. Aden above all ports must be visited. Not for its beauties, for transparently it had none, but for the astonishing bargains in cameras, watches and radios to be found in its duty-free shops. Serafino went with the last launch, sitting at the back behind a group of British migrants who were chattering shrilly in the forward seats. Loudest and shrillest was a fat, elderly woman upon whose frizzled grey hair perched an imitation Mexican sombrero of pink and peppermint-green straw purchased, almost certainly, at Port Said.

"Ow, she was lookin' so pretty that day! Jest like the pictures! She was wearin'—now let me see—yes, she was wearin' a pelisse—that's what they said it was in the papers—an embroidered pelisse, greeny-like. An' a toque—a toque with an egret plume. An' 'er jewell'ry! You never saw the like of it. Well, 'er 'usband was there too, of course—the Prince. What a really lovely gentleman 'e is, ain't 'e, Mrs. Throsby? You never seen 'im? Not close-to, like? I 'ave. *Twice.* Once in 'is admiral's suit, only it was rainin' 'ard an' 'e was lookin' damp-like an' a bit put out—natcherly. An' once up in Scotland while I was up there for a week 'elpin' Cyril while Edna was in 'ospital. 'E come to open this playin' field—leastways I *think* it was. Proper fond of the kiddies 'e is, the papers say. 'E was wearin' a kilt with one of them fancy fur bags 'angin' from it like in old pictures, an' there's a dirty great knife stuck in 'is sock. Proper 'Ighland laddie 'e looked, for all that 'e's really a Greek—as I says to Cyril."

The launch swung in to the landing-stage and the passengers clambered ashore, protesting with appalled, wondering disbelief at the Aden temperature. Serafino loitered at the jetty's edge until they were all safely past the port gates with their landing-cards checked and punched before he followed them. Passing the polished wooden *houri,* the Red Sea fishing canoe, on its stand, he glanced inside. None of the passengers had thrown in any coins, despite the notice requesting them to do so. Not that Aden was the sort of place in which one expected to find flourishing charities: a town of pumice stone and porous, slaty rock, lying beneath towering mountains of purplish slagged coke, it was awesome in its utter, burnt-out aridity. One felt that under the thin crust of ashes and furnace dross there could be no earth but only smouldering fire. It was always a relief to re-embark, to leave the land for the sea, where the gleaming jade-green water seemed a far friendlier element than the dusty, desiccated lava of the shore.

Serafino walked slowly past the Crescent, with its curved row of shops all selling the same wide assortment of duty-free manufactured odds, mostly Japanese, at prices lower than anywhere else in the world, except perhaps Hong Kong. Here, on the way back, he would buy a watch for Silvio, a couple of shirts for Salvatore, and something for the rest of the family. Now that *San Ramòn* was also on the Australia run, it seemed probable that quite a large collection Aden-bought goods would in future find their way into the Vic' Re Galantuomo.

Walking slowly, limping a little, along the narrow, dusty pavement, his face rendered still more enigmatic than usual by his large dark sun-glasses, Serafino stared into the shop windows with envy and interest and a certain dry amusement. Owned and operated mainly by Indians, these places were all named with such sycophantically extravagant British imperialism that even the Suez conspirators must have been slightly nauseated by it: The King-Emperor's Bon Marché, The Royal Union Jack Stores, Her Glorious Majesty's Bazaar, The God Save the Queen Emporium. And from large coloured pictures in their windows, pictures reverently draped and tinselled, all the members of the Royal Family and their associated hangers-on bared their fangs in grins wide enough to boost the sales of even the least popular kinds of tooth-paste.

Passing the pictures, Serafino thought of Japheth Wendlandt doing the same the day before yesterday, thought of his disgusted comments and smiled. " . . . All that Coronation crap. Say, I read in one of their news-sheets that the limeys think we *envy* them their goddam King or Queen—envy them, for Chrissake! Why the hell they think we threw the last bastard out?"

They had met two years ago in a shoe shop in La Guayra. Entering from the humid glare of the street, Serafino had found a very small American officer with long, honey-coloured hair and large glasses with honey-coloured frames trying patiently but with inadequate Spanish to buy a pair of children's white sandals. Seeing another young man in the white of the mercantile marine, the American had eyed him a moment doubtfully and then asked in his halting Spanish, "*Habla Vd Inglés, señor?*"

" A very little I speak—yes."

" Thank Christ! Will you kindly tell this dope I'm buying these shoes for me—not my granddaughter or my great-nephew or something."

" For yourself?"

" For myself. Look, I know it's funny, but I got terrible small feet. So I generally buy kid's shoes when I buy them in a store. I get them specially made for me when I'm back home, though."

Later they had gone to a bar and Serafino had ordered Compari-sodas which the American took to at once. "I'm not drinking P.J.'s beer or his goddam rum. Why should I put my dough into his pocket—he's got plenty. Say, have you heard the new P.J. story?"

Serafino had sighed deply. " Listen, *amigo,* this trip I hear already four new P.J. stories—last trip, five. They do nothing in La Guayra only to tell P.J. stories. In Caracas it is for some the all-day job, I think."

" Sure—why not? They say he makes a lot of them up himself. No, but I mean this one about old P.J. and the yucca root and the two-headed calf—heard that?"

" No."

" Fine. Well, it's this way . . ." And the American had launched with zest into the newest of the many stories about Venezuela's gaudy President, General Pérez Jiménez, towards whom he seemed to have a sort of mocking proprietorial affection.

They had become friends almost immediately, largely because of the fascination which persons of different nationalities but the same profession inevitably feel for one another. They were also both undersized, both third officers of the same age, and with a touch of the same odd, stubborn fatalism; it was enough to hold in common.

Moving past a shop window on which was painted in gold lettering "Suppliers of Toilet Requisites to His Grace the Duke of Dunbar and Consort," Serafino wondered how Japheth would have liked working under the command of Captain Onestinghel and felt that they would probably have been a source of perpetual delight to each other. He had not heard from his friend for nearly four months. The American had a habit of writing letters and leaving them with the proprietors of dockside bars to be delivered if and when the recipient's ship called in. In this way he kept up an erratic correspondence with a variety of mercantile acquaintances all over the world. It was not a foolproof system, but, as he said, it was more reliable than putting messages in bottles and chucking them over the goddam side. Under no circumstances did he consider using normal postal facilities.

It was in the hope that he might find a letter waiting for him in Aden that Serafino had come ashore. Now he turned right at the end of the Crescent and walked uphill, along a street full of goats and beggars, towards the Star of Hellas bar. It was a small, shabby place run by a Greek family, but it was the only one in Aden which did not insult Japheth's republican and egalitarian principles by being named after a British prince or duke or displaying royal portraits above the counter.

The Star of Hellas stood on a corner, and this morning it was comparatively crowded. Pushing aside the bead curtain in the doorway, Serafino glanced round the small room with its bare wooden tables, curved zinc bar and inevitable chromium coffee machine. There were a dozen sailors of different nationalities in dungarees, two British soldiers in khaki drill, a group of slender young Indians, probably from the Crescent stores or perhaps clerks from shipping offices, and, getting up to go, a ship's officer in white. Taking off his dark glasses, Serafino blinked in the sudden glare of pale light and caught a glimpse of the man as he pushed through the bead curtain that gave access to the street on the other side of the bar. It was Gil Sotomayor. Serafino stared with speculative interest as the bead curtains rattled into place behind the broad-shouldered white back. What was the owner's son doing in a place like this? There were plenty of smarter bars; there was even a hotel to visit if he wanted a drink. And anyway, should he be ashore at all? Onestinghel had said nothing to his Chief Officer concerning any restrictions on Gil's movements, had not mentioned him at all throughout the voyage. Onestinghel was known to be a friend of Don Ildefonso's, and in this matter of Gil he was presumably acting in that capacity rather than as a senior employee of the Flotta Soto. Gil's passage to Sydney was a strictly private matter between the owner and his senior captain in which no one else need concern himself, yet, as was the way on ships, conjecture and rumour mixing and fermenting together were distilled by a few logical minds into an approximation of the truth. Gil was in deep disgrace, he was being exiled for a period of years to the offices of the Sydney agency in O'Connell Street, and he was forbidden to leave the ship at any port because of a known reluctance to fall in with these plans for his future.

There was no letter for Serafino at the Star of Hellas, and, walking back to the jetty, he kept a lookout for Gil—in vain. It was half-past eleven and the last launch to *San Roque*, packed with sweating tourists excitedly clutching duty-free cameras and radios, was just leaving. Serafino went with it, dourly wondering how the Throsbys the Micklems, the Ampels and the other British tourist-class passengers managed to buy gold watches, precision cameras and tiny transistor radios when they were only able to find ten pounds each for their fares to Sydney and had the remainder made up by the Australian and British Governments.

Gino was at the head of the gang-ladder and Serafino asked him if Gil had returned. "No, signore. I did not know that he was ashore. He didn't leave while I've been on duty."

"Who was before you?"

"Petelli."

Serafino nodded, frowning, and went up to the bridge. He would casually mention to Onestinghel that he had seen Gil in the town. Probably the Captain would say that he knew it, that he had given Gil permission. Serafino devoutly hoped so, for it was already a quarter to twelve and *San Roque* was due to sail at noon. If Gil was coming back he would hire a private launch; he would not be accustomed to using public transport. But he had better be quick.

The Captain did not appear on the bridge until the moorings were being cast off. He was in a good humour at the imminent prospect of quitting the vicinity of the *Ivan Setchenov,* and asked his Chief Officer how he had found Aden.

"The same as ever, signore, though I was a cadet when I last went ashore here. I think I saw——"

"Did you find a letter from your American friend?"

"No, I——"

"So? Ah, well, you may meet him on the voyage back. Malestroit, I want you to organise a full boat-drill tomorrow morning. And——"

A harbour launch had unhooked the bow cable from the great buoy and a slow, clanking rattle from a forward winch told that it was coming aboard. Desperately Serafino said, "*Signor Capitano, scusi*——"

"One minute, Ciccolanti. Malestroit, I want to emphasise most distinctly that——"

"*Capitano!* I think Signor Sotomayor may still be ashore."

The Captain swung round as if he had been hit on the side of the head. "What! What's that?"

Serafino swallowed. "Signor, I saw Don Gil Sotomayor in—in the town and I don't think he's back aboard ship yet."

Onestinghel's face was rigid, a hard, cold mask; only his pale eyes gleamed narrowly. "You saw him ashore—when?"

"About half an hour ago. Maybe a little longer."

"You are sure?"

"I—I *think* it was him."

The Captain turned abruptly to Malestroit. "Run down to Don Gil's cabin. See if he's there. As fast as you can."

Malestroit disappeared down the ladder like a monkey, and Onestinghel seized the telephone and shouted angry orders to Petelli in the stern to halt the casting off of the after cable. No sooner had he replaced one phone than another rang. The Captain snatched it from its holder. "So! All right, Malestroit, go forward and stand by to take out the boy cable again." Putting down the phone, he strode across to the ship's broadcasting transmitter, switched it on and snapped, "*Il Commissario, per cortesia al Ponte Comando—subito!*" And from the starboard bridge wing Serafino heard the deck amplifiers below echo curtly "*—subito—ito.*"

Then Onestinghel beckoned to his Chief Officer. "I'll

want you to take a letter to the Aden police headquarters. Wait, though—your English is not sufficient. Malestroit had better take it. Go forward and tell him to report here with you in——" the Captain glanced at his watch—" eight minutes' time."

"*Si, signore.*" Serafino saluted and left the bridge, smiling grimly to himself. Semprebon was about to receive a very unpleasant eight minutes at the hands of his irate Captain in the little office behind the chart table, and Onestinghel wished that it should be in private.

Climbing back to the bridge eight minutes later, followed by Malestroit, Serafino found the Captain in a state of grim, controlled anger. When Malestroit had been despatched with his letter, he called Serafino into the bridge office and shut the door. " Well, now we can only wait. I think Don Gil will soon be found. Aden is not a big place." He looked appraisingly at his Chief Officer. " You've done me a distinct service to-day, Ciccolanti. I'm grateful to you. I suppose I should have told you earlier that young Sotomayor is forbidden under all circumstances to set foot ashore until we reach Sydney. But the whole matter is, of course, a delicate family affair of the owner's and nothing to do with the Line. I did not wish anyone but myself to become in any way involved in it. Also, until to-day Don Gil has shown no inclination to disobey his father's wishes."

Serafino nodded. " I understand, signore." Inwardly he was delighted with the praise he had received and the confidence the Captain now plainly felt in his discretion. His endemic fear of losing his job, that taut, ever-present worry at the back of his mind, eased and slackened. Perhaps—who knew? —Onestinghel might report so well of him that he might be retained permanently as Chief Officer on *San Roque* and never revert to his official position as Second on board the smaller *San Ramòn*. If Onestinghel really liked him as well as approving of him. . . . Onestinghel was the senior captain and a friend of the owner. . . . Under those circumstances Don Ildefonso might overcome his well-known distrust of youth. It was possible. It could happen.

But the Captain was still talking. "I fear that on this occasion the boy undoubtedly meant to leave the ship. If you had not seen him we would have sailed without him. His absence might not have been discovered for hours, and by that time it would, of course, have been quite impossible to do anything about it." He paused. " Semprebon is much to blame—as I have just informed him. Gil certainly had a landing-card, or he could not have passed the gatehouse on the quay. Yet the Purser knows perfectly well that a landing-card may only be handed over in exchange for a passport, and that boy's passport is in my safe and the key is in my pocket. He says that Gil was hanging about the vestibule while the passengers were collecting their cards and probably stole one himself." Onestinghel's voice was coldly sardonic. "Perhaps—and equally, perhaps, Semprebon turned a blind eye to the theft. Things are not supposed to get stolen from the Purser's office; it is supposed to be as secure as a bank. But young Gil is the owner's son, of course!"

He paused, his lips turned down angrily. "While we are on the subject, Ciccolanti, I want to say this. Don Ildefonso is our owner—*not* Don Gil. Don Gil has nothing at all to do with the Flotta Soto at present, and he will have very little to do with it for many years to come. Under no circumstances is he in a position to give orders to anybody on board this ship. Beyond his sole privilege of living in the Captain's quarters and the fact that he is not allowed ashore, he is in exactly the same position as a first-class passenger and is to be treated as such. When we reach Sydney someone from O'Connell Street will come aboard, either Mr. Bembrose or Signor Bevilaqua, and take charge of him. And——" added the Captain dryly—"I sincerely hope he will give the Agents less trouble than he has given his unfortunate father or myself. Anyway, you understand the position now, Ciccolanti?"

"Si, Signor Capitano—senz'altro."

3

The incandescent sun, hanging poised in the mid-heavens over Steamer Point, enveloped the iron ships becalmed upon the warm, sluggish sea in a glare of gluey heat and eye-searing light; then, very slowly, it began to arch westwards. On *San Roque* the passengers, at first fretful at the delay, began to grow angry. If only the ship would leave, would sail out to sea and away from this cindery, heat-radiating, mountainous shore, there would surely be a breeze. They would be able to stand on the upper decks and let the wind cool them, lifting the damp shirts and blouses from sweating bodies already itching and smarting with prickly heat.

First-class and tourist, they besieged the vestibule counter with querulous demands and inquiries.

"Purser! I say, Purser! What are we hanging about for? We were supposed to leave at twelve, weren't we? I said, we were supposed to leave at noon—eh?"

"If we'd known we was goin' to be all this time 'ere we could 'ave stayed ashore an' all!"

"Mr. Semprebon, will you please tell me *when* we're leaving? I don't want to know *why* we're still here, I want to know *when*. . . ."

". . . ain't fair on the kids."

". . . if you don't know, why don't you find out?"

"Why the devil *don't* you know?"

"Somebody ought to see the Captain."

"This heat's killin' the kids, poor little baskets!"

"Look here, Semprebon, this just isn't good enough!"

By two o'clock Cavaliere Semprebon was in such a state of nerves that he nearly lost his temper with Mrs. Crambatch. "Madam, we shall go *when* we go. Beyond the fact that this matter appears to be the Chief Officer's doing, I can tell you nothing—nothing at all!" And he had slammed the shutters across the counter and gone to his cabin to take a double dose of heartburn pills and a glass of milk of magnesia.

At three-thirty the passengers, angry, despairing and mystified, had seen the port police-launch *Margaret* shoot out towards them from the jetty and slow down alongside; then the Chief Officer had hurried down the gang-ladder, climbed into the boat and returned with it to the quay.

Entering, some five minutes later, the white charge-room of the port police-station, Serafino felt both pleased and a little anxious. He was flattered at the way in which Onestinghel was confiding in him over this affair, first telling him privately of the instructions he had received from Don Ildefonso and now sending him to bring Gil back. For the first time since the start of the voyage, he really felt he was Chief Officer of *San Roque* and the Captain's trusted second-in-command. And yet—he did not quite like acting as Onestinghel's emissary in this way and becoming too closely associated in Gil's mind with his elderly jailer. It was true that Gil would not be of any importance in the Flotta Soto for a considerable time, not, at any rate, until after Captain Onestinghel had retired. But for himself it was different: if Gil took a dislike to him over this matter, it could, in time, have serious consequences. He would have to be as tactful as he could; but he was uncomfortably aware, at the back of his mind, that his was not a naturally tactful nature.

There were no signs of Gil in the charge-room, and Serafino looked round questioningly. "Where——?"

"In here." A young English police officer turned from a couple of native constables and led the way, grinning, towards a row of iron doors at the end of a wide passage. "He's not very pleased at being picked up, I'm afraid. He says he won't go back to your ship. We can make him, of course—in fact we shall—because his landing-card expired at noon and he has no passport. But I think it might make matters easier if you had a talk with him first and tried to make him see a bit of sense." He opened a cell door, quickly ushered Serafino inside, and then shut it behind him.

A small, whitewashed room, square and unfurnished save for a plank bench against the far wall: a high, barred window letting in some of the vivid light of day; Gil rising from the bench, his sweat-soaked white shirt clinging to his broad chest, his dark, hot, oddly familiar face breaking slowly into a savage grin. "So——! He sent *you*, did he?" They were the first words the owner's son had ever addressed to Serafino, and they were heavy with menace. "You saw me in that bar. I thought you did. And then you went back and told him—that's it, isn't it? Haven't you learnt that sometimes it's wise to keep your ugly mouth shut, you stupid fool!"

Serafino's face reddened. He suddenly felt totally unsuited to this kind of interview. He was far too close to Gil's age, for one thing; probably there was little more than two years between them. If he had been Parodi, of course . . . He tried to remember that he held Parodi's rank and position, that he was Chief Officer of *San Roque* and the Captain's trusted second-in-command, but it did not help a great deal: he felt much more like a schoolboy about to have a fight with another stronger than himself who would probably beat him.

Ignoring Gil's remarks, he said with an attempt at firm politeness, "Don Gil, the Captain has sent me to bring you back. He says——"

"He can say what he likes. I'm not going back."

"Listen, Don Gil——"

"For Christ's sake stop calling me Don Gil like that!

You're not an old family servant any more than that imbecile Semprebon!"

Serafino swallowed. "Well, Signor Sotomayor, then, or whatever you like—you've got to come back. The police are refusing to allow you to stay."

"They can't. I've got a landing-card."

"It expired at noon." Serafino smiled, anxious. "You need not worry that anything will be said. The Captain says he won't refer to this incident at all, or tell your father, if——"

But Gil, who had pulled the crumpled green landing-card from his pocket and studied it carefully, must have seen the expiry hour for the first time and realised what it implied. His face flushed a dark crimson, he tore the little card violently in two, flung the pieces into Serafino's face and followed them up with a vicious swing of his fist which smashed into Serafino's mouth and sent him spinning across the cell. Then they were locked together, gasping and grunting, reeling about the stone floor and cannoning off the bare white walls. They grappled breathlessly and wordlessly, neither wanting, for different reasons, to attract the attention of the police outside.

Serafino, dazed by the blow in his face, feeling blood dripping over his mouth and chin, was entirely on the defensive, desperately trying to grab Gil's flailing arms and somehow halt the rain of fierce blows that thudded into his body. Panting, coughing, spraying blod from his battered mouth, he gasped, "You—you don't understand. Look, when Onestinghel——" And then Gil had him by the throat and they fell over the plank bed with a crash and were rolling on the floor. Serafino, his throat held in an iron grip, his breathing stopped, felt his arms weakening as they grappled him close to Gil. Blind instinctive panic filled him, and with the last of his strength he brought his knee up sharply between Gil's legs, felt a galvanic jerk in the body so close to his own and the loosening of the hands about his throat. Then the door was thrown open, there came the clatter of boots on the stone floor, and the young Englishman in the khaki police uniform was lifting him to his feet, while two black constables gripped the groaning, retching Gil and twisted his arms behind his back.

"My God! I'd have come in with you if I'd thought this sort of thing was going to happen. I'd no idea he'd get violent. Are you okay?" The police officer was supporting him with an arm, gazing at him with concern and apology written clearly on his face.

"I—I'm all right." Gasping, trembling, Serafino jerked himself from the policeman's arm and, leaning against the wall, pulled out a handkerchief and wiped his smarting, bloody face.

"You sure? You don't look too good, you know."

"No. I'm okay." Serafino took his hat which the police officer held out to him and stared bitterly at Gil, who glared back from a sick face to which the blood was patchily returning. "I am sorry if I hurt you, Signor Sotomayor, but it was your own fault. You had no reason to attack me. I had to defend myself. I don't know what the Captain will say when he hears about this."

"Or what my father will say when he does. You can kill people, doing that to them."

Serafino shrugged helplessly and turned to the police officer. "Will you allow, please, for two men to—to come with us back to my ship?"

"Yes, of course. Look, shouldn't you sit down for a little? I mean, you look a bit——"

"I am all right! And we have made to wait too long already."

Still breathing heavily, deeply conscious of his limp and his battered face, he turned away. He felt suddenly sick and exhausted, his legs seemed to be made of weak rubber. In a mirror on the wall of the charge-room he caught a glimpse of himself: a small, blood-stained figure in torn, dirty shirt and trousers, one black epaulette hanging from its gilt button, his cap alone immaculate, seeming, with its big gleaming badge and gold strap, a ridiculously incongruous headgear for the battered scarecrow beneath. And from the wall his reflection glared at him despairingly, mocking him with the broken hopes for the future with which he had been deluding himself one short hour ago, telling him that something like this had been bound to happen, that he should have known by now that he could never with impunity steal an advantage from the fate that harried him. Now he had fallen into the trap and as good as thrown away his job. And behind that realisation he sensed all the old weary fears and worries awakening from their short sleep and clamouring to be heard: Naples and the family's food; the rent; the winter coming and the fuel bill; making ends meet somehow, and no job—no job, no job.

4

It was past midnight, and Serafino, who had just relieved Bressan, stood out on the starboard bridge wing, waiting to see the pinpoint flash of light from Cape Gardafui. The cool breeze of the open sea rustled his shirt and gently caressed his stiff bruised face. Behind him in the darkened bridge the quartermaster stood motionless at the wheel, a ghostly figure limned in the phosphorescent greenish glow reflected upwards from the big compass dial before him.

Leaning over the rail, looking back along the length of the ship as she drove her smooth, powerful course through the calm sea, Serafino thought of Gil lying almost directly beneath his feet in the Captain's quarters and wondered if he was asleep. Very probably he was; he had not seemed unduly worried at his reception on board this afternoon, nor had he any reason to be so. Miserably Serafino recalled the quick trip across the harbour in the police launch, the curious faces staring from the other ships—even the Russian officers on the bridge of the *Ivan Setchenov* had peered down with interest as the launch passed below them—and then the crowded decks and closely lined rails of *San Roque*. The loud, excited buzz of speculation as he and Gil had come aboard up the gang-ladder beat again in his ears, then there had been Petelli's red, worried face at the ladder's top, and his obvious, unnecessary message: "The Captain wants you both in his cabin at once, signori."

Onestinghel's behaviour, once they were in the big comfortable day cabin, had come to Serafino as an uncomfortable surprise, embarrassing, disappointing, infuriating. He had expected Gil to be given a ferocious dressing down phrased in the bitterly sarcastic manner for which Onestinghel was notorious when deeply displeased. Instead, the Captain had been mockingly genial, almost oily. Affecting a sort of weary amusement, as if a friend had persisted in playing a foolish joke, he had tried to make light of the whole thing. "My dear Gil, you really must try to grow up! This sort of escapade is all very well at fourteen, but it is somewhat ridiculous at twenty-four, do you not think? What would your father say! And if you want to fight with someone, why pick on my unfortunate, hard-working Serafino Ciccolanti?"

Gil had laughed. "Serafino? He's no seraph, Captain, I can tell you! You have no idea what he did to me! I doubt if my father will ever have any grandchildren now."

"So?" Onestinghel had turned from taking a bottle of liqueur brandy from a locker. "Ah, these Neapolitans—they are indeed barbarians!" He had laughed silently, pouring out three glasses. "Here. I think we all need a drink. This is an Armanac your father gave me, Gil. If anything can restore you to your natural fecundity it will be this." He lifted his own glass and glanced mockingly over it at them both. "I drink to that wish; to Ciccolanti's peculiar prowess in battle—and Gil, to the fervent hope that you will behave yourself a great deal better for the rest of the voyage."

Onestinghel's amused indifference to Gil's attack upon him had filled Serafino with a burning resentment, which drove out the despair he had felt at the police-station when he had realised the full enormity of actually having come to blows with the owner's son. Onestinghel could have said things to Gil which he himself dared not say, but it seemed that he saw no reason to do so. Probably his old-fashioned Tsarist background caused him to consider that if a Sotomayor wanted to beat up an employee of the Line, there was no reason to make a fuss about it. Half a century ago he had probably whipped his own serfs whenever the inclination took him. Serafino, staring sourly at the short-stemmed, bulbous brandy glass had been temped to refuse it. But what was the good of such a gesture? Gil would merely laugh and Onestinghel would smooth the matter over with some suavely derisive banality; both would manage to make him look a fool. He gave his Captain one glance of complete contempt, drank a little brandy and put down the glass. Gil grinned slowly. "You missed a chance, Serafino. I thought you were going to throw it at me." His voice had held an amused, contemptuous derision. Serafino had not replied. Silently picking up his cap, he had given a brusque nod to Onestinghel—a gesture he would never have dreamed of making twenty-four short hours ago—and had strode from the room.

After dinner that evening Onestinghel had sent for him again, ostensibly to speak to him of some small matter concerning the watch-keeping routine, and had quickly reverted to Gil. "I fear you do not feel very forgiving towards him, Ciccolanti," he had said, carefully selecting a cigar from a large box—a box, thought Serafino angrily, which had probably been given to him with the liqueur brandy by Don Ildefonso. "I doubt if that worries him, *Signor Capitano,* since you have forgiven him yourself."

Onestinghel had started to laugh. "Oh, yes, I have forgiven him completely. After all, I am an old friend of his father's—and besides, he did not hit *me*. However, he bears you no ill-will, I am happy to say. He has not a bad nature really, that boy, I think."

Serafino had stared sombrely at his captain. "Thank you, signore. I am glad to hear that Signor Sotomayor has forgiven me for being attacked by him."

But Onestinghel, smiling, had held up a hand. "Yes, yes, yes. He has punched you and knocked you down and you are black and blue all over—spare me, please, the gruesome details! But remember that for your part, you spoilt a cherished and long-thought-out scheme of his. I know what he was trying to do, though he has not of course, admitted it. He does not in any way share the desire of the rest of our passengers to sample the delights of life in Australia; in fact, the thought of that peculiar land repels him intensely. He wishes, therefore, to frighten his father into forgiving him and allowing him to return to Naples. He could have done this by simply disappearing for a few months. After we had left Aden without him, he would have gone to the Spanish consul, explained that he had missed his ship by mistaking her time of departure, and requested—and doubtless been given—some temporary identification papers. Then he would have gone—oh, to Africa, I expect, or perhaps South America. I think he has some money with him though he is not supposed to possess any. Very soon his father would have become quite wild with anxiety, for he is passionately devoted to Gil, even though he is very angry with him at present. Then Gil would have appeared again, repented like the prodigal son, and, I am certain, been forgiven completely by his father. And there would be no more talk of Australia and our agency at O'Connell Street." Onestenghel paused. "You see? But no. A young man barely two years older than himself, a young man who is in no disgrace, but, on the contrary, has recently received some rather quick promotion, a young man who is *not* being exiled to Australia by an angry parent—this young man, I say, decides to prevent Gil's so well-thought-out plan and does so. You cannot expect the boy to be pleased. He is no saint, as he has very adequately proved. Had I taken a—shall we say, a sterner attitude towards him this morning, Ciccolanti, it would have been an addition of insult to injury. He would not have blamed me because I am so much older—so old compared to you or he that often I must seem to represent quite a different species—but he would never have forgiven *you*. You are both southerners—Latins; you know how easily enmity can last for life. The vendetta—eh?"

" Not to-day, signore. Italians are more civilised than that, now."

Once more the Captain had started to shake with silent laughter. " Is that so indeed, Ciccolanti? I rejoice to hear it. I am sure, therefore, that in any further relations you may have with young Gil you will demonstrate this high degree of Italian civilisation for us to admire."

Serafino's face had broken into a sulkily reluctant grin. " *Signor Capitano*, you laugh at me."

" I? Not I, Ciccolanti, I assure you! I seldom laugh at people, and never at young ones—they do not deserve it."

Despite his relief at hearing that he had not, as he had feared made a disastrously powerful enemy, Serafino left the Captain's cabin with an unhappy feeling that on this voyage everything was going wrong for him. Semprebon, the English passengers—and now Gil. He felt confused and harried and wished passionately that he was back in his old subordinate position on *San Ramòn*. Here, on *San Roque*, he was not getting a single extra lira for the higher rank that he held, and every mistake that he made placed his job in peril. There was something, too, about this ship which he found uncomfortable and even ominous, something elusive which could not easily be expressed in words but which filled him with an irrational sense of foreboding. She was too new, too crowded, too flashily smart for her size and her function; her crew were still more cosmopolitan and less reliable than on either of the other two ships of the Line, and with her odd and enigmatic captain . . . He grinned painfully, feeling the cool night breeze stiffening his sore face, and then, far away on the starboard bow from miles across the dark, still sea, came the sudden pinpoint-flash of light. A pause, and then once more the bright gleam, like a winking star. Cape Gardafui, the last light on the Horn of Africa, was shining its indifferent farewell to *San Roque* as she drove her steady southward course down into the wide, empty expanses of the Indian Ocean.

IX

"*Sehr geehrte Gräfin!*" It must have been the fifth or sixth time that Bella Zapescu had reread the letter she had received at Aden, the letter from the Prince of Sebelin-Rukenthal, with its Paris postmark dated only four days ago. It was difficult to concentrate because everything about the letter brought Paris and the Prince so vividly back to her; the tall, thin writing in very black ink on thick white paper smelling faintly of eau-de-Cologne, the old-fashioned phrasing and carefully elaborate style, in which a courteous respect was softened by touches of polite affection and friendship. It was the sort of letter which could have been written only by someone of her own generation and background, someone who had studied those manuals of etiquette and correspondence which had been so widely in use when she was young but which one never saw now: "A Specimen Letter to a Gentleman who has paid you a discreet Compliment at the Opera"; "Ditto, a Nobleman"; "A Letter of Felicitation to an Elderly Relative upon his/her Saint's Day"; "A Letter to a Person of Rank upon the receipt of a Gift of Game."

This letter would not have been found in such a book; the Prince would have had to design it himself; yet it might well have found its place between the covers as "Specimen Letter to an Elderly Friend announcing Complete Disaster." For Dorothea von Reichenbach was dead, knocked down and killed by a military truck three weeks ago in Melbourne. The last letter the Prince had written her had been returned unopened with a brief explanatory note from her landlady. And now . . . "I cannot but fear that this most distressing news will affect you, my dear Countess, with something more than deep sorrow at the untimely death of our old friend. You chose to inform me at our last meeting that poor Dorothea was making arrangements for your reception and entertainment at Melbourne, and I cannot do otherwise than take the liberty to feel disturbed at the thought that these arrangements may no longer be available to you upon your arrival in that city. . . ."

No, they would not be available. When the ship docked at Melbourne there would be no one there to meet her, nowhere to go, no apartment to share, no job—and no money. Had this letter been delivered to her before the ship left Aden she might have disembarked and attempted to return to Paris; somone—the French consul, perhaps—might have lent her the money. But there had been some sort of trouble which had caused the Purser's office to shut down until after the ship had left the harbour, and no mail had been delivered until they were once more upon the high seas. But even so, what could she have done if she had returned to Paris? Practically her last franc had gone on the cost of this voyage. Momentarily panic clutched her. Dear God, would she land, then, in this foreign city across the world and starve there? It seemed inevitable. Would it not be much better to leave the ship in mid-ocean, to fall overboard and drown? Distractedly her mind played with the thought, and rejected it because of Brown. Perhaps if she gave Brown to someone first . . . but that would arouse immediate suspicion, and in any case there was no one to whom she felt like giving him. She could not abandon him among strangers, among Italians particularly, for they had no idea of how to look after animals, though it was true that they were treating Brown quite nicely; even over the episode of the aluminium paint she was prepared to admit doubt—it *could* have been those British children.

She had managed to get a key of the kennel from the young cadet on the firm promise that she would never let Brown stray from the stern of " C " deck, and consequently Brown now lay beside her on her bunk chewing a small bone which one of the crew must have given him. He was looking so well these days, almost too fat from the big meals he was getting and the scraps constantly fed to him by the sailors. Thinking of Brown calmed her fears a little; he was so much a part of her life—they had never been separated from each other once in his whole twelve years—that he represented a silently devoted, reassuring permanency. While Brown was here—and he always was here, under a chair, curled up in his basket by the fire, sprawled in a patch of sun from the window or sniffing dejectedly at an old mouse-hole in a corner—she had a friend, a child, a dependant, an ally against all that life might yet try to do to her: she was not alone. Absently she started to fan him with her old tortoiseshell and lace fan. " No, no, your old mother will not abandon you, Brown. No, no. Never."

2

Bronwen said, " We're supposed to go to her cabin after the boat drill to have a drink and be shown her souvenirs."

" Oh, God, no! No, Bron. I'm damned if I will!" Roger turned from the open port-hole out of which he had been moodily gazing at the glittering calm of the morning sea. " Strega and chocolates at eleven-thirty and yak-yak-yak about Dunedin and that bloody shop and Leslie. The only good thing about Leslie is that he's safely underground with twenty tons of granite to keep him there.'"

" None the less, we're going——and you're going to behave properly." Bronwen's voice was cold and her back, turned to her husband, was stiffly uncompromising. She pursed her lips at the mirror and started to fill in a small Cupid's bow with deep rose lipstick. When she spoke it was flatly and with pauses to turn her head and study the progress of her work. " Everything's going very well at present and I've practically got her eating out of my hand. She's secretly dying for us to go on with her to New Zealand. She's already half suggested it."

" That doesn't mean she'll offer me a job. People like that don't. I've met one or two before—nothing quite so revoltingly vulgar, but the same sort of thing. They all seem stupid and they *are* stupid, stupid as hell about everything except their incomes. Crambatch wants us to go and live in Dunedin so that she can show us off to her frightful cronies of the Women's Darts Club or the Female Wrestling Society, or whatever it is she goes on about all the time. We'd be just like her other souvenirs. That's how she thinks of us, Bron—like her wooden camels and ivory elephants. But when it came to a job, then she'd say we must talk to her Mr. Smith or her Mr. Jones in whose hands all such decisions are always left. Then——"

" Listen, I'm going to get an offer of a job for you—and a good job, too—out of Crambatch before we get to Sydney!" Bronwen's voice was briskly confident. " But you've got to help."

" Not if it means sitting and listening to hour after hour of the most unutterable trash——"

" Of course it does mean that! And if everything goes well we'll be listening to it for the rest of her natural life."

From the bunk Roger stared up at his wife in startled disbelief, but Bronwen's round face was unsmiling: she had not been joking. " You haven't anything else to do all day, in any case. You don't like the other passengers and you can't even get on with the ship's officers, it seems."

Roger scowled. " They're such a stupid bunch of swabs."

" They've at least got jobs. At least they're working and earning. All you do is criticise everybody else. You tell everyone that you could do the Captain's job infinitely better than he does it him——"

" I do not! I merely said that if that shabby little cripple of a Number One——"

" Well, at least he *is* Number One. And *you* wouldn't look so good, either, if you'd had a couple of bombs dropped on you when *you* were ten! Why didn't you get a job like his yourself if you're so keen on it, instead of wasting——"

" Because, my good woman——"

" Don't ' good woman ' me!"

" Then don't ask such bloody silly questions!"

" They're not silly. Just because you're bone idle and——"

" I am *not*!"

" —and absolutely green with jealousy because——"

" Damn you ! I am *not* jealous of that little bastard!"

" You bloody well are! I've seen it. Oh, yes——"

" Now shut up!"

" Shut up yourself! You make me sick and tired——"

" Shut up!"

3

" A little more Strega, Cavaliere? No? How about you, Professor van Staedtler? Roger, be a good boy and pour the Professor a little more. Oh, that life-jacket! It's made me itch all over. It was so hot!" Mrs. Crambatch speared a small crystallised orange from the box on the table before her and looked round contentedly at her five guests over the little silver fork. " I do hope we never have to use them."

The Purser crossed his long legs and smiled. " My dear madam, that is most unlikely, I assure you. None the less, an occasional practice is demanded by the regulations. It is tedious, I admit, and to-day it was much protracted owing to a rather folish idea of the Chief Officer—the swing from the—the holders."

" The davits."

"Of course! Thank you, Commander Lannfranc. The swing from the davits of the boats. I myself informed him that this should be done later, after all was finished. I informed him that because of the heat much inconveniency would be caused to the passengers which it was unnecessary. He said that this was not my work. I said, 'I beg your pardon, Mister Ciccolanti, but I consider that all things concerned with the passengers' conveniency and happiness is my work—*all* things!'"

"Dear Cavaliere! You're so thoughtful. Really, you spoil us!"

"I do, in my poor way, all I am able. It is a pleasure always. I like to think that it is the most valuable part of my work to make the voyages not voyages but *holidays*—you comprehend? But the officers of the deck have the responsibility of the safety of the ship and the passengers. They must in all things be obeyed. Still . . . No, no, thank you, Mrs. Crambatch. No more, if you please. It does not entirely agree with me."

"Well, now," Mrs. Crambatch rose heavily to her feet. "I promised to show you some of the beautiful things I bought in Europe, didn't I? Now let me see—what shall I show you first? My chessmen, I think. They really are quite fascinating!" She opened a locker under the window and took out a large, flat box. "I found them in a shop in Brussels. They're German and very old, of course." Lifting the lid, she displayed a set of large, ornate chessmen carved in the form of Roman soldiers and accoutred in gilt and silver armour. "Their shields are *real* silver—*solid!*" Her guests produced the required exclamations of admiring pleasure and Mrs. Crambatch beamed. "And now look at these little jugs. They're Irish peasant work—*genuine*—from Killarney. And this I found in the quaintest little out-of-the-way shop in Dublin. And—wait a minute, you'll never guess what I've got here. Look!"

It was only when every available inch of space was covered with the miscellaneous bric-à-brac of the past four months and all her many secular souvenirs were exhausted that she fell back upon the ecclesiastical pieces. She had not intended to display them, for neither the van Staedtlers nor the Lannfrancs were Catholics, but so appreciative had everyone been that she could not resist exhibiting the silver-box pyx and the old Greek thuribles. "And—well, really, I hardly know whether I ought to show you my *own* relic—my little holy relic!" She giggled playfully. "After all, except the Cavaliere you are all unbelievers, I'm afraid, aren't you?"

Bronwen said enthusiastically, "Oh, do show us, Mrs. Crambatch, please! I've never seen a relic and I've always wanted to."

"Yes, yes," echoed both the van Staedtlers with only slightly less enthusiasm. "Let us, by all means see this relic." They were a mild old couple, so bored with each other's unceasing company after forty devoted years of marriage that almost anything, even of the most meagre interest, was capable of giving them pleasure so long as it appertained to someone else.

"What," asked Roger, "is it a relic *of*?" And at once received a glance of warning rebuke from his wife.

But Mrs. Crambatch was unworried. "Of a saint, dear. It's a relic of St. Vera of Castel Baldini in Italy. It wasn't at all easy to get and it was very expensive, but when I'd seen the village and the church and found out that the saint's name was Vera, like mine—well, I couldn't resist it. I felt she *wanted* me to have it, somehow. There seemed, in a way, to be a bond between us. Of course St. Vera has been dead for centuries. She was middle-aged when she came to Castel Baldini and she was a widow and very rich. She gave all her money away, though."

"Really? What a very kind woman," said Bronwen appreciatively. "Who did she give it to"?

"To God, dear. She founded a convent."

"Oh."

"She lived a very holy life and performed several miracles. Her most famous was when she went round the taverns and inns of Castel Baldini one Christmas Eve and found the inhabitants drinking and singing when they should have been inside the new church she had built for them, praying. She turned all their wine into water."

"That," said Roger carefully, "must have made her rather unpopular."

"It did, dear. *Very* unpopular. In fact, she was martyred shortly afterwards by being stoned to death with empty flagons."

"They have a mineral water factory there to-day," remarked Cavaliere Semprebon as Mrs. Crambatch went into the second cabin to get the relic. "The mineral water of Castel Baldino is most famed. And on each bottle there is a picture of this saint. None the less, though of good quality, this water is of all mineral waters the most expensive. There is, because of this, a saying about it. ‘Those who can afford to drink the water of St. Vera's well can also——’ ”

But suddenly Mrs. Crambatch was among them again, her face anxious and flushed. “I must have left it here, after all. It's not in its usual drawer. Cavaliere, please give me my bag. It's beside your chair. Thank you. Sometimes I—No! Oh, dear, where *can* it be?”

There was a note almost of panic in her voice, and immediately Bronwen leapt up to be of assistance. “Now don't worry. It's bound to be here somewhere. Tell us what it looks like and we'll soon find it.”

“It's in a little gold box—like a small cigarette box with legs. There's a sort of medallion on the lid with a picture of St. Vera on it and rosette made of rubies—only small ones, of course. I had it yesterday, I *know*.”

“A little gold box.” “A box—gold—with small legs.” Everyone began searching among the piled-up objects in the cabin, lifting cushions, peering behind chairs. The search, complicated by the presence of so many other souvenirs, was carried on to the accompaniment of Mrs. Crambatch's increasingly worried and angry comments. “I can't *think* what's happened to it . . . No, no, Mr. Semprebon, it's not likely to be in the washbasin, now is it? Do please let's use some common sense! . . . Of course it's very valuable. I mean, the box is largely gold—not *solid*, of course, but still—and the little rubies. But of course——” Turning, she saw Roger, who had early become bored with the search, clicking the trigger mechanism of an old flint-lock pistol. “Commander Lannfranc, do please put that down! If you don't want to help me you might at least not fiddle with my things!”

Roger flushed and Bronwen's face paled with anger, but when, a few minutes later, the search had to be declared over and the relic unfound, it was an ominously different Mrs. Crambatch who faced her guests from the happy, garrulous woman who had welcomed them an hour ago. Trembling a little, her face red, her eyes narrowed spitefully behind her glasses, she said: “Well, it's obviously been stolen. It's been stolen, either from one of these cabins or from my bag on deck or in the saloon or somewhere. That isn't a very good advertisement for your Line, is it, Mr. Semprebon?”

“My dear lady, I assure you that it shall be discovered!

I think perhaps that it has been not stolen but—but forgotten in some place."

"Nonsense! Some thief has taken it. I'm not really surprised, I must say. I've had plenty of lessons about the dishonesty of Europeans——" she almost spat the words—"in the last few months. Well, I'll just have to see the Captain, that's all."

Roger glanced covertly at his wife. Surely this exhibition of vicious malice would demonstrate clearly how impossible her scheme was. But Bronwen avoided his eyes and stared out of the window, and Roger, realising her implacability, felt a quick stab of panic.

The Purser, flushed and ruffled, was saying, "My dear Mrs. Crambatch, it is not a matter for Captain Onestinghel. I am the correct official in such a matter. And I shall indeed——"

"I shall see the *Captain* nevertheless, Mr. Semprebon! And if it is not given back to me very soon I'll have to see my lawyers when I get home. I shall see that this has very serious consequences for someone—for quite a lot of people, perhaps."

4

Next morning Captain Onestinghel sat at his desk in his big day cabin, examining the broken pieces of a small gold box. "And Petelli saw one of these boys with it you say, Ciccolanti?"

"Yes. One of the children of these Ampels. He was breaking it by bashing it against a hatch combing." Serafino's mouth turned down at the corners disgustedly. "It is typical of them—always they like breaking things."

"And there was nothing inside?"

"Apparently not. The boy *said* he found the box under the drum of one of the boat winches, and it was open and empty."

"And what exactly is *supposed* to be inside?"

"The relic is a knuckle-bone from this saint's hand, signore."

"So?" Captain Onestinghel's eyebrows lifted dubiously. "I wonder how she got it into her possession? Such things are not easily—or legally—come by."

"If it is genuine."

"If, as you say, it is genuine. Probably it is not. One

would have very little difficulty in selling Mrs. Crambatch a pair of book-ends and a set of ashtrays, all made from the true Cross."

Serafino gave the Captain a startled glance. Like many deeply religious people, Onestinghel was capable of saying things which struck the less devout as closely approximating to blasphemy, and though Serafino had ceased to be a practising Catholic since that day—barely a fortnight after his first communion—on which God had betrayed him among the bombed rubble of the school buildings, he still retained an Italian deference towards the vast edifice of Christianity.

"However, she now demands that we investigate further, so, Ciccolanti, you had better go and see this boy. Take Mrs. Crambatch with you. At least they speak the same language."

5

By mid-morning the tourist passengers were mostly congregated on the after-end of "B" deck, the younger ones in, or upon the edge of the swimming-pool, their elders in deck-chairs under the surrounding awnings. By a kind of instinctively tacit agreement the English migrants kept to the port and the Italians to the starboard side of the deck; only in the water of the swimming-pool did they mix, and then with reluctance.

The Ampel children did not use the pool. Coming from a city of the industrial midlands, they had never learned to swim and entertained an extreme distrust of water. Serafino, followed by Mrs. Crambatch and Petelli, found them disembowelling a doll which they had stolen from the youngest Ricciotti child, with all the ghoulish relish of three Japanese war criminals at work. They looked up, scowled at Petelli and bent once more over the mangled doll, while one of them, the smallest, growled menacingly, "This is ourn—see? You try to take it an' Dad'll get the lawyers on yer."

Mrs. Crambatch said quickly, "No one is going to take it. We've come to ask you about that little gold box you found. We want to know whether there was anything in it."

"There weren't nothin' in it."

"Are you quite sure?"

"I tell yer—*there weren't nothin' in it*!" An Ampel looked up, his face screwed into aggressive irritation. He jerked his thumb at Petelli. "I tol' this bloke s'mornin'. Rocky 'eard me—dincher, Rocky? 'Ow many more times we got to f—ing tell yer?"

Mrs. Crambatch had never had language of this sort used to her in her life. Her colour deepened, but she persisted. "There was something in it when I lost it, you see. Something very important to me. A little bone."

"A bone?" The three small boys looked at her incredulously and then broke into jeering laughter. " 'Ere that? Bone, she says! She kep' a *bone* in it! Cor, a bone! Whatcher want a bone in it for, missus?"

"That's not your business!" Mrs Crambatch was trembling with affronted dignity. "And you are three very rude little boys! I don't know *what* your parents——"

" Now, now, now!" Mrs. Ampel, in a pair of outsize boy's jeans and with an American sailor hat on the back of her tousled head, loomed up angrily. "You can lay off them kids for a start, see? An'——"

"One of these children had my box! My small gold box was stolen and one of these——"

"Oho—so you're by way of callin' them thieves, are you? That's a matter for me 'usband, that is. Come 'ere, Norman! This *lady* from the first-class is libellin' us in public!"

Norman Ampel, a skinny figure in a pair of ancient Army shorts, slouched up scowling, and behind him came Ted Condron, the Throsby family and the Micklems. In a few moments more than a dozen of the British migrants were edging in ominously round the Ampels, their knobbly, malformed faces—faces at once vicious and cringing, exemplifying to the full that horrible, squat pillar of the nation, the British working class—staring with a blandly cunning threat, their voices raised in the repetitious whine of the industrial slums! ". . . ain't done nothin' . . . kids is kids. . . . Ain't got none of 'er own, don't suppose. . . . Libellin' other blokes' families . . . 'Ave the law on 'er strite away, *I* would!"

Encouraged by this chorus, Norman Ampel snarled aggressively, " What you sayin' about my kids—eh, missis?"

Mrs. Crambatch, whose violently anglophile sentiments had been based throughout her life on a mental picture of the Royal Family decorously having tea in one of the great drawing-rooms of Buckingham Palace, was now faced for the first time with the real England—the gruesome four-fifths of the iceberg. Pop-eyed, she stared round the ring of glowering, jeering faces and turned impulsively to the Chief Officer beside her. " Mr. Ciccolanti, one of these children *did* have my box, didn't he?"

Serafino nodded. " The *Capitano d'armi* finds him with it."

" 'E found 'im with it, did 'e?" Gladys Ampel's voice was shrill with scorn. " An' that means 'e stole it, of course! An' which one was it, eh? Our Rock, was it? You say our Rock stole it?"

Petelli shrugged and muttered something to Serafino. " It is not said that this boy steal anything." Serafino stared disgustedly through his dark glasses at the three sneering, grinning children. " The *Capitano d'armi* says also that it is not Rock he is finding with this box. It is this other—this —this Dirt."

" Dirk."

" So. Yes. When it has been lost inside this box there is one small bone of the hand."

" A *'uman* bone?"

" A bone from the dead of a sacred woman."

" Cor!"

" Listen to 'im!"

" Well, I never! *Some* people——!"

The British migrants stared at Serafino and Mrs. Crambatch with disgusted amazement written plainly on their florid, peeling faces, and Ted Condron, knowledgeable as ever, pushed to the front. " Now look 'ere, mister. Just take this in, see? We ain't got your bone. We don't want no bone. We ain't cannibals nor yet ignorant 'eathens. We don't 'old with narsty practices such as worshippin' bits of old corpses, though I know it's done where you come from Not that you can 'elp that yourself of course, so no offence meant an' none taken, I 'ope." He turned to his friends. " I know 'ow it is—see? I was there in the war. They got these things—bones an' such—in boxes in their churches. All got up very fancy, like bleedin' Christmas trees, too —real 'orrible—ugh! An' they prays to 'em—gabble-gabble-gabble-gabble—an' throwing their arms about. Fair gives you the creeps to watch 'em."

But now it was Hogben's turn. Towering protectively above the Ampels, his huge red face glowing with the effects of sun, beer and righteous indignation, he pointed across the deck at the Italian migrants. " Why don't yer ask *there*, mister? What you got in your loaf 'stead of brains—sea-water? What yer think *we* want with a Cath'lic bone? We ain't your religion—if you calls it a religion, an' I suppose you does. But *they* is—over there—ain't they?" Suddenly he raised his voice to a hoarse shout. "Armander; Armander, what you done with that bone?"

There was a roar of derisive laughter from the English migrants, and Hogben, grinning, bellowed again. "'And over that bone I says, Armander, 'fore I comes an does somethin' narsty to yer with it!" But Armando was not on deck and the other Italians, not recognising Hogben's pronunciation of his name, merely tittered.

Serafino turned shrugging to Mrs. Crambatch. "So——"

But Mrs. Crambatch of Crambatch's Emporium, Dunedin, Mrs. Crambatch, the President of the Ladies Arts Guild, the pillar of the Parents and Citizens Association, and the P. and O. Line's Favourite Passenger, had collapsed on to a deck-head, where, her empurpled face crumpled into a dreadful soggy mask of shocked misery, she wept and shook with fear and rage and distress. "Oh, oh! These dreadful, horrible people! English, too! I can't believe it—I can't! Oh, let's go away *quickly*, please!"

Serafino, looking from the fat, quivering figure on the deck-head to the ugly, grinning faces of the British passengers, felt the deepest stab of envy for Japheth Wendlandt that had ever pierced him. Oh, for the life of a tanker officer with high extra pay and a cargo of nothing but oil—placid, silent, untroublesome, innocent oil! He sighed deeply. "Petelli, take this lady to her cabin. It is useless to make any further inquiries here."

6

"So Giselda is going to send you a telegram on your saint's day, is she, Tino?"

"*Si, signora.* She always does. And I to her on hers. It is for us a special day, you see." Augustino smiled ruefully and shrugged. "We are so far apart."

"And what will she say in the telegram? That she still loves you desperately, I suppose?" He blushed and nodded; his eyes would not meet hers. "Put that tray down, Tino, and come here."

Reluctantly he placed the worn metal tray with the early morning tea things on the top of a locker and then approached the bunk. Flora McKenrick took his wrist and ran her hand up his bare arm to the elbow. "I'd like to give you something on your saint's day, too. I'm in a better position to do so than Giselda—though I suppose her precious telegram will mean more to you than anything else. What would you like? A watch? A camera? I could get them at Colombo."

"No, no."

"Well—what, then?"

"Nothing—I want nothing, signora."

Flora smiled thinly. "It's like that, is it, Tino? I thought—since you've become such a shy boy all of a sudden—that you might feel happier if I gave you presents instead of money." But she could see that he did not understand her, he just stared down with a frightening deprecating smile on his sun-browned face and tried uncomfortably to loosen his arm. She knew perfectly well that all he wanted of her was to be left alone, but this knowledge only excited her and made her more determined than ever to force him to her will. "How about another ten pounds—seventeen thousand lire? You'd like that, Tino, wouldn't you? I know you need money."

Yes, he needed money—to get married. So that he could have this *fidanzata* of his. The more money she gave him, the more quickly she helped him to his Giselda. And one night next year, when she herself would be lying alone in her small bungalow at Gyana, he and Giselda would be pressed together, their legs entwined, their naked young bodies straining, in some big Italian double bed in a room in Livorno. In a spasm of fierce desire she gripped the arm within the circle of her fingers, thinking bitterly that it belonged to someone else. It was Giselda's—like the broad, bronzed chest under the open-necked white shirt, the narrow hips and smooth, strong thighs. But before that they must be hers once more—at least once more. She had lain sleepless for nights past, thinking of Tino's body, imagining her own hands holding, gripping, pressing. . . . "Twelve pounds, then," she said, and turned the sum into Italian currency with the deftness of an arithmetic teacher. "Over twenty thousand lire."

Agostino gulped, and for a moment he was tempted. After all, it wouldn't be quite so bad the second time—he'd know what was going to happen. He could short her light-switch too, so that she could not look at him in that horrible way. In the dark. . . . He glanced down at her, and at the sight of the naked burning desire in her face he shivered. No, no, not again—he couldn't do it again. And yet he was angry with himself because of this. Other boys of his age at home made almost a part-time profession out of obliging summer tourists. They earned thousands of lire, talked of "a good season," and annoyed the older men who had to work by boasting and showing off in the clothes they were given. And some of the women were old and ugly—far older and uglier than this one—and it wasn't always only women who were obliged in this way, either. Yet the first time he tried his hand it had all gone wrong, somehow—he had caught a Tartar. Now the other mess-boys were mocking him about it. "When are you going to do it again, Tino?" "Didn't she think you were any good, then?" "Has she asked for her money back?"

Resentment at his own bad luck, or his incompetence, or his lack of the usual blandly innocent sexual extroversion of his countrymen overcame his normal placid good nature. He frowned and pulled his arm away quickly. "No, signora. I am not wanting——" He could only think of one English word for what he needed to say, and though he guessed it might not be a very appetising one, he used it. "Not with you. I am sorry. For me the first time is—is bad. *Capisce?* Is not like. Is no good for make again." He smiled, opening his hands in a gesture of apology. "I am sorry."

Flora gave a bark of amusement and tried to recapture his arm, but, still smiling unhappily, he backed away. "Poor Tino, you really are rather sweet! I know you didn't like the first time—that's why I'm going to pay you more now. And it will be different. You're a dreadful little prude for an Italian, you know! You didn't like it because I kept the light on when you were undressed—that's one thing you didn't like, though I really can't think why, because you look twenty times better without your clothes. And I suppose I didn't flatter you enough and tell you how beautiful you are. And I won't hurt you—honestly I won't hurt you this time!"

But it was no good; he just shook his head, grinning unhappily. "No, no, signora. Please, no."

"Fifteen pounds—twenty-five thousand lire. I can't afford any more, Tino, really, I can't."

"No, no! It is not for money. I not *want*, signora—please!"

And now it was her turn to get angry. Her hard face hardened still further, she stared at him unsmilingly, and he, as if hypnotised, stood miserably in the middle of the cabin, holding his tray. "You've got to learn that sometimes you must do things that other people want, even if you don't," she said, as if rebuking a schoolboy in her class at Gyana. "Supposing that I was to tell Semprebon that I'd seen you come out of Mrs. Crambatch's cabin with that thing she's lost? I know they've found the box, but you could easily have thrown that away in a fright now there's such a fuss about it all—couldn't you?" He did not understand and she had to repeat her threat slowly twice more. But it had the desired effect. She saw his eyes widen and his hands begin to tremble. It was easy to guess that an accusation of theft would leave him defenceless. Like so many of his kind, he had obviously stolen occasionally before and would be an immediate object of condemnation, however much he protested innocence.

"All right then, Tino. Give me my bag. And come here. No, no—I'm not going to do anything to you now." From her purse she carefully took six pound notes, held them up for him to see, folded them and thrust them quickly into his trouser pocket. "Right. You see, I trust you, Tino. You'd better prove I'm correct in doing so. Nine o'clock to-night, in here. Nine o'clock. All right, you can go now."

7

Flying fish slipped furtively out of the blue swell, hovered low over the water, stiff, shining and seemingly motionless like silver toy gliders, and then disappeared abruptly. Ocean bats, glimpsed generally from the corner of the eye rather than in a direct glance, they had none of the friendliness of the Mediterranean dolphins leaping and playing beside the prow, but only a mindless, perhaps venomous, inquisitiveness—they looked as if they stung.

Flying fish, parrots, coral islands—the lure of the sea. Yes, yes, when one was very young. Cavaliere Semprebon, his back to the vestibule, stared morosely out across the blue swell of the Indian Ocean. One would have done better to have stayed ashore—far better. Gone into a government office—some ministry or other. It would have been dull at first, of course, and naturally when one was young one would have been very bored; youth hated that sort of thing. Take young Pavanoli, for instance; happy as the day was long, running up and down to the bridge and monkeying around with a sextant or a pair of binoculars—flying fish, parrots and coral islands were still exciting realities to him. If one took away his white uniform with its gold anchors and put him into a clerk's dark suit and sat him at a desk in the general office of a ministry from nine till five, he'd be absolutely miserable. But that's what I'd do if I was his father, thought the Purser gloomily; that's what I wish my father had done with me. By now I'd be *somebody*—a respected civil servant with an office of my own, a secretary, and perhaps even an official car. And safe, quite, quite safe, with a secure salary and a pension coming in a few years' time. And there would have been Mafalda's cousin's influence to help, too. As it is, the best I can hope for is to marry a widow with some money before I lose this job. Someone like Vera Crambatch. I *had* thought of calling her "Vera" soon—before this wretched business of her relic. I was going to start with "Signora Vera," of course, over a drink in the bar. It might have worked—no use now, though. Oh, my poor, foolish father—why did you let me go to sea?

Flying fish—three to-day—coming out—in the air—going in. If I see six in the next hour I'll pass all the navigational exams straight off. If I see eight I'll be a second officer before I'm twenty-four. If I see . . . And they wanted to put me in an office in some dreary ministry or other. "A good opening. If you'll only work hard and stick to it you'll be *somebody*, some day." I said that I wouldn't work hard or stick to it, and I didn't want to be *somebody*—not in a ministry at any rate. Being *somebody* and wearing pin-striped trousers and going bald and looking like old Semprebon, probably, and getting a hell of a kick out of signing letters "your obedient humble servant, etc., etc., etc." God! "But the future of Italy's mercantile fleet is by no means assured, and if——" But they're building new ships all the time—big ones, too. Anyway, what's the use of saying "and if" all the time? And if they drop an atom bomb on the ministry I won't be so well off there, will I—even if I am *somebody* just before it explodes? "And you should think of the future. You're young now but one day you'll be sixty." But not for hundreds of years yet—well, more than forty, at any rate. To start worrying about being sixty before one has even reached twenty! I said I was not going to waste all my life hanging around some government office waiting to be sixty. I *made* them let me go to sea. Holy Virgin, there's that damned dog again!

8

Coming out of a bathroom on the starboard corridor of "C" deck, Agostino heard an urgent voice shout "Stop him—quick! Don't let him get past!" and saw Countess Zapescu's dachshund galloping down the narrow strip of red carpet towards him, pursued by Pavanoli. "Quick! He mustn't get into the vestibule!" The cadet's voice held an agonised urgency, and Agostino dropped the broom he was holding and set down the pail of dirty water with such a jar that half of it jerked out on to the floor. He made a quick grab at the dog as it shot past, but his wet hands slipped off the smooth shiny coat, and Brown was past him and on towards the vestibule with no hope of recovery.

"Fool!" snarled Pavanoli slowing down to a trot. "That dog's looking for Semprebon—it always does if it gets the chance. He gives it cough-drops or something and it loves him. And he'll tell the Captain, and then——"

"Fool yourself! Why do you let him out if you're not supposed to?" Agostino glowered down at the spilt water. "Look what you've made me do!"

"Ah, what does that matter! Come and help me get him back."

Together they walked sulkily towards the vestibule, and Gino said, "I have to let him out when she wants to exercise him. And I can't stand around watching him lift his leg against every stanchion on 'C' deck—I've got other things to do."

"Poor, poor Ginetto!"

"Don't call me that!"

"Of course not, Signor Pavanoli. I beg your pardon deeply!"

"Or that, either!" The cadet grinned and punched Agostino in the ribs. "I've been hearing some horrible things about you. *Oh, Mamma mia,* Semprebon *is* there!"

The tall figure of the Purser stood in the middle of the vestibule with Malpiero beside him, and at their feet Brown sat puffing and staring up with glazed devotion. The Purser looked coldly at the two boys as they came in. "Pavanoli, I thought that the Captain gave you strict orders that this dog was not to be allowed off the stern of 'C' deck—is that not so?"

"Well, he did but——"

"Can you think of any reason why I should not report your disobedience to the Captain? Really, if you are unable to control a small dog I cannot see how you imagine you will ever be able to control a ship." Gino scowled. That was the sort of ridiculously illogical remark old people always made. As if there was anything in common between a dachshund and a liner! But surely Semprebon was—yes, Semprebon was laughing! "Look, my boy——" he held out a well-manicured hand in which lay a small, narrow bone, brown with age and unlike any bone Gino had seen before—"we have it back—the famous relic!"

"No!" They all peered at it incredulously. "Is that really it, *Signor Commissario*? Are you sure?"

"Quite certain. To anyone with an elementary knowledge of anatomy . . . Oh, yes, Pavanoli, I'm quite a man of parts though I know you think I'm an old martinet!" Gino had never seen the Purser in such a good humour, and he guessed at once that Semprebon was thinking of the time when he would present the bone to its delighted owner—probably on a silver salver or something. "So this time—just this once—I think we may overlook your neglect of your duties. Yes, I think we may do so. I cannot imagine where the Countess's little dog found this, but all bones attract dogs, I suppose, and as the unfortunate animal goes along with its nose barely three centimetres from the ground . . ." Hitching up his well-pressed white trousers, the Cavaliere bent down carefully and patted Brown, then, pulling a small flat tin from his hip pocket, he took out a white tablet and gave it to the dachshund, who crunched it with a look of agonised pleasure.

"What are those, *Signore Commissario*?" asked Gino interestedly.

"These? H'mm—pills I take for a minor stomach ailment."

"And Brown has the same trouble?"

"No, certainly not! At least, I imagine not. He just likes the taste. Now take him back to his kennel before anyone else sees him."

9

The news of the recovery of Mrs. Crambatch's relic soon passed round the ship. It was greeted with considerable relief by the service staff, with open derision by the British migrants, and with discreet amusement by all the first-class passengers except Flora McKenrick. She, when she heard of it, went straight to her cabin, where, as she expected, she found six one-pound notes lying carefully folded on her dressing-table.

X

Under a sky of low clouds and with a light breeze from full astern, *San Roque* drove steadily on through the pitch-black night. Because of the following wind which exactly matched her speed, she was enclosed in an atmosphere of her own making, a gaseous mixture of exhaust smoke from the funnel, acrid fumes from the fuel tank ventilators, a greasy reek of cooking, and, permeating all these, that inevitable smell of new paint which hangs about a ship even on the brightest, windiest days.

Third Officer Malestroit, standing the watch, walked from end to end of the bridge, hoping to find some relief from the soggy humidity of the still night. But there was none to be found, and as he leant over the chart table, meticulously entering time and course in the big ruled log, drops of sweat fell from his face on to the page and his hand left a damp imprint on the blank white paper below his neat figures. Turning away, dabbing at his face with an already damp handkerchief, he wished that Gino or Petelli or someone unable to sleep would come up on to the bridge. Then they could sit beside the chart-table light and talk. It was so boring by oneself to-night, oppressive and vaguely, indefinably sinister. There was something—a feeling of brooding heaviness, as if dark wings hovered over the ship, drawing it along a sea-furrow by a sort of magnetism from the hidden moon, while a hot, fetid breath from above held it in a malodorous effluvium.

He shrugged and, whistling soundlessly through his teeth, opened a drawer in the chart table, felt carefully under a pile of radio forms and took out a small, flat, glass-fronted puzzle. A blob of quicksilver had to be guided round two curved glass tubes to fill five small holes. It took a lot of careful manipulating, and it was agreed among the deck officers that when one of them succeeded he was entitled to note it in the log—very faintly, so that the Captain should not notice—by putting five small dots under his latest initialled entry. The puzzle belonged to Bressan. It was one of several of the same sort which he kept in his cabin.

2

"*We Nikolai, by the Grace of God Emperor and Autocrat of All the Russias, King of Poland, to All Our Faithful Subjects make known. . . .*" War—and the crowds cheering before the great façade of the Winter Palace and then suddenly silent, a forest of arms removing hats, as the massed bands of the Imperial Guards crashed out the first slow, sombre, magnificent bars of the anthem in a deep, surging swell of sound. "*We Nikolai. . . .*"

Onestinghel tossed uncomfortably in the hot darkness of his cabin and the dream changed abruptly. He was running down that iron alleyway in the *Tsaritsyn* with the feel of the filthy fireman's overalls—the saving disguise which Dolka had thrust with him into the cupboard—gritty on his shoulders. Other figures were running too, laughing, shouting, pressing him on—"*Tovarich! Tovarich!*"—down now, through the engine-room hatchway, and the spidery ladders with their oily, polished iron rungs were slippery under his hands. He must get back; it was only a dream, he knew that—but he must get back. With a fearful effort of will he made the ladder disappear, and he was lying in the Naval Hospital at Cronstadt and he was eighteen and a midshipman and his leg was broken and the Fleet had sailed without him—sailed round the world to Tsushima and total destruction—and he was saved for the first time.

A long convalescence, a long period of leave: the hunting-sledges breaking from the forest edge, the baying of the dogs. Bright sun on the snow, fur-capped peasants, a bearded priest lifting his hand in blessing from the door of his cupola'd church—Holy Russia. A glow of fire in a dark background of a gloomy winter afternoon; somewhere on the frozen harbour a crowd of laughing, drunken sailors were sawing holes in the ice, watched by a guarded group of ashen-faced, manacled officers. But he was not there, for it was spring and he was driving out to the Karienovskys' *dascha* with Dmitri and Nadia beside him, and Dolka in his sailor's uniform perched up on the box next to the driver. . . . "Mikhail Fyodorovitch, my dear friend! And how is the General?" . . . The glittering uniforms of the Imperial Cavalry at the

Easter ball. The *nagaikas* whistled over the shoulders of the staggering line of Red prisoners as his *sotnia* of cossacks trotted along the slow column, and a cold voice from nowhere said, " Officially, the family will perish during the evacuation." Then he stood again in the deserted Ipatieff house at Ekaterinburg—doors open, everything in indescribable confusion, the stoves full of half-burnt clothes, charred buttons, bits of brushes, hooks and eyes among the ashes. The growing horror of the continued search, the basement and that room with the small barred window where the walls were pocked with marks of bullets and in one place there was a large, gaping hole. "*We Nikolai. . . .*"

The slippery rungs of the ladder were once more under his hands. Dolka's frightened face beneath its coating of coal dust and grease was following him down, and, gripped now in the full nightmare, he was in the fire-room of the *Tsaritsyn*—renamed, two hours before the *Bakunin*—and the furnace doors were open and in the hell-like glow crimson-lit figures dashed laughing across a flaming scarlet stage. Dolka's hard hand on his arm, his bloodshot, blue peasant's eyes glaring in the red light. " Laugh, fool—laugh!" The bunch of officers, mostly gory with facial mutilations—an eye hanging out on a cheek, a nose cut off and leaving merely two red holes between the eyes, a tongueless mouth babbling blood—were groaning and screaming as they were tied stiffly with wire round the ankles, round the knees and wrists. Then a shout—the first one lifted, swung once—twice—and flung into the seething, incandescent heart of an open furnace. A short, soaring, unearthly scream, and a convulsion in the heart of the fire. Now the next. And another. And again. "*Tovarich! Tovarich!*" Now he and Dolka were holding a body, swinging it one—twice—and he was staring into the madly rolling eyes of Dmitri, his own cousin, his almost younger brother. There was appalled recognition, surely, in that moment. Despite the mask of coal dust smeared across his own face, despite the maniac death-terror in Dmitri's, there had been recognition. Surely that last, breathless scream as the living body had shot into the roaring flames had been " Pavel! Pavel!" Then a flood of fiery darkness closed mercifully over the scene, and somewhere within it a slow, windy, booming voice intoned "*We Nikolai, by the Grace of God. . . .*"

3

"*We, by the Grace of Heaven Emperor of Japan, seated upon the throne of a line unbroken for ages eternal, enjoin upon you, our loyal and brave soldiers. . . .*" Colonel Chelgrove stood again in the front rank of prisoners, listening to Lieutenant Tonomaki Itagaki's accurate but ugly English as he translated direct from Imperial Army orders. He too knew he was dreaming and he too wished to get away—to break out of the sticky web of nightmare before the *rottang* cracked across the shins of those four bound prisoners whose eyes were already sealed shut with strips of pink sticking-plaster, before they fell moaning to their knees and Itagaki drew his sword. But it was doubtful if he could make the effort required, he felt so weak—as if he really had been living for three years on a little daily rice and an occasional bit of vegetable. Yet the dream changed, just as a voice in the second rank said, unnaturally loudly, "How did Toni find out about those *durians*, Chelgrove?" And he was one-quarter awake, lying in a queer, unreal state of partly controlled reverie, lifting and sinking on an uneven flow of semi-consciousness.

He was a boy again, back on the parade-ground at Sandhurst on a fresh autumn morning, and old Sergeant-Major Brand was shouting at him: "Mr. Chelgrove, sir! Your rifle's idle! Your 'ands is idle! You're idle all over! You're a bloomin' 'orrible sight, sir! Sargint 'Ills! Put that cadet's rifle *properly* on 'is shoulder 'fore I 'as twins an' triplets where I stands!"

"Yessir!" And Sergeant Hills coming up smartly and seizing the rifle and staring into his face from a pair of narrow, hot brown eyes and saying softly, "*Shelgrove, I do not want any more troubles from the prisoners. You I make responsible, Shelgrove. Next time. . . .*"

Why had he joined the Army? Why? He struggled to think against a tide of weariness. Family promptings. "There's always been a Chelgrove in the Queen's Rifles." Father saying it? Yes—and Paula too—continually. "But, Perry, there's *always* been a Chelgrove in the Queen's Rifles. Father would hate it if you . . ." "*No, we do not hate you, Shelgrove. Nippon does not hate you. Major Yamu does not hate you. I do not hate you. We do not hate such poor things—soldiers who run away, who are afraid to die. We are sorry for you!"*

But the Life—the Life. That was it, really. The British Army as a Way of Life. Ancient Traditions. He liked that, knew it all, studied it, was—what had Colonel Forbes-Stanford called him jokingly—" almost a military antiquarian." India—Bicester barracks—the Bahamas—Ireland—Bicester barracks. A conversation overheard in the mess while he had been taking a short rest half-asleep on a sofa: " Oh, he's *not* brilliant—nobody less so. I'll even agree that he's lazy as hell. But he's a *nice* man, a thoroughly nice man. He's not one of these damned enthusiasts—he won't want to *innovate* all the time. Chelgrove's a good regimental man, if you see what I mean. He's the sort who lets things alone and doesn't want to turn the Army upside down every ten minutes. And since there *is* this majority going . . ." " *Shelgrove, I am promoting you. Now you have a hut to yourself. And you will tell me anything more that you hear, please." " Yes, Itagaki san, of course."*

Bicester barracks—India—Ireland—Bicester barracks. . . . " I—I feel tired more quickly than other people, I think, Doctor. Nothing you can find wrong? More exercise? Well, the more exercise I take, the more tired I feel. I should have thought more *rest* would have been better." The old King's Jubilee and Paula urging him to finish his book, *Regimental Traditions of the British Army.* " Perry, you've been saying you'll finish it for years! Now couldn't be a better time. Think of the kudos—and not only for yourself but for the family! " By then, though, the family had really meant Paula. It was she who ran the Manor House—and Rallstead village too, for that matter. In the end he had published it—or the bits of it which he had already written—as a series of articles in an old-fashioned, high-class magazine. " Why the Queen's Rifles carry White Staves through Bicester on Shrove Tuesday " ; " Why the Royal Cornish Hussars wear green laces in their boots " ; " Why the Durham Fusiliers drink the Duke of York's health over crossed swords by candlelight." And it had got him his lieutenant-colonelcy—the command of a battalion of his regiment. " The very best type of British officer " a correspondent had termed him. " *Shelgrove, did you not write 'Why Japanese officers carry two-handed swords?'" " No, Itagaki san. But I know why now, of course."*

" There's an old Moulmein pagoda . . ." The Far East—

Maugham country rather than Kipling. "They're not the right *jaht,* that's the real trouble with these war-time officers, Chelgrove—not really *sahibs,* if you see what I mean. I wouldn't say it to anyone else of course——" Tommy Malcolm-Bruce's voice had lowered slightly as he glanced round the club bar "—but what the Army wants—what it *needs*—is more people—well, like you and me, if I may say so."

"If you were a soldier, Shelgrove, you would not, of course, be here. Soldiers do not surrender—only coolies. You are a coolie pretending to be a soldier."

How very young the first court had seemed. And there was hardly a Regular soldier among the faces behind the long wooden table. It wasn't fair! He was entitled to be tried by his peers, wasn't he? That meant by other Regular officers who understood about the British Army as a Way of Life and drinking the Duke of York's health over crossed swords by candlelight, and important things like that.

". . . in the face of the enemy in that he ordered his battalion to lay down their arms before—I wish the Court to note this well—*before* action had been joined—*before, in fact, a single shot had been fired."*

But it had been a mistake—a complete mistake. He would never have done it if he hadn't felt so tired, and if he had guessed that it would entail three years under Tonomaki Itagaki—never!

". . . and under interrogation the recently executed Japanese lieutenant stated that the accused was in the habit of giving him information concerning his fellow prisoners' doings, talk of escape or denigration of the enemy, in exchange for extra food or excuse from working parties. . . ."

"The Court will retire . . . despicable cowardice . . . your age and health can be considered only partial palliations . . . literary work of some value to the Crown . . . a Regular officer or it would go harder with you . . . ignominious dismissal, with forfeiture of all decorations, pension and allowances. . . ."

So at last Rallstead Manor House on a cold, wet autumn day. Putting down his suitcases in the antler-decorated hall. Paula's frozen face. "Perry, I—I don't know what to say to you! The scandal! The disgrace to the family name!" It was queer how easily he had persuaded her that the court had been biased, the trial a miscarriage of justice. Or had she persuaded him? Coldness, drabness, post-war England. Paula giving him money for cigarettes and clothes—he had none of his own now. Lonely walks through the wintry woods and country lanes—not lonely enough though, for there was generally someone with him, someone just out of sight behind his left elbow. . . . "*Shelgrove, you are really quite as dead as I—only you have no rest.*" Conferences with old Finnemore, the family lawyer. "Time—give it time. In ten years or so these things will come to be seen in a different light." "But my brother is quite innocent!" "Yes, yes, Miss Chelgrove—but still, I advise you to wait."

Years of waiting. Years alone with Paula—if one did not count the company of a ghost who none the less soon became more real than Paula. Sometimes one spoke aloud to someone whom no one else could see—asking to be left in peace. "*But why should I go away, Shelgrove? It was your evidence that convicted me, was it not? When you came down into the pit where I swung slowly round and back, and round and back, my eyes were wide open, you remember? I was not saying good-bye, Shelgrove. Oh, no!*"

And at last the arrangements with the War Office for a retrial. A visit to a cheerful, rubicund staff colonel in Whitehall. "So old Malcolm-Bruce is a friend of yours, is he, Chelgrove? Well, well! It must have been in '32 that he and I first . . . Yes, I think we can help. Yours is a difficult case, of course, because of your comparatively junior rank. If you'd been a general it would have been simple. Cowardice in the face of the enemy, eh? My dear man, we recently fixed up a full general who'd had *hysterics* in the face of the enemy! Ordered an immediate retreat of his army in two opposite directions, flown off in his private plane, and been found four days later in his club bar severely criticising the conduct of someone else's campaign in another part of the world. You never heard——? Of course not. We keep these things under our hats. Professional discretion, as the lawyer chaps say. Well, anyway, we cleared him all right—made him a K.B., actually. That's what we call using a Royal cover-upper. But you've got to be a general for that particular treatment. In your case the best thing would be a medal—a D.S.O., perhaps. We could try . . . This business about selling information to the Jap officer might not look too good in the citation, admittedly. He's dead, though, isn't he?"

"Well . . ."

"And not a nice man, by all accounts. We could overlook his evidence, I think."

"My sister wants a retrial, actually."

" Frankly, I don't advise it. Much better keep the thing in the Army—in the family, as it were. Let me try for a D.S.O."

" I'm afraid she insists."

" Oh."

" . . . little that the years have altered to mitigate his unsoldierly conduct. . . . We cannot but consider that the appellant was treated leniently rather than otherwise . . . story of shocking cowardice . . . painfully obvious . . . the first court's findings are confirmed."

" Cowardice Appeal Fails!—Chelgrove Collapses in Witness Box while Sister Shouts Defiance at Court—Cowardice in Face of Enemy—Read Full Story in our Sunday Edition."

" Perry, we must get away! I can't stand it here any more. Right away on some small ship—as far as we can go!"

Far, far away into the South. A land of wide blue skies and palms—and a voice. A voice translating into accurate, ugly English the ceremonial suffix to Imperial Japanese Army Orders before the ranged ranks of prisoners and guards. *" . . . Hallowed spirits of our Imperial Ancestors guarding us from above, we rely upon the loyalty and courage of our soldiers in the confident expectation that the task bequeathed by our forefathers will be carried forward, and that the sources of evil will be speedily eradicated and enduring peace immutably established in Eastern Asia, preserving thereby glory of our Empire."*

4

Triumphantly Malestroit made five small dots under his last initialled entry in a corner of the log. He put the puzzle back in its drawer and carefully covered it with radio forms. Then he jerked erect from the chart table. Was that a shout? He walked quickly to the starboard wing of the bridge and peered back along the empty, sparsely lit decks towards the stern. Silence. After a few moments he turned, shrugged and wandered back to the chart table. Then there were steps on the port ladder and Ansaldo, the fireman, came on to the bridge, glanced round for the officer of the watch, and coming over to the chart table, gave a furtive, apologetic imitation of a salute. " Signor Malestroit, I want to report something."

" Well, what? Surely not a fire?"

" No. I was checking the stern boxes a few moments ago when I heard a noise." Ansaldo paused. " A splash."

" A splash! You mean——" Malestroit jumped to his feet.

" It wasn't a very big splash, signore."

" Look, Ansaldo, for God's sake! Are you trying to tell me that someone's fallen overboard or aren't you?"

The short, swarthy fireman shrugged and opened his hands, a look of unhappy perplexity on his face. " I don't know, signore. I mean, it could have been someone throwing rubbish over—or—or anything. It wasn't a very big splash—not really."

" And no sound—no shout or anything?"

" No."

" Are you *sure*?"

" Yes, quite certain, signore."

Malestroit's snub-nosed, cheerful face creased into an expression of painful doubt. If someone had fallen overboard he must act at once, the ship must turn immediately, search-lights, lifeboats. . . . But if not—one could not circle all night looking for floating rubbish. Angrily he said, " You shouldn't have reported it if it wasn't a case of man overboard."

" I didn't say it wasn't, Signor Malestroit. I said it *could* have been." Ansaldo politely, a little reproachfully, handed the responsibility deftly back. This gave Malestroit the idea of doing the same. After all, why not? He was only Third Officer; why should he accept the task of making such a serious decision? His face cleared. " Well anyway you'd better come and tell this silly story of yours to the Chief Officer. We'll see what he makes of it. If he tells you to go to hell and fines you two days' pay I shan't be either surprised or sorry."

Ciccolanti sat up in bed, blinking in the strong electric light. He looked ridiculously young like that, his hair rumpled, his hands clasped round his knees, in his cheap pyjamas—almost certainly from UPIM, the multiple chain stores, thought Malestroit as he stood listening once more while Ansaldo told his halting, uncertain story. " . . . and I reported the matter to Signor Malestroit."

" You ought to be able to tell by the splash if it was some-body, or not."

" I've never heard anybody fall overboard, signore," said Ansaldo virtuously, " so I wouldn't know what it sounded like."

" Was the splash a big one?"

"Well—biggish. It depends on what you mean by a *big* splash, signore."

Serafino thrust his fingers wearily through his hair. He had been dreaming too. Dreaming that he was back in the ruins of the bombed school while the planes, with their big red, white and blue roundels, roared in formation high above him, dropping big black bombs the size of houses. Lying amidst the rubble, pinned on his back and worrying stupidly about the dirt on the clean white shirt Mamma had given him that morning. . . . She would be very sorry. . . . He shook his head and sighed. "Well," he said coldly at last, "there's no point in doing anything now, is there? If anyone fell over he'd be drowned by this time. You've left it too late to do anything, between you both."

Malestroit said, a little shamefacedly, "A person could swim, perhaps. . . ."

"*If* anyone went overboard he probably jumped on purpose—you know what migrants are like. He wouldn't try to swim. Now go away and leave me in peace."

5

Early next morning it was discovered that the ship's doctor was no longer aboard. His cabin was neat and clean, but the bunk had not been slept in. On a locker stood a half-empty bottle of whisky and a large but unopened tube of morphine pills. A fully-charged hypodermic syringe lay clean and shining on a pad of cotton-wool upon the lid of the doctor's desk, and in a drawer below a loaded revolver gleamed dully. "Poor Gavanian! He was the most undecided man I have ever known," remarked Bressan to Serafino, with a vain attempt to repress a hysterical giggle. "But in the end he chose the sea!"

Serafino stared glumly round the cabin at the polished furniture shining softly in the early light from the scuttle. "Why did he do it? His job was quite safe, after all."

Bressan glanced at him with interest. "Oh, yes, his job was quite safe—why not? He was not at all a good doctor, but then ships' doctors seldom are, of course. No, no, it was his wife—yes, undoubtedly that was it."

"His wife?"

"Yes." Bressan pointed to a framed photograph on the locker beside the whisky. It showed a big, darkly handsome girl, with a thick mass of black hair descending to her shoulders, heavily made-up eyes and a sullen mouth. " They'd only been married two years but she gave him a dreadful time, poor man. She was a Greek—and much younger than he, of course. He introduced me to her once. I went with him to Cairo. For the first ten minutes she was all over me." He giggled again at the memory. " Not that it did her any good, of course. When she saw I wasn't interested she shut up at once and started to sulk. She hardly took any notice of poor Gavanian, except to complain that he hadn't brought her the things she'd wanted from Naples. She used to make him bring her all sorts of things on each voyage. And then—you know he went to Cairo again while we were in the Canal?"

" Yes."

" Well, she'd gone. She'd sold his car—it was one of the new baby Fiats and he had not made even half the payments on it—and all the furniture and the television set he'd bought her—even his clothes! She'd gone off with a young Syrian—an air force pilot, I believe."

" He told you this?"

" Yes. Poor Gavanian! It was a shocking thing, of course." Bressan shook his head, but his light voice was breaking on a tittery edge of nearly uncontrollable laughter. For reasons which Serafino was unable to understand, he seemed to find the doctor's tragedy irredeemably comic. " He couldn't get over it. ' She sold my medical books,' he said, ' every one! And my gramophone records, and even the little clock my old father gave me once when I had done well at school. . . .' "

None of the rest of the crew seemed particularly surprised: they had all, it seemed, known something of the doctor's betrayal. " He was a fool!" said Petelli with callous contempt to his deck gang later that morning. " If any bitch did that to me I'd go and find her and then I'd hang her up by the ankles and take every centimetre of skin off her body with a tarred rope. And as for the man she'd gone with . . ."

" At any rate," remarked the Chief Officer dryly to his colleagues, " Ansaldo will now know what sort of splash someone makes going over the stern."

X I

Bright, sparkling sea under a sky of clearest blue, a light breeze from the south-west rippling out the big red-and-blue-starred flag of Panama on *San Roque's* stern, dispelling completely the warm, greasy miasma of the past night. Coming up to the bridge nearly an hour later than usual, Captain Onestinghel listened coldly to a report of the doctor's suicide from his Chief Officer. "Why did you not inform me of this at once?"

"Wake you up, signore?"

"Of course, wake me up! In a case like this there should have been no hesitation—none at all!"

"But—*con permesso, Signor Capitano*—there was nothing to be done," Serafino submitted respectfully. "By the time——"

"And don't answer me back!" The Captain's voice snapped like a whip. "You've been at sea long enough to know that *everything* of importance must be reported immediately to the captain. Or don't you think the suicide of the ship's doctor a matter of importance? Quite a normal occurrence, doubtless, on a passenger ship. One merely enters it in the log 'One-thirty a.m. Doctor leaps overboard. Sea calm, light wind from the south-west.'"

"Signore——"

"If there is any further failure on your part to report things to me, Ciccolanti, you will find yourself changing epaulettes with Bressan before this voyage is out! Now send for Malestroit and Ansaldo at once!"

Serafino said hesitantly, "*Scusi, Signor Capitano*—but Malestroit is probably still asleep. He——"

"*Almighty God! Will you obey my orders!*" The Captain's voice had risen, for the first time in anyone's experience, to a shout and his face became an odd, livid white. Everyone on the bridge jumped as if he had been stung by a hornet, and *San Roque* veered two or three degrees from her true course as the startled helmsman jerked the wheel.

In an astonishingly short space of time both the Third Officer and the fireman were on the bridge, where, together with Serafino, they received a long and bitterly sarcastic rebuke. None of the three could understand why they had merited such treatment or what the Captain imagined would have been gained had they followed any other course of action on the previous night. You were never able to stop people drowning themselves at sea if they had set their minds upon it. They could not know that in his own mind, a mind which, despite its wide cultivation, vast experience and depth of intellect, still retained a strong inherited tint of the occult mysticism of the Slav, Onestinghel connected the doctor's death leap with his own recent dream. He was now firmly convinced that Gavanian had jumped at the very moment when Dmitri's rigid body had swung from his hands into the furnace, and that in some timeless and supernatural way he was involved in both deaths. Fire and water—the anithetical conection added a further disturbing touch to the gruesome business. Also, he was feeling unwell. The recurrence of that ghastly nightmare was always, with him, a sign of bodily sickness; it attacked like a waiting ruthless enemy as soon as it detected some physical weakness, and he had always known with brutal clarity that it would re-enact itself again, more horribly than ever, across the screen of his fading consciousness during his last earthly moments. That the doctor's suicide should have taken place without his knowledge added an ominously evil significance to his dream.

It was not until Petelli appeared on the bridge, notebook in hand, that the Captain turned from his two scarlet-faced officers and his frightened little fireman. "Well—and what in Christ's name do *you* want?"

Petelli whipped the cap off his bullet head and bowed. "*Signor Capitano, buon' giorno!* I am reporting for the inspection."

"What do you mean, idiot?"

Wide-eyed, Petelli stammered, "The—the inspection, signore. To-day is Sunday."

"So!" Onestinghel glared round at the ring of frightened faces in the bright morning sunlight which poured in through the many-windowed bridge. "To-day there will be no inspection." He paused a long moment. "This unfortunate business of last night is, of course, to be kept from everybody—particularly the passengers—for as long as possible. Perhaps we will be able to make it believed that the doctor was urgently recalled on private matters and disembarked at Colombo to-morrow—but I doubt it. Ciccolanti, you will radio Naples at once, informing them of what has happened and requesting a replacement for

Gavanian as soon as possible. Now I am going to my cabin. Send Tomei to me. And do not forget what I have said. Everything is to be reported to me—*everything*. Since I must work this ship with a gang of boys for officers, it is, of course, necessary that I supervise them continually!"

"He has dreamed again," remarked Malestroit in the uncomfortable silence after the Captain had left the bridge. "Oh, yes, I know how it is. I have not served under our so interesting captain for nearly a year without becoming acquainted with the signs. He has a will of iron—but still he dreams. Of what he dreams one does not know, but one assumes of something formidably unpleasant." He shrugged. "Ah, well, *à chacun son enfer*. I myself do not dream ever. I have been told that in this way I miss much. At least I am able to keep an equable temper when I awake. Unlike Monsieur, I do not find it necessary to fly into an Oriental rage because of my nocturnal hallucinations." Turning away to the bridge ladder, he grinned angrily. "*C'est amusant, quand' même*. Now I myself shall return to bed."

2

Half an hour later Malpiero looked up from his desk behind the counter in the vestibule to see his chief approaching in an obvious good humour. Cavaliere Semprebon was normally as irritable and nervous on Sundays as most of the crew of *San Roque*. Though he did not accompany the Captain on his inspection, those of his premises which were visited often earned him a suavely sardonic reproof on its termination. To-day, however, there was a certain playful jauntiness about the Purser's manner and bearing, a slightly swaggering upward tilt of his cigarette-holder, which surprised his saturnine assistant. "Good morning, Malpiero! Now tell me—what day is it?"

"Sunday," said Malpiero defiantly, but without apparent effect.

"Yes, yes, I have a calendar. One of many presented to me by grateful tradespeople. I am also aware that yesterday was Saturday and that it will be alarming and confusing if to-morrow is not Monday. I meant the date."

Sensing that Semprebon expected him to smile at this sally, Malpiero refrained from doing so. "Sixteenth of August," he said briefly.

" Exactly! The sixteenth of August. And this date means nothing to you? Stirs no echo of childish days when you were doubtless under the instruction of some good priest in—where was it? Calabria, I think? No, I see it does not. The sixteenth of August, my good Malpiero, is the day of San Rocco—in Spanish, San Roque—a shepherd saint whose peculiar privilege it is to be the patron of earthquakes. If sufficiently devout—are you devout, Malpiero? Never mind, that is between you and God—if, as I say, one is sufficiently devout one offers to him one's prayers against these unpleasant occurrences. Pass me that ashtray—thank you. To-day, therefore, is the ship's Saint's Day. Yes, it is the day of our patron saint and I intend that we celebrate it accordingly."

" For the passengers?"

"For whom else?" The Purser carefully ejected the end of his black cigarette into the ashtray. " Now let me see. What film have we to-night?"

Malpiero picked up a list. "*Chica del Barrio,* with Pepe Blanco and Lolita Sevilla."

"I am not interested in the cast." The Cavaliere frowned. "That is one of the Spanish ones handed over from *San Ramòn,* I suppose, eh? I do sincerely wish that now the whole Line is off the Venezuelan run we could abandon these vestiges of the past."

" All films must be shown on all ships," quoted Malpiero mechanically. " Besides, they were cheap."

" Malpiero, sometimes I think you have the soul of a fishmonger. Indeed, I believe your father was a member of that elevated profession, was he not? No, no—I do not wish it confirmed or denied. The sub-titles of this film—are they in English?"

" Italian."

" So. I am not happy about these Spanish films. I received a small deputation of protest from the British migrants last week when we showed that one about the seminarists of a teaching order."

Malpiero raised his thick black brows. "*Por un Mejor Mundo?* What grounds could they have for protesting over that picture? It was a religious documentary. They said it was dull, I suppose?"

"They said it was indecent. Or to quote them verbatim, '*downright disgusting—all about clergymen and small boys.*' Yes, yes, Malpiero, you may well look shocked. When you are my age you will become accustomed to the most astonishing reactions of diverse humanity. Meanwhile, have we no British films left?"

"Only two." Malpiero glanced at his list. "*Moonlight Marauders*—a war film about British raids on the Norwegian coast. And a thing called *Riviera Rendezvous*—about amorous indiscretions on the French one. Neither appears to feature priests and the sub-titles are in Spanish."

"Show the second this evening. The first we can reserve until later in the voyage." Cavaliere Semprebon fitted a fresh Russian cigarette into his holder. "The best method of marking the day will be in the field of catering. We will improve the quality of the first-class passengers' dinner and increase the quantity of the tourists' 'tea'—as they call it."

"More cake," said Malpiero, and earned a nod of approval from his chief.

"Exactly. Much more cake. Now, for the first-class dinner I have sketched a menu. It is in French." Semprebon took a slip of paper from one pocket and his hornrimmed glasses from another. "To start with—a French soup."

"*Consommé Julienne*," said Malpiero as if he was making a response in church.

"So. But to-night we term it '*Consommé de la Reine Elisabeth*.' Now, the fish?"

"The fish is haddock. Steamed, I suppose?"

"You suppose correctly. It is not a fish that can be termed *soigné*, but it will be served with a suitable sauce and called '*Poisson de la Mer du Sud*.' We have a few fowl still, I believe. I want them to extend sufficiently both for to-night and the—ah, the small Gala Dance I hope to arrange later in the voyage. Serve some of them, therefore, with plenty of rice. That is '*Pilaff Royale de San Roque*.'"

"Very well."

"Then a coloured jelly with the contents of a can or so of fruit salad—'*Gêlée des Milles Fruits de Panama*.' And then some of those canned Spanish mushrooms which we took over from *San Raphael* last year. I intend this course as a small compliment to the Captain; it will therefore be termed '*Cèpes Onestinghel*.'"

"The Captain is said to be unwell. He has sent for Tomei."

Semprebon raised his eyebrows. "So? Then there will be no inspection?"

"I understand not."

"H'mm. Well, then, Malpiero, we must trust he recovers in time for dinner. If not, my little compliment will be wasted."

"Oh, yes—mushrooms by all means. Ah, well, 'a rose by any other name'—Shakespeare, I believe. Do you read him, Malpiero? No, no, I see you do not. If the Captain is unable to dine to-night we will call this dish—er—'*Cèpes Semprebon.*'"

3

Wandering down the boat deck at noon, a stocky figure in his ex-naval whites, Roger Lannfranc found his wife sitting under an awning and watching a sedate game of shuffle-board between Mrs. Crambatch and Colonel Chelgrove on the other side of the deck. "Why don't you come forward, Bron? There's much more of a breeze up in front." He sat down near her deck-chair and beside another which contained Mrs. Crambatch's large handbag and larger box of chocolates.

Bronwen said quietly, "She doesn't like it up in front. The crew sun themselves on the prow when they're off duty—or the younger ones, at any rate. She says their bathing-trunks are indecent, and I'll admit they *are* pretty skimpy; they don't leave much to the imagination. It wasn't like that on the P. and O., of course, so she's going to complain."

Roger scowled. "Why shouldn't they sunbathe if they want to? After all, they spend practically all the time working. All *we* do is sit about and eat and sleep."

Bronwen smiled slightly. "That's what Flora McKenrick said. She's always up there. She got quite angry on their behalf. So Crambatch said, 'Well, dear, there's no accounting for tastes. In N.Z. our boys *adore* the sea but they wouldn't dream of lolling about exhibiting themselves like that in front of women. In Australia you may have different ideas, of course.'"

"If old Crambatch was on a warship she certainly *would* have something to complain about, but——"

"But she's not. And nor are you."

"Worse luck. Bron, I—I've been talking to Bressan."

"Who?"

"Bressan—the Second Officer. The fat fellow with the silly laugh."

"What about?"

"Well——" Roger looked uncomfortable and his voice held a defensive sulkiness—"about ships and jobs and so forth. I mean I thought I'd just inquire a bit."

"I see," said Bronwen ominously. "Well—go on."

"Well, naturally I was careful about what I asked, and fortunately Bressan speaks good English. He told me that while this Line demands the usual mate's and master's tickets from its officers, there are other Panamanian ships which don't. He didn't know much about them—or if he did he wasn't telling me. They wouldn't be this sort of thing, of course, but smaller and on much shorter runs—African or West Indian coasters, probably."

Bronwen opened her bag and searched inside for cigarettes with hands that shook slightly. "And what good do you imagine that is to us? If you got a job on one of those sort of boats, what would you be? Third mate on a filthy little down-at-heel tramp ship. And you'd get about as much pay as an ordinary sailor on this boat." She kept her voice pitched low so that her words were inaudible at the other side of the deck, but she glared at her husband from eyes dilated with anger. "My God, I think you must be going crazy! One minute you say you despise this ship's officers because they aren't like naval ones, and the next minute you want to get a job in which they would have every right to despise *you*!" She lowered her voice still farther. "Listen, Roger, I know what the trouble is with you: it's quite obvious. You're on a ship again for the first time since you left the Navy and it's gone to your head. You——"

"It's not that!" Roger's anger matched his wife's. "And anyway, I wouldn't take a job as third mate or anything like that at all! I'd expect to have command of a ship. It's a lot better to be commander of a small craft than an ordinary officer on a larger one. Don't you see, you fool, that it's something I *can* do! Not like running round after Crambatch, carrying her bag and lighting her cigarettes. If you want to know—I'd rather be a gash-hand on a leaky Hong Kong scow than work in Crambatch's foul shop!"

"Then you shouldn't have married! What you are saying is that you wish I wasn't here so that you could go on lazing about until some job that pleases your fantastic vanity turns up. This talk of what you can do makes me sick! You can't do *anything* except run a submarine, and as there aren't any more for you to run, you've *got* to do something else

—you haven't any choice. You've got a wife and you'll soon have a child. Don't you think it's time you stopped behaving like an irresponsible schoolboy and started to grow up mentally? If you——"

But the game of shuffleboard was over and Mrs. Crambatch waddled across to them, beaming. "I won! I did indeed. I beat the Colonel! What a charming man he is. Thank you, Roger, dear—just a little farther into the shade, if you will. Ah—that's better!" She settled herself comfortably and opened the big box of chocolates on her lap. "What—all here! You sinless young couple! Why, at your ages I couldn't have resisted a box like this for two minutes. But I'm forgetting what I wanted to say to you. I understand that we arrive in Colombo soon after breakfast-time to-morrow and remain there all day. I thought it would be nice if we all three took a car and went up Mount Lavinia through the tea plantations and had lunch there. I don't suppose Bronwen has ever seen a tea plantation, have you, dear?"

"No—but I should love to. It sounds a delightful idea."

"I'm so glad! Then we'll do that. I saw the plantations on the way over, of course, but I'd like to visit them again. You really are the most accommodating young people—always falling in with my plans." She giggled happily. "I fear I rather monopolise you, you know! But I'll miss you dreadfully if you stay in Australia—you see I say 'if.'" Smiling complacently, she took off her spectacles and began to polish them. How delightful the Lannfrancs were. Such a good-looking young couple, so well matched. And soon to have a baby—what could be nicer? If only Bronwen were one's own daughter, one need never fear loneliness in old age. One would have a family to look after one, and——

"We shall miss you too, you know, Mrs. Crambatch."

"But, my dear, there's no reason why you should, you know. You've only got to come on to N.Z. with me. I've told you how much nicer it is for an English couple than Australia. You'd feel at home at once, I promise you."

Bronwen gazed up with a little-girl frown of distress between her slightly too heavy eyebrows and an expression of innocent bewilderment in her big eyes. "Yes, yes, I'm sure we would. And we'd love to come on with you. Only it's so difficult. . . ."

Mrs. Crambatch put on her glasses again, the world clicked back into clear focus, and as it did so she noticed Roger's sunburnt fingers give his wife's hand a sharp, twisting pinch. "Difficult," she repeated slowly, "yes, difficult." What were they up to? What was the meaning of that sudden vicious pinch? Had something been said that should not have been? Was it some kind of warning—against her? All her latent suspicion of Europe and Europeans stirred uneasily in her mind. She gave the Lannfrancs a sharp, shrewd glance. Did she detect some peculiar embarrassment? "Difficult in what way, dear?" she asked carefully.

"Well, you see, Roger's got to get a job—and so have I, until the baby comes."

"I'm sure you'd find it just as easy, if not easier, to do that in N.Z."

"Yes—perhaps. But you see he's got some introductions he can use in Sydney which could probably lead to at least one really *good* job there, with luck. After all, he's been a lieutenant-commander, as you know, and naval officers just can't take any old job that's going. He's qualified for a really good post."

"If that's the case, if he's *qualified* for a good post, then I'm sure he won't find any difficulty in getting one in either Australia or N.Z. Both countries are simply crying out for qualified men. Only you had rather given me the impression that Roger wasn't qualified in that way—in any way outside the Navy, I mean. I'm very glad to hear that's not so, for it's sometimes worried me rather for your sakes."

Flushing slightly, Bronwen said lamely, "I didn't mean in any technical sense, you know. I meant—well, qualified by his whole past, his background and training and personality. Qualified in that sense to organise, to take decisions, to—well, *lead*. I mean, he'd be terribly useful in dozens of positions really, if he was given the chance—and he ought to be and he probably will be. Naval officers don't grow on trees, you know."

"No, dear—and nor do really good jobs, unfortunately. Have a chocolate? No? You, Roger?"

Dumbly taking one of the big, expensive, gold-wrapped things from the box, Roger felt, for the second time in his adult life, a sense of such bitter, desolate degradation that he could easily have cried if he had not, like so many Englishmen of his class, forgotten how to do so somewhere around his sixteenth birthday. That Bronwen should have to try to sell him to this awful woman and that he should have to sit and listen to her doing it—doing it so badly and failing and being snubbed. She was trying for him as much as for herself. She only wanted what other wives wanted—a home for her child, some security; and if she saw these always in terms of wealth and success, which to her were one and the same thing, it was only a personal idiosyncrasy. And he wanted to give her these things, despite what she had recently said, and inwardly she knew, surely she knew, that he wanted to do so. She had only spoken to him like that because she was frightened that he would fail her. And it was true that by her own standards of relentless, unswerving dedication to the goal of worldly success he had failed her, though he could not, *would* not, agree that it was through any fault of his own. He had been somehow—how he did not quite know—cheated out of the means to give his wife any of the things for which she craved. He could not even afford to give her chocolates like these. He jumped quickly, resolutely, to his feet.

"Bron, I'd nearly forgotten! I promised that we would have a drink with the—the Second Engineer in the bar at twelve-thirty. Come along, or we'll be late."

Mrs. Crambatch looked up disappointedly; despite her newly acquired suspicions of the Lannfrancs, she hated being left alone. "Why, Roger, you greedy boy! You can't eat chocolates *and* drink at the same time!"

"I know—I'd quite forgotten." Quickly he stooped and put the big gold-wrapped chocolate back in the box. He grinned at Mrs. Crambatch with queer, hot-faced venom. "I'm very sorry. You see, I promised we'd go."

"Oh, well, then—I suppose you must."

"Yes, really we must. Come on, Bron!"

4

"The English alphabet," said Bressan, "has twenty-six letters; four more than our own. These always seem to me to be rather unnecessary when it comes to talking the language, but you will certainly never be able to read it unless you can recognise them. This is what they look like." He carefully drew a "K," a "W," an "X" and a "Y" on a clean page in the exercise book and handed it to Armando. Then he glanced at his watch and noticed with surprise that it was nearly seven o'clock. Beyond the two open scuttles, the night was falling fast over the calm opalescence of the sea.

He rose and clicked the bulkhead switch, flooding the dusky cabin with bright light. It was a comfortably furnished yet very neat room. Bressan never cluttered up the place with Oriental souvenirs or quantities of family photographs, as other officers were apt to do. There was nothing, save his rows of carefully shelved books, that bore any personal association whatever. Except for the books, it could easily have been the cabin of some unusually tidy passenger.

Now he slumped back in his chair, watching Armando through half-closed, heavy lidded eyes, one pudgy hand rapping the pencil gently against his knee. Armando was not, on the whole, a satisfactory substitute for Gino. His background was too different: it cast a sombre shadow from which he could never wholly escape, even in his gayest moments. While to Gino life meant adventure, to Armando it meant survival. Where Gino was interested in himself as a living personality and valued himself accordingly—in fact, over-valued himself with the healthy egotism of youth—Armando thought of his whole being as merely an instrument for his economic existence, something to be worked, used and driven—for some time at the will of others and later, with any luck, at his own—irrespective of its mental or physical needs or desires. Gino knew he was young and healthy and handsome, and gloried in the knowledge, hating the thought of increasing age, possible ill-health and the physical coarsening of the years. Armando would willingly have exchanged his own youth, health and southern good looks for financial success and security. He looked forward eagerly to his fifties and sixties when these might be his, and saw the years between then and now as merely a long period of heavy, unceasing labour. It made him servile where Gino was impudent, fatalistic where Gino was resilient, and it would work on and on within him, this grim inheritance of struggle, increasing with the years until he possessed his big dry-goods store, his shipping wharf or his fleet of hire-cars, and was enclosed at last in the deadly peace of the commercial counting-house which passes all desolation.

It was considerations such as these, considerations which came all too easily to Bressan's analytical and introspective mind, which saddened him and made him compare Armando's polite, grateful and touchingly eager company invidiously with that of the evanescent, lighthearted, sometimes mocking Gino.

He sighed softly and Armando, looking up from the study

of "K," "W" and "Y," said suddenly, "There is an Englishman called 'Ogben——"

"Hogben. Breathe out sharply to make that 'H' sound."

"H—Hogben. He says they will make rules for us in Australia so that we cannot work more than they do."

"Then certainly you will be leading lives of leisure," remarked Bressan sardonically. But, as he guessed at once, humour of this sort was lost on Armando, who only looked scared and worried. "No, no. What he says is not true. At least, it is only a little true. The English, as the Captain once said to me, have a habit of saying things that are not true but which they would like to be true. They hope in this way to make them come true. It is not a system that works well and they have recently had a few sharp lessons to this effect. Don't worry about what you are told—wait till you get there."

"This man H—Hogben hates me."

"So?" Bressan pushed some cigarettes across the table. "Help yourself and keep the packet. No, no, I get them duty-free, it is nothing." He paused. "I expect this Hogben only hates you because he is frightened of you."

"Of me?"

"Probably. Of you and what you represent. If you and other Italians work as hard as you like—as hard as you are accustomed—then he too must work as hard, or perhaps his employer will prefer to dismiss him and to engage you in his place. And he is not accustomed to working hard; not because he cannot, but because—because——" Bressan frowned—"because it is against all his principles to do so, against everything in which he believes." He saw Armando's blank incomprehension and smiled. "Never mind. You will win, because—oddly enough—it is a great deal easier to work hard than not to. Now let us turn to some of these peculiar but easy verbs. For example, to want to work. See in how many persons you can conjugate that."

But Armando was not quite ready for further instruction. "Signor Bressan, it is true that someone jumped overboard last night?"

Bressan gazed at him expressionlessly for a long moment. "Yes, it is true. How did you hear of it?"

"From some other passengers; they said one of the crew told them." Armando's face had paled, his eyes widened unhappily. "Why should anyone want to do that—drown himself?"

"Who knows? A darkness descends upon the spirit and it despairs. Then it finds cause enough for death in reasons which to you and me would not seem reasonable at all."

"But——" the boy's voice was urgent with distress—"to jump over like that—alone in the night . . ." He shuddered. "The sea is so deep! I could never do that."

Bressan shrugged. "These things happen. It is probably best not to discuss them, for it can do no good." Privately he cursed the garrulous member of the crew—he thought it was probably Ansaldo—who had talked. There was nothing, as he knew well, which created a worse atmosphere on a ship at sea than a suicide by jumping. Firmly he said, "It's done now, and what's done cannot be undone. Don't let it——" He broke off as the telephone buzzed beside his bunk.

Armando jumped to his feet. "Signor Bressan, I must go. You are busy."

Bressan smiled. "All right, Mando. You're getting on quite well." He put a hand on the boy's shoulder. "Look, don't get upset about Hogben or what the English migrants say. They're just as worried about Australia as you are—and they know no more about it. If——" The telephone gave a long, angry buzz and, cutting short Armando's thanks, Bressan picked it up as the boy left the cabin, quietly shutting the door behind him. "Second Officer here."

From against his ear he heard Ciccolanti's deep voice. "Good. Look, Bressan, I've just had Tomei up here telling me the Captain's ill and ought to have a doctor—a doctor!" he repeated with angry sarcasm. "That is a fine thing to say just now, is it not? Anyway, the Captain told him he was being a fool, but he says——"

"The Captain hates Tomei. He once caught him cleaning the surgery implements with an old dish-cloth. What is supposed to be wrong?"

"Pains in the stomach."

"Appendicitis. We must get ready to operate," said Bressan at once.

"That's just what Tomei said, and it annoyed the Captain extremely because apparently Gavanian always said that whenever anyone had stomach pains."

Bressan giggled. "Yes, he did. He was always getting ready to operate and asking for the ship to slow down and so forth. It made him feel important, and he enjoyed feeling important more than anyone I have ever met. So then it became a joke among us: 'Appendicitis! We must get ready to operate!' We mocked him terribly, I'm afraid. Poor man! He was a bad doctor and a most ineffective husband, yet he always meant so well! Anyway, the Captain knows a lot more about medical things—much more than Gavanian did, I am sure. Tomei, of course, knows nothing —nothing at all. Do not take any notice of Tomei. Even Gavanian only used him to wash the surgery floor."

5

The celebratory dinner in the first-class saloon was not the success it might have been. Neither the Captain nor the Chief Officer were at table and though Cavaliere Semprebon viewed the seat of the latter with indifference he felt it to be unfortunate that the master of *San Roque* could not be present at his ship's official birthday party. The passengers too, with the exception of the van Staedtlers who were disembarking tomorrow at Colombo, seemed depressed and irritable, and out of tune with the festivity of the occasion. Perhaps they had been quarrelling among themselves or perhaps they had heard rumours of the doctor's suicide on the previous night —it was nearly impossible, as the Purser knew from past experience, to keep such occurrences secret on a ship; at any rate, there was a glumness in the atmosphere of the gaily-lit saloon which neither the Cavaliere's elaborate jocularity nor the frothy, second-rate Asti Spumante which he had daringly served from the ship's stores was able to dispel.

The dinner, too, proved itself a disappointment by refusing in any way to fulfil the hopes raised by the brightly decorated menu cards. The "*Consommé de la Reine Elisabeth*" was only to be distinguished from a rather tasteless *bouillon* by a few peas and some strips of faded carrot afloat in it; the "*Poisson de la Mer du Sud*" was so thick and stale and leathery that one felt it could never have been really fresh, even before it was caught; and the chicken for the "*Pilaff Royale de San Roque*" had been used with such economy that the shreds of flesh were hardly visible in the mounds of sticky rice. The fruit jelly had been taken from the refrigerator too early and was sloppy in consequence, and if the Purser had hoped to retrieve his reputation as a caterer with the production of the canned Spanish mushrooms, now named "*Cèpes Semprebon,*" he was singularly mistaken. "An old family recipe," he explained genially as they were handed round, and then gazed with slight alarm at the soggy, soot-black substance on a piece of toast which was placed before him. But it must be brazened out somehow. "Yes, my family had the secret from a titled ancestor of ours over a hundred years ago. At home we serve them only on important feast days. To-night, I felt——"

"What *are* they, Mr. Semprebon?"

"They are mushrooms cooked in a very special way."

"They don't look like any mushrooms I've ever seen."

"I doubt, Mrs. Crambatch, if you have ever, in fact, seen this species of mushroom. They grow only in the woods near my home."

"All mushrooms that aren't mushrooms are toadstools."

"I assure you that these are very special mushrooms—most prized by the tenants on my family's estate. Early in October it is the custom——"

"They taste of tar!"

"They have," said the Cavaliere, whose genius for improvisation was being severely strained, "a somewhat bitter flavour—it is customary. They are a small, fragile mushrom of a delightful dark colour with—with green stems."

"Ah, yes!" Professor Staedtler interjected from across the table. "I also know these mushrooms."

The Purser shot him a grateful glance—but it was premature.

"They grow," pursued the Professor in his slow English, "at the edges of the mangrove swamps in southern Java. They are not at all good to eat. Often the native cattle consume them in error and become most ill. They have a native name which would, I think, translate into English as 'Froth from the Lips of a Dead Goat.'" He put down his fork decidedly, and the rest of the diners at the Captain's table hurriedly followed suit.

"Really, Mr. Semprebon! I can't imagine what——"

"No, no, no! I assure you these are not of what the good Professor speaks. These are most nourishing and edible mushrooms. Allow me, please, to know best . . ." But it was no good; the dinner had been a failure from the start and the "*Cèpes Semprebon*" were merely the final touch that ruined it.

6

In the Captain's sleeping-cabin Serafino and the plump, bald sick-berth attendant Tomei stood unhappily beside the bunk from which Onestinghel stared up at them, his parchment face strained and seeming for once to express his true age. Every now and then he caught his breath and his narrow mouth contorted with pain. When he spoke it was in quick, short sentences between these spasms. "All right, then—call for—assistance. I suppose—it is best. I cannot diagnose what is—the matter with me. No! It is *not* appendix trouble, Tomei!" With a weak nod of his head he indicated two thick red textbooks lying open on the locker beside him. Serafino saw that they were old-fashioned French medical manuals. One showed diagrams of the interior of the human abdomen, the alimentary tract and cross sections of the large and small intestine. "Can you—read French, Ciccolanti?"

"No, signore."

"Ugh!" It might have been an exclamation of contempt or one of pain.

"Well, whatever is wrong with me—is not what—this fool thinks." The Captain paused, and for a moment there was no sound in the cabin save his harsh and continually interrupted breathing. Then he said tiredly, "All right. Call assistance from—the nearest—ship. Change course towards her—as soon as she answers. Don't forget—to inform the—agents at Colombo and——" the pain must have been growing more severe for he raised his knees and the breath hissed sharply between his teeth before he grunted—"the Naples office."

Less than four minutes later *San Roque,* steaming through the night on a direct course for Colombo at her cruising speed of sixteen knots, sent out her call for medical assistance. In the small, hot, brightly lit radio room aft of the bridge Radio Operator Aldo Brighenti clicked out the message on the Morse key, sending rapidly, confidently, with the peculiar nonchalant dexterity of the experienced signalman. "*Emergency illness. We need a doctor.*" *San Roque's* message rayed out from Brighenti's key across great wastes of water to where other men sat in other hot, brightly lit radio rooms behind other bridges. "*Emergency illness. We need a doctor.*" And soon, from ships scattered like tiny seeds across the vast indifference of the Indian Ocean, came the replies. Brighenti scribbled on his pad, waited, clicked the key and scribbled again—waited, eyebrows raised, scribbled once, twice more, and then turned to the Chief Officer, small and gaunt behind him. "That seems to be all, Signor Ciccolanti."

"Only four?" It was a small enough response, and as he examined the scribbled messages Serafino's brows drew together in a worried frown.

The nearest ship to answer was the Spanish freighter *El Buen Pastor,* homeward bound from Colombo to Barcelona. She carried no doctor but her captain asked if he could help in any way. Next, from far back somewhere off the coast of Socotra, *San Roque's* call had been answered with speed and precision by an American tanker, *Sovac Swiftsure,* bound fully laden from the Gulf. She had a doctor—had two, as it happened—and a fully equipped operating theatre and hospital. Could she be of any help? She would change course at once if required to do so, but she presumed that she was too far away. Serafino nodded grimly and turned to the third. This was the Portuguese destroyer *Sao Paulo de Loanda,* outward bound from Goa to Lourenço Marques. She offered her naval surgeon, but as she had partially broken down with engine trouble and was limping back to port at something under four knots, *San Roque* would have to turn and steam all the way to meet her. It would take all night and much of the next day: that was out of the question. Lastly, the Egyptian ship *Istiqlal,* which gave no information regarding position or course, kindly but haltingly offered the services of a passenger about whom she gave profuse details. He was a certain Abbas Mehib el Habakli, a first-year medical student from Cairo University, training to be a forensic pathologist. He was twenty years old and placed himself at the full disposal of *San Roque,* subject only to the limitations of his present skill. If there was a legal aspect to the trouble he felt he might perhaps . . .

Serafino shook his head. " No good, Brighenti. Try again. There *must* be some other replies. Send them straight up to me on the bridge."

On the bridge he found Bressan, still in his full white uniform from dinner, strolling up and down smoking a small cigar. He nodded to him brusquely, went over to the chart table and began to plot *San Roque's* present position. It left him in no doubt that unless Brighenti called up a ship within a radius of some one hundred and fifty miles, the only thing to do was to press on towards Colombo at full speed, and when, five minutes later, the radio operator reported that his message had brought no new answers, Serafino rang the engine-room. "*Ponte Comando*—I want Signor Aafjes."

"Signor Aafjes is off duty. Signor Zocco is on watch at present."

"Very well. Tell him the Chief Officer wishes to speak to him."

A pause. Then Zocco's voice. "*Buonasera, Signor Ciccolanti.*"

"*Buon'sera, Signor Zocco.*" The carefully polite form of address indicated that on *San Roque,* as upon all mechanically driven vessels on the high seas, the "deck" and the "engine-room" were two different worlds inhabited by two different races whose only link was their common rule by one king. "How many knots can we make at top speed, please?"

Zocco hesitated. "I do not think that under full power we could give you more than twenty-two."

Serafino glanced at his watch and calculated quickly in his head. Twenty-two knots, a calm sea with only a mild swell—they should reach Colombo at early dawn. "Very well." He was about to order full speed when he remembered Onestinghel's rage that morning, remembered also the parsimony of the owner and that a ship under full power was not running at its most economical speed. "All right, Signor Zocco, thank you. Please stand by to give us all the power you can. I am now going to ask the Captain's permission to give the order."

Standing once more beside the bunk in the big sleeping cabin, Serafino was appalled at the deterioration in the Captain's condition. Onestinghel's face was no longer a pallid, parchment mask, but suffused and swollen and perspiring heavily. The pain, too, must have increased terribly, for the Captain was groaning and twisting in agony so that the bunk below him creaked and rattled. He stared, for a moment seemingly without recognition, at his Chief Officer from small bloodshot eyes. "Full speed? Yes, yes. At once."

Serafino snatched the phone and this time it was Aafjes who answered from the engine-room. Zocco must have sent for him on being ordered to stand by. "From the Captain's cabin? I see. Yes. Yes, all we can give you. Immediately.

Yes. Very well, Signor Ciccolanti. Er—may we assume then, that for all practical purposes you are now in command of the ship?"

Serafino stiffened. In command of the ship? Responsible—solely and alone responsible—for *San Roque*, the pride of the Line, and all the souls, passengers and crew, aboard her? Responsible in the eyes not only of the owner, but of every maritime body, every Admiralty Court, every Port Authority throughout the world? But of course he had really been responsible—been in *de facto* command—since that morning, since the Captain had left the bridge and called Tomei to his cabin. He glanced quickly at the groaning, contorted figure of Onestinghel on the sweat-soaked bunk. Yes, he was in command now—at least, for all practical purposes.

"Yes, Signor Aafjes, you may assume that. All orders will be given by me until the Captain is sufficiently recovered."

"Very good, signore." Serafino gave a slight start. Aafjes, the Chief Engineer, addressing him as "sir." Of course—for he was no longer chief of a part of the ship—the "deck"; he was commander of the whole. He put down the telephone, and as he did so Onestinghel gasped, "Ciccolanti!"

"*Signor Capitano?*"

"This means—this means no answers to the—emergency call?"

Serafino nodded unhappily. "We have received only four. None is suitable." Carefully he told the Captain of the four replies Brighenti had received and of his own reasons for disregarding them. It seemed that between the convulsions of pain Onestinghel was trying to follow him, for an occasional "yes" hissed between the tightly drawn lips. "So this seems the only way, signore. We shall be at Colombo by dawn." For a long moment there was silence, save for the Captain's grunting, spasmodic breathing. Then with a sudden swift intake of breath the harsh, barely-controlled voice cracked, "That fool—probably right, I suppose."

"Tomei?"

"Yes. It must be. What is—the time?"

"A quarter to ten, signore."

The Captain said with sudden distinction, "You'll have to operate by 'Medrad.' Tomei—will give the anaesthetic." He seemed for a moment to be trying to smile, but the pain caught him, his legs jerked up and the breath whistled from his nose and mouth.

Serafino looked dumbly down at the bunk, looked from the

panting figure of the Captain to the incomprehensible medical books on the locker and shook his head. Operation by medical radio, by continued stage-by-stage instructions spoken into a microphone by a doctor far away in the great C.S.I.R.O. building in Rome? He shuddered painfully. *He* to open a human body, to delve about among the infinitely complex and delicate human organs with instruments whose uses —whose very names—he did not know in his untrained hands? No, no, the Captain must be joking. He did not look in a state for joking, admittedly; but then, as Serafino had learnt in the last weeks, Captain Onestinghel was a most unusual man.

With a weak attempt at a smile he said, " We shall be in Colombo in a few hours, signore. Can I tell Tomei to give you something to stop the pain?"

Then the Captain turned his head on the sweat-soaked pillow and looked at him—a look oddly like that with which he had examined him on the evening he had reported aboard at Naples, a carefully appraising, probing scrutiny, trying to estimate his capabilities, sum him up, decide upon his reliability and value. Under that queer, searching gaze Serafino felt again the blood heating his face, and for a moment he was no longer Chief Officer, acting captain of a liner at sea, but just a young Italian from a poor home, undersized, lame, struggling to keep a large family on his inadequate wages, respectful towards his betters (which meant everyone with more money than himself) humbly accepting his own poverty and all the weariness and humiliations that went with it as part of his ordained lot—a Neapolitan. He shrugged, still smiling wanly, and opened his hands.

Then Onestinghel's head turned impatiently on the pillow. He started to speak, was convulsed for a moment by a spasm of breathless pain and, as it ebbed, said with a weary impatience, " Yes, yes. Send Tomei with something, then. You are—in command now. Go to the bridge."

For a long moment Serafino hesitated. There had been something in the Captain's voice, in that tired, impatient dismissal, which disturbed him deeply, filling him with a miserable sense of his own inadequacy. He waited, hoping that Onestinghel would say something more—make some request that he could fulfil, give some order that he could obey. But the head on the damp pillow did not turn again towards him, the half-shut, bloodshot eyes stared upwards at the ceiling. Awkwardly he said, " *Va bene, Signor Capitano.*

I will send Tomei at once." And, bowing quickly, left the cabin.

7

Down below—far below the water-line in the depths of the ship, in the engine-room—Aafjes had given a few brief orders, hands had spun wheels and shifted levers, while eyes had watched needles creeping up pressure gauges. There was little outward sign among that mass of complex machinery to indicate that it was now developing maximum power. Perhaps the soft roar of the oil furnaces increased, but only to a degree which could be noticed by ears attuned to such things, while the great humps of the turbines where the extra power was being manufactured, where the raw material of superheated steam was being turned into the finished product of thrust, remained to outward view as static and motionless as ever. It was only by her increased vibration that *San Roque* indicated that she was now steaming at full speed. She shook and shivered from keel to mast-head with a continual rapid trembling which jingled all the cutlery in the dining-saloons, made the glasses tinkle on the shelves of the first-class bar and rattled loose any object not firmly secured to the juddering decks or bulkheads.

On the bridge Serafino, feeling that vibration through the soles of his feet, took some comfort from the fact that with a light breeze on the port quarter and a calm sea, *San Roque* was probably travelling as fast as she ever would. The elements, at least, were not against her.

From beside him Bressan said, "Poor Gavanian—what a mischance! Had he but waited this one voyage he would have been able to remove the Captain's appendix. It would have made him quite unbearable with triumph afterwards, of course, but still, I am sorry for him. I imagine an appendectomy to have been the only operation of which he was capable." He giggled. "Even so, I have little doubt that Tomei would have managed to leave most of the surgical instruments, and doubtless a packet of cigarettes and a few other oddments, within the Captain's abdominal cavity at the conclusion of the affair. Yes, perhaps for the Captain's sake it is best that things are as they are. None the less, we must trust that we arrive in time to avoid a ruptured appendix. Peritonitis at the Captain's age—he is, as you know, approaching his seventy-third birthday—would be no——"

"Bressan," interrupted Serafino quickly, his deep voice holding an odd-sick note, "if you wish to go below you may do so."

"I'm on watch."

"I know. But I am here and I intend to stay here until we reach port."

"Oh, I see." The Second Officer sounded slightly offended. "Of course you are in charge now, I suppose."

"Yes."

Bressan did not go below but walked over to the chart table and sat down beside the soft blue light. There was silence on the bridge which lasted for half an hour. Then Tomei telephoned from the Captain's cabin. "Signor Ciccolanti, can you come down? I—I do not like the look of things at all."

"*Subito*." But it was with a feeling of the deepest reluctance that Serafino left the bridge, and with a sensation almost of dread that he once again entered the Captain's night-cabin.

Tomei turned as the door closed behind the Chief Officer and shook his bald head unhappily, the shaded light gleaming from his spectacles. "I fear—yes, yes, he is unconscious, signore—I fear that it has ruptured. His belly is as hard as rock. Come—you shall see what I mean."

"No, no." Serafino drew back from the bunk where the Captain, his face a lined, livid mask, lay still except for the stertorous breathing from his open mouth. "If you say so, it is so." He stared down at the figure on the bunk. So old—he looked so old. It was as if suddenly all the years, all the fabulous experiences of the long life which he had worn so lightly, had at last descended upon Captain Onestinghel, crushing him beneath their accumulated weight. It was an ancient man who lay there now, not—not the Captain at all.

Knowing what the answer would be, Serafino said slowly, "For us—you and I, Tomei—to do anything now—to try to operate by 'Medrad'——"

The sick-bay attendant shook his head decidedly. "Quite out of the question, Signor Ciccolanti. Only a skilled surgeon—and a great deal of luck—can save his life." He lowered the wrist, whose pulse he had been feeling carefully, to the smoothed sheet. "Yes, only great good fortune, I think, can save him now."

XII

"... beyond expressing my sympathy for you." The English doctor glanced speculatively at the ship's officer rising from his seat at the other side of the desk. He was certainly extremely young for the rank he held, but it was the doctor's experience that Panamanian ships were often manned and officered by adolescents or senile old dodderers—presumably because they cost less than men in the prime of life. And how thin he was, this boy! There seemed to be no flesh on his small body; his waist was as narrow as a girl's, the white doeskin belt encircling it nearly twice, and his bronzed arms were stick-like below the short sleeves of his shirt. But it was his face that drew the doctor's attention most strongly: a broad-browed face with wide-set brown eyes, wide mouth and small, firmly angled jaw, a face at once aloof and sombre, with a sullen stubbornness which perhaps would look less bitter when he smiled—if he ever did. Despite his outlandish name, this was not at all an Italian—a southern—face, but a northern one; except for the warm brown of the eyes, it could have fitted a Scotsman.

Standing now, in the bright, pale tropical light pouring through the tall hospital windows, there was an indefinable shabbiness about this short, gaunt figure. His white shirt and trousers were clean enough, but it was difficult for anyone so small and bony to look smart in such light clothes—particularly as he limped, due to some damage to his right foot. What a little scarecrow! Yet an oddly attractive little scarecrow, somehow. The doctor started to smile, remembered of what he was speaking, and coughed quickly instead. "Of course, at that age—but even so, had you only been able to reach a doctor in time there's no doubt his life would have been saved. There was nothing in the least complicated about it—a perfectly simple case of acute appendicitis. It was just a question of getting the thing out in time—child's play, really. Yes, all most unfortunate. Mr. —er—I'm not quite certain how you say your name——"

"Ciccolanti. He—he speaks before he dies?"

The doctor glanced up sharply; there had been a note—a distinct note—of fear in that oddly deep voice. He paused. "Well, most of the time he was unconscious, of course. Oh, and for goodness' sake tell that infirmary fellow of yours to go easy with the morphine. He'll put somebody to sleep for good one day, if he behaves as if he's handling out cough-drops. Those drugs are dangerous. Tell him that, will you?"

"Yes, *Signor Dottore*."

The doctor suppressed a quick smile. "Where was I? Yes, of course. Well, Captain Onestinghel came to, despite the morphine, just before the end. But—well, he wasn't in his right mind, I'm afraid. One cannot be surprised at that, of course—in the circumstances. He *did* speak—yes. But it was all in Russian—or perhaps Italian—I don't know either language myself."

"He—he did not say my name?"

The doctor looked up, looked down at his desk, and shifted a paperweight. "No," he said firmly, "he didn't." He rose with a slight sigh. "Well, Mr. Ciccolanti, we'll fix up the death certificate here of course, and naturally you must notify your Consul who'll deal with the other formalities." He paused, then smiled openly. "I fear this has all been a considerable strain on you, hasn't it? I would prescribe bromide—not morphine, please—and bed. Is that impossible?"

And for the first time that queerly arresting face broke into an uncertain, humourless grin. "I have much work. I must leave here. Many thanks for your assist—for your help."

"Not at all. I wish it had turned out differently. And—er—if you can't go to bed, at least——" the doctor lifted an imaginery glass to his mouth—"a couple of good strong ones, eh?"

2

The death of Captain Onestinghel was not generally known aboard ship until that evening. All day *San Roque* had lain at her moorings near the east end of the sea wall, oiling from lighters for the long haul across the Equator and down into the southern hemisphere. She had arrived several hours earlier than scheduled and had been at anchor offshore before the first of her passengers rose from his bunk. After breakfast, most people had left the ship by launch for a tour of the town or a trip up through the tea plantations. It was a day of typically equatorial weather, humid and windy and drained of colour—intensely enervating to the unacclimatised European. The harbour, the low white town and the long palm-fringed coastline of the island, all had a shabby, washed-out appearance, as if they had been soaked over-long in a steam bath. Many of the passengers returned early, clutching boxes of cheroots or bunches of stumpy, yellow-green plantains, and then, finding much of the ship still enveloped in the acrid stench of fuel oil, wished they had stayed on shore.

At five o'clock the amplifiers all over *San Roque* spluttered and crackled warningly and a voice, which most of the passengers recognised as the Purser's, called: "Attention! Attention, please! It is with the very most regret that we have to inform you of the—the decease of the Captain. Captain Onestinghel was found last night to be most deeply ill. The ship progressed at its fullest speed to reach Colombo for assistance. Captain Onestinghel was taken to hospital immediately upon our arrival and all effort was made to save him. To our great sorrow this failed, and he died this morning at the hour of ten twenty-five. This event will cause the ship some slight delay so that it is not expected to depart to-day. For passengers who wish to return ashore for the evening an arrival of launches will be in half an hour. Thank you." And then in Italian. "*Attenzione! Attenzione, per favore! . . .*"

Comment—shocked, worried, superstitious or annoyed—broke out at once all over the ship. "Cor! Poor old bleeder! Wonder what done for 'im? Not sayin' though, is they?" . . . "S'long as it's nothin' catchin'—gotter think of the kids." . . . "Think they're 'ushin' somethin' up? P'r'aps 'e done in the doctor bloke they says jumped over, eh? Went nutty-like an' done for 'im an' then done 'isself?" . . . "Could be, I s'pose. *Anything's* possible on this boat if you ask me." . . . "An' what's to 'appen *now*, eh? Tell me that. Nice state of 'ealth this is, I *must* say! Pays our bleedin' fares an' now we ain't got no bleedin' skipper!" . . . "'Oo's gettin' us to Australier, then? Think young 'op-and-go-one'll take over?" . . ." Now—not 'im. We'll be 'ere until they flies someone out." . . . "Mrs. Throsby! 'Ere a minute, Mrs. Throsby! 'Ave you 'eard? Captain's 'ad 'is chips!"

Mrs. Crambatch, returning with the Lannfrancs from the expedition to Mount Lavinia, was not in any case in a good temper. She had wanted Roger, who had told her that he had once been stationed for several months in Ceylon, to help her buy some of the island's famed aquamarines and topazes.

He surely would have some idea of the correct prices and know the genuine from the counterfeit, for her recent European experiences had aroused her deepest suspicions concerning the goods people sold her. But Roger had been gloomy all day. The island, it seemed, held memories of his naval past, and despite a few sharp remarks from Bronwen, who plainly did not like to see him behaving so morosely, he had been almost completely unhelpful. " Looks all right to me." " You probably won't do any better anywhere else." " Why worry? They all *look* alike, don't they?" So that if they had not found the Second Officer, Mr. Bressan, buying a new watch in one of the many jeweller's shops which they visited, she would have had no help at all. But he, in his queer, shy way, had tried to assist her and had pointed out one or two shops which he considered more reliable than the rest. None the less, there had been none of the spectacular bargains she had hoped for, and it was in an irritable frame of mind that she once again boarded *San Roque*—to be greeted by the news of the Captain's death.

She took it as a personal affront. " Well, really! This is *too* bad! *Now* what's going to happen—tell me that?" But no one could. She sought out the Purser. " Mr. Semprebon, I really must complain. I've paid for two-first-class cabins all the way to Sydney, and now this has happened!"

" Madame, I assure you——"

" It's no good assuring me of anything! If Captain Onestinghel was in poor health he shouldn't have been allowed to command a ship in the first place. When I pay my fare I expect to—to—well anyway, I exepect things to be done properly. What's going to happen now?"

" A new captain will be found—undoubtedly."

" Where?" demanded Mrs. Crambatch, staring accusingly round the vestibule as if to emphasise the lack of captains behind the potted palms or under the chairs.

" Doubtless he will be flown at once from Naples."

" That would take *days*."

" Perhaps, then, from Australia."

" That would take still longer. The fact is, you've no more idea than I have about it! I wish now that I'd waited for my passage on the P. and O. At least *their* captains don't die in the middle of voyages!" She scowled viciously at the unhappy Purser, and her garish spectacles trembled on her bulbous nose. "This is a *horrid* little ship; badly run and smelly, and the food is—is *revolting*!"

3

Only to Colonel Chelgrove and his sister was the Captain's death an event of secondary importance, for here, at Colombo, the Malcolm-Bruces were to join the ship.

"Yes, Paula, you're bound to like him—and his wife too. Of course he was Indian Army—Wellington, Sandhurst, Hoskin's Horse—and so we didn't meet often before the war." The Colonel wandered slowly up and down his cabin while his sister sat on the bunk. He had spent nearly all day below decks, for the sight of the town depressed him intensely: it was here that the first court martial had taken place fourteen years ago. "We met originally in London. At the Cavalry Club. I was having lunch with Percy Tancred of the Blues when suddenly Malcolm-Bruce came over—he was a friend of Percy's—and when I was introduced he said, 'You're not the chap who wrote those damned good articles on regimental tradition, are you?' I said I was, and—well, after that we always kept in touch."

"Who are his family?"

"The Malcolm-Bruces? Oh, Scots, of course."

"Naturally. I mean are they the Bruces of Glenlivet? Or the Drumlithie Bruces?"

"I've no idea, Paula, I never can get the Scottish gentry right. So many similar names."

"Not if you use intelligence," said his sister sharply. "Let me see: I know there are some Macdonald-Bruces at Carnoustie who are connections of the earls of Glenrowan. Father used to know——"

"These are *Malcolm*-Bruces."

"Yes, yes, I know. None the less——"

But the Colonel was not listening to her; lost in a slow wave of reminiscence, he strolled and turned and strolled again. "We became close friends. He wanted to write about Indian Army traditions—often asked my advice. Then the war. His men let him down—badly. Poor chap, it quite broke him up at last. 'I'd never have believed it, Chelgrove!' he kept saying to me afterwards. 'Never. And I wouldn't tell anyone but you. The fact is that there had been a queer sort of feeling in the regiment ever since we went up to the front. I can't account for it unless the rice issue was wrong, or something. A queer, jumpy feeling—everybody had it. And the men were sulky and started to get ill. They complained of pains in the stomach and said their feet always felt cold—though it wasn't the rainy season, or anything. Well, you know as well as I do that you can't do much with sick troops. We had to retreat. It wouldn't have mattered so much if we hadn't left all our armoured cars and equipment behind. They were irreplaceable, of course. So now *we're* off to garrison the Bahamas.' Yes, cut up badly he was, poor fellow. But he was back at the time of the first court. He did his best for me. I remember him giving evidence: 'Chelgrove is the best sort of Regular officer,' he said. 'He knows the Army like the palm of his hand. But his health's not good. He's always suffered from tiredness ever since I've known him. In a staff position, where he could have had proper rest, he would have been invaluable—*absolutely invaluable!*' Yes. And later he was always on my side. He thought I'd been treated shamefully. He was a deep thinker, you know, too. 'After all, Chelgrove," he once said to me, 'one doesn't join the Regular army to fight wars oneself. One's there to make sure the other fellows—the emergency people—know how to do it when war comes. *A specialised cadre.*' Yes, he was very fond of that phrase, I remember. I think you're going to like him, Paula."

And then, far away down the corridor outside the cabin, came the first faint notes of the xylophone heralding dinner. The Colonel turned to his sister with a smile. "Well, let us go down. I've asked the Purser to put the Malcolm-Bruces at our table to-night—if they've come aboard in time. Both them and their children, though I've no idea whether their children are old enough to stay up for dinner, of course."

Cavaliere Semprebon was waiting for them at the entrance to the dining saloon. He was looking tired and a little harassed, but he greeted them with an attempt at his usual urbane jocularity. "Ah, Colonel—and Miss Chelgrove! Good evening to you. Yes, your friends are here. Allow me." He led the way between the tables of the thickly carpeted saloon, halted and stepped aside, smiling. "This is indeed a pleasure to me—to be permitted to—to reunite old friends. Mr. Malcolm-Bruce, here is Colonel Chelgrove!"

From behind a table laid for six, four slit-eyed yellow faces regarded the Colonel and his sister with polite but impassive interest. Then one of them rose affably to its feet, and for a ghastly second the smart, pale-grey suit appeared to Colonel Chelgrove to turn into a stained, shabby uniform, and a shadow at its waist—a shadow thrown, doubtless, by a chair-back or some piece of furniture—seemed a heavy, two-handed *samurai* sword. A voice, an affable genial voice, said, "Colonel Shelgrove? I do not think we have met before. But——" And then changed to quick concern: "Purser! The gentleman is ill!" Then Semprebon and Paula were supporting him, and if there had been a low chuckle just behind his left ear no one but he had heard it, and he was saying meekly, "No—no thank you. I'm quite all right. But I think there's been some mistake. I——"

Then Paula's voice cut in, outraged and accusing the standing yellow-face. "*You're* not Brigadier Malcolm-Bruce?"

"I? No, madam, I am not a brigadier. Dear me, no! But my name *is* Malcolm-Bruce. Allow me, please, to present my wife—and my son, Ian, and my daughter, Fiona. I'm sure we're delighted to renew your acquaintance. Frankly, I can't remember meeting you before—most remiss of me. My memory isn't what it was. Doubtless we met in Singapore. I have a house there."

Cavaliere Semprebon—a little nonplussed, nodded at once. "But yes, indeed, Colonel. Mr. Malcolm-Bruce is a most important citizen of Singapore. A gentleman of the very greatest standing and importance in that city. And now—please excuse me." And before either of them quite knew what was happening, the Colonel and his furious sister found themselves sitting down opposite a courteous, handsome and obviously very wealthy family of Straits Chinese.

4

"CHIEF OFFICER SAN ROQUE

YOU ARE APPOINTED TEMPORARY MASTER. FURTHER INSTRUCTIONS ON SHIP'S ARRIVAL SYDNEY. *Sotflot.*"

"MASTER SAN ROQUE

SYDNEY AGENTS ARRANGING DISPATCH DOCTOR MEET SHIP FREMANTLE. MEANWHILE DOCTOR ON PASSENGER LIST FROM COLOMBO. MAKE SUITABLE ARRANGEMENTS. *Sotflot.*"

The new master of *San Roque* sat in the Captain's cabin, gloomily studying the two radio messages on the Captain's desk. So Naples were intending to supply neither a new captain nor another doctor until it was quite convenient for them to do so. It would cost money to fly either or both to Colombo, and the owner's almost patholigical loathing of spending money upon which there was no likelihood of a substantial return was a byword throughout the Line. For a moment Serafino seemed to see that heavy-shouldered, bulky figure behind the big desk in his comfortable Naples office, to hear the growling voice speaking in its perpetual tone of irritable contempt: "Let Ciccolanti take her on to Sydney. What does he think a master's ticket is for? And can't the young fool *see* he's got a doctor on board?"

So now—he shrugged helplessly—he must take *San Roque* to Sydney as her master. The thought filled him with a resentful, despairing gloom. It was not the navigational work that he feared—he understood that well enough and would have done most of it himself in any case; it was the responsibility. As master, he would be responsible for literally everything, from the amount of cotton waste which the engineers used to clean their oily hands to the making up, in so far as it proved possible, of the delayed ship's schedule. There was nothing now that could not be laid upon his narrow shoulders—and nothing that would not be. Less than a month ago he had been Second Officer on the small, single-screw *San Ramòn*. That was still his official position and he was being paid accordingly. He could still afford to use a new razor blade only once a week, still possessed only four white shirts and three pairs of trousers. But now, if he made a single mistake between here and Sydney—and if that mistake cost the owner a few thousand lire—he would probably be dismissed. Then he would find himself back in Naples, trudging up and down the Via de Pretis from one shipping office to another without a reference and with very little hope. . . . And he could not afford to wait for jobs—not with the family in the Vic' Re Galantuomo depending on him for almost everything. It was quite possible that in another six months he would be kneeling on the well-deck of some old freighter, chipping rust from her ironwork under the supervision of someone like Petelli. All because he was now acting master of *San Roque*.

He smiled wryly, suddenly remembering the books he had once seen in Japheth Wendlandt's cabin in La Guayra—books on self-improvement, success, *How to Get On*. He had opened one at random. "*Never shun Responsibility, attempt rather to acquire as much as possible.*" . . . "This word 'shun'?

How does it mean?" "'Shun'? Oh, I guess it means to avoid—not to want. The guy's saying that you always got to *want* responsible jobs, see? So you can prove yourself and all." Japheth, it was evident, took those books quite seriously; probably all his countrymen did. Those vigorous maxims enshrined important basic American beliefs. If Japheth saw a chance to take command of the *Sanvac Stronghold* he would seize it joyfully—and if he ran her aground or into collision, if she caught fire and had to be abandoned or if her crew mutinied and deserted *en masse* at a foreign port, he would not be unduly perturbed, for his conscience would be clear; he would have followed the advice of his self-help books.

Two or three muffled blows, as of someone attempting to open a jammed door, came to Serafino from across the short corridor of the Captain's quarters. That was Gil. He had been locked in his cabin ever since the arrival of the ship at dawn two days ago. Colombo was Gil's last chance to escape before being handed over to the O'Connell Street agents, and Serafino was grimly determined that he should not be allowed to avail himself of it. Whatever happened, Gil should make the full journey. It had been obvious at Aden that Onestinghel, the owner's old friend, had realised that even he would not easily be forgiven if he failed to hand Gil over at Sydney, and it was equally obvious to *San Roque's* new master that he himself could hope for no forgiveness at all in such an eventuality. His future in the Flotta Soto depended on getting both the owner's ship and the owner's son to Australia.

Serafino sighed angrily. To him Gil was a problem which it was impossible to solve—a continual threat to himself, and therefore to the family back at Naples. It might perhaps be possible, given sufficient resources, to serve both God and Mammon, but it was undoubtedly impossible to serve both Don Ildefonso and Gil: their desires were contradictory. Yet contradictory only for the moment—that was easy to guess. Sooner or later Don Ildefonso would forgive his son, recall him from O'Connell Street and establish him in the Naples office. And on that day anyone against whom Gil bore any sort of grudge had better look for another job. Gil was a Spaniard, and Spaniards, as Serafino had noticed during his ten years at sea, were implacable about paying off debts of revenge. Since those five minutes in this cabin with Onestinghel when, bloody and bruised, he had brought Gil back from the Aden police-station, they had avoided each other, looking away with uneasy embarrassment if they met by chance on deck or in the ship's corridors. At least, Serafino corrected himself, *he* had been embarrassed; Gil had seemed to find such encounters a cause for amusement, generally smiling in his odd sidelong way, and once stopping as if he would have said something if Serafino had not hurried past.

But it was different now. You could not lock somebody up in his cabin, even if it was a large, comfortable, self-contained state room, for over forty-eight hours and expect him to be pleased. Petelli, under the threat of immediate dismissal in case of failure, had been made responsible for Gil's safe-keeping, but now that the ship was about to leave . . .

Serafino telephoned for the *Capitano d'armi* and when he came, sullen and scowling, told him to unlock Gil's door. "Signor Ciccolanti, Don Gil has threatened to have me dismissed because of this! It is your fault if this happens to me."

"It will not happen."

"It was not work which I engaged for, signore. Captain Onestinghel dealt with this matter himself. He did not depute others to——"

"Oh, go away, Petelli, and let him out! Kiss his hand and tell him you are his slave for ever. Doubtless he'll forgive you."

"This is no joking matter," grumbled Petelli obstinately, but he went out and Serafino heard him unlocking Gil's door across the corridor.

Five seconds later Gil was in the Captain's cabin. He stood, hands in pockets, in the doorway, staring down at Serafino sitting at the Captain's desk. "So you decided to let me out at last?" His voice held a quiet menace, sounding a far more ominous note than the sudden harsh rage in the cell at Aden.

Serafino got to his feet. "Listen, Don Gil—I mean Signor Sotomayor. I——"

"You might as well call me Gil, might you not? As you treat me with no respect in any other way, it would seem to be natural."

Serafino swallowed. "You make things very difficult for me," he said weakly.

"Do I?" Gil approached him, hands still in pockets but bunched tightly into fists which could be seen clearly through the tight cloth. "Do I, then?" His eyes were narrowed with glinting anger. "I think you will find that I shall make them much more difficult in future."

Serafino took a step backwards and Gil followed implacably. So it was to come to that again, was it? And this time there was no one beyond the door to rush in with help. Desperately he said, "I have to do what your father wishes—that is what I am paid for!"

"He gave orders that I was to be treated as a first-class passenger. You haven't locked all *them* up, have you?"

Another step back and again Gil came forward. "What will my father, of whom you are so frightened, say when he is told about this?"

Serafino found the wall against his back. "He—he will have to be told also why it was done. What happened at Aden."

Gil's face became suddenly convulsed with rage. He whipped his hands from his pockets and seized Serafino by the elbows, pinning him against the wall. "You're not to mention that—ever! That was your fault. And now you have meddled with me again! Don't you understand, you stupid little fool, that this whole affair is a private one! Onestinghel—yes, that was different. He was an old family friend and he had personal instructions from my father. But you! *You!* He wouldn't offer you a cigarette—let alone give you a personal instruction! If you knew what he thinks of his junior officers! 'I take them because no one else wants them and therefore they're cheap. But I never give them any real responsibility.' Yes, I've heard him say that often! That's why he pays you about half what you'd get—or, rather what you *couldn't* get—on Italian ships. That's why none of you is ever made a captain—they all come from other Lines. And now, because Onestinghel's dead—and you didn't do much to save him, as far as I can see—you don't imagine you're going to take over, do you? He'll fly another captain out and——"

"Go and look on the desk."

"What?"

"Go and look. That radio signal. I *am* captain—at least until Sydney." Serafino lay back against the wall, his heart thudding with a sick fury of mingled rage and fear and shame. What Gil had told him was quite true—everyone knew it. The Owner never attempted to disguise his contempt for his officers. But to *say* it out loud—that was something else. Thickly he said, "You see? I am captain."

Gil threw down the radio form. "Well—God help us all! We need a priest on board now, rather than a doctor!" He laughed with angry contempt. "Do you seriously think you can take this ship to Sydney?"

Serafino breathed deeply. When he spoke his voice was bitter with hate. "Of course I can. I've got a master's ticket. What do you suppose I was learning this job for, all the time while you were chloroforming little girls and . . ." Then they were on the floor and rolling over and over, but the smashing blows which had thudded into him at Aden did not come, and it seemed to Serafino, his chest pressed hard to Gil's, that Gil was laughing.

In less than thirty seconds he was once more pinned helplessly—this time to the floor. Gil sat on his thighs, panting, grinning triumphantly. "Now—apologise! Go on! Or I'll do what you did to me at Aden!" He lifted a fist poised to strike downwards. And suddenly, looking up into that hot, dark face with its slightly tilted eyes and wide, oddly unconfident grin, Serafino was standing again in the Vic' Re Galantuomo, staring at the poster advertising the Modena Acadamy on the wall beside Dr. Gallifuoco's door. And from the crudely overdrawn picture the same hot, southern features, the same, sly, prurient leer touched with something more—an uneasy mockery, a troubled knowledge—stared down at him. Suddenly all his fear of Gil, all his anger and shame at what Gil had said, left him. Gil could no more be taken seriously than that erratically inspired picture, and, like it, he lost all value, all importance, except the most valuable importance of all, and became a human being. Serafino laughed. "All right, all right. I apologise, then." And as Gil shifted from his legs, he got quickly to his feet. "After all, if you *like* doing that sort of thing to children it's up to the police to stop you—not me. I quite realise that."

Gil grinned. His anger too seemed suddenly to have evaporated. "Listen, do you want a real beating-up? You shouldn't start fights, you're not big enough or strong enough." He spoke with amusement rather than malice and pulled a cigarette-case from his hip pocket. "Did the English bombs really do that to your foot?"

"Yes."

"So? You and Italy have a lot in common, you know. You're both small and not very strong, and you both start fights you can't possibly win. Then you get hurt and you don't like it."

"At least we don't go around murdering each other like the Spanish. Praying like saints and sharpening knives on the altar steps at the same time!" Serafino picked up his hat. "So now you are quite free again to go where you wish—on the ship."

"Thank you." Gil's voice was sardonic. "Are you not going to get out the brandy and drink to the hope that I behave better during the rest of the voyage?"

Serafino laughed and walked to the door. "I have to do what your father tells me. So, I think, do you. I agree that you have more reason to complain, but I do not care how you behave for the rest of the voyage. Short of jumping into the sea, there is no choice for you except to come to Australia. We leave now."

5

Serafino was still thinking of Gil as he mounted the ladder to the bridge. He was filled with the same queer mixture of relief and embarrassment and humiliation that he had felt at Aden when Gil had grinned at him over the brandy glasses in the Captain's cabin. To-day the pattern had been repeated—only without Onestinghel: his own fear of Gil and the consequences of Gil's enmity, the attempt at placation followed by the fierce physical attack (twice now he and Gil had rolled interlocked about a floor like urchins in a gutter, and his face reddened at the thought), and then Gil's sudden startling reversion to good humour and a sort of genially mocking forgiveness, as if he himself had been the victim rather than the aggressor. No, as Onestinghel had said, Gil was probably not bad-natured, merely quick-tempered and arrogant and with more than a full share of the insensitive brutality of the youthful rich who fear no one and consequently despise everyone. A year in prison, which, Serafino remembered sourly, several newspapers had suggested that Gil deserved, might have taught him some self-control.

He nodded briefly to the salutes of the bridge personnel, and forgot Gil in the business of giving the orders that would take *San Roque* on the last lap of her journey to Australia. It was a slightly overcast afternoon, with a strengthening breeze blowing from the south-west and an incoming tide. Since finishing oiling two days ago, *San Roque* had been anchored in the roadstead outside the harbour half a cable's length from the end of the mole, thus saving the extra harbour dues which the forty-eight hours' delay would otherwise have cost her owner. Now, as he gave the order to weigh anchors, Serafino glanced back across the harbour to the low grey-green shore and the grey-white of the town. Onestinghel lay there in the Catholic cemetery, had lain there since early yesterday morning. That shore, that town, that hot, dull, overcast sky—these were to be his last and permanent home. *San Roque's* foghorn blasted out its long, windy roar of departure; the strong breeze would carry that melancholy booming note back across the choppy sea to the town and out to the cemetery beyond, a quiet place of palms and ornate monuments and little patches of grass. Would he feel lonely there by himself when the grey, humid day faded into night and his ship, his last ship, was hull down over the horizon and driving on and on into the great southern ocean?

Turning, with a sick ache in his heart, Serafino acknowledged the report of anchors weighed, glanced round, saw Bressan looking at him with an odd, slight smile on his perpetually open mouth, and gave the order, " Half ahead on both engines." For a moment he thought the seaman at the telegraph was going to say something, but the man changed his mind and rang down the order to the engine-room. The ship vibrated to the commencing churn of the screws, and Serafino, moving to one side of the bridge, lifted his binoculars for a last look at the town. Onestinghel . . .

And then something, the odd sixth sense of the trained sailor made him lower the glasses. He frowned momentarily over the side. What was happening? The ship was not moving forward, although the engines were throbbing steadily—he could feel their vibrations under his feet. He glanced quickly aft. Yes, the sea was boiling whitely around the stern. Yet *San Roque* was—was moving backwards and sideways, while the mole, with which she had been parallel a minute ago, was now off her port quarter and growing steadily closer. He leapt back into the bridge. " Half *ahead—ahead*, I told you!"

" Signore!" The seaman at the telegraph stared unhappily and pointed to the big dial. The brass indicator stood at *Avanti—Mezza forza.* What in God's name were they up to down below? Serafino seized the telephone. "Engine-room—quick!"

"Engine-room here."

"Why aren't you obeying the bridge telegraph? I ordered half ahead on both engines!"

A puzzled pause. "But that is what we are giving you, signore. Half ahead on both turbines."

"You can't be!" Serafino heard his own usually deep voice rising in an exasperation that was approaching panic. Out of the corner of his eye he saw the end of the mole beginning to appear off the port beam; they were drifting obliquely but steadily towards it. "We're getting no *power*! We're moving *sideways*!"

"But that is impossible!"

"Give me Full Ahead—at once! Full Ahead on both engines!"

He turned, and with Bressan beside him, ran to the port bridge wing and looked back along the length of the ship, aware at the back of his mind of the crowded rails below him lined with faces. The ship's stern was barely fifty yards from the small sharp waves slapping the foot of the heavy stone wall of the mole. His heart contracted with fear. *Christ! What's happening? I don't understand what's happening!*

Then the white water below *San Roque's* stern increased into a wide carpet of milky, churning froth as the twin screws began to revolve at full speed. Now, surely—*surely* nothing could hold the ship back. But the extra power, the immense power that had recently driven the ship and her dying captain at twenty-two knots through the night towards Colombo, made no difference whatever. *San Roque,* shuddering and trembling under the enormous force of her twin turbines, continued to drift sideways and backwards towards the mole—blown leewards by the wind, sucked back by the tide.

The mole—*the mole.* In an agony of spirit such as he had never known before Serafino visualised the mole. The steep wall descending into the water and built upon a great shelving glacis of tumbled boulders which spread out to form a broad base on the sea bed. He could not risk a close approach to that rising mass of rocks—not with the screws in motion. One blow and a blade—perhaps an entire screw—would break clean off and then . . . Well, it wouldn't matter what happened then—not as far as he was concerned, at any rate. He would be back in Naples outside the employment exchange before *San Roque* was ready to continue her voyage. He was beating his hands on the bridge rail hard enough to break the bones, his mind a whirl of tortured, uncomprehending despair. He glanced back into the bridge —Malestroit, Gino, even, fantastically, Zocco from the engine-room, everyone staring at him with wide-eyed, frightened perplexity. Their livelihoods too might hang on his decisions of the next few seconds, for if *San Roque* was badly damaged Don Ildefonso was quite capable of dismissing every officer of both deck and engine-room.

Then, from somewhere deep within his subconscious memory, the blurred page of a textbook he must once have read as a cadet glimmered slowly up into focus: "*. . . in the days of sail a ship in this situation would be said to be 'in irons.' . . . To-day, under conditions of modern steam navigation . . . normally quite unknown . . . except in certain cases when a vessel equipped (which is not usual) with twin inturning screws. . . .*" He swung round to face Zocco. "The screws! The screws—are they in-turning ones? Quick!" His voice was almost a scream.

Pop-eyed, Zocco nodded wordlessly, then started to stammer, "*S-s-si, Signor C-Ciccolanti.* They are in——"

"Stop engines! Down with both bow anchors—quick!"

Everyone leapt to transmit the orders. Alone on the port bridge wing Serafino waited shivering, staring dully at the still approaching mole. Thirty yards—no, barely twenty-five. "*. . . not to attempt to get under way with both engines on an angled turn. . . .*" The threshing, boiling water at the ship's stern subsided slowly. "*. . . in these circumstances the action of each in-turning screw may nullify that of the other, thus, in fact, leaving the ship powerless. . . .*" Twenty yards. "*. . . and at the mercy of wind and tide. . . .*" The rocks would be climbing steeply in great jagged piles from the sea floor towards the wall. The sudden roar and rumble of the anchor chains. Fifteen yards. But yes, she held. Thank God, thank Christ, thank the Holy Virgin, she was holding!

Shakily he walked back to the bridge centre amidst an awed, frightened hush. Everyone was avoiding his eye. "Well——" with an enormous effort he tried to speak calmly —"we will try again. This time——" he glanced expressionlessly at Bressan—"with *one* engine."

Down in the vestibule Cavaliere Semprebon, turning back towards the counter, took the long cigarette-holder from his mouth and glanced at the crowd of interested passengers. "There was no danger—none at all, I assure you." He shrugged contemptuously. "It was merely that—well, evidently we have *two* apprentices on board: Pavanoli and the Chief Officer."

XIII

"Mad dogs and Englishmen go out in the midday Sun . . ." sang Noël Coward jauntily over the ship's amplifiers. This record had recently become a favourite of the steward in charge of the gramophone and, followed or preceded by another favourite—an Italian version of the Londonderry Air, it was to be heard several times each day and would probably continue to be so until its constant repitition grated on the Purser's ears and he ordered it to be laid aside.

Aft on "B" deck the British migrants looked up angrily and grumbled among themselves. They took the words of the song as a slight upon their nationality, a subtle mockery of them by the foreigners by whom they felt themselves to be surrounded. Since leaving Colombo three days before, their normal xenophobia had been deeply inflamed by the presence of—as Ron Hogben put it—"a collection of bleedin' Chinks an' Niggers up there in the first class!"

Such education as the British migrants had received or been able to comprehend had been the usual outdated mixture of Chauvinistic nationalism, historical half-truths and politically perverted geography which pass as "schooling" among the English proletariat. It had induced in them the firmly held belief that while all foreigners were their social inferiors, coloured people were so much more so as to be almost on an equal footing with domestic animals. Social inferiority could only be visibly estimated by degrees of poverty, and in this respect the Italian migrants, who were undoubtedly poorer than themselves, ran true to the expected form. It followed that the Malcolm-Bruces and Dr. Sessabandrian and his two small children should have been still poorer than the Italians —so poor that they would travel steerage down on the stern of " C " deck beside the kennel. But they were not. Though the Sinhalese family were probably of merely moderate means, the Malcolm-Bruces were plainly very rich indeed. All four, but particularly the two children in their early teens, had about them that peculiar gloss, that illusive but unmistakable patina which only the accustomed and unembarrassed use of wealth can give. This unsuitable affluence was apparent not merely in their excellent clothes and all the expensive teen-age toys—radios, cine-cameras, record-players and tape-recorders—with which the boy and his sister were surrounded, but in their voices and gestures, the confidence of their laughter, the nonchalant freedom of their movements.

To Hogben, to the Ampels, the Micklems, the Throsbys and the rest, this unholy combination of opulence and pale golden skins was as infuriating as it was unnatural. These people's lands had been taken by Britain, they were ordained to be for ever subject to the British rulers, to be coolies and sepoys—yet here they were, persons, as Mrs. Throsby indignantly put it, " not 'ardly fit to clean me shoes," up there on " A " deck, while their lords and masters were confined to the more restricted space of the tourist deck below.

" 'Course," said Ted Condron knowledgeably, " it wouldn't be allowed on a British boat. Now. On a British boat they'd be put somewhere down in the 'old—kep' in their place. Wouldn't make no difference 'ow much cash they 'ad—down they'd go in the 'old where they could eat with their fingers an' 'ave all their filthy 'abits without doin' other folk inconvenience, see? 'Course you can't expec' anyone to know 'ow to treat 'em proper on a foreign boat like this. It's only the English knows 'ow to treat blacks an' such. We got the experience, see? Like the Prime Minister says, we got the moral superiority an' the experience."

But beyond glowering up at " A " deck whenever a Malcolm-Bruce or a Sessabandrian appeared, there was nothing the British migrants could do about it until, on the morning of the second day out from Colombo, they found the four coloured children in the swimming-pool. This was too much to bear, for as it was one of the periods reserved for juveniles some of their own children were in the water as well. These were called out at once in tones of the deepest indignation. " Marleen! Lauren!" " Philip! Elizabeth! Come outer that immediate! *Immediate,* I say!" " Marleen —yer mother wants yer! Did'jer 'ear me! *Marleen Throsby* git outer that water or yer Dad'll give yer a 'idin'. None of yer to play with them darky kids ever, see?"

A deputation went at once to the vestibule and sought out the Purser, who listened with a certain mystification which he was at pains to conceal from Malpiero, nearby. " But I can assure you that these children you complain of are perfectly healthy. You are quite mistaken. They are not ill in any way and there is no danger to anyone."

" 'Tisn't that. We don't say they *is* ill. We says we don't want them in the pool with our kids, see? 'Snot *nice*—if you see what we mean. An' 'snot right, either—we bein' British an' they bein'—well, whatever they is."

Cavaliere Semprebon sighed vexedly. Apparently the British disliked bathing with foreigners—a peculiar national idiosyncrasy of which he had until now been unaware. " These children are of the first-class passengers," he said coldly. " They have every right to use the pool at the correct times."

" Then our kids can't use it."

" That is your own affair."

" Is it?" Mrs. Micklem thrust her huge bosom forward menacingly. " Is it, then? We paid our fares—well, the Governmint 'as, anyway—an' we got our rights. If you won't do anythin', then *we'll* 'ave to!"

" You can, of course——" began the Cavaliere haughtily, and then stopped abruptly. He had been about to suggest that they complain to the Captain before suddenly remembering that the Captain was dead. " I cannot argue further concerning the swimming-pool. I am too busy." He turned away from the counter, strode back to his office and shut the door firmly.

2

Armando Lodigianni was no longer the only passenger to find refuge from unwelcome company on the stern of " C " deck: Colonel Chelgrove had recently discovered the place and now made considerable use of it. The few square yards of roped-in space covered with deck machinery made a safe retreat from Paula, for they bore a notice forbidding entry to passengers and Paula had always possessed an almost Teutonic scrupulosity in such matters.

Paula was becoming more and more difficult as the voyage began to near its end. She had never quite got over the shock of meeting the Malcolm-Bruces; she seemed, despite his vehement denials, to believe that her brother had been playing a trick on her. "You must have had *some* idea, Perry! This Brigadier friend of yours—was he *really* white?"

"Of course he was! Tommy Malcolm-Bruce is just as British as you are. I tell you these people are not his relations!"

"But the name. They can't possibly be called Malcolm-Bruce if they're Chinese! Chinese have names like Wang and Chang."

And wearily he had tried to explain that many Straits Chinese had European names and European blood in their ancestry. Probably in this case the original ancestor had been some Scots soldier of the garrison in Victorian times. Probably, too, the name had not been hyphenated. A private Malcolm Bruce of the Camerons or Argylls had kept a Chinese girl, and had children by her who had taken his name. Despite later Chinese marriages, diluting their European blood to virtual extinction, the family had clung with typical Chinese tenacity to the name of their ancestor and their semi-mythological Scots descent; that was why both children wore those dreadful tartan ties at dinner. Mr. Malcolm-Bruce's Christian name was Torquil. It was very likely that he had equally well-to-do brothers and cousins called Andrew, Fergus and Wallace. "But they have no connection at all with *Tommy* Malcolm-Bruce, I assure you." Paula was not convinced and merely said that the whole thing was disgraceful, managing to imply that her brother bore at least some of the responsibility for the disgrace.

So that when, on the day after they left Colombo, Colonel Chelgrove had suggested that from Sydney onwards he would prefer to drop the military rank to which he had not been legally entitled for the past fourteen years and become plain Mister Chelgrove, there had been an outburst of fury which had exploded over his trembling head like a freak electric storm. Was he so utterly stupid, so spinelessly silly, so—so *wet* that he could not see that by jettisoning his title—which in any case he had earned before the war by regimental soldiering of a high order and by his literary work—he was tacitly *agreeing* with the decisions of the Court. And everyone knew—well, everyone with any sense knew—that the two trials had been gross miscarriages of justice. He was going to New Zealand as *Colonel* Chelgrove; let him make no mistake about that! Why, if the second Court had not obviously been suborned by his enemies he would have been reinstated like Dreyfus and promoted to the rank he would normally have achieved at his age. If Paula heard him mention that *wet* suggestion again she would make him take the rank of Brigadier, which was the very least he would have risen to if . . . Rather than suffer retrospective promotion at the hands of his sister, the Colonel had hurriedly agreed to retain his present title even unto death and, truthfully pleading a severe headache, had gone to his cabin to lie down.

But headaches did not last for ever, or even as long as Paula's rages, which fed continually upon her inflammable pride and smouldered dangerously near eruption for days on end. The only way to attain any peace or quiet, both of which the Colonel valued more highly than anything else in life, was to find a safely hidden retreat from his sister.

It was the sight of a small boy sitting beside the kennel beyond the roped-off area of the stern which first induced the Colonel, mooning dejectedly about the lower decks, to consider the possibility of a retreat behind some of those winches and tarpaulin-covered objects like the stumps of ventilators. He hung about a little longer, peered carefully over his shoulder to see that he was unobserved, and then climbed creakingly over the low ropes. The boy beside the kennel glanced up startled, rose quickly to his feet, smiling widely and placatingly. The Colonel nodded absently and strolling down to the stern rails peered over them at the wide wake of beaten, foaming water which spread away, subsiding slowly across the swell, almost to the horizon. From somewhere below on "E" deck a scullery-hand tipped a bin of kitchen refuse down a rubbish chute, and stale rolls, empty beer cans, grapefruit rinds and a fish crate tossed violently in the churning water and then spread out bobbing into the wake. The Colonel watched them with absorption. To what far lands back there over the horizon would they eventually drift? Lands of palms and steamy, bright jungle; of old, rather fusty clubs where electric fans rattled in the ceilings and *stenghas* were served at evening on long verandas—and where somewhere a short, bandy-legged skeleton with a broken neck lay grinning in a shallow grave. The Colonel had turned from the rail and seen Armando sitting down once more outside the kennel. He was glad the boy was nearby for he did not want to be quite alone—merely free from Paula.

He came to the stern of "C" deck several times after that.

He even fell into the habit of saying hallo to Armando and receiving a wide grin and a "*Buon' giorno, signore*" in return. They made a queer couple, the elderly, melancholy Englishman in his ancient Panama hat and old-fashioned tropical suit, and the over-deferential little Italian in his striped T-shirt and crumpled white shorts, as they wandered vaguely about the deck among the machinery, for Armando felt it wrong to sit down before the English signore and Colonel Chelgrove was often undecided where to sit. Generally, however, he lifted himself over the wooden pen that held the great stern hawsers and reclined across their coiled bulk. And, seeing him do so, Armando would resume his seat beside the kennel and soon, if there was a stern wind that day, a smell of peculiar fragrance would indicate to him that the Colonel had lit his big curved pipe. Armando liked the smell of the Colonel's tobacco and he used to sit and sniff the odd waft of scented smoke with pleasure.

One day, however, after a dreamy hour spent in the long, swaying reverie, the peculiar, tenuous thought sequences of youth that are part daydream and part planning, Armando sniffed and decided that the old Englishman must have changed his tobacco—this new sort smelt much more strongly and unpleasantly; it smelt, in fact, like burning rope. Armando rose curiously to his feet and looked round the kennel. The old man lay on the hawsers and he was obviously asleep; his mouth was open and his pipe had disappeared, though a rising cloud of faint blue smoke showed that it had not gone out. There were two red fire buckets near the kennel. Armando lifted one and, quickly dodging round the wooden pen, emptied its contents on to the smouldering glow that smoked and rustled among the bottom coils of rope. The sharp hiss and splutter of the extinguished fire woke the Colonel. For a moment he stared at Armando with frightened eyes. "What—what——?"

"Signore . . ." Armando leant over the wooden pen, dived a hand down amongst the wet coils and brought up the Colonel's charred pipe. "This. Make fire."

"Oh—oh, dear! Yes. I must have gone to sleep. Well, I hope no great harm's been done." Colonel Chelgrove got quickly off the pen and together with Armando stared gravely down at the heavy cables. But fortunately the boy's promptness had prevented any serious damage; near the floor of the pen two of the light cords which bound the great ropes in firm coils to iron rings in the deck had been burnt nearly through, but the stern cables themselves were undamaged. "Well, I don't think that's very bad. I don't think we need worry about that. No one's likely to notice, eh?"

Armando did not understand all the words but he realised their meaning completely and nodded agreement. Like the old Englishman, he valued his retreat on this part of the deck and had no wish to be turned off. "Well, well, you did quite rightly. Very well indeed." Colonel Chelgrove fumbled in his trouser pocket, searching vaguely for something to give this polite and helpful foreign boy.

Armando watched him with distress. It was wrong that this old man should try to give him money for what he had just done. In the garage people had often tipped him small amounts for his services and that was quite all right and in order; he was, after all, a tradesman in his own right; but it was humiliating to be offered money for something which had nothing to do with his work. If he had been Gino Pavanoli—whom he admired and envied and with whom, rather than Signor Bressan, he would have liked to have made friends—the Englishman would never have thought of giving him money. But he was too shy to say anything or even to walk away; he stood wriggling his shoulders self-consciously while Colonel Chelgrove fumbled endlessly in his pocket. But when at last he drew out his hand he held only a few loose keys and a safety pin. "H'mm—ha." He glanced from them to the crimson-faced Armando and flushed deeply in his turn. They were both horribly embarrassed and avoided looking at each other, and that afternoon when Colonel Chelgrove wandered down towards the stern of "C" deck and caught sight of a blue-and-white striped T-shirt beside the kennel, he gave a despondent, sighing grunt and turned away. Nor did he visit that part of the ship again.

3

Next morning Roger Lannfranc stood staring morosely at the Malcolm-Bruces' Cadillac, a tarpaulin-covered shape lashed securely on the forward end of "C" deck between the two modern electric-hydraulic cranes which, on *San Roque*, replaced the more usual old-fashioned derricks and donkey engines. Then he turned away and wandered slowly towards the stern. The oily, sickly smell of cooking was borne up to him from the deck below as he gazed over the rail at the endless expanse of blue-grey sea under the depressing, whitish equatorial sky. Yesterday they had crossed the line of the Equator, and now they were plunging deeper and deeper into the vast emptiness of the southern ocean. The sea itself seemed to be on a larger scale here, the slow swells which gently lifted *San Roque* and lowered her were immense—great rolling downs of water—and, as he watched, a huge flat shape like a monstrous black carpet flapped heavily out of one of them and fell back with an explosive crash in a sheet of spray—a giant manta. He waited, hoping that it would surface again, but it did not. It had come up to smash the sea lice from its leathery skin by that colossal belly-flop and was now flapping rhythmically downwards—down, down into the unimaginable depths. "Diving stations," muttered Roger with sardonic bitterness, remembering the blaring klaxon, the swift clamber through the hatch, the crowded control room. . . . "Stop main motors. Out engine clutches. . . ." The men at the hydroplanes carefully adjusting their wheels, guiding her down. . . .

"You see that?" demanded an excited voice behind him, and he turned to see Gino Pavanoli staring over the side in the direction from which the manta had risen. Roger, his cherished reverie broken, regarded the cadet with distaste. "Only a giant ray. Nothing to get in a flap about," he said dourly.

"Yes—ray," confirmed Gino exasperatingly. "For me it is the first time I see one ray so big."

"I expect it's the first time you've seen a lot of things."

"Oh, I have seen many, many things. I have been on the sea for nearly two years. In two—no three—months it will be two years I am on the sea!"

But Roger was not in the mood to find Italian naïvety in the least appealing. He stared Gino up and down coldly. "So I suppose you think you know enough to be a bloody admiral, eh?"

Gino's sallow olive face flushed slightly; he grinned with a sort of mocking insolence. "There is not admiral in this fleet. But why are you not admiral? You are so great hero of the *sottomarine*. For me, I think is better on the sea—under I do not wish." He turned and started to climb the steps to "B" deck, whistling nonchalantly.

Scowling, Roger walked on towards the stern. What that boy needed was a good dose of discipline. But he'd never get it, of course—not on an Italian-manned ship where youth, instead of something to be snubbed and corrected, was treated with an amused indulgence. At the moment he would be climbing up to the bridge—the bridge from which Roger, a mere passenger, was barred. Of course he would have no work of real importance there, just a few minor navigational chores for the other officers; nevertheless, he would be working as a sailor on a ship. And in front of the boy stretched a lifetime of such work. By the time he was Roger's own age he might well be a Chief Officer with the prospect of his own ship one day. With a sudden shock Roger realised that his envy of the other officers extended even to Gino, and he reddened with mortification. He, Lieut-Commander Lannfranc, R.N., to actually covet the life of a cadet on a foreign passenger ship!

He shrugged angrily, dismissing Gino from his mind. There were other, weightier matters to be considered. In about ten days *San Roque* would be docking in Sydney harbour, and before that time the struggle between himself and Bronwen over Mrs. Crambatch would have to be resolved. So far, despite Bronwen's hints, the old woman had not come forward with the offer of a position for him in her business. Yet sometimes she appeared to have such a suggestion under consideration. Bronwen, who as usual had everything worked out, was sure of this. "It's *you,* Roger! You're holding things up. Before Colombo she adored you. If only you'd gone on behaving nicely to her it would all have been fixed up by now. We'd have been going on to New Zealand and she would have found us a house in Dunedin and we'd have had everything. Honestly, I could have got *anything* out of her in time—a good car, and very probably a position for myself advising on the buying side—glass and silver and materials. And in due course if we'd made enough fuss of her I think it very likely that she would have made us her heirs—she's got no one else. In fifteen or twenty years we might have been really rich—*really* rich, Roger. If only you hadn't been so bloody sulky and stupid that day on Mount Lavinia. . . . Now she's starting to take up with the Chelgroves. She doesn't really like them because Paula Chelgrove's such a rude old snob, but at least they are going to New Zealand, I suppose. . . . But if you'll only pull yourself together we can still get her back—there's still time. Look, if only you'll *try* I'll promise to make her get you a motorboat or a yacht or something within twelve months. It's like having to bribe a child, I know, but . . ."

But he had not given any definite promise to "try." The thought of fifteen or twenty years spent making a fuss of an ageing, increasingly querulous and increasingly demanding old woman—an old woman who could, and certainly would, use their dependence upon her to blackmail them ruthlessly—was too horrifying to contemplate. He had tried to explain this to Bronwen and had reminded her of Mrs. Crambatch's swift change from cosy geniality to spiteful malice on the day her relic was lost, but he had only succeeded in bringing home to both of them the total divergence of their views on living. Both of them, of course, wanted "success." Both came from that great English upper middle-class which, rising to comparative affluence on the flood tide of the late industrial revolution, was now stranded, nostalgic and more or less impecunious, in the backwaters of the mid-twentieth century. For such people, brought up in the fading refulgence of a Golden Age now past, reared to accept dusty old beliefs and shop-soiled values stored lovingly in the mental attics of their families since 1910, life was bound to be difficult. Success, worldly success, could alone make tolerable the conditions of modern life which were so bewilderingly at variance with the imaginary ones that their upbringing had led them to expect. For such as they "success" meant either honours or riches; pessimists from birth, few would be sufficiently sanguine to hope for both. Roger wished honours—naval ones, of course—not only for themselves but for the life they would allow him to lead, the life of uniformed command and authority which he felt to be his due. His wife wanted wealth and felt that to be here. She considered that as Roger's ambitions—in any case childish ones—were now unattainable, he should discard them and join her in her single-minded determination to become rich.

"Of course she's a horrid old woman," she agreed. "Simply foul. But that's got nothing to do with it."

"But—fifteen or twenty *years* of her!"

"Well, you've got to work at something all that time, haven't you?" Bronwen would win, sullenly he saw that; for she was in a much stronger position than he was.

Climbing up aft on to "B" deck, he noticed that the swimming-pool was for once practically empty. Only the two little Sessabandrian boys swam gently round and round like well-behaved, skinny black frogs under the careful supervision of young Fiona Malcolm-Bruce. Roger, hands in pockets, was watching them moodily when an aggrieved voice at his elbow growled, "Took that pool right over, they 'as." And he turned to see a very large, red-faced man whose dirty flannel trousers were strained across a bulging belly.

"Those children, you mean?"

"Yers—them." The big man glanced at Roger and noticed the silk scarf he wore. "You bin in the Navy, then, mister?"

Roger nodded. "I've only been out of it a year."

" 'Ave you now? I was a matelot meself for a bit in the war. Long time ago that seems, don't it?"

"Were you?" Roger's voice quickened slightly with interest. "What ship were you on?"

"Weren't on no ship—not me." The man chuckled and his great stomach shook. "Issuin' stores and equipment at Davenport. Petty Officer 'Ogben I was them days." He shook his nearly bald head. "Ah, well, I might not done so bad for meself come I'd stayed in. Wouldn't be f—ing off to f—ing Australier, at any rate. I dunno." He grunted morosely and returned to the subject of the swimming-pool. "Just like bleedin' Port Said, it is. All we need 's a few pennies to chuck 'em, eh?"

Roger grinned. Hogben was hardly an attractive person to claim as an ex-colleague, but by now the Navy and everything to do with it had become sanctified to Roger, the background of the long serial story of the doings, actual and imaginary, of Lieut-Commander Lannfranc. He pulled a hand from his trouser pocket and displayed five pennies. "My last English ones. They may as well have them. Here!" The children in the pool looked up and Roger lobbed a coin between them. It sank, glimmering darkly in the clear water. "Go on—catch it as it goes down!" He threw another, and one of the little boys made a politely half-hearted attempt to catch it in the air. "No, no—as it *sinks*. You dive for it," Roger instructed, laughing, and threw in two more. Pink soles waved in the pale-green water, and one of the children appeared triumphantly on the surface, spluttering and holding up the coin. He lifted his arm to throw it back to Roger. "No, no—you keep it. Here! Try again."

"Put it in yer mouth," advised Hogben, grinning, when a high, furious voice cut in, "Athelstan! Edwin! What is it that you think you are doing? Give that man back his money at once! At once!" Roger looked up as a small, dark-skinned, thin-faced man in a neat tropical city suit came rapidly round the side of the pool. He was the father of the two children and his narrow, spectacled, bad-tempered face was a yellow-grey mask of distraught fury. He approached Roger, one trembling finger pointed in outraged accusation. "You, sir! Yes, you! How dare you! How *dare* you throw money to my children—*copper* money! You think they are beggars, do you? Diving children from a bumboat, perhaps? You think that I, their father, am a beggar? You are wrong! I am a very qualified man and of perfectly adequate financial position. You have chosen to deliberately insult me without any provocation whatever! I—I—I shall see the Captain! At once! I shall tell him——"

"Can't," said Hogben succinctly. "'E kicked the bucket 'fore you come aboard."

"Then—then, in that case I shall—I shall——"

"*Signor Dottore, scusi*——" They all turned to find Gino Pavanoli standing behind them. "The Chief Officer says his compliments. When it is convenient to you he would like, please, to speak with you in the Captain's cabin."

Dr. Sessabandrian glared at the cadet, his spectacles trembling on his thin, arched nose. "So? And what, pray, if it is *not* convenient?"

Gino smiled deprecatingly and opened his hands. "Then—when you are ready. It is for you."

But the Sinhalese was not easily placated. "I am not sure. Perhaps I will not trouble to see this man. Why should I, if I do not wish?"

"He says only when it is a good time for you."

"I do not know. I have just been criminally insulted. But never mind, you are only a boy and could not understand. Now go. You have delivered your message."

Gino went quickly. Dr. Sessabandrian's sneering, violent way of speaking had frightened and upset him. He had never been spoken to in that way before.

Nor had Roger. "Look here," he said, now at last able to get a word in, "I don't know what's biting you or who the hell you are, but nobody's insulted you or your children."

"'E's barmy, that's what it is," said Hogben. "Crazy as a shithouse rat, if you ask me." But Dr. Sessabandrian, turning his narrow back, took no notice of either of them. "Athelstan! Edwin! Get out of that water and go and dress. Immediately! And you are not to enter this place again under any circumstances!"

"Well," said Hogben loudly to Roger, "if *that's* so you can reckon you done a good day's work, mister. We're grateul—me and me mates. You got the worst ones out. Chinks s bad enough, but I can't stand niggers—makes me bleedin' lesh creep just to look at 'em. Come on down to our lace an' 'ave a wet. What say?"

4

Here—look at this!"

"I have seen enough."

"No—look!" Holding the wide photograph album open, Gil pushed it on to the desk in front of Serafino and pointed o a picture on the left-hand page. Six shaven-headed men in agged, tattered uniforms leant weakly against a wall, staring rom contorted faces at their severed hands which lay before hem on the trampled, blood-stained snow. Other soldiers, Cossacks by their dress, stood laughing beside a tree-stump hopping-block, and in their midst, holding a heavy butcher's leaver, was a slight, smiling, slender officer with high Kal-muck cheekbones and pale eyes.

Serafino shuddered and pushed the book away. "Why did e keep this sort of thing? No wonder he had bad dreams. couldn't sleep at all in a cabin with those books—even if hey were locked in a safe."

"I don't suppose he kept them in the safe all the time. He robably took them out and looked at them at night when he as alone." Gil shrugged. "Civil war—you see? It is like hat. All revenge and reprisals."

"But after forty years—to keep on wanting to remember!"

"He had a reason of his own. My father told me about ."

"I don't want to hear."

Gil grinned. "I wasn't going to tell you. It's a family ecret." He gazed round the big day cabin at the piles f books, clothes, papers, the two swords, the Cossack whip, he daggers and the beautiful old sporting-gun. Onestinghel ad been a man of few but impressive possessions. "I hink that's everything." He picked up one of the daggers, n ornate, heavily inlaid weapon from some tribal region f remotest Russia. "Here—you can keep this to remind ou of him. He probably used it for disembowelling his risoners." He laughed, seeing Serafino's expression of dis-gust. "No? Very well. I am going to take this pistol, though. I've always wanted one." He lifted a black auto-matic from the desk and unclipped the magazine.

There came a brief, sharp, single knock on the door and Dr. Sessabrandian entered the cluttered room, smoking a cheroot. He glanced round him coldly. "Well, I have, as it happens, been able to find time to visit you. But I have other things to do so I must ask you to be quick."

Serafino got to his feet. "*Dottore—Doctor Sessabandrian?*"

"Yes, yes. You know quite well who I am."

"This is Signor Sotomayor."

The doctor acknowledged Gil with a cold stare and briefes of nods. "Well——?"

"You like to sit down?"

"No."

Serafino glanced uncertainly at the dark, bad-tempered little Sinhalese. This interview, he felt, would not be easy. "I ask for you to come because we have on the ship no doctor."

Sessabandrian's narrow, arched brows rose a little. "No ship's doctor? But that is *most* improper! That is scandalous Why have you not?"

"It—one accident happens and he dies."

"So? And what, then, if a passenger becomes ill?"

Serafino glanced at Gil; after all, it was Gil's father who had made the suggestion. But Gil merely grinned and thrust the butt magazine back into the pistol.

"It is—is thought perhaps you, Doctor, will assist. W perhaps will make a—a adjustment." Serafino smiled un-happily. "You perhaps will like to make the voyage i position of doctor of this ship, not passenger?"

Dr. Sessabandrian stared at him for a long moment, the took his cheroot from his mouth and examined it silently At last he said slowly, "I think you are mad—unless you ar trying to be funny at my expense. If it is the latter, then I sha write to the ship's firm as soon as we land."

"*Signore Dottore,* I——"

"What else can I think except that you are mad or tryin to insult me, when you need a physician for your ship an ask for me, a well-known doctor of civil engineering on h way to an important international conference, to take th post? And as for your friend——" Dr. Sessabandrian pointe the inevitable, accusing brown forefinger at Gil—"if h does not put that pistol away he will undoubtedly shoot him-self—or worse, someone else. And having no medical ma aboard, it will probably be fatal. And now I have no more time to waste on either of you!"

5

Half an hour later Serafino, descending to his own cabin directly below the Captain's quarters, heard the sound of angry voices—Gino's and another's—lifted in accusation and protest at the end of the narrow corridor leading to the deck officers' rooms. Turning the corner, he came upon the cadet and the young Italian who was sometimes to be seen sitting by himself down on the stern of "C" deck by the kennel. Gino held the boy firmly by the arm, and at the sight of the Chief Officer he burst into excited denunciation. "Signor Ciccolanti—look! I was coming down to my cabin when I saw this—this little thief coming out of Signor Bressan's cabin with these!" Triumphantly he held up three packs of cigarettes. "When he saw me he tried to get them in his pockets but they wouldn't go. I saw him!"

Serafino, looked at the boy, saw that the dark eyes were full of angry tears. A Neapolitan all right—a *scugnizzio*, too, for all that his clothes were neat and clean. So now there was going to be trouble with the Italian migrants—as if he had not got enough on his hands as it was. "Well," he said wearily, "where did you get them?"

"From Signor Bressan—he *gave* them to me!" The voice, at once frightened and pleading, took him back to Naples—to his own childhood. In those days all the children had seemed to be involved in thefts and illegal dealings in cigarettes. "He gave them to you? All three packs?"

"Yes."

Gino laughed scornfully and Serafino shook his head. "No, that is not likely, I am afraid. These are cigarettes which we get specially cheap. It is forbidden to give them away. Also it is forbidden for you to be in this part of the ship."

"He did! He *did*! Because to-day I have written entirely out three correct English verbs. He bet me three packs I could not!"

Serafino and the cadet loked at each other blankly. "You mean Signor Bressan is teaching you English?"

"Yes."

"In his cabin?"

"Yes."

"Do you go there often?"

"Once every two days—sometimes more. Look, he's there now. Come and ask him."

"Certainly I will!" said Serafino grimly. Bressan—he had heard some odd things about Bressan; the name had not been entirely unfamiliar even before he joined *San Roque*. He turned, and followed by Gino who still held the boy's arm, went down the short corridor, knocked on Bressan's door and heard from within that peculiar light voice call "*Entrate!*"

Bressan put down a book and rose to his feet as they came in. In the confined space of the cabin he appeared taller and fitter than he was; he loomed above all three of them, and as his heavy-lidded eyes took in the situation, the blood slowly mounted to his flabby cheeks.

"Well?"

"Pavanoli found this boy coming out of your cabin with these." Serafino pointed to the packs of cigarettes. "He says you gave them to him."

"I did."

"That is forbidden."

"Possibly."

"He says he comes to your cabin and you teach him English."

Bressan lifted his eyes and glanced—with a total lack of expression—at the boy. "Does he?"

"Do you?"

"Why not?"

Gino gave a short, contemptuous laugh and the colour drained from Bressan's face, leaving it pale and yellow. He started to tremble slightly and his voice, when he spoke, was high and shaky. "I do not see that this is your affair—in any way!"

Serafino turned to the cadet. "All right, Gino, let him go. No—first put those cigarettes on the table." He jerked his head at Armando. "All right—get out of here. And you're not to come to this part of the ship ever again—you understand?"

"Yes."

"All right, then. You can go too, Gino."

The door closed, leaving him alone facing Bressan. The Second Officer said furiously, "Will you kindly stop meddling with my affairs! Who I have in my cabin is nothing to do with you. And if I give cigarettes away—well, everyone else sells them. You know that!"

"That's not the point. Can't you see you're playing with fire—taking up a boy like that. He's only got to get the idea of blackmailing you into his head and you're finished. I live in Naples. I know that sort and how it is with them. They are capable of anything."

Bressan picked up the cigarettes and, opening a locker, threw them inside.

"Yes. You may in general be right." His voice was coldly vicious; he had lost Gino for good, now. "I would not have your knowledge, I realise that. I was not brought up in the *bassifondi* of Naples among the gutter garbage and the pimps and the pickpockets. Therefore those are things which I do not know. None the less, I doubt if that boy was whelped and reared in quite such a wretched kennel as you! At least he seems to have had enough to eat and his manners are quite adequate."

Serafino disregarded him with an effort. "Listen, what I have told you is for your own good. And anyway, you are not to have him in here again. That is an order. If he is found with you again I shall write about it in my report to Naples."

"You are behaving like some filthy-minded Englishman!"

"And you are behaving like a fool! Can't you understand what people think about such 'friendships'—if that's what you call them? Couldn't you see what young Gino thought, just now?"

Bressan's normally drooping eyelids lifted suddenly, making him appear oddly pop-eyed. His high voice lifted almost to a shout. "All right! All right, then! I'm going to leave this ship at Sydney. I'll explain to the agents that you are impossible to work with and I'll write personally to Naples as well. They'll be interested to hear about the way *San Roque* left Colombo roads, won't they? And now get out of here! Go on—get out!"

XIV

Why did every deck officer the world over hope and live for the day when he would become a master—captain of his own ship? Even in one's first days as a shy little cadet, hardly able to distinguish bow from stern or port from starboard, one had one's secret, supremely confident dreams of the future, the day when in the newspaper sailing lists one's name would appear in brackets after the name of some ship. In those youthful days one seemed destined only for the biggest and best of liners: *Cristoforo Colombo* (Capt. S. Ciccolanti); *Marco Polo* (Capt. S. Ciccolanti); but even later, when one's ambitions assumed more reasonable proportions, it was towards the lodestar of captaincy that they unfailingly pointed. The dignity, the pay, the authority that went with a master's position; the comfortable quarters from which one delegated the dull routine of ship management to one's subordinates. Yes, that was how captaincy appeared as seen from below.

But it was not really like that at all, thought Serafino frowning uncomprehendingly at a routine fuel consumption report from Aafjes that lay on the desk before him. It was a compendium of every job afloat and most of those ashore. There was nothing which a captain was not expected to know and, when necessary, to do. God-like, he was supposed both by his owner above him and his crew below, to be infallible, and he could expect no understanding, mercy or sympathy if he failed them in any way. No wonder shipmasters were invariably elderly: a lifetime—two liftimes—would hardly be sufficient to acquire the necessary breadth and diversity of experience.

Three days ago there had been that business of Bressan and the Neapolitan boy. He had mishandled that badly. Onestinghel would have done much better—would have treated what was, after all, unimportant if unwise behaviour on the part of the Second Officer with the surest and lightest of corrective touches. While he himself—Serafino felt his face reddening at the remembrance—had behaved, as Bressan had said, like an Englishman. He had spoken in the sort of way that Lannfranc, the British naval throw-out, would have spoken to one of his officers in the circumstances. It was true, of course, that, unlike Onestinghel, he knew of what Neapolitans were capable and that he feared and distrusted them and had done so ever since the far-off day that his family had left Certaldo and moved south. Also, he had been worried and angry over the ridiculous interview with the Sinhalese engineer and the fact that *San Roque* still had no doctor aboard. Yet whatever excuses he might make, he knew that his conduct had been almost as grossly tactless and clumsy as Gino's—and that had been another mistake, for Gino should never have been allowed into Bressan's cabin, holding that wretched boy as if he were a policeman arresting a criminal! No wonder Bressan said he was intending to leave the ship after such treatment. And when Naples heard about that they would be very displeased, for it would not be easy to find a suitable replacement at Sydney in a hurry.

Now, here was another difficult case, and this time he had better try to handle it with some sense if he wanted to keep his job in the Flotta Soto. He glanced up at the tall, dark-haired mess-boy standing on the other side of the desk. "And how long has this been going on?"

"More or less since we left Naples, signore. Though—well, I think she had it in her mind soon after we left Southampton—before you came aboard, that is."

"Before I came aboard," repeated Serafino sardonically. "I see. Has she offered you money?"

"Yes."

"How much?"

"Twenty-five thousand."

"And you did not accept?" Serafino looked up, frowning. "Why not?"

"You don't know what she's like, signore. She's—she's——"

"Of course I don't know what she's like! It's you she's interested in, Cavagni—not me. I don't know what you're making such a fuss about, though. How old are you?"

"Nineteen."

"Well, what's wrong with you, then? Or are you so rich you don't want to earn an extra twenty-five thousand?"

Tino blushed a deep crimson. "You see, Signore Ciccolanti, I'm engaged and—and—well, it's not very nice, is it?"

"Isn't it? I would not know."

"I don't mean being engaged, signore," said Tino hurriedly. "I like that. I mean this happening now."

Serafino sighed irritably. He wished that this big, handsome fool of a boy would go to bed with McKenrick and earn his twenty-five thousand instead of creating trouble about it. It was what Onestinghel would certainly have suggested.

"Look, Cavagni. It wouldn't hurt you to oblige this woman, would it?"

Tino's face went sullen. "I won't. I don't want to. She is like a bitch on heat."

Serafino sighed again. "All right, then. Well, you say she's threatened you. How?"

" She says that if I will not—will not come to her to-night she will report that I have assaulted her and tried to—to force her."

" She said that!" Serafino's wide, thin grin spread slowly across his face and he shook his head wonderingly. Even Tino chuckled a little shamefacedly, but then they were both silent, both realising the extreme difficulties in which the execution of such a threat could place them.

" Do you think she meant it?"

" Oh, yes, Signor Ciccolanti—she meant it! She is terrible. She would do anything—anything at all!"

" I see." Serafino opened a drawer and took out Onestinghel's tiny portable typewriter. " I am going to put down what you have told me, Cavaliere. Then you will sign it in front of myself and Signor Malestroit and we will note the time. That is for safety." He paused, his light-golden eyebrows creased in a frown of concentration. " Yes—for safety. Then to-night I will come with you."

Tino looked astonished. " To her?"

" Yes. You report to me here at nine o'clock."

2

At five past nine that evening Flora McKenrick sat on the side of her bunk in the softly shaded light of the bedside lamp, longing to smoke a cigarette but refraining from doing so. She did not want either herself or the cabin to smell even faintly of tobacco smoke until Tino arrived. She had no idea whether Tino had taken her threat seriously—little idea, for that matter, whether she took it seriously herself. At moments she felt that she really would carry it out if he disappointed her again, at others she realised that it might do her almost as much harm as it would do him. Her position might be nearly as certainly lost as would be his job if the matter was sufficiently publicised—as it would be if she knew anything of the habits of the Australian Press. But Giselda, too, might perhaps be lost to him, and that would be revenge at its sweetest. The day after to-morrow was Tino's saint's day, and Giselda would be sending him the promised telegram.

" Dear, darling Tino, I love you for ever and ever "—something like that, probably. And he would beam over it and go all starry-eyed. Ugh! At the thought of Tino's girl in

Livorno waiting for his return, waiting confidently, complacently, for marriage and the big Italian bed and night after night in Tino's arms, she stiffened, felt the sweat break out under the thin silk dressing-gown which was all that she wore, and vowed to herself that somehow—whatever she had to say or do—she would put an end to *that* dream.

Yet if Tino came to-night she would make everything as pleasant for him as it had been unpleasant on that evening in the Canal. She had frightened him then, and hurt his odd, prudish adolescent vanity. To-night she would encourage him to sit and talk and smoke—she had cold beer ready for him, too; she knew he liked that. She would listen to descriptions of Livorno and his parents' house, and even of Giselda if she must. Then she would give him the four shirts she had bought at Colombo for his approaching saint's day, and later, the silver cigarette case. Then she would turn out the lights, despite her longing to look at him, and even when they were together in the bunk she would try to remember not to be impatient or demanding. When it was all over she would give him his fifteen pounds—God, what an expense that boy was!—and—and who could say? He might be quite happy to come back another night, if Giselda's stilted little love message did not make him go all chaste and virginal like some overgrown Boy Scout.

If only she had behaved that first time as she vowed she would behave to-night, she might have had several nights with Tino already. She caught her breath sharply at the thought. It had been her fault—coldly she knew that. She needed young men and she needed to dominate them; any other form of gratification seemed to her repellent and dull. Yet they could hardly be expected to enjoy the process; which, of course, was why she was prepared to pay so generously. But with Latins this, it seemed, might not. . . .

There was a light knock on the door and her heart leapt as she heard Tino's voice—low, a little frightened. "Signora?" Gladness—a blazing happiness—suddenly filled her, and she realised that she had not really expected Tino to come. Poor, frightened Tino! Dear, funny Tino, with his big shocked eyes and half-hearted smile! "Come in!" she called, aware of an unusual huskiness in her voice. But the door did not open. He could not have heard her for he said again, a little louder but still tentatively, "Signora?"

"Come in, Tino! I'm here. It's all right."

And the door opened, the main lights clicked on, and Ciccolanti was in the room with a blinking, hang-dog Tino beside him. She stared at him wordlessly for a long moment and he stared impassively back. His eyes, she noticed dully, were a lighter brown than Tino's, a flecked, tawny brown. At last with a slight jerk of his head towards the mess-boy, a jerk which made the gold badge and cap-strap on the high-fronted hat glitter and sparkle in the strong light, he said coldly, "This steward—he has told me what you say to him this morning." The deep, hard voice seemed full of menace, frightening her.

"I don't know what you're talking about," she said shakily. "You—you've no right to come in here like this. It was Tino who knocked."

"Yes." And now he grinned widely, humourlessly. "Yes, it was Tino. And it was Tino for which you wait, is it not?" He turned with brusque contempt to the scarlet-faced mess-boy beside him. "*Allora, Cavagni!*"

Swallowing painfully, his eyes on the floor, Tino stammered a short, set speech in English—a speech he had plainly learnt by heart. "Mees McKenrick. I ask to-day to be transfer' to the tourist-class work. I will be on this deck no more. I ask, please, you do not—not——" forgetting the word he shrugged helplessly—"not to me any more."

Then Ciccolanti's voice dryly: "You understand?"

And now the whole squalor of the scene suddenly came home to her. Tino standing there against the wall, blushing, stumbling over his shabby little prepared speech in which he had probably been tersely coached by this thin, small figure in white to whom everything had been secretly explained earlier in the day. Ciccolanti, coldly contemptuous, knowing all about her now—how much she had paid Tino, what she had made him do—everything. Armoured in the sour, resentful chastity of the sexually unattractive young male no less than in his officer's uniform, he stood there, aloof, bitter, condemning. If only she could have had him to herself for ten minutes! She was twice as big and strong as he. . . . She stared at him, her eyes wide with hate, and he asked again, carefully, "You understand?"

And then, since physical violence was out of the question, the dam of her fury burst into a cataract of words. "You filthy-minded, dirty little beast! You skinny, half-sized little rat-bag! What do you know about anything? You've never had a woman—and you never will. It's obvious that you couldn't, anyway. I've had boys like you in my class and

I know all the filthy, furtive games you get up to. I can tell by just looking at you the sort of things you do. I know." She stormed on in a choking diatribe of mixed sex and psychology, the ill-digested fruits of a great deal of miscellaneous reading in both subjects. That he probably understood none of it, that she was speaking much too fast for his limited comprehension of English, meant nothing to her. She went on and on, and somehow, in the detailing of the more obscene and unlikely sexual acts, she seemed to find relief for her agonising disappointment.

At last she paused for breath—and once more he grinned widely, mirthlessly. "Yes—now I understand. I think first Cavagni make trouble for nothing." He shook his head. "But no! He has, I understand now, much, much reason to complain. Now, signora, you will please let him alone. That is understood. So now—good evening."

3

Though the beautiful young partisan had recently undergone forty-eight hours of intensive interrogation at the hands of her sadistic captors, she was led into the giant radio station looking as if she had just emerged from an expensive beauty salon and was now at work modelling ski suits. In the circumstances it was hardly surprising that the monocled German colonel began to make evil insinuations concerning the possible sparing of the hero's life if she would be his. He went so far as actually to offer marriage, though how he imagined he was going to be able to keep the partisan in the extreme luxury to which she was obviously accustomed on anything less than a field-marshal's pay, was not apparent. A scornful rejection averted economic disaster, but threw the colonel into an icily insulted rage. He ordered executions all round, and wooden-faced firing-squads appeared suddenly among the towering electrical impedimenta. The partisan and her lover were straining against their chains for a last viscous kiss when, with a gay shout, the hero's best friend, at the head of an indefinite number of humorous cockney soldiers, rushed in among the generators to rectify the situation with all the hearty yet whimsical *élan* which the British believe their army officers to display on such occasions. The German colonel, attempting to escape through a stained-glass window, fell into a nameless but lethal piece of machinery and perished horribly; the great radio station was smashed to pieces with sledge hammers, and a droll sergeant placed a small Union Jack on top of the wreckage. Then everyone fled hilariously to a submarine waiting under a lamppost at the end of the driveway, where they linked arms with the bearded skipper, drank rum (the partisan, now disclosed as a W.A.A.F. officer, wrinkling her nose prettily), slapped one another on the back, and sang a comic song with patriotic fervour as the screen dimmed to blankness. *San Roque's* last British film, *Midnight Marauders*—or *Midnight Murderers,* as it had appeared in Malpiero's erratic spelling—was over, and as the lights went up in the long darkened saloon on "B" deck, chairs were pushed back and everyone rose blinking and made for the doors. The film had done little to dispel the gloomy boredom of six humid days on an empty, slow-heaving, grey-blue ocean. It had annoyed Roger Lannfranc by its wild inaccuracies in the submarine sequence; it had mystified Colonel Chelgrove who could not decide to which unfortunate regiment the humorous cockneys belonged; and the British migrants—most of whom had seen it years before—made loud and rudely sarcastic comments, thus annoying Mrs. Crambatch who otherwise would have enjoyed it immensely. But it was upon Flora McKenrick, who had been in a darkly sullen, vengeful rage since yesterday evening, that the film seemed to have had its greatest effect. When the lights went up she was still smiling broadly and had even forgotten to eat the bar of chocolate she had brought with her. So, finding it still in her hand, she looked around until she found the Ampel children engaged in breaking the back of a chair, and called them over and gave it to them.

Half an hour later Serafino, on the bridge, was listening to a ribald account of it from Malestroit when the telephone buzzed urgently behind them. Malestroit turned, still talking, and lifted it. ". . . So then this woman who, one must understand, belongs secretly to the female flying service and whose hips are independently sprung. . . . Yes, *Ponte Comando* . . . Why? . . . Well then, Petelli, *mon brave vieux*, why do you not stop them? For what do you suppose you are being paid? . . . Yes, yes, yes, I will tell him. Hold on." He turned to Serafino. "Petelli says there is trouble in one of the tourist dormitories between the British and the Italians."

"That is for him to deal with."

"Yes. But he thinks an officer should be there too. In fact, of course, he is frightened."

" Very well. I will go down."

The acrid smell of sweating male bodies mixed with tobacco smoke and the sharp odour of carbolic disinfectant from the nearby washroom greeted Serafino as he entered No. 2 dormitory on " D " deck a few minutes later. He hated these long low rooms with their packed rows of multiple-tiered bunks, their bare, steel-caged electric bulbs, forbidding lists of rules and soulless lack of privacy. A mixture of prison, chicken battery and filing system, designed to pack the maximum amount of human flesh into the minimum space, they negated the dignity of humanity as effectually as a seventeenth-century slaver's 'tween decks, and were, he considered, among the more heinous of the forbidding catalogue of sins which was alleged to burden the soul of Don Ildefonso Sotomayor. He agreed with Malestroit when the Third Officer suggested that the Owner deserved to spend eternity voyaging, like some unhappy Flying Dutchman, endlessly over a rough sea, and packed in one of his own dormitories with a crowd of seasick demons.

To-night the long room seemed hotter, noisier and smellier than ever. Serafino made his way over the piled suitcases, valises, tangled orange lifejackets and stacks of tattered magazines which cluttered the narrow spaces between the bunks. Among the growling snarls of angry male voices he heard Petelli's sharp "*Basta!*" and coming at last into the middle of the room, he found the Master at Arms gripping the wrist of a dark, thin, trembling Italian in singlet and jeans. On the floor lay a pearl-handled spring knife; Serafino bent quickly and picked it up. He looked round the crowd pressing between and through the tiers of bunks. As he had suspected, it was sharply divided into a large group of English, surly and muttering, and a smaller, stiller, tenser one of Italians. Well, they had not come to blows yet, at any rate, and the sole thing that could be said in favour of Don Ildefonso's dormitories was that they were very nearly impossible places in which to stage effective fights.

Petelli said quickly, " It is over a watch. The English say that one of these has stolen a watch."

" Which one? This one?"

" No, signore. That boy."

Serafino turned his head to see Armando kneeling on a bunk behind the owner of the knife. " What—you again?"

" No!" Armando's voice was shrill with fear and anger.

" I haven't stolen anything! We came back after the film and then this 'Ogben comes over and says——"

" Now, now, now." A heavy hand fell on Serafino's shoulder and pulled him round so that he stared up into a round, red moon of a face whose snub nose, bloodshot eyes and tiny mouth pursed above a roll of chins lent it the look of a sinister clown, an ogreish comedian who threw hand-grenades rather than custard pies. " Now, Mister Whatsit —you just stop listenin' to that jabber, see? You listen to me a minute." Serafino tried in vain to shake the hand from his shoulder, but the big fingers only tightened their hold more strongly. If he jerked away he would merely rip the epaulette from his shirt, leaving it in that heavy fist. Petelli did nothing; the English closed in behind their huge leader.

" It's this way, see. Ted Condron 'ere come in durin' the picture—wants to get somethin' from 'is case, see? An' 'e finds Armander near me bunk. Don't say nothin'. Kid don't seem to be doin' no 'arm, like. Nex' thing, when we come back I finds me watch is gone. Well, I mean to say —simple, isn't it?" Hogben rocked Serafino gently back and then pulled him forwards. When he spoke again his voice held an odd, grim geniality. " You speaks a bit of English, mister. I know you does. So now, just tell me—do you understand what I bin sayin'? 'Cos if you doesn't I'll say it all again—very slow, like. An' if you *still* doesn't catch on I'll say it again an' again—all night, see? 'Cos I'm goin' to 'ave me watch back an' you're stayin' 'ere until I does."

A man close to the one whom Petelli had been holding said urgently, " Signore, this Englishman has always hated our cousin—for no reason at all. He wants to start a fight. He has tried before but we have managed to avoid it. Now he is pretending this theft and we can do nothing except fight him. If we allow it to be thought that our cousin is a thief they will not allow him into Australia."

Serafino said rapidly, " If you fought him with that knife they would not allow you into the country, either. That is quite certain."

" Well, what——?"

" Let the *Capitan d'armi* search your cousin's things. Then, when nothing is found there can be no further trouble."

The Italians muttered angrily among themselves, and from the bunk Armando protested shrilly, " No, no, no! Why should I allow it? I tell you, Signor Ciccolanti, I have not got his miserable watch!"

"Then you need not worry if Petelli looks for it in your baggage," said Serafino coldly. He realised that the decision did not lie with the boy but with his older cousins. "Well——?"

For a long moment they hesitated. Then one of them shrugged his thin shoulders. "It is very wrong that such an accusation should be made, but—all right, I suppose so."

"No! No!" shouted Armando furiously, but he was completely disregarded. His cousins pulled his fibre suitcase and rucksack from under the bunk and, opening them, stood back.

Petelli knelt down and carefully, quickly, lifted out some folded shirts, a pair of workman's overalls, a pair of heavy boots—and there, upon three violently coloured silk ties and six packets of duty-free ship's cigarettes, lay two wrist-watches, one of ornate imitation gold, the other neater and smaller.

A sighing shudder went through the group of watching Italians and a roar of triumpuh came from Hogben and his friends. "Two f—ing watches!" "Which is yourn, Ron? An' where's 'e get them fags, eh?" "Dirty thievin' little bastard!"

"That there's mine—the big 'un." Hogben's voice was quiet, matter-of-fact and darkly sinister. "You like to give it back, Armander, eh? Or shall I come an' get it?"

Sensing the threat in that voice, Serafino snapped, "Give him the gold watch, Petelli—quickly!"

He turned to the shivering, white-faced Armando. "Now—this other watch. Whose is it?"

"Mine! And I did not take 'Ogben's. He must have put it there!"

"If this other watch is yours, why don't you wear it?"

Trapped, Armando stared blankly at the Chief Officer. "It's mine," he repeated, and started to sob.

Serafino looked at the boy's grim-faced cousins. "Is it his?"

"No."

"Very well. I'll take it and we will see if we can find the owner. Give it to me, Petelli."

"Well, now, mister——" Hogben's voice was eminently, ghoulishly reasonable—"nex' thing is, what we goin' to do—ain't it?"

"Not what *you* do. What *I* do. You are not the master of this ship."

"Never says I was, chum. But 'ave it your own way. I'll tell you what I'm goin' to do——"

"You are going to do nothing."

Hogben put his hands on his hips and stared down at Serafino from his full six feet six inches. In his small, hot eyes something mad seemed momentarily to flicker, and Serafino took a quick step back. Hogben's tiny mouth writhed into a pursed grin. "Keep your 'ead, boy. Nobody's goin' to 'it you. You ain't done nothin'—yet. But what I'm goin' to do—I'm goin' to wait till we gets to Aussie an' off this perishin' boat. Then I'm goin' to the coppers, see? I'm goin' to tell 'em all about it and let 'em deal with young Armander—if they allows 'im to land at all, that is. An' another thing: I'll be seein' me Union, too. I'm a good Union man an' always 'ave been, an' I'm goin' to ask them to make—make what's-it?—representations to the Government about this boat. It ain't good enough, this boat ain't, not for British workin' chaps. Not with Niggers an' Chinks in the first-class an' thieves all over the place. Me Union's got a lot of push—you'd be surprised. Come to that, you prob'ly *will* be. Prob'ly find yourself out of a job in a few weeks, cock. Meanwhile we're not 'avin' Armander in this room, see? You gotter lock 'im up so's our things is safe."

Very little of Hogben's English was comprehensible to Serafino, and, guessing that it was some sort of dialect, he gave up the struggle to understand more than a few words. This was only the second time during the voyage —during his life, for that matter—that he had been in any real contact with the English proletariat, and he was as shocked and appalled at the experience as are most foreigners. These people radiated evil. Fleetingly he remembered some words Onestinghel had once spoken: ". . . rain—rain and soot and cold fog and a heritage of sunless misery. . . ." He shuddered. Thank God he was an Italian and these were not his countrymen!

Then he turned to Petelli. "This boy can't stay in here any longer. They're quite capable of murdering him now. Take him and his baggage to the sick bay. Put him in the isolation berth—and if he wants to have his meals there, he can. It would be better if he did so, I think." He turned back to the Italians. "Now—you have only five more days before we reach Fremantle. It is not long. For your own sakes you must avoid fighting with these English." He paused, glancing from face to face among the sullen group before him. "The Australians *want* these English. They have a scheme called 'Bring out a Briton' under which they import them, but it is said that it could more properly be termed 'Keep out an Italian.' You will receive no sympathy from Australia if you damage one of these apparently so desirable animals before it is unloaded. So be careful!"

4

Had it not been for the presence on board of the Malcolm-Bruces, Cavaliere Semprebon might well have cancelled the Gala Dance which he had promised earlier in the voyage to Mrs. Crambatch. She had been insistent, as she always was in matters concerning her own pleasure. "They have them on the P. & O. A voyage isn't a voyage without a Gala Dance, if you see what I mean, Mr. Semprebon."

He had agreed with her, of course, and despite his knowledge of the Owner's dislike of shipboard festivities, he had allowed himself to be persuaded. Together they had settled down like two elderly and rather greedy children to plan the dinner menu.

But that had been nearly a fortnight ago and things were very different now. Mrs. Crambatch—he had still not got around to calling her Vera—had shown herself to be gluttonous, bad-tempered and spiteful; worse, she was undoubtedly possessed of all the narrow vulgarity of the colonial-bred *petit bourgeoisie*. It was doubtful whether a jobless, impecunious retirement to Mafalda's cold stone cottage under the bleak Apennines would not in the long run prove a less intolerable fate than marriage to Vera Crambatch.

Also, the Cavaliere really did not think it proper to hold a Gala Dance during a voyage on which the Captain had died; it seemed disrespectful even to consider doing so. And there was an unpleasant gloom about the ship—a sense of brooding trouble impossible to pin-point, though often the focus seemed to be Ciccolanti. That had to be taken into consideration too. Spending so many of his working hours between the kitchens, the storerooms, the pantries and the vestibule, which, from a social viewpoint was the heart of the ship, the Purser knew far more of the moods of the passengers and the feelings of the crew—the general tone of the voyage—than the deck officers up on the bridge or the engineers, remote and uncaring, down in their oily depths. And here, halfway through the long haul between Ceylon and Western Australia, the atmosphere he sensed was such as to leave him profoundly thankful that in something less than five days *San Roque* would be at her berth beside Dalgety's big wool store ir Fremantle harbour.

It was natural that the death of the Captain should have thrown a dark shadow over the spirits of the crew, and, tc a lesser degree over those of the passengers. It was alsc quite usual for most of the latter to become a little tense and nervous as the end of the voyage came within sight They were about to start a new life in a far country among strangers; they were, or should be, bracing themselves for the effort, the struggles, and the unexpected but inevitable obstacles which must be overcome. Yet he sensed something more than depression among the crew or anxiety in the passengers—an air of furtive, smouldering anger, of glum vindictive malevolence which seemed to pervade all those parts of the ship to which his duties called him. The officers had fallen out among themselves and that naturally upset the crew, who even at the best of times were a tricky lot—the sort of human material one expected to find in a ship flying the red and blue stars of Panama. The falling out wa Ciccolanti's fault; he had it seemed, insulted Bressan in a most uncalled-for way, which was only what one migh have expected from an upstart Neapolitan guttersnipe. Cava liere Semprebon, a Roman born and more or less bred had no use at all for the concept of United Italy. Piedmon was full of vulgar, purse-proud industrialists, and as for th erstwhile Kingdom of the Two Sicilies—well, one coul only say that Ciccolanti was typical of what they produce down there. He would never make a captain, that youn man. Not only did the crew distrust him—and after tha shameful exhibition of incompetence when leaving Colomb who could blame them?—but the passengers seemed t detest him as well. He had taken to having his meals in th Captain's day cabin—strictly against the Owner's new regu lations—and it was amusing to listen to what was said abou him in the first-class saloon.

Yes, it was a thoroughly unhappy voyage, and if th Chief Officer was very largely to blame—well, that was point of interest, perhaps of use—but it made things n better. It seemed almost too late to do anything to rectif the situation now, but still—the Gala Dance should be giver Cavaliere Semprebon lived almost entirely for the social sid f his position, which, as a Purser in the Flotta Soto, was nfortunately a very small one. He sometimes daydreamed istfully of the big transatlantic liners with their never-ceasing ocktail-parties and dances—floating palaces throbbing with usic in which the sea was all but forgotten in an atmos- here of gilded champagne bubbles and an aroma of hothouse arnations and cigars. As Chief Purser on such a ship . . . e sighed and reluctantly returned to reality and the present -to *San Roque,* to the inadequate stores cut to their grudg- ng minimum by the Owner, to the ancient worn-out films paringly exhibited, a job lot of scratched, chipped gramo- hone records in a cardboard box, and always and wherever ne looked the vast panorama of the swaying ocean.

Alone, quite out of place, strayed apparently from one of is own wistful dreams of sea-going grandeur, were the alcolm-Bruces. He had heard Commander Lannfranc rumblingly telling his wife that the Malcolm-Bruces " stank f money." An odd and unpleasant expression, for why should ne deprecate wealth? It was true, though, that the Singapore amily smelt of riches. They moved about the ship in a de- ghtful aroma of expensive scent, excellent soap and hair il, like four benign golden deities visiting, for their own bscure purposes, their earthbound subjects. Cavaliere Sem- rebon had become deeply enamoured of the whole family lmost as soon as they had come aboard. As an Italian, he iewed all marks of wealth with pleasure and admiration rather an with the envious malice normally displayed by Anglo- axons on contemplating persons more affluent than them- elves; as a Roman gentleman, he appreciated the genial ourtesy of the parents and the cheerful good manners of the hildren; and in his official capacity he esteemed their lerance of what must have been a distinct lowering of their ormal living standards. Also, he noted with deep approval at wealth called to wealth, for though the Malcolm-Bruces ere unfailingly polite to all their fellow passengers, it was ith Gil Sotomayor that they seemed most at ease. It was nly because Mr. Malcolm-Bruce's heart was adversely affected y altitude and his doctors therefore forbade him to fly that e family were upon *San Roque,* which at the time happened be the quickest alternative means of reaching Australia. et since they were here something, however poor, must be one to entertain them.

So that evening—an evening which the Purser had earmarked ays ago on finding that it was Mrs. Crambatch's birthday

—the first-class saloon was decorated with streamers anc extra artificial flowers, and the kitchen staff made a heroic and not altogether unsuccessful attempt to produce a fairly adequate dinner. So anxious was Cavaliere Semprebor that everyone should be present that he went so far as tc write the Chief Officer a short note informing him of th dance and hoping rather pointedly that he would see fi to put in an appearance at dinner. It meant altering all the seating arrangements, but with Ciccolanti, seated as he wa now entitled to be in the centre of the Captain's table looking as common and badly dressed as ever, but, it mus be admitted, talking quite pleasantly with Countess Zapescu the Purser felt that the trouble had been worth it. His ow best moments were when Mrs. Crambatch actually went so fa as to compliment him upon the food. ("You see you *ca* produce it when you want to, you wicked man!") And whe at the end of the meal the large birthday cake he ha secretly caused to be made for her was ceremoniously carried in by Meschia, the fat, elderly chief steward. By a earlier arrangement of timing and signals it was the momen when the amplifiers should have softly relayed the Gigl recording of "*Santa Lucia,*" and it was a disappointment whe the seemingly inevitable "Mad dogs and Englishmen . . . flooded loudly into the dining-room. But Mrs. Crambatc was too touched to notice the music. "*Dear* Mr. Semprebon How *did* you know?"

"Ah, we pursers find out all things! There is no end to ou desire for information that may allow us to convenience ou passengers!"

"And look—all those little pink roses!"

"One for every year."

"But you couldn't have guessed my age. And you haven't There are far too few!"

"There are precisely forty, Mrs. Crambatch. I refuse t believe that you are a day older than that."

It was a triumphant touch and one, moreover, which seeme to please everyone else in the room. For a moment th rivalries and animosities which divided the group of officer and passengers seemed to fade and lose something of thei malice, and it was with a certain amused benignity that everyone watched Mrs. Crambatch cutting her cake, while Semprebone took the opportunity to beckon to the cadet. "Gin run down to the vestibule and get that fool of a stewar to put on some dance music. Select the records yourself if necessary."

"*Subito, signore.*" Even Gino, it seemed, was on his best behaviour this evening.

After dinner there was some rather laboured dancing in the first-class lounge. The Chief Officer, who naturally did not dance, had gone to take over on the bridge, leaving his colleagues to entertain the passengers as best they might. The Purser had ever managed to induce a couple of the engineer officers and Brighenti, the radio operator, to quit their own mess and take part. They were not the sort of people he would normally have invited—not *signorile*—but their presence added to the numbers. For himself, as he explained to Mrs. Crambatch with whom he was dancing, he had never been *amoreux des masses*. "To people of our age this modern idea that the lower orders are important must seem most absurd. Do you not agree?"

"Yes, indeed." Mrs. Crambatch attempted to forget that New Zealand was the only important member of the Commonwealth which still had a socialist government. "In Dunedin—well, of course we're broadminded. But still, we know what's what. There aren't many titled people among us, but there are some very old and respected families. Why, I have some friends who can trace their family tree almost as far back as the Battle of Waterloo! And though Leslie—that was my husband—started in quite a small way, he was one of Nature's gentlemen. Everybody said so."

The Cavaliere nodded gravely. "I have no doubt it was as you say. My own family, though no longer rich, have a most ancient descent. The name Semprebon, for example, comes from the Latin *Semper Bonus*—always good. In our case——" he smiled archly—" it refers to birth rather than behaviour, I am afraid."

"Oh, I'm sure it means both!"

"You are too kind. But none the less we have a certain—how does one say?—fastidiousness. For me to go among the plebeians, as I so often must in the course of my work, is a real distress." He shrugged sadly. "*Noblesse oblige*—yes, perhaps. Yet I often feel like retiring. I have a small country estate, of course, and——" The dance music stopped in the middle of a slow waltz and, coming to a halt, the Purser frowned whimsically. "Doubtless our young Gino has found another record which he prefers—these boys are so impatient!" He smiled at Paula Chelgrove who had been distastefully dancing with the Chief Engineer, whose breath this evening smelt still more strongly than usual of rum. "I am sure it will not be long before we may resume."

The couples stood about on the floor uncertainly and then Gino entered, looking hot and apologetic. He smiled sheepishly at the halted dancers. "I have some small trouble with electricals. Signor Brighenti will make it to go quickly."

The Purser sighed wearily; this was just the sort of thing one might expect to happen on a Panamanian ship. "All right, Gino. Signor Brighenti will, I am sure, accompany you and put things right. In future I advise you not to fiddle with machinery, however simple, of which you know nothing."

But five minutes in the vestibule examining the record-player in company with a puzzled Gino made Brighenti shake his head. "There's nothing wrong with it at all that I can find."

"The amplifiers?" suggested Gino doubtfully, but Brighenti rejected the idea at once. "They don't function from down here; they're connected up in the radio room. It might be the wiring." But further examination eliminated that possibility too. Gino looked at his watch. "We've been here nearly a quarter of an hour. I don't think the Cavaliere's going to be very pleased."

Brighenti, wiping his hands on a duster, grunted disgustedly. "Well, it must be a fault in the amplifier system after all. There's nothing else wrong. We'd better check from the radio room first, I suppose."

Four minutes later Serafino left the bridge on an urgent summons and came quickly down to the radio office. "What's the trouble, Brighenti? I can't come running all over the ship every time——" Then he drew in his breath in appalled wonder. "What in the name of God has happened here!" He stared from Brighenti's furious face to Gino's wide-eyed one, and from them round the ruined office. Every dial on the great front panel of the powerful transmitter had been shattered into fragments, every wire torn from its socket, every connection, handle, lever and button wrenched, battered and broken. Brighenti's typewriter lay upside down on the floor, spilling its entrails over the brown linoleum; even the novel he had been reading between calls was ripped from its binding. Silently, except for their heavy breathing, all three gazed upon the havoc, and then Gino, his face crimsoning with the effort to control a sudden hysterical surge of laughter, pointed upwards.

"L-look, *signori!* That film!" On the very top of the battered transmitter, sticking out of the uppermost broken dial, was a small paper Union Jack. "Those ch-children!"

5

Armando woke shivering from a dream in which Hogben had been pulling out his fingernails with a pair of garage pliers. For a long moment he crouched on the bunk motionless, aware only of the fact that somewhere on the ship Hogben moved, talked, thought. There was no sound in the isolation berth of the sick-bay except a slight creaking from one of the bulkheads and the soft, rhythmic throb of the turning screws far below. Had it not been for that reassuring steady engine pulsation he could have imagined the ship abandoned while he slept—by all except Hogben. Hogben would be coming slowly along the empty corridor now, taking his time, moving very quietly, a coil of rope in one hand and some surgical instruments in the other. . . . "'Cos we got to make sure you don't work too 'ard, Armander, see? So just to make certain you can't we'll cut out a muscle or two, say, in one of your arms. An' if your thumbs is gone too you won't be able to 'old anythin' proper. . . ." Once more Armando woke and this time he slid trembling from the bunk and, with breath held, tried the door. It was locked; he had locked it himself and kept it so at all times, only opening it when he heard the voice of the steward who brought his meals. But it was not a strong lock; a big man pushing from the outside could easily snap it. And it was a very simple lock; a little manipulation with a piece of bent wire could open the door easily and quite silently. Armando had been in the isolation berth nearly two days, but he had hardly slept at all except in short, dream-filled snatches which left him continually more exhausted and drew ever more narrowly the hysterical line between reality and hallucination. He dared not take his eyes off that door, and fought a desperate foggy battle with his straining nerves to stay awake.

When he had first been brought here by Petelli forty-eight hours—or weeks or months—ago, everything had been quite different. He had been frightened, certainly, but not of Hogben so much as of his cousins Emilio and Niccolo and of the future. And as well as fear there had been rage and shame and bitter resentment. It was obvious to him that

Condron, on Hogben's instructions, had hidden the big man's watch in his suitcase. He himself had only been passing Hogben's bunk—the quickest way out of the dormitory, but only used by him when Hogben's absence was certain—when Condron had come in and the planting of the watch must have been effected. Yet even so the trick might easily have failed. Had he not been frightened of the discovery of the second watch, the one Signor Bressan had given him the day they left Colombo, he would not have objected to the searching of his case, and then, even when Hogben's watch had been found, Emilio and Niccolo would probably have believed him and stood by him. That might have meant a fight, but a blade through the middle of Hogben's right hand—a Neapolitan tactic which either of the elder Lodigiannis could have been relied upon to use—would have quickly settled it, and prevented any further violence from Hogben for the rest of the voyage.

As it was, however, the circumstances had all been against him, and the first stretched back nearly two years when, a fourteen-year-old newly at work in his cousins' garage, he had taken a radio from an American car that was undergoing maintenance. He had heard that the Americans were so rich that they hardly noticed the loss of personal possessions; that they tacitly approved such thefts and never reported them because they received nearly twice the value of the stolen property from their insurance companies; that they were so accustomed to losing things in Naples that they were resigned to it as a normal occurrence. He had been rapidly disillusioned. The theft had been reported at once, Emilio had accused him, and he had broken down and confessed. The matter had been put right with considerable difficulty and he himself had been in the deepest disgrace for months afterwards. Neither Emilio nor Niccolo had ever really trusted him since that day, and the finding of the two watches had undoubtedly confirmed them in the belief that he was a born thief.

He could, he now supposed, have told everyone that the second watch had been given to him secretly by Bressan, but he realised immediately that no one would have believed him unless Bressan corroborated the story—and it was very possible that Bressan would not. Since that scene in the cabin with the Chief Officer and the cadet, Bressan was frightened and was avoiding him. The Second Officer had become something of an enigma to Armando over the past weeks. At the time of their first meeting by the kennel he had been in no doubt as to what sort of person Bressan was. The shyness, the sad kindliness, the odd, nervous giggle —one did not spend one's first sixteen years in Naples without learning the meaning of such signs. Yet later Bressan had shown no inclination towards any unusual or unpleasant behaviour. He had given his English lessons with a lethargic air of boredom which had concealed a surprising ability to teach, but mostly he had seemed to want Armando to talk and had sat slumped in his chair, listening, nodding, leading him on to tell of his life in Naples and his hopes of Australia. But since the affair of the cigarettes everything had stopped abruptly. Bressan had withdrawn with the suddenness of a snail when its horns are touched. It was obvious that as far as he was concerned the odd, unusual, enigmatic little affair was over. And somehow Armando had known that the Second Officer would never speak to him or of him again. Later, on that first evening in the isolation berth, when the first shock of fear and anger had left him, he had realised that what had occurred could not now be undone; no one would believe his denials and it was pointless to hope that they would. So there had remained the question of the future. Pacing to and fro in the narrow cabin, he had thought distractedly of the ship's imminent arrival in Australia. Would he be allowed to land? If so, would he not be deported again once Hogben went to the Australian police? Who would pay his fare back to Italy? Neither of his cousins —that was certain. Even if, in some way, he managed to stay, Emilio and Niccolo would have no more to do with him, for he had endangered their own position. And there was Hogben—he would be there too.

Hogben. He had not thought of him, save as the cause of what had happened, since he had entered this cabin an hour —two hours—before. But now the shiny, bald, pink head, the huge moon-face with its ridiculously tiny features, jolted back into his memory, filling him with dread. Hogben—Hogben, perhaps, had not yet finished with him. Perhaps this evening's affair had not been merely a single act of spiteful malice on Hogben's part, but a preliminary manœuvre —towards what end? He had stopped pacing the floor then and had turned the key in the door. The reassuring click of the brass ward had calmed him a little—sufficiently to realise how tired he was. He had lain down on the narrow bunk and within a matter of seconds, or so it seemed, the evening's events had begun to disintegrate into a swaying pattern of indifference. Sleep was closing over him when, with a painful jerk of exhausted nerves, he was awake again to see the brass handle of the door move gently round, to see the door itself shiver slightly as it was stealthily tested from without. The sweat prickled out all over his body and he lay utterly still, holding his breath—waiting. Once more the door shook slightly, then stilled. For what must have been half an hour he had lain motionless in the bright silence of the cabin, controlling his breathing, watching the door. He must have been dreaming after all, for surely nothing had happened, no one was there. Then, very softly, the door shook again, the handle turned, and quiet footsteps moved away down the corridor.

And from that moment he had begun to guess—slowly at first, faster later as sleeplessness and fear picked and pulled at his nerves—what Hogben intended. Hogben had demanded that he should be sent away by himself out of the dormitory. Hogben had probably realised that with no doctor he would be sent here—to the quietest and remotest part of the ship. Now Hogben had him trapped—and alone.

Throughout his life Armando had never spent a night by himself: in overcrowded Naples there had always been at least one and often several others sharing whatever room he slept in. Now, entirely alone for the first time, he fell rapidly yet unevenly into a state of despairing panic, enhanced to unnatural proportions by the unaccustomed isolation. During that first night he had lain staring at the door, hardly thinking: a small, terrified animal crouching in its burrow. With daylight, much of his fear had ebbed, leaving only a dull, uneasy despondency. After all, what could Hogben do? Murder him? That was ridiculous, surely. And probably last night's shaking of the door had taken place only in his own overwrought imagination. Now that it was daylight he would sleep. But he had not slept; he had found that he could not shut his eyes. All day he had lain or sat on the bunk doing nothing, hardly thinking, waiting emptily in a foggy confused dullness for something inevitable to happen. Footsteps had come and gone, but the door had remained motionless, unshaken.

But that night, his second in the isolation berth, he had slept. He had not wanted to, had not even, or so he thought felt sleepy, but he must have dozed for a few minutes, for when he awoke the cabin was in darkness. For a moment he had wondered where he was, and when realisation flooded back he had crossed quickly to the door and switched on the light. It had worked instantaneously, there had been no breakdown, then—no blown fuse. Yet he knew that he had left it burning when he had lain down. And the door was locked. He had started to sweat freely. Had someone—and there was only one possible person—unlocked the door while he was asleep and switched out the light—as a sort of ghastly warning that the lock was no longer a defence?

And then—surely he had *not* slept. He had sat on the bunk's edge, not even lying down. Yet suddenly he had been staring straight at Hogben standing in the open doorway, framed in blackness. And as suddenly he had been staring at the closed and locked door. But there had been no retreating footsteps this time.

When the surly steward brought his breakfast he had asked timidly to see the Chief Officer. Ciccolanti, it was said, came from Naples; perhaps he would do something for him, find another, safer cabin or even tell Hogben that his plans were known. But it was, of course, an act of extreme presumption on his own part to ask to see an officer at all, particularly the Master—just as if he was rich and a first-class passenger instead of a penniless migrant, and in disgrace at that. He was not in the least surprised when at lunch-time the steward told him that the Chief Officer was too busy at present but would try to find time to-morrow. He had nodded, smiling weakly, saying nothing, knowing with a horrified despair born of some dark inward knowledge that to-morrow would be too late.

And now evening was falling again. Once more a sombre fading of light was apparent over the endless blue-greyness of the ocean. It was occasionally possible, if one was very quick, to take one's eyes off the door and to glance out of the open scuttle for a second. It was a good thing to do to keep oneself awake. For now at last an overwhelming desire for sleep had descended stiflingly upon Armando. His eyelids were so swollen he could hardly keep them apart, and his whole body ached with weariness as if he had been working strenuously instead of sitting or lying on a bed. Worst of all, a part of his brain seemed numb: that part which thought and ordered his actions was no longer functioning properly. He could not think at all, but merely register impressions. He knew, for instance, that it was getting dark, that the sky was a lower, deeper pearly-white than it had been before, the sea a deeper, duller pewter. There was something one did when it became dark—what was it? He could not remember. He sat staring at his upturned hands on his knees, trying to think, and then, slowly, laboriously raising his eyes a little, he saw that the door was different. How? He was only looking at the bottom, but it seemed—a pair of legs. He jerked his head upright. Hogben loomed in the dusk, filling the open doorway, motionless, staring.

Then Armando was standing on the bunk, trying to scream but knowing that no sound came from his open mouth because there was no breath in his lungs to make it. He felt something hard pressing into his back—the brass edge of the porthole. It was the only way out. He did not pause to think at all, there was no time. He bent, thrust his head and shoulders through, and was falling before his exhausted mind could tell him what he had done. He awoke fully for a brief second before hitting the water—a second of passionate relief in which he knew he was free—before being grasped, spun round, sucked down and thrust into the beating, churning whirlpool of tortured water under *San Roque's* stern.

XV

All that night the wind, which had risen at dusk, blew strongly, steadily and with increasing force—the south-east monsoon blowing out of the Pacific, out of the Islands, taking *San Roque* squarely on her port beam and making her pitch and roll uncomfortably as she wallowed over the great whale-backed swells. But by dawn, when Serafino came on to the bridge, it had dropped to little more than a gusty breeze laden with occasional squalls of thin rain. Malestroit, in a dark-blue raincoat and with drops of water glinting on the black peak of his cap, greeted him with a slightly ironic salute. No one had yet evolved a satisfactory method of dealing with Ciccolanti's new position. To be at once Master and temporary Chief Officer of *San Roque* while at the same time being Second Officer on that old tub *San Ramòn* was a complexity of rank too difficult for his present subordinates to resolve in terms of their own behaviour towards him.

"Well, so that is that. I thought two hours ago that we were going to experience quite a gale. The wind force at one moment was six and looked like rising higher. However,

I was wrong, it seems. A pity." Malestroit grinned. "I should like to have seen the effect on our British migrant passengers. What a *bouillabaisse de merde!*"

Serafino nodded absently; he was checking the barometer readings in the log and now he compared them to the glass. Falling. He turned and stared out at the dull pewter of the sky and the leaden green of the waves. Away beyond the port bow a big seabird hovered on wide wings, seeming to hang almost motionless, grey against the grey clouds. He recognised it as a Great Wandering Albatross and shivered slightly, remembering the old belief that these huge birds which swept endlessly and always alone over the tossing wastes of the vast southern oceans were supposed to be the souls of drowned sailors. "You may get your gale, I think. But I hope not. We have quite enough to contend with as it is."

But there was to be still more. Two hours later in the Captain's day cabin a worried Petelli was reporting that someone had gone overboard.

"That boy, signore. We cannot find him anywhere."

"You have searched properly?"

"Everywhere—crews' quarters and even down to the tank tops. As soon as we got the door of the isolation berth open I felt it was no good, though. The scuttle was wide open and had been so for hours. The bunk below it was drenched with water. Well, Signor Ciccolanti, who would keep their scuttle open during half a gale like we had last night? And another thing: the steward who brought his food tells me that he had been behaving more and more queerly. He seemed to be frightened all the time, Consolini says. Consolini is not at all an imaginative man, but he says that all yesterday the boy seemed terrified. You could almost smell the fear in the cabin, he says."

Serafino nodded sombrely. "Yes. Yes, he was frightened. He thought there was going to be trouble for him over that watch."

"Two watches," corrected Petelli.

"One. I found out that the second was a present from —from someone else. Even so . . . And he wanted to see me yesterday." Serafino's deep voice was bitter. "I should have gone, of course. I was going to-day. Now it is too late." There was silence for a long moment. Then, without looking up, he said, "All right, Petelli. Do what you can to keep the matter quiet. And search once more, very thoroughly. After that I will have to tell his relations."

"Very good, signore."

But for nearly ten minutes after Petelli had left the cabin Serafino sat motionless, staring down at the desk before him. Onestinghel's desk. Onestinghel's big blotter, ivory paper-knife and pen-tray. If he had propped one of those old medical books in front of him . . . Tomei would have said, "All right, signore, he's unconscious now" . . . a controlled hand cutting firmly . . . eyes on the big diagram . . . Perhaps he could have done it—crudely, clumsily, but done it. It would have been very dangerous, yet the human body was more toughly tenacious of life than most. But he had not done it and therefore Onestinghel had died. And now this boy. Consolini had said, "He wants to see you, Signor Ciccolanti."

"What for?"

"I don't know."

"Well, I'm busy. I cannot possibly see him to-day. Perhaps to-morrow. . . ."

And now it was to-morrow and there was no one to see. Twice death had waited patiently for him to intervene between itself and its victim—given him every chance to do so—and twice he had failed to grasp the opportunity. A grave in a Colombo cemetery, a small body sinking slowly down into the black depths—these were the results of his failure. And both deaths had been horrible. The first a gasping defeat under agonising pain; the second a lonely, terrified act of hopeless despair. Officially neither death could be laid at his door, yet he would be implicitly blamed for both—and with justice, for he could have prevented either had he tried to do so. Guilt weighed so heavily upon him that his narrow shoulders sagged as if it was a physical burden that lay across them. With an effort he turned his mind to other matters, matters for which he could be held openly responsible and certainly would be Bressan's impending resignation at Sydney, for instance. *San Roque* was already being run on a diminished staff of deck officers, but it was a strain on everyone and meant treating young Gino as a fully qualified watch-keeping officer which he was not. Once Bressan left it would be impossible to take *San Roque* to sea without a replacement, and satisfactory replacements in foreign ports were neither easy to find nor cheap to employ.

Then there was the damage to the radio room. Fortunately this had proved, on careful examination, to be less extensive than had appeared at first sight. But it was bad enough. Both the main radio and the emergency set had been put out of action, though Brighenti said he could probably have the latter working again before they reached Fremantle. The costs of the damage had not yet been totalled up, but they would obviously run into a large sum. And of course it was quite impossible to pin the crime on to the Ampel children; practically every English tourist-class passenger was prepared to swear to an unshakable alibi for them, and unluckily no member of the crew had seen them enter or leave the radio room. Serafino had questioned them—a useless and humiliating undertaking but one which in view of the Owner's imminent wrath he had known he must perform. For a moment he saw again those three simian faces, either empty with an evil pretence of uncomprehending innocence or crinkled and contorted into shrill, foul-mouthed denial. And, always at hand, the parents. "You mind what you say, mister! . . . Libel, that's what it is. Defermashun of character! . . . Yes, we know 'ow it is! You thinks 'cos we're workin' folks you c'n take advantage, don'cher? Well, you'd better watch your f—ing step, mister! We c'n go to law just as quick as anybody else. An' we will, too! . . . Libellin' our kids—that's what it is!"

Then this Hogben, it seemed, was going to complain about *San Roque* to his union. Serafino had little idea of the power of British trade unions, but Malestroit who, as a cadet, had touched continually at British ports, had explained their supreme importance in that country. "They are thinly disguised semi-Communist organisations. I found them a most interesting study. You must understand that the English worker has a completely split mind on this matter of Communism. He strongly desires it for the opportunities of loot which it offers and because he is, of all persons, the most bitter and malignant, hating greatly that anyone should have any more than he himself possesses. Yet he has discovered that applied Communism means, among other things, hard work and discipline, both of which are, to him, the greatest evils in the world. He has therefore shown the so famous English spirit of compromise by taking the parts of Communist doctrine which please him and disregarding the ones that do not. This is socialism as the English understand it. Of course it does not work, but then neither does the English worker. Instead, the country lives upon what I believe it calls 'invisible exports' or 'intangible assets'—terms which in practice appear to mean the cheap labour of other peoples and loans from America. Then also they have a system called 'Imperial Preference' by which they acquire the produce of their own empire for next to nothing Oh, yes, my friend! The English manage very well without working, as I have seen. And the trade unions of England are there to regulate these proceedings—and they are most powerful. You have seen Hogben. I have seen Hogben. These trades unions are Hogben's multiplied many millions of times."

It was a deeply unattractive thought, but Malestroit was almost certainly right: he had been there, he spoke the language, he knew. In that case some sort of representations against the Flotta Soto were going to be made at Government level, and Don Ildefonso would perhaps be forced to spend more of his hoarded money to keep his ships on the Australian run. For that, too, he would certainly blame the temporary master of *San Roque*.

Bressan—the radio—Hogben's union. There was no hope: he was certain to be dismissed. This voyage, his first as master of a ship, would also be his last as a mercantile officer. For Don Ildefonso never gave references or testimonials to dismissed staff; he knew it was unnecessary, for if they were not good enough for the Flotta Soto it was quite certain that no other Line would employ them.

Bowed over the big desk, staring down gaunt-faced at the blotter under his hands, he saw Naples in October—it would be October when they got back—and winter coming on and nothing to do and the streets crowded with workless. A cold wind in the Vic' Re Galantuomo—thin grey rain and the roof leaking. They would have to give up the fourth room—the only one in which nobody slept and in which the cooking was done—but that would be only the first step of the journey downwards into the hungry, dirty poverty of Naples which lurked perpetually, a dark shadow of fear at the back of his mind. Yet greater than that fear was his despairing sorrow at losing the sea and the sailor's life to which he had escaped from the city ten years ago. If he left the ship at Sydney, could he perhaps find a third mate's berth on a coaster—and later move back to the ocean service? But it would be too risky, for what would happen to his family if he failed and could not get back to them? For the family were in Naples, they belonged to the city and, Italian that he was, he knew he could never desert them.

Back on the bridge half an hour later he found Malestroit nd Gino. The cadet, flushed with excitement and pleasure, vas arguing hotly. "It was, it was! If it was not, then what vas it? You saw it too."

"Gino," said Malestroit, this time deciding not to salute he Chief Officer, "has just seen a sea serpent."

"Yes, truly I have! We both saw it."

Serafino's wide mouth broke into its accustomed humour-ess grin. "So?" He went over to the log on the chart table nd the grin faded. "Gino! Did you put this in: 'Sea-erpent sighted one hundred metres off starboard bow?'"

"*Si, signore*. It was so close—and so big! If it had sur-aced dead in front of us we would have collided."

"You are not to do this sort of thing! You're seventeen, ren't you? It is time you started to behave like a respon-ible person. What do you suppose people will think when they ead this?"

"What people always think," remarked Malestroit dryly, when sailors talk of these things. I saw it myself, however. nd, as you see, I am quite sober."

"*What* did you see?"

The Third Officer shrugged. "I do not know what it was. omething lifted out of the swell and curved very slowly in gain. It was the back of some sea animal because it had long dorsel fin running its full length. It was certainly ot a whale. It was excessively large and it appeared go on a long time—more coming out and more going ." He shrugged again. "I do not know what it was. Ve have all seen queer things surface at times—things hich presumably only come up from very far below on rare ccasions. It was one of those."

Serafino nodded. It was true that once in a way a sailor ould glimpse some strange and enormous sea animal of n unclassified and therefore nameless sort. It was con-dered by some people that these things only rose from the rofound depths when weather conditions on the surface ere deteriorating. He glanced quickly at the barometer. It as still falling. Turning away, he said coldly, "Yes, yes, ut we do not refer to them as sea-serpents. Officially the iggest living creature in the sea is a whale. Change your ntry to 'whale,' Gino. It will look silly, but not as silly as hat you have written. And—yes, you will put underneath Sighted by L. Pavanoli, aged seventeen years.' That will xplain it to the curious-minded." He grinned sardonically.

" But it *was* a sea-serpent. And Signor Malestroit saw i and——"

"Don't agree!" Frowning, Serafino walked out to the por wing of the bridge. The wind was rising once more; i caught him full in the face with unexpected force. He looke up at *San Roque's* small house flag far above him—a whit square with a big red " S " in its centre. It was strainin hard and flat against the grey sky. The wind seemed to b veering round to the south, and though it was no longe raining, the sky was low and dark, the sea almost black an licked and spotted with foam on the rolling crests of th swells.

He moved back into the shelter of the bridge and wen over to the chart table. How long ago it seemed sinc he had last been in these latitudes. What was it? Six—no seven years. He tried to think back to those distant days but it was difficult for there was so much between then an now—so many harbours and ports, tricks of the weathe in certain latitudes at certain times, prevailing winds acros other oceans. Years of the Caribbean and the South Atlantic of reefs and lights, shoals and shallows. He had been onl nineteen, in his ultimate year as a cadet, when he had las sailed these waters. It had been in a small old freighte the *Bar-le-Duc*—a ship taken from France in 1940 and some how still retained in the Italian service twelve years later. Sh had seen better days and so, as he continually complained, ha her captain, Leando Pergher, a mild, gin-sodden old mar dirty, religious and given to holy visions which he liked t recount, sometimes mixed with nautical instructions, at grea length to his subordinates. "Last night I was privileged t see Paradise and the Throne of God. I was escorted thithe by the holy martyr St. Luciano. . . . Yes, Ciccolanti, in thes latitudes we may expect sudden tropical disturbances at thi time of the year. The warm South Equatorial Current meet the cold West Australian Current coming up from the south and this is highly conducive to cyclonic conditions of a gene ally powerful but short-lived nature. . . ."

Well, if there was going to be a cyclone he would certainl rather ride it out in *San Roque* with her powerful moder twin turbines than in the *Bar-le-Duc* with her cranky old triple expansion engine. In any case the weather reports woul warn them of anything really bad in the vicinity and measure could be taken to avoid—— But a small, cold hand seeme suddenly to touch his heart: the radio was out of action here would be no weather reports and there was no way of ontacting other shipping. Deaf and dumb, *San Roque* was linded too.

2

' I am doing all I can. It is not easy—and the sea is not making t any easier." Brighenti, a pair of pliers in one hand, sat n his chair with his legs hooked round the iron supports of he emergency set to steady himself. He glanced irritably at he Chief Officer, who stood bracing himself in the frame of he doorway. "And what is more, there is nowhere where I an put anything. Once something is unfastened it falls o the floor and bounces around like a pea on a drum. You an't treat radio parts like that, Signor Ciccolanti. As I told ou earlier to-day, I may cause more damage working on the adio in these conditions than if I left it alone."

"That is a risk which we must take."

"It would be more sensible if we waited until the wind lrops," grumbled Brighenti.

Serafino grinned. "It shows no signs of dropping, howver. It may interest you to know that the barometer has een falling steadily since before dawn. It is now standing t 29.62. Perhaps that explains the motion of the ship—yes? want weather reports and I want to contact any ships hat may be near us. How long will it take to get the mergency set going?"

Brighenti swore as a particularly steep roll sent a small ox of insulators crashing to the cabin floor. "You see what mean? Those things cost money. And that's by no means he worst I have to contend with. If——"

"I asked how long——"

"At least thirty hours. More, probably, in these condiions. I cannot do miracles, Signor Ciccolanti—even for ou!"

"You must try."

It was just past noon and blowing a full gale. The wind ad veered three points to the west and was now taking *an Roque* on the starboard bow, so whatever else it might e, it was certainly not the seasonal monsoon. Serafino would ave liked to discuss the vagaries of the weather with Bressan, ut since they were no longer on speaking terms this was mpossible. For the present, in any case, there was nothing he could do. *San Roque* was, if not new, at least very recently reconditioned. For her size she was extremely powerful and though a gale of the strength of the present one would certainly delay her arrival in Fremantle by some hours, supposing that it continued long enough, it would not otherwise inconvenience her. It would inconvenience her passenger considerably, but that was another thing altogether and one in which Serafino felt no interest at all. What worried him deeply was his inability to communicate with the outside world. If the radio had been working he could have contacted other ships in the vicinity and asked about their weather He could have contacted the big radio station on the Coco Islands some seven hundred miles back to the north-east, and even Fremantle right down in the south nearly a thousand miles away. He could have charted the weather condition along his route and all around him. He could have found out where this wind came from and what it was going to do Then he could have altered course, had it seemed advisable instead of pitching and wallowing on indefinitely in the teeth of this gale.

But by four o'clock that afternoon it was becoming something considerably more than a normal gale. The baromete had dropped twelve points and now stood at 29.50, while the wind-force was closer to nine than eight, with occasional gust reaching ten—and the wind itself had veered still farthe west. It was now taking *San Roque* directly on the starboard beam and heeling her over steeply enough to make walkin from left to right across the vestibule like climbing a shor but steep hill. Not that there was anyone to walk across the vestibule, for the ship was pitching and lurching in a way which ensured that the majority of the passengers were rollin miserably in their bunks, as apparently inanimate as sack of potatoes.

Cavaliere Semprebon, whose digestion had been upse by the increasing violence of the ship's motion and who wa consequently suffering from heartburn, phoned the bridg and informed Bressan, the officer of the watch, that it would be impossible to serve dinner, let alone eat it, unless something was done to steady *San Roque*. They had already, he explained angrily, had fiddles on the table at lunch, and even so a plate of soup had been thrown into the lap o Dr. Sessabandrian, who believed it to have been done on purpose. The motion was now considerably worse; the bridg would do well to remember that this was a passenger ship and act accordingly.

Bressan relayed the message to the Chief Officer. He had to shout to make himself heard above the whistling roar of the wind, which, high up here on the bridge, had already produced that peculiar muffling deafness in the ears consequent upon prolonged exposure to a continuous thundering noise. Staring out of the thick-glassed windows, Serafino nodded. He would in any case have given the order to heave-to within the next half-hour. It was no longer possible to stand on any part of the exposed deck, and the seas were becoming tumultuous—great hills of dark water laced with foam over which *San Roque* swooped and plunged like something in a fun-fair. It was a useless strain on the ship to force her onwards through such weather. He would turn her bows full into the wind and hold her there under whatever engine power was necessary until the cyclone passed. For that *San Roque* was now on the edge of a cyclone there could no longer be much doubt, though on which edge and how far from the centre and whether she was being thrown out or sucked in were questions which it was impossible to answer. All that could be said with any certainty was that somewhere within a probable radius of fifty miles or more of the labouring ship a system of high velocity winds rotating ever faster round a centre of low pressure was moving across the ocean floor. It was unlikely to be moving very fast—not more than six or seven miles an hour, probably—but, bereft of her ability to check with shore stations and other shipping, *San Roque*, holding her course for Fremantle, might as easily forge straight into it as steer clear. So at four-fifteen Serafino gave the necessary orders, *San Roque* turned slowly a full ninety degrees to starboard and, steadying herself with her sharp prow splitting the gale, prepared to ride it out.

3

By seven o'clock that evening the growing fury of the storm had produced a nervous air of spurious comradeship among the first-class passengers. It also considerably enhanced the position of Roger Lannfranc, who ceased in their eyes to be yet another impecunious, discontented ex-Naval officer migrating in search of a better job and became Lieut-Commander Lannfranc, R.N., an experienced sailor who could explain to them what was happening and assure them that they were in no danger. Roger accepted his new status with gusto. Balancing on wide-set, well-accustomed legs in the middle of the first-class saloon, he held forth on storms at sea in general and those which he had weathered in particular. "Of course in a sub. we'd go down to about twelve fathoms and say there until it was all over."

"That's just what we *don't* want to do," said Paula Chelgrove, who, alone among the other passengers save for Dr. Sessabandrian, disliked Roger's newly acquired arrogant *bonhomie*. She had found no mention of the Lannfrancs in either the Burke or the Debrett with which she always travelled; they were nobodies, really.

Roger's face broke into his once-famous, slow-motion grin. "There's no danger of that," he said confidently, but then, not wishing to lose his audience through too definite assurance, he added, "Unless the officers lose their heads and do something stupid. With our little lot on this ship anything's possible, of course."

"But, Roger, dear, surely they're fully qualified, aren't they?" Mrs. Crambatch's voice was almost a wail. She had spent most of the afternoon praying and bitterly repenting taking her passage home in such an awful little boat, but despite St. Vera's predilection for water, the sea had become still rougher.

"Qualified? Oh, I suppose they're qualified all right. But what they're qualified *for* is quite another thing, isn't it? So long as you can drive a trolley or a tricycle or something I imagine you can get an officer's berth on a Panamanian ship. But I think it most unlikely that they can navigate. I imagine that the main reason we have touched at each port so far is so that someone can ask the way to the next. I——"

"Now, Roger, you're being silly!" Bronwen turned comfortingly to Mrs. Crambatch. "Don't let him upset you. It's only his fun. You see, he *knows* there isn't any danger, really."

"I do hope you're right! I just can't bear to look out of the windows at the sea. And I've been so ill!"

"Poor Mrs. Crambatch!" Bronwen was sympathy itself. "Would you like to go back to your cabin and lie down? I'll come and sit with you."

But Mrs. Crambatch somehow thought she felt safer

in the saloon. She liked being near Roger, who in an emergency would surely do something to rescue her. Surely in the depths of an arm-chair securely fastened to the deck and thus padded against the pitching and rolling of the ship, she pondered on whether or not to suggest a position for Roger in the Emporium at Dunedin. Early in the voyage she had determined to do this, had longed to sound Bronwen on the matter and had prayed fervently that Roger would accept. Later, finding that, as with so many of their class, the appearance of the Lannfrancs was a little deceptive, she had become hesitant. For on closer acquaintance it became lamentably plain that under his genial, breezy manner Roger was neither very clever nor particularly charming. An exasperated, impatient, rather bitter man showed increasingly through the cracks in the decaying façade of carefree naval youth. Bronwen—well, she could not have put herself out to be nicer, but one could not quite believe that a good-looking, intelligent girl, married to a handsome husband with allegedly excellent prospects and numerous friends, would spend so much time attending an elderly widow, a mere travelling companion on a ship, unless she had a good reason of her own to do so.

Mrs. Crambatch was not a fool where her own interests were concerned. Once she had sensed what the Lannfrancs were after, her natural caution and obstinacy warned her to be careful. Mentally she reduced Roger from the position of assistant to the general manager with prospects of an early directorship to manager of a small department—sports, say—on probation. Later she decided that even that position must be earned—and learned, for Leslie had always been a great believer in starting from the bottom. The day before they left Colombo she had decided that she would wait until Bronwen actually proposed the idea herself, and then, and only then, offer Roger a job as a salesman—a representative of the Emporium—travelling over a sector of the islands and selling something—kitchenware, probably—strictly on a commission basis, of course. After all that was how Leslie had started. But by the time they were across the Equator she had decided no. She did not really think she liked the Lannfrancs enough—not Roger, certainly. She would not offer him a post and she would cease to suggest that they both came on with her from Sydney.

Now, however, the position had once again altered. Now it might be expedient to bind the Lannfrancs to her. She knew nothing of storms at sea, but she held a vague belief that sailors could control them in some way—do something about them, anyhow. She was old, she was overwrought, and she knew herself to be physically incapable of any serious exertion. If something nasty happened she would be helpless unless somebody assisted her, and Roger, in the circumstances, seemed the ideal choice. If she was now to suggest to Bronwen that she had quite a good opening in mind—one did not have to be specific, after all. . . . But caution still held her back; this storm would probably die down soon and she would regret any hasty action.

The rest of the first-class passengers, with the exceptions of Countess Zapescu, who felt that in the present circumstances Brown could be kept openly in her cabin or the saloons without anyone objecting, and the four children who were staring raptly out of the windows at the terrific waves and squealing with delight, were by no means unworried. Mr. Malcolm-Bruce in particular was upset. His wife was suffering from violent sea-sickness and he could do nothing for her; both his children were on board and sharing any danger that might possibly arise; and despite its protective tarpaulin, his new Cadillac must be taking a terrific battering down there on the foredeck. Earlier in the day he had seen some sailors doubling the lashings and had discreetly encouraged their efforts with a few Australian pound notes, but even so . . . He wished ardently that he had brought his last year's Ford with him instead.

Dr. Sessabandrian was angry because he believed the ship was bound to be delayed—perhaps more than a whole day. In that case he might miss the opening of the conference. Of course no one said anything important on the first day, but there was the allocation of seats. If he was late he might be given a poor seat—and people might think it was because he was a coloured man and unimportant. Then there was the soup over his trousers at lunch to-day. It must have been some fault in the plate; doubtless its bottom was not flat but slightly concave. It was obvious why *he* had been given a faulty plate. No European had had soup spilt over his trousers.

Paula Chelgrove, whose family had always looked down a little on naval men—the best people joined the Army or, on occasion, the Church—felt that Roger Lannfranc ought somehow to be put in his place and that a show of complete imperturbability was called for, whatever might happen. In a way she hoped that the storm might get worse, so that young Lannfranc became frightened—or "windy," as they had called it in 1915. Then Perry could demonstrate his *sang-froid* and cheer the trembling passengers with the courteous courage that she never doubted he really possessed. There would be something afterwards in the papers, perhaps: "At Height of Storm British Colonel Calms Fears. . . ." She glanced at Perry sitting beside her, and to her irritation saw that he was sound asleep.

4

Down in the tourist-class accommodation the position was made much more unpleasant by the overcrowded conditions and the venomous hostility between the British and the Italian migrants which the disclosure of Armando Lodigianni's suicide had brought close to flash point. But for the rolling and pitching of the ship there would almost certainly have been an all-in fight during the afternoon, and despite their superior numbers the British would have fared badly, for the Italians were in a savage mood. Yet as the storm increased in strength and darkness fell, hatred slowly gave way to fear. It did not, as in the first-class, draw the passengers together but drew them apart. They huddled in groups of their own nationality and there banded, as it were, into small self-help communities. Signora Valpatena would sit up with the two youngest Ricciotti children, who were terrified and whose mother was prostrate with sea-sickness. Also Lombardi would try to find out the position from the *Capitan d'armi,* while old Signor Trimeloni who had been a sailor once—though admittedly only on Lake Garda—would try to explain to the wives that these storms were really not at all dangerous on modern ships.

It was the same with the British. They got together and joked about the Blitz. "Bin through a lot worse things than a *storm*!" as Mrs. Throsby said with a contemplative sniff. "Thing is, I don't trust the skipper. Silly-lookin' bleeder, I reckon—an' a lot too young, come to that."

"If we was on a proper ship . . ."

"Proper British ship, properly run, like . . ."

"No use you sayin' that now, Ted Condron. We're 'ere, ain't we?"

Shortly they deputed Ron Hogben to find out how long the

storm was going to last. "So's we know when the kid's c'n get a bit of kip, poor little baskets!" But Hogben was not going to approach an Italian. "Fair sick of dagoes, I am, I tell you strite! Thievin', lyin' bunch of dirty crooks! Gets right on me tits, it does, just to 'ear 'em jabberin'. Tell you what, though. I'll go along a bit later an' 'ave a word with a bloke in the first class. Naval bloke name of Lannfranc. Snooty bastard, like all them officer types. Still, 'e'll prob'ly 'ave some idea of what's 'appenin', like."

He found Roger in the first-class bar where, with his legs twined round the chromium stem of one of the fixed stools, he was drinking whisky and attempting to encourage Ettore, the barman, who had been very seasick all day and now had the appearance of a miserable little marmoset that someone had left out on a cold night. "This ship—*questo nave*—very *buono.* Perfectly *sicuro. Non avete* reason to flap—*panico.* I know. I've been a *marinaio* for years—*troppo anno.* The *capitano* is not *molto buono,* I agree, but——"

Ettore put a hand inside the open neck of his shirt and pulled out two small medallions. "*Allora—siamo tutti nel mani di Dio!*" he said, smiling unhappily, as if the hands of God were not the place he would personally choose to be in the circumstances.

Then Hogben lurched in through the doorway and brought himself up heavily against the bar. "'Scuse me, Commander," he said, his tiny mouth slit into an ingratiating smile. "I've come from down below. It's the women. They're gettin' a bit scared, like. So they ask me to come an' 'ave a word with you. No use talkin' to any of these 'ere dagoes, is it? But you bein a naval man we kind of thought you'd 'ave an idea what's goin' on—if you see what I means."

Roger was delighted to reassure him. He even bought him a double whisky. After all, Hogben was an Englishman and an ex-rating. He explained matters in very much the same way as he had done earlier in the evening in the first-class saloon. ". . . So that, as long as everyone keeps his head there's nothing at all to be alarmed about."

"Ar," said Hogben, with a significant glance towards Ettore, "but will they, though? That's the burnin' question Commander, ain't it? I mean, it's not as if we 'ad a proper captain, is it? The old bloke what passed out at Colombo was all right, I s'pose, but now we got this young feller with the wonky leg runnin' the show, ain't we? An' I've never liked the looks of 'im. In with the dirty little tyke what stole me watch, 'e was. Stood out a mile. 'E'll like as not drown the lot of us if somethin's not done to stop 'im—that's what I think."

Roger laughed. "Well, your guess is as good as mine." He paused, frowning thoughtfully. "Look, I think I had better go up to the bridge and find out how they're—how everyone's getting along. Then I'll let you know how things stand."

Hogben looked relieved. "That's a f—ing good idea! You do that, Commander—an' tell 'em for Chrissake to act sensible!"

5

Up on the bridge, high above the decks, the motion of the ship was such that it was impossible to stand without holding hard to some support. The officers clung to stanchions, while the quartermaster gripped the wheel and dug the heels of his rubber shoes into interstices in the wooden grating on which he stood. In order to keep *San Roque* hove-to, the turbines were working at nearly three-quarter speed and it seemed that shortly they might have to go still faster. For the wind, the officers reckoned, was now blowing with a velocity of nearly a hundred miles an hour, and with the barometer down to 29.11 there seemed no immediate prospect of its decreasing. It was too dark now to see the waves, but it was not necessary to see them in order to have some idea of their size and speed: they could be felt. *San Roque* was a passenger ship and was therefore comparatively light; she rode high and lifted quickly. This saved her from much of the terrible pounding a laden freighter would have taken in the circumstances. The *Stanvac Stronghold*, full of oil, would have lost most of her deck machinery by now, and her big after-castle would have been in the process of being hammered into its component parts. Yet *San Roque* was not escaping all the worst seas; from time to time she shuddered and reeled under a stunning blow as some great mass of water reared up and flung itself upon her out of the howling darkness. Her pitching was becoming acute, she seemed sometimes to be trying to stand on her stern. Up—up—up the bows lifted, every nut and bolt creaking and groaning in agonised protest; a short pause, then—crash! And down—down—down as if they were about to plunge below the sea into the gloomy stillness of the depths. It became monotonous and tiring; particularly when, like the deck officers gripping their handholds on the bridge, one visualised every part of the ship and seemed to feel in one's own body the strains and stresses to which the hull and the hatches and the superstructure were being subjected. Up—up—up. . . .

At ten to eight—Gino was glancing at the bridge clock at the very moment it happened and was thus able to note the exact time in the log afterwards—something seemed to rush out of the night and strike the bridge window in front of the helmsman. There was a crack like a gunshot, a crash, and the quartermaster was flung back screaming from the wheel in what appeared to be a shower of ice. But it was not ice: it was a torrent of thick splinters of jagged glass hurled at him by a hundred-mile-an-hour cyclonic gale. For a single second Serafino saw the man's face as he crashed back against the bulkhead. It was hardly a face any longer, it was all in ragged pieces. Lips, cheeks, chin, forehead were laid open in great flaps of flesh showing the white bone beneath, and the wind was tearing them still farther away from the skull—flaying the face by pressure. Then the blood gushed, masking the horror in crimson, and the man slid down the bulkhead to the floor. But there was no time to attend to him. One and all, the officers flung themselves towards the wheel, struggling in the grip of the thundering, almost solid wind before they could lay a finger upon it. Malestroit got there first and grappled himself to the spokes, then Serafino was beside him, holding partly to his body, partly to the binnacle. The wind blew their eyes shut, but, by cowering their heads into their chests, they were just able to open them sufficiently to glimpse the compass and Serafino saw with quick relief that *San Roque* had not started to turn; they had got to the helm in time. Malestroit, now in control of the wheel, nudged him and, letting go too suddenly, he was flung back to the blood-stained bulkhead at the rear of the bridge.

Then Petelli and four sailors were up from below, entering by the interior companionway through the Captain's quarters. Orders were screamed against the roaring flood of air, and planks, ropes, bolts, were rushed to the bridge for the gaping window frame from which every fragment of glass had been blown must be closed. Until then the wind would continue to pour into the bridge with the force of a pressure hose. Already the place was a shambles of ripped charts, tumbling signal flags, broken glass and blood. Already Malestroit, grappled to the wheel, was being stripped of his clothes. First his raincoat went; the wind got inside it, tore out the buttons, burst the seams and jerked out the cloth in long shreds which rippled out behind him, suspended in the whistling stream of air; then his epaulettes flew off his shoulders like flitting black bats and his shirt was ripped away as if someone had him by the collar. But slowly, with everyone thrusting and pushing, the planks were secured across the empty window frame. The wind whistled and hissed between the cracks, but it was possible to move about again and to stand properly at the helm.

The quartermaster whose face had been sliced to pieces by the hurtling glass was mercifully dead; there was a ten-inch splinter embedded deeply in his throat just under the chin. His blood had been sprayed by the wind in all directions and this, in conjunction with the scattered signal flags from the overturned lockers, gave the bridge something of the macabre look of a carnival held in a slaughterhouse. Petelli covered the man's head with one of the flags and motioned to two of the sailors to take him below; then he approached Serafino with something in his hand. "Look, signore." It was a four-inch horseshoe shackle-bolt and attached to it was a shred of brown tarpaulin. "From the motor car!" He had to shout to make himself heard. "The cover must have torn loose and been flung up here. It was this shackle which smashed the window."

Still slightly stunned by the wind, their lungs aching with the air that had been forced into them, their ears dull with the continuous thundering of the storm, the bridge personnel stood panting and swaying, feet braced, gripping any likely handhold on the swooping bridge. The officers' hats were scattered among the wreckage of charts and smashed navigating instruments on the deck, their clothes were ripped open, and Malestroit was naked to the waist, his bare chest scarlet and gleaming with the atomised spray which had beaten and rebounded from his flesh during his eight minutes at the exposed wheel. It was thus that Roger Lannfranc, entering the bridge from the interior companionway, saw them.

6

"Well?" Serafino motioned Roger to precede him into the small office behind the chart table and a lurch of the ship slammed the door. Silence—comparative, at least, to the whistling roar of the bridge, suddenly enclosed them. They stared at each other for a moment, each deeply aware of the other's hostility. Then Serafino said coldly, "To ascend to the command deck is forbidden to passengers." His deep voice came with an odd breathlessness. His lungs, blown up with air like balloons some minutes before, had left him with a queer ebullient giddiness; he would have liked to laugh at his own words, but dared not for fear this Englishman would think him hysterical.

Roger braced himself carefully against the small table. He had been surprised and alarmed at the state of the bridge and its occupants. It had brought home to him with a disturbing force which, despite his earlier remarks in the first-class saloon, he had not felt before, the fact that this ship was manned and—far worse—officered by foreigners. Perhaps because of the international sameness of sea-going uniforms, particularly tropical whites, Roger had up till now thought of *San Roque's* crew as seamen first and foreign nationals only secondly. He had criticised them in their former rather than their latter capacity, judging them by the yardstick of his own professional experience. Now, suddenly, the precedence became reversed—they were first and foremost foreigners, and an education composed largely of British naval history had left him with a genuine contempt for the sea-going qualities of any nation other than his own. And now in the middle of a particularly severe storm—as bad as any he had ever known—his life, Bronwen's life and the lives of a great many other English people were entirely in the hands of this skinny little Italian, hatless, dishevelled, in a grubby civilian mackintosh, who faced him across the table. It wasn't good enough. He began to get angry.

"Now, look here, Ciccolanti, I've been asked by all the passengers—the British ones, at any rate—to come up here and have a word with you. So for a start I think we'll drop this 'command deck' talk. I want to know what's happening."

"So?" This time Serafino could not prevent himself from

grinning. "You wish to know what happens? If you are to look from the window you are seeing what happens, I think. We are in a storm."

"We're in something a hell of a lot bigger than a storm, let me tell you!"

"*Va bene.* We are in a *ciclone*—I do not know the English word. But there is no reason to terror. You are in good safety."

Roger controlled his growing anger with an effort. When he had told Hogben that he would come up here he had been comparatively unworried concerning the safety of the ship. He knew, far better than the other passengers, just how powerful and seaworthy a modern turbine liner was. Properly manned, carefully handled, *San Roque* could ride out the worst storm that had ever been recorded with no more than superficial damage to her deck gear. It was only now, when he was confronted by Ciccolanti and after he had seen the state of the bridge, that he remembered the Panamanian flag and began seriously to take the human element into account. For first-class officers and seamen did not sail under the red and blue stars and never had. It was generally only the second-rate, the failures or the incompetents, who found themselves forced to accept the lower pay and unstandardised conditions of the "flags of convenience." If there was any real danger of disaster it lay, not in the ship herself but in her crew—and most of all in her captain. He said firmly, "I want to know one or two things. Firstly, is the wireless still out of order?"

"Wire——?"

"Oh—radio then, or whatever you call it."

"It is soon to operate."

"But not yet?"

"At present—no."

"I see." Roger jerked his head in the direction of the closed door. "And what happened out there?"

"One window breaks."

"How? Not the wind, surely?"

"Not wind. From the automobile below is torn the cover. One piece of iron break the window. You will say to Signor Malcolm-Bruce that I am sorry, but I think his automobile is —is *kaputt.*"

Roger grunted. "I couldn't care less, personally. What about all that blood. Was someone hurt?"

"Small hurt—yes."

"Small! Christ, whoever bled like that wasn't 'small hurt'!"

"That is not for you. And now, please——"

"I haven't finished yet. Look—you've got her head-on and you're going to ride it out, aren't you? I want to know a bit more about that."

Serafino's mouth set thinly. "What I do is for me. I am captain. You are one-time captain of *sottomarino*—but there is very much difference. You cannot, I think, to understand about the ship on the sea. So now——"

Roger said grimly, "I probably know a hell of a lot more about navigating every sort of ship than you ever will. And that doesn't necessarily mean I know a lot! I want to go down and tell the passengers that everything is all right——"

"All is right."

"But I'm certainly not going to unless *I* think it is. I want to assess the position on the full information available. I want to know the wind force and the barometer reading and what engine power we're under and——"

But Serafino had had enough. An hour ago Gill had come up to the bridge, but he had done no more than ask a couple of brief questions before sardonically wishing everyone good luck and returning to his cabin. That this pompous, arrogant Englishman should take it upon himself to demand technical information and question bridge decisions when the Owner's son had the sense not to, was too much.

"So? Then, you say to the passengers what you like. I tell you all people are safe. More things I will not tell you for you also are only a passenger. You forget this many times, I think, Signor Lannfranc, but it is so. You are passenger, *not* officer of this ship! Now you will go from the command deck where it is forbidden for you to come again."

XVI

Dawn broke almost imperceptibly over a wildly mountainous sea ripped and torn by the screaming wind until the air for thirty or forty feet above the waves was largely spray. The utter blackness of the past night slowly became a pearly greyness, a semi-opaque, whistling fog of atomised brine. Now the officers on the bridge were at last able to get a partial view of what had been happening to *San Roque* during the past ten hours. It was fortunate, perhaps, that it was only a partial view—the spinning disc of the clear-vision screen had gone with the centre bridge window and the remaining windows were shimmering fogs of rebounding spray—otherwise it would have been sufficient to frighten them badly. They had all been through storms at sea, even Gino had once spent several hours in heavy weather off Cape Matapan, but none of them had seen anything like this before. The wind was producing a screaming, thundering roar through which nothing else could be heard; it had continued to increase all night and had now reached an acceleration far higher—probably twice as high—as Force 12, the highest register on the Beaufort Scale. There was no longer any means of assessing the velocity of such a wind.

At the back of the minds of the bridge personnel small cold visions of drowning glimmered behind the more controlled and conscious thoughts which told them that their position, at least at present, was not as dangerous as it looked. For *San Roque* was riding out the cyclone magnificently. She had been under full engine power since just before midnight, when the bridge had guessed the wind to have reached the tremendous velocity of nearly one hundred and fifty miles an hour, and she had stayed head-on to the storm. Even so, it appearerd likely that they were being blown slowly backwards—with no radio and neither stars nor sun upon which to take sights they had no idea of their present position—but at least the twin turbines were powerful enough to keep the ship's sharp prow firmly pointed into the teeth of the wind, and while it remained thus there was no real danger to be anticipated.

Though the waves were often sixty or seventy feet high, vast cliffs of water bearing down upon *San Roque* with nightmare speed and force, she swooped up them, staggered, buried her nose in the boiling foam of their crests, and slid, shuddering but buoyant, down their backs. For she was not only a complex achievement of modern engineering skill, but also the produce of centuries of human sea-going experience. The lines of her hull were beautiful, but this beauty was incidental to the designer's main object of stability and the endurance of conditions such as those in which she was now placed. Even when, as sometimes happened, she was struck obliquely rather than head-on by a water-mountain of some hundreds of tons, the stresses and strains of the blow were artfully distributed and evaded by these lines in such a way that all but a minimum of their slamming force was nullified.

But with dawn came a change in the weather. The wind seemed to swing back towards the south and became uneven. An hour later it had ceased to be a solid, roaring stream of air and was blowing in gusts. And as the pearly light increased, these gusts could be seen as sudden tunnels in the spray-filled atmosphere, tunnels screaming swiftly down out of nowhere and striking with the force of dynamite charges and from directions covering half the compass card. *San Roque* could not possibly be kept head-on to every angle in an arc of 180 degrees at the same time, nor could she be manœuvred so that her sharp, curved prow slit the centre of every tunnel as it bore down upon her. She was buffeted from side to side like a cork, but like a cork she bobbed upright again as soon as each gust had passed.

Despite the uncertainty and the jarring frequency of such blows, the officers on the bridge welcomed the change in the weather with relief. It meant one of two things: either *San Roque* was approaching the calm, low-pressure centre of the cyclone, in which case they might hope to be out of the system or at least in a part of its navigable semicircle by this evening, or they were already on the periphery and could expect to be finished with the storm completely within a few hours. None the less, the wind, though it had fallen considerably, was still blowing with a velocity which to a landsman would have seemed a tremendous gale, and these gusts merely constituted a further danger for certain parts of the ship. The great hull and much of the superstructure were of thick, welded steel and indifferent to any wind force, but there was the lighter deck machinery to think about, the boats, the funnel and the remaining bridge windows. When they saw a gust bearing down on them the bridge personnel, all too mindful of the dead quartermaster's face, bent down below the level of the windows until it had passed.

But the first casualty of these new conditions was the Malcolm-Bruces Cadilac. Somehow, miraculously, it had survived the night—not undamaged, certainly, for its windows were gone and its body buckled and bent until it resembled corrugated zinc—but it was still in its place. Now a great gust from the starboard tore it from its lashings, hurled it on top of the port hydrocrane, and heeled *San Roque* so far over on her beam that both car and crane crashed overboard into the sea. "As the Scottish people would say," shouted Malestroit to the Chief Officer, "bang goes sixpence."

But Serafino, glancing automatically at the bridge clock to mark the time for the log entry, was unamused. He cared little more than Roger Lannfranc for the fate of Mr. Malcolm-Bruce's car, which was, presumably, well insured and in any case was being shipped at its owner's risk as far as the Line was concerned, but the hydrocrane was another matter altogether. The new hydraulic-electric cranes which on *San Roque* took the place of the conventional noisy old derricks and donkey-engines were one of the ship's showier and more costly pieces of equipment. Until the port one went over the side the storm had only cost *San Roque* the breakage of a bridge window; one did not count the death of a quartermaster, for by Don Ildefonso's reckoning that was a matter of complete indifference. The window could be replaced in Sydney for some twenty Australian pounds or so, but a hydrocrane cost thousands. Its loss finally set the seal on Serafino's conviction of coming dismissal. For Don Ildefonso would probably overlook the bridge window, though he might well stop the money from Serafino's wages to pay for it; and as far as the damage to the radio went, that was, after all, an act of wanton destruction on the part of some passengers' children and could equally have occurred on either of the other ships of the Line. But the loss of a hydrocrane . . . No, that was too much; that had finished off any slender chances he might still have had of retaining his job. So it was going to be the useless trudge up and down the Via De Pretis, after all, and the inevitable questions: "Your last position? . . . With which Line? . . . And why did you leave? . . . No, no—we have nothing at present . . . keep your name on the books . . . let you know if we should find ourselves able to . . ." And then . . . Gripping the hand-rail, bracing himself with feet wide apart, Serafino stared through the spray-slashed window and saw nothing of the monstrous seas but only the black despair of a jobless future. A future without the sea. Someone else would be on this bridge soon—probably an elderly man, an ex-chief officer from another Line who was prepared to accept Don Ildefonso's pay and the Panamanian flag in order to achieve captaincy before he retired—while he himself would be back in Naples, wandering miserably about the street with nothing in his pockets. . . . But then something happened which made it unlikely that he would ever see Naples again or that *San Roque* would ever have another master.

At eight minutes to six a gust-tunnel appeared off the port quarter, rushing upon the ship with the speed of a racing car but the force of a dozen bulldozers. *San Roque* lurched, heeled, shuddered, then righted herself easily enough as the gust passed on into some far oblivion over the empty tossing sea. But forty-five seconds later the ship began to turn slightly to starboard. "Keep her steady, Ruggiero!" Serafino shouted angrily at the helmsman, and obediently the man swung the wheel. But the turn to starboard continued—surprisingly, for the roar of the wind was already lessenin perceptibly. "Steady! Steady, I said!" Serafino thrust the sailor out of the way and took the wheel himself, hearing as he did so, the bridge telephone ringing urgently behind him Under his hands the wheel seemed dead. *San Roque* was no answering to it at all. Had the steering-engine broken down? The turn became greater as the wind caught the ship on her exposed port bow and Serafino felt pani prickle out all over him. In a very few moments *San Roqu* would be broadside on to the weather, and then nothing not even the great power of her twin turbines, would turn her again until the storm died. Then Bressan, white-faced was shouting in his ear, unnecessarily loudly it seemed "Aafjes says something has fouled the screws! He's ha to stop both engines!"

For a second Serafino's mind refused to understand, rebelle at accepting such a catastrophe and all its terrible implication He spun the wheel furiously while a numb voice in his brai repeated dully, "Both engines stopped . . ." Then his eye slid to the propeller revolution counter and his stomac contracted: both needles were back at zero. *San Roqu* was at an angle of 50 degrees to the weather now, and sea were beginning to take her broadside, breaking over he decks in roaring cataracts of white water. "Both engine stopped . . ." That meant that they were helpless in the gri of the cyclone. There would be no more riding it out, holdin her head-on into the weather, waiting for the inevitable lu and the chance to forge out into the sunlight and the cal once more. Without power, *San Roque* would be sucked alor indefinitely in this roaring, pearly gloom, until, beaten a last almost to pieces, she foundered. And suddenly, seein all too clearly the lethal hopelessness of their position, h wished with a savage, childish anger that brought tears to h eyes that she would go down now, at once, so that it could all be over without any of the further useless efforts and agonised waiting as she broke up under his feet.

There was nothing he could do—he or anyone else—and turning from the wheel, he saw the fear in the faces of the other two officers. He supposed he too should be frightened, but he was not—he was too angry. For it had always been like this—always. Nothing ever went right for him; he was dogged by a malignant fate which delighted to torture him. In childhood it had smashed his foot; in early youth, just as his apprenticeship was over, it had laid upon him the whole burden of supporting his family. It had seen to it that he did not get a position in an Italian line but must sail under Panamanian colours in the employ of a sinister racketeer. Then—Onestinghel—Gil—the radio—that boy—the hydrocrane. It was not even content to thrust him into a cyclone without ensuring his ultimate destruction. All right, then: he would try no more. He would not lift a finger to save himself, the ship or her company. It was no good—everything was hopeless! His wide mouth set stubbornly like a sulky child's. He would not play any more.

Then Gino, whom Bressan had sent aft on some errand five minutes ago, suddenly reappeared on the bridge. He was dripping wet, his black hair plastered over his forehead, his shirt ripped open. He shouted, Patelli says it's the stern hawsers! That last gust sent them over the side and he says the lashings must have broken somehow."

So that was it. Serafino had a sullen vision of the great hawsers snaking over the stern, the ship, thrust slowly backwards, overriding them as they unravelled in the furious waves. An end touching the propellers—the inward-turning screws—and being seized, wound, flung from one to the other; in ten seconds there would be a ghastly tangle, a gigantic cat's-cradle under the stern, steely taut, jammed and completely motionless.

Yet the fact that he now knew what had happened somehow eased the sullen bitterness of his despair. It was ridiculous, for the knowledge could be of no value to him, yet it made him feel slightly less the blind victim of his fate. And Gino—Gino who seemed excited rather than frightened, who plainly did not realise the implications of what had happened; it would perhaps be worthwhile fighting a little longer on the off-chance of some miracle saving him.

They were nearly broadside to the wind now, and the

next gust striking on the port side might finish everything. Before that . . . But then it came. It struck *San Roque* with a slamming punch that shuddered through every plate, plank and bulkhead, it thrust her through the last few degrees of the right-angled turn to lie sideways to the weather, and it heeled her over on her starboard beam farther than it was possible for any ship to heel without capsizing. The officers' feet skidded from under them as the bridge deck lifted almost vertically; everything loose on the bridge, including Gino who had lost his handhold, was flung into the starboard scuppers. Through the whistle and roar of the wind could be heard crashes and booms as heavy ship's fittings not made to resist such an angle tore themselves loose and feel to starboard. But the officers noticed none of this. Hanging by their hands from stanchions and rails they stared with whitening faces at the clinometer clamped to the rear bulkhead. The needle swung swiftly across the numbered dial: 38°—39°—40°, slowed but moved steadily on past 45°—46°—47°—48°——Serafino shut his eyes. This was the end. No ship with a superstructure like *San Roque's* could be expected to return from a roll of 50° in this sea—it was impossible. And now anger and despair were brushed aside by the sharp, cold, animal terror of imminent death; all the fears and anxieties and doubts were swept from his mind, leaving it empty of all but the single piercing call, "I'm alive—and I'm going to die!"

Yet something—it must have been another, contrary gust from starboard—held her when her starboard rails were awash, and slowly, groaning, shuddering, cascading water from her flooded decks, she reeled back to lie wallowing in the troughs of great waves, listed by the wind to 33° and awash both fore and aft.

On the bridge the awestruck officers stared silently at one another from grey faces. They knew that they had escaped death by a couple of degrees and a single fortuitous gust of wind. They knew that they could not expect such a random chance to be repeated. Any further miracles must be wrought by them alone.

Ballast—that was the first thing. It probably flashed into all their minds simultaneously, and though nothing could be heard from where they stood save the thundering of the wind and the appalling crash of the great seas on *San Roque's* port side, they knew what orders Serafino was shouting into the phone to Aafjes. All ballast tanks to port must be flooded, all possible fuel pumped from starboard to port. They would lie lower in the water, present less exposed surface to the artillery salvoes of the wind, and though this would reduce the chances of capsizing by adding to those of filling and foundering the first danger was by far the greater at present.

And there was one thing more—a thing which Malestroit remembered before the others. He grappled his way slowly up to the port bridge wing, crouching on hands and knees below the wooden top of the bulwark over which whistled air almost solid with spray. Then, anchoring himself to the stem of the port alidade, he turned and gazed up at the funnel. *San Roque's* funnel was of the modern type, low, wide and tapering from fore to aft with a rakish slant that added a fine look of windswept speed to her smart lines. It presented very little resistance to a wind from ahead but far too much to one from the side. And now, as Malestroit stared up through the haze of flying spray, he saw that it was actually rippling. Its comparatively thin fabric was trembling into corrugations under the enormous pressure of the gale. At best it could only last until another strong gust hit it—and when it went it would carry the foghorn with it. The thick steam pipe of the foghorn ran up, for appearance sake, inside the fore part of the funnel and emitted its cloudy, booming blast of sound from a spreading set of circular louvres eight feet from the top. That steam must be cut off—and at once. Malestroit shot back down the canted bridge so fast that he rolled head over heels against Serafino's legs. He clambered up breathlessly and shouted, "The funnel's going! Quick—the steam!"

It was incoherent enough, but Serafino understood immediately and screamed another order down the phone, then waited a few seconds and replaced the instrument. Even as he did so there came a deep, groaning rumble, a growling shriek of tearing metal, and a heavy crash from above.

Well—that was that. Serafino glanced round at the bridge clock. One minute to six. Seven minutes ago *San Roque* had been a live ship riding the cyclone, confident in the power of her great turbines and with little more to fear than some damage to her superstructure and external fittings and the destruction of most of her Purser's crockery. Now she was dead—a broken, listing hulk, wallowing awash in the tremendous troughs of the battering waves like a water-logged corpse full of frightened and completely helpless maggots.

2

It took the passengers, the service staff and all those members of the crew who were not on watch far longer than the bridge personnel to realise what had happened and what it meant. Cavaliere Semprebon, whose sea-going experience was both long and varied, worked the matter out for himself as soon as he heard the bare fact of the fouled screws. He had been in the vestibule all night, calming, albeit with a harassed air, such passengers as from time to time staggered up to the counter for reassurance. He had somehow contrived a dinner which no one wanted to eat and had even had sandwiches handed round at midnight, for despite his reassurances, very few of the passengers had felt inclined to go to bed.

As the night wore on and the storm had increased in violence, his usual bland air of suave geniality had given place to abrupt, nervous exasperation. Twice before in his life he had survived tempestuous storms at sea, both times in ships older and less powerful than *San Roque*—but he had been younger then. It angered him that it should happen again now that he was getting on in years and in poor health. But that was the sailor's life for you! Seafaring held no seemly rewards for old age and long service; savage and brutal, the sea had no respect for either. To master it you had to be an Onestinghel, as alert and tough and resilient at seventy as you had been at seventeen. But Cavaliere Semprebon knew himself to be no such man; he was getting old and he felt every year of his age. Well, even if Don Ildefonso did not dismiss him at the end of this voyage, he himself would probably hand in his notice. He decided to consider this step most seriously—once the storm had died down.

Meanwhile, there was his own staff to calm as well as the passengers. Malpiero was steady enough, though he was sweating like a horse; his shirt was soaked; but the mess-boys and the stewards were another matter. Some of the former were on their first voyage, and those who were not being ill were becoming stupid and panicky. One of them had fallen with some china, had cut his hand slightly and was now weeping and shivering like a baby. Another was furtively crossing himself in a corner behind the vestibule counter where he had no right to be, and when Malpiero informed his chief that a third—the bar-boy, Ettore—had fallen down the service lift on "C" deck and broken most of his bones, Cavaliere Semprebon raised his eyes to the lurching ceiling in angry despair and would have raised his hands as well had it not been necessary to cling to the office doorway for support. "In first-class ships, Malpiero, the service staff do not become entirely incapacitated in the middle of storms!"

"First-class ships don't get into storms, Cavaliere—not ones like this, at any rate. They have captains who know their jobs too well. It is my intention to leave the Flotta Soto at the end of this voyage."

The Purser glanced at his assistant with interest. "So? And you will seek a position with another Line?"

"I shall return to my uncle's restaurant in Cosenza."

When dawn broke with the storm still at its height, the Purser decided that he too would resign from the fleet when *San Roque* once more reached Naples. Contemplating the crumpled ruins of his potted palms which slid about the floor among scattered earth and broken china, he told himself that he was too old, far too old for this kind of thing. Mafalda's little cottage under the Apennines began to seem a rather desirable retreat, not at all unsuitable for a retired seafaring man whose health made it necessary for him to lead a very quiet life. And it could probably be made quite cosy in the winter with a good oil-stove—one of these new British oil-radiators, perhaps. . . . He was still pondering the heating of his stone cottage when the news of the fouled screws was shouted to him by the telephonist in his box of an office ten feet from the counter. For a long moment he stared blankly and unbelievingly at his informant, and then, without a word to Malpiero, he abruptly left the vestibule and made his way to his cabin. He told himself that he was only going to fetch his lifejacket, yet once among his own things, his old, shabby, but originally expensive possessions, he sat down on his bunk for a short rest and remained there for quite some time.

3

Roger Lannfranc was the next to grasp the situation. It took him somewhat longer, for unlike the Purser, he was not officially notified of the facts. During the past night he had been engaged on the schizophrenic twin attempts of telling such of his fellow passengers who were not rendered practically unconscious by sea-sickness that they were in no great danger, while at the same time hinting darkly at incompetence on the bridge. In the latter he was successful, and before dawn he had managed to add considerably to the panic of the more timorous and the misgivings of the less impressionable. And this annoyed him, for what he really wished was to stand out as the calm, experienced sailor, knowledgeable and unworried. If Ciccolanti had given him the information for which he had asked, had treated him as an equal—and after all, he was several years the elder and with much more time at sea—he would have been delighted to assist, both by calming the passengers and giving Ciccolanti the benefit of his own experience in a little quiet and encouraging advice from time to time. As it was, however . . .

The cessation of the wearisome pitching and tossing, the continuous shuddering swoop and fall over the huge waves had puzzled him. Were they trying to turn? If so, then in God's name why? How did that little ape on the bridge think he'd ever get her bow on again? Then came the first dreadful roll to starboard. He was in a corridor at the time and coming up from his cabin where he had gone to demonstrate his naval imperturbability by shaving. At first he fended himself off from the bulkhead with one hand, then with both and then—Christ, they were going right over!—he was lying on the wall which had become the floor. So this was it. And suddenly, lying there listening to the cries and crashes from above and below, he knew that the prospect of imminent death did not distress him more than the knowledge that he would be going down in someone else's ship, not his own.

Then, miraculously, the ship recovered and he was running down to the vestibule. A scared Malpiero faced him over a piled litter of papers, smashed gramophone records and broken office equipment. "What's happened? Where's the Purser?"

"Cavaliere Semprebon goes, I think, to his cabin. For what happens I do not know."

"Then let's find out!" Roger climbed over the counter, skidded on a patch of spilled ink, and reached the phone. "*Ponte Comando—subito!*"

"*Momento. Non è libero.*"

So Ciccolanti was on the line already, was he? With a flash of prescience, Roger guessed that he was talking to the engine-room.

Then he was through. "Ciccolanti?"

"Si. Chi parla?"

"It's Lannfranc here." Excitement, tinged strongly with fear, made his voice loudly overbearing. "Look, what the hell are you playing at? Are you trying to drown us all?" There was a long pause. Impatiently Roger shouted, "You've got her broadside, haven't you? Christ, you don't have to tell me, I can *feel*! Listen, have the engines failed?"

"We have some trouble—yes."

"Have the engines failed?"

"For now they are stop."

"Oh, Christ! Well—look, I think I'd better——" But then there came a distinct click and Roger smashed the receiver furiously back on its hook.

In the saloon he found a scene of chaos. Though prac-ically all the furniture was supposed to be secured to the leck and those pieces which were movable had been roped o the rails, the major part of it had been hurled to the star-oard bulkhead, where it lay piled in a jumbled mass of mashed wood, torn material and protruding springs. The rand piano, though screwed firmly to its dais, had snapped its egs like matches and slithered down to rest on top of the eap; something loose within its interior produced a plain-ive arpeggio of top notes at every lurch of the listing hip.

The first-class passengers, badly shaken, dishevelled and leeding from minor cuts and scratches, were clustered ogether round Mrs. Crambatch who had been tipped from her hair and rolled under a window-seat. She was unhurt, but vas crying bitterly with fear and self-pity, while Bronwen, ale-faced but exhibiting the almost professional calm of a aval wife, tried to comfort her.

Roger saw that despite their growing fear throughout the ast night, culminating in the sudden shock of that dreadful oll to starboard, none of them had any idea of the extreme anger in which the events of the last few minutes had placed em, and the knowledge that he alone understood its true xtent filled him with an odd exhilaration, a sense of power. hey turned to him at once.

"Commander, what has happened? I thought we were oing to roll right——"

"What has gone wrong? Something has gone very wrong I——"

"What should we do? Should we go on deck or——

"We drown—yes? *Mein Gott! Mein Gott!*"

"Oh, Roger, help me! Please, *please* do something!

Roger bent and, grasping Mrs. Crombatch, heaved her t her feet. "Bron, help her into a chair. Yes—there. Now Malcolm-Bruce—yes, your wife's okay. Get her into chair too, and—— Oh, God, can't someone stop that do barking!"

"He is most, *most* frightened! Poor Brown, he gooc now!"

Roger raised his voice above the crashing and bangin that still echoed throughout the ship. "Now calm dowi everyone! You're none of you hurt. Just keep calm an you'll be all right. There's been some trouble with——"

Then the door of the saloon burst open and Hogben, hug in an orange lifejacket, burst into the slanted room, followe by Condron and half a dozen white-faced tourist passenger "What the f—in' 'ell's 'appening, Commander? What the 'e they up to upstairs? What's s'posed to be goin' on?" H voice was high with fear and anger, his small, hot ey glinting with the uncontrolled hysterical rage which gri animals forced together in dangerously confined spaces.

Roger had once seen the same thing in members of a su marine's crew in a moment of acute danger. Automatical he raised his voice and spoke with a slow, loud authorit "They've had some trouble with the engines—that's wh has happened. I expect the engineers will have them goi again in a few minutes. And it's not going to help matte if the passengers start running all over the ship like a lot scared hens in a farmyard! Nobody's drowning yet."

"Bloody soon will be, I reckon!" growled Hogben, b the note of hysteria left his voice and he anchored himse to a pillar with one bear-like paw. When he spoke agai it was with a half-threatening, half-pleading urgency. "Con on, Commander, let's 'ave it all! You got to tell us where stands. We sinkin'?"

Roger glanced quickly around him and licked his li Suddenly he realised that he was going to do something; did not quite know what, but this was an emergency a a large amount of his training had been in dealing wi sea-going emergencies. Of course he was going to do som thing, for here at last was a situation with which he cou cope. The knowledge filled him with an extraordinary sense of well-being, and that old trick of viewing himself from a short distance in front and a little above his normal height came back to him after an absence of nearly a year—Lieut.-Commander Lannfranc, R.N., dealing with an emergency. Disregarding Hogben's last question, he said loudly, "I've told you what the trouble is—temporary engine failure. Now let's get things sorted out. First, how many people have been hurt down in the tourist decks?"

"Two or three, I reckon, but——"

"Well, for Christ's sake get somebody to go and find out!" Roger's voice struck with all its old authority. "You've been in the Navy, Hogben. You should know better than to rush up here like a scalded cat just because we do a roll!"

Hogben's little eyes narrowed ominously. "Now, see here, Commander——" he began, but Roger cut him short and turned to Condron. "Look, you go down and find out how many are hurt. And get everyone into their life-jackets and ready to come up here when I tell them."

"Okay, Commander," agreed Condron promptly, and staggered across to the door. Like Hogben and the rest of the British migrants, he had a natural and inbred detestation of Roger, both as an officer and as a representative of a hated and decaying class system, but he also possessed a streak of cynical common sense which told him that for the present, at any rate, Roger would prove invaluable so long as his orders were obeyed with the promptness to which he was accustomed. As soon as he had gone Roger turned once more to Hogben, whose size and ferocity made him the obvious leader of the British migrants, despite his friend's quicker intelligence. "We'd better get the women and children up here as soon as possible. They'll be completely trapped down there in the dormitories if anything happens. We must get them up carefully and slowly, or they'll get hurt. I don't know where the hell all the bloody crew have got to, but——"

"Prayin' mostly—like the dagoes down with us," grunted Hogben. "Look 'ere, Commander. We got to do somethin' about it. Somethin' more'n just bringin' the women and kids up 'ere." His eyes, small and hot, met Roger's with a message that was unmistakable—perhaps because it had been in Roger's mind all the time, just below the surface. He nodded. "Yes, I know. But first things first. We can't do much till we're sorted out and organised. Now I'll come down to the mess decks with you."

It was entirely due to Roger that the incipient panic among the passengers was repressed before any harm was done. Leaving the first-class saloon in company with Hogben, he climbed with all his sailor's nimbleness down the heaving, canted companionways to the migrant accommodation. In the messy litter of the listing dormitories, among scared men, weeping women and howling children, he moved with a brisk certainty, a coolly genial assurance—a symbol of order and safety whose presence steadied snapping nerves and brought some sense of security to the most terrified and hopeless.

It was Roger who sorted out those passengers, both British and Italian, who had been hurt at the time of the great roll to starboard, and he who bullied trembling Tomei out of the surgery and down to the dormitories with the necessary medical equipment to deal with them. It was he, aided by Condron and Emilio Lodigianni, who ordered and assisted the slow lines of life-jacketed women and children carefully to the upper decks and marshalled them into their correct boat groupings in the listing saloons. And during all this time no officer or responsible member of the crew was to be seen. The few scared mess-boys and stewards who appeared were as useless for practical purposes as any of the passengers and, realising this, Roger treated them in the same way, saw that their life-jackets were properly adjusted, and made them fall in with the rest. In fact, busy and happier than he had been for twelve long months, Roger was hardly aware that he was doing work which should properly have been performed by the ship's officers and petty officers until Hogben brought it home to him. "All up 'ere now, Commander," he said, "an' no thanks to any of the bleedin' crew, either. Question is, what we do now. Isn't it?" They stood panting, sweating with the heat of their exertions and the stifling bulk of their life-jackets, gripping the side rails in the first-class saloon and surrounded by passengers of both classes.

Roger nodded, his eyes sliding over the faces around him, faces worn with fear and exhaustion and sea-sickness, faces framed incongruously in the kapok-stuffed collars of the life-jackets. For the first time for hours, it seemed, his thoughts turned to the bridge. What was going on up there? Why had no one come down to give information, issue orders or take control? Were they all dead or something? As far as he knew the engines had not started again, though with *San Roque* lying pinned down to starboard in the troughs of the waves their proper functioning might not perhaps have made very much difference to the present situation. Yet there were things that could be done—that *should* be done now. But were they being done? He gravely doubted it. He himself, assisted by two passengers, had been doing the jobs of both Semprebon and Petelli for the last hour. God alone knew what anyone else had been up to. And his life and the lives of all these people were in the balance.

"Yes." He took a deep breath, and when he spoke again it was loudly and with the intention of addressing not only Hogben but everyone around him. "We'll have to take things in hand from now on—properly in hand. It's no use pretending that this ship is being handled or run properly because it obviously isn't. Ever since we lost the Captain at Colombo I've been frightened of something happening—and now it has. I had a talk with the acting captain last night —Ciccolanti. He's too young and he's got too little experience, and at the same time he's obstinate and a bloody-minded little liar. He's got to be made to listen to reason, to take sensible advice and act on it, or—or else let someone more responsible take over. We've got a right to have a say in things now because of what's happened and because——"

"'Course we 'as!"

"Yes, indeed!"

"Too bleedin' true!"

"—because——" Roger's voice rose with quick triumphant anger—"I wouldn't put it at all past Ciccolanti to sink this ship in an hour or two if left to his own devices!"

A hubbub at once broke out across the crowded saloon. "Sink the ship!" . . . "Drown us all!" . . . "Of course it's quite possible, really. I mean, look at the things that have happened!" . . . "And that odd business when we left Colombo." . . . "Out of touch . . . no wireless . . . just another example of what Commander Lannfranc means." . . . "You just can't trust foreigners—that's what I says an' always 'as!" . . . "Is no *goodt* that man! I am knowing always is no goodt." . . . "Oh, Roger, dear, *how* I wish you were captain of this ship! I should feel so completely safe in your hands." . . . "'Course 'e oughter be! 'E knows it all—they gotter know it all in the Navy, see? This other bloke—'e don't know nothin'. It's obvious, ain't it? Otherwise we wouldn't be where we is."

There was a chorus of agreement and Roger, seeing Bronwen looking at him adoringly—surely for the first time in twelve months—raised a voice in which a less distressed and harassed audience would have noticed an unsuppressed note of jubilant triumph. "Very well, then. We'll rout out a seaman or—no, I'll go and phone from the vestibule."

4

On the bridge it was Bressan who answered the phone. He listened carefully to Roger's sharp, demanding voice, shouted, "One moment!" and turned to Serafino. "It's the passengers. They want to see you. They want to know what's going to happen next."

"Do they?" Serafino was staring down at the foredeck. Twenty minutes ago the starboard hydrocrane had been torn out by its roots and hurled across the tilted deck. Before it went over the side into the sea it had ripped the tarpaulin off the foredeck hatch, and now the hatch timbers themselves had gone. The hatch was unusually large—one of *San Roque's* several peculiarities of design—and as the waves broke regularly over the foredeck, ton after ton of solid green water poured through its gaping mouth. *San Roque* had already been heavily ballasted when the hatch cover had gone. Now, although the pumps were working at full pressure they could make little impression upon the ponderous and rapidly increasing weight of water in the bow. Already the ship was listing still farther to starboard, and, ominously, her rolling was growing less and less as she became heavier and settled deeper.

Serafino turned a face devoid of all expression to Bressan. "I can't go. I must stay up here. Your English is better than mine—you go. Unless——" He looked doubtfully to where Gil stood beside Malestroit, staring down with a stiff, horrific grin at the seas flooding through the foredeck hatch. But no; it would be better to send a ship's officer even though there was little that he could say. "Tell them we may be out of the storm soon. Say the wind is dropping." That, at any rate, was true enough. The wind force was falling rapidly, the air was clearer of spray, and

The gusts no longer tore roaring tunnels through a fog of driving sea-water. Had it not been for the list of the ship and the waves smashing over the foredeck, it would have been possible to get men out to cover that hatch.

On his way down to the saloon Bressan considered what he should tell the passengers. Not too much, obviously. It was a principle of the mercantile service never to let passengers think they were in danger if it was possible to induce them to think otherwise. But something must be said, and it was doubtful if a mere reassurance of safety, couched in general and non-technical terms, would suffice. Then, too, there was this ex-naval officer. . . . Bressan shook his head wearily. He was not strong, was easily tired and had been without sleep for the best part of two nights—and even down here the wind still seemed to be bellowing in his brain. Ciccolanti should have gone to the passengers himself; it was the Master's duty to calm them in an emergency and he was doing no good standing up there watching *San Roque* slowly fill by the head. Ciccolanti. He was responsible for everything; since he had come on board at Naples nothing had gone right; to everything he touched he brought disaster. Armando's death, too. . . . "The sea is so deep." The boy's words sighed softly in the back of Bressan's mind, filling him with a confused, angry despair.

Once in the saloon, however, he found that it was unnecessary for him to say anything. Lannfranc did all the talking, while Bressan himself stood listening expressionlessly, his bloodshot eyes half-shut, his stubbly jowl drooped on his chest, to the forceful English voice demanding to know, demanding to be consulted, demanding, it almost seemed, to take command of *San Roque*.

". . . so that is the way we feel about things at present . . . whole way this ship has been handled . . . just not good enough . . . Ciccolanti doesn't seem to realise . . . won't, or more probably can't . . . too young . . . second officer on a smaller ship, I've heard . . . our lives in such hands . . . children. . . ."

As soon as the quick voice stopped on an angry note of interrogation there was a deep fervent chorus of agreement, and then Bressan found himself facing an impatient, hostile audience. Aware, as ever, of his lack of presence, of his ugliness and his poor speaking voice, he felt no match for these people, and least of all for the ruddy-faced, stocky man straddled dictatorially before him. What was more, he understood their feelings and largely agreed with them. It suddenly struck him that there was no reason why he should defend Ciccolanti and every reason why he should not. The loss of Gino—poor little Armando—his own forthcoming resignation. He said slowly, "What do you want us to do?"

It was a question which nobody had expected and temporarily it silenced even Roger. It seemed—it sounded—almost like an abdication of responsibility on the part of the bridge and while it shocked the British passengers, it also bore out all their national theories. Here was the Second Officer a dirty, unshaven, exhausted foreigner, slumped heavily against a bulkhead, admitting himself and his colleagues to be at a complete loss and prepared, if not secretly anxious, to turn over responsibility to someone more competent and resourceful.

Hogben was the first to state their real desire, for he saw no reason to prepare a tactful reply. "We want Commander Lannfranc to take over—that's what we want, see? Our lives is in danger and we want someone we can trust like. Someone 'oo *knows* what to do. We don't trust this Ciccolanti feller—nor you, come to that, though you prob'ly ain't so bad, but——"

Roger interrupted quickly, sensing that Hogben was going too fast. "Well, perhaps we don't mean quite that exactly——"

"Don't we? We does, Commander. We means just that!" Hogben scowled and said something to Condron, who at once started to edge his way out of the crowded saloon.

Roger was saying, ". . . so we insist that we have a voice in what's to be done. I want to come up to the bridge, and —well, check up on everything and try to organise the proper handling of the ship in this emergency. You've got to listen to my advice and act upon it. The three of us together you and I and Ciccolanti, can get together and see what can——"

"If——" cut in Paula Chelgrove—"there is to be some sort of managing committee, I think my brother ought to be asked to join it. After all——"

"If only out of a reasonable desire for politeness, I too——" began Dr. Sessabandrian, but no one took any notice.

"Colonel Chelgrove isn't a sailor!" snapped Bronwen

furiously. "I can't see that he would be the slightest use in the present circumstances!" Like the rest of the passengers, with the exception of Roger, she had no idea of the ship's true condition, knowing only that the dreadful rolling and pitching had become much less, but she was not going to stand for this long, horse-faced bitch stealing any of Roger's limelight, and certainly not in front of Mrs. Crambatch to whom, she saw clearly, Roger was now appearing in the guise of a heroic saviour.

But Roger needed no assistance when it came to holding his own. He had just realised that the full command of *San Roque* might really be within his grasp. If Ciccolanti took the same supine and despairing attitude as Bressan there should be no difficulty at all. And he very well might, for Roger believed that all foreigners, particularly southerners, were prone to collapses of this sort when faced with frightening emergencies. Ciccolanti would probably be immensely, if secretly, relieved to hand over command and to slide out of the mess he had created by his own lack of competence. He was probably waiting up there, biting his nails and longing for Roger's cheerfully reassuring voice and calm confidence. In his mind's eye Roger saw himself entering the bridge with an air at once firm but encouraging. "Well," he would say, summing up the position with a practised eye, "this is certainly something of a shambles. But if we all get cracking I dare say it won't turn out to be so bad after all. . ." Meanwhile, he had plenty of backing and he was not going to stand for any interference. He glanced contemptuously at Paula Chelgrove. "If we were arranging a church bazaar I'm sure your brother would be most valuable—but we are not!"

Paula had never been so openly insulted in her life, but before she could reply Dr. Sessabandrian cut in hotly, "It is sometimes thought polite to listen when others speak—even persons of different races! What is more to the point, I have two small children with me. I am their sole maintainer. Probably Mr. Malcolm-Bruce will agree with me that as the fathers of children we have a special responsibility which——"

Mrs. Crambatch turned a shaky, red-eyed glance upon him. "Oh, do be *quiet*! Mrs. Lannfranc's going to have a baby too. I should have thought an unborn child is just as important——"

"Madam, I am not used to being addressed in that manner!"

"The ship," remarked Roger, who was receiving his firs lesson in the disadvantages of popularly elected leadershir "is almost certainly sinking while you argue. If we don cut out this talk and *do* something, there won't be any child ren or parents to get hot under the collar about!"

"And who's been doing all the talking?" came Flor McKenrick's voice unexpectedly. "It hasn't been us—it' been you." She turned to the Second Officer. "The ship' not really sinking, Mr. Bressan, is it?"

Bressan, who had been trying to compute the amount o water the pumps were capable of ejecting compared to th probable amount coming down the foredeck hatch, looked u with pallid surprise. He hesitated a long moment, torn b the conflicting emotions within him. Then he said quietly "Yes."

There was an appalled hush, and Roger, determined t retrieve his position at all costs, snapped, "Of course she is Can't you see this list? Can't you feel the waves hittin her? Can't——" But then he stopped suddenly. The lis yes, that was there; it was as bad as ever with the saloo deck tilted at something like 30° to starboard; but the wave were no longer striking the port side with their heavy muffled thuds, and the dull roaring of the wind, which her in the saloon had been heard as a deep, low hum, had entirel vanished.

XVII

The wind had gone. The ship lay heeled to starboard an down by the bow in a sea dark, silent and heaving in a deep troubled swell. A lifeless quiet had suddenly and mysteriousl taken the place of the thundering roar and whistle of the gale the crash of the waves and the whining groan of the labourin hull. Slowly, carefully, in ones and twos, then in small, trailin groups, people clambered up the sloping companionways t the canted decks; first-class and tourist, British and Italian passengers, service staff, deck crew, even one or two boiler suited engineers—all pouring out into the damp, humid ai like ants from a nest when a thunder-shower has passed.

They came from surroundings which, though dirtied an disordered, were at least thoroughly familiar into a worl they did not know and had never imagined. For the firs time they were able to see what the cyclone, and in particular the last hour, had done to *San Roque*. Practically everything remaining on the decks seemed to be broken or twisted or bent out of shape. To port, five of the ship's twelve new lifeboats had disappeared from the boat deck, leaving nothing but torn ends of rope trailing from their davits, while a sixth sagged broken-backed in the falls. The mast had vanished, the ventilators were nothing but holes in the planking, while the port side-light and part of the radio aerial lay in the swimming-pool in which a large dead seabird floated among minor wreckage. More horrifying still, the huge funnel, broken wide open, lay, a great crumpled sheet of metal, across the starboard side of the boat deck, while from its black and gaping hole protruded a few broken pipes and indistinguishable stumps.

Sticky oil filled the scuppers and ran in glistening black streaks from port to starboard; rags of canvas awning and bits of rope were twisted and knotted in rails and crevices, and the contents of a crate of oranges gleamed here and there among the débris like decorations from an abandoned Christmas tree. Worst of all was the angle of the ship. Far more noticeable above than below decks, it was quite sufficient in itself to frighten even the least impressionable among the passengers. That great tilt to starboard was a fearful indication of *San Roque's* defeated helplessness; it brought home to them, as nothing else could, their insecurity and insignificance on the empty, heaving expanse of the ocean.

Had they emerged into bright sunlight, had the sea been its familiar blue, the air fresh and clean and the sky clear, they might have felt at least partly reassured. Despite that alarming list, there would have been a sense of danger averted rather than present, a feeling of hope rather than foreboding. As it was, the state of the weather was not less ominous than that of the ship. For the cyclonic atmosphere still enveloped them in a humid, breathless silence. The sky seemed lower than ever and was a dull, steamy grey; the horizon was a close but indefinite line where ocean and sky dissolved mistily into each other. The air was thin, intensely enervating and so soggy with humidity that they were all perspiring heavily before they had been on deck two minutes. But it was the sea itself which was the most horrible, for it was black—as black, almost, as ink, yet with a glassy translucence which made it possible to stare down through fathoms of dark clarity to where scraps of foam and torn, ravelled strands of spume lay embedded like bubbles in a glass paperweight far below the rocking surface.

By far the greatest proportion of the passengers were migrants; poor people from poor homes who had never before been at sea. They had possessed none but the vaguest idea of ocean storms, and with no technical information save the small amount filtered down from Roger Lannfranc's remarks in the first-class saloon they had been quite unable to guess the severity of what they had just been through. Had *San Roque* still been herself, still on an even keel with her engine vibrations pulsating gently through the deck planks beneath their feet, they would never have guessed that she had been riding out a full-scale cyclone. Now, however, there could be no doubt in any of their minds that something most unusual and disastrous had occurred.

The British in particular were scared and consequently angry for unlike the Italians, they felt themselves to be in the hands of foreigners—and untrustworthy, incompetent foreigners at that. Gathering by habit at their accustomed place near the swimming-pool, they stared appalled at the messy wreck of *San Roque's* superstructure and shuddered at the grim, darkly glassy sea. Twenty minutes ago they had listened to Ted Condron as he moved from group to group explaining what he and Hogben had heard in the first-class saloon ". . . so that's what we think gotter be done, see? Now this bloke Lannfranc: I know what you thinks 'cos I thinks the same. Me an' old Ron, we don't like that officer-sort any more'n you do. Most of us as is old enough 'as 'ad our bellyful of that in the war. Fact is that's one of the reasons I'm going to Aussie—to get right away from all that shower 'cos they makes me sick an' always 'as. But as things are now we think—me 'n Ron—that we gotter 'elp 'im see? Lannfranc's a bleedin' bossy sort of bastard, but at least 'e ain't a dago and there ain't no one else who can get us outer this f—ing mess-up these dagoes 'ave got us into. So we gotter 'elp 'im."

Now, with their own eyes, they saw what had happened to *San Roque* and at once laid the blame for it and for the peril in which they stood on the foreign officers whom for the past weeks they had seen from time to time, quick-moving white figures going about their duties on the ship—and whom slowly they had begun to recognise individually—

" the lame one "—" the fat one "—" the tall old bloke in the office "—" the kid with the gold anchors." These were responsible for what had happened; these must be called to account. Marshalled by Condron and Hogben, they left their usual part of the ship and, picking their way carefully across the sloping planking, slipping and skidding on patches of viscid black oil, made their way up to the boat deck.

Roger, standing with the other first-class passengers, below the great black hole of the funnel just aft of the bridge, watched them coming with feelings of mixed satisfaction and guilt. He realised that Hogben was bringing them to form a clamorous background to his demands, but he would much rather have managed without them; he did not wish to give anyone the impression that he was using force. That was, he told himself uneasily, the last thing he intended to do; it was only a question of bringing reasoned pressure to bear. . . . None the less, he was determined to achieve command of the ship; it must be his completely and undividedly. The damage above decks had at first shocked him only slightly less than the rest of the passengers, but on closer inspection he had realised that it was mainly superficial. Superficial—but very spectacular. If he could get *San Roque* to port—he saw himself bringing her, storm-beaten but triumphant, into Fremantle harbour, saw the crowds on the docks, the photographs of himself in the newspapers—surely he could rely upon the gratitude of the Line and the insurance companies to help him to a sea-going position once more. He turned to Bressan, who had already sent a sailor to bring Ciccolanti from the foredeck where he was supervising the repair of the hatch. "I hope you'll impress upon him the sense of what I'm suggesting. There's bound to be some sort of inquiry over this affair. If he can say that. . . ."

Bressan said wearily, "I do not know what he will say or do, Mister Lannfranc. I have told you that I hardly know him at all. He only came on board at Naples, as you know." Bressan was growing more and more worried at the position into which Lannfranc seemed to be jockeying him. He had intended to adopt a negative attitude in this affair. He would neither help nor excuse Ciccolanti, nor would he abet the passengers in the making of unauthorised demands. He was exhausted and confused; the worry, the general unhappiness he had felt during the voyage, the fear and strain of the past twenty-four hours, had made clear thought an effort and action or decision of any kind a weary burden. Unlike Roger, towards whom he was beginning to feel an increasing antipathy, his nature was cast down rather than buoyed up by disaster. He felt himself groping in a fog of unreality.

Then Ciccolanti climbed into view at the forward end of the tilted boat deck and, with Malestroit following him, came down towards the group of waiting passengers. It was surprising what little effect the dangerous and exhausting events of the past twenty-four hours seemed to have had upon him. His eyes were red-rimmed, his clothes creased and dirty, but there was about him none of the weary dejection of Bressan. He seemed perfectly sure of himself, and were it not for the ruinous evidence around him might have been thought to have the situation well in hand. At his approach a growl of anger and complaint went up from the crowded British migrants behind Hogben, but Roger angrily motioned them to be silent and a hush fell over the boat deck as the officers approached.

There was no doubt, Roger realised at once, that Ciccolanti had some idea of what was going to be demanded, and less doubt that he meant to resist it. His face was cold and grim and he moved with a wary tenseness which disguised his normal limp. So there *was* going to be a struggle. Ciccolanti was not, after all, secretly longing to hand over responsibility for *San Roque* and her passengers to a British naval officer. Roger's own determination to get command of the ship hardened rapidly at the prospect of a battle, and his bitter envy and dislike of Ciccolanti turned to fierce hatred. He would willingly have seen *San Roque* in a still worse condition if this would have reduced Ciccolanti to the exhausted, supine state of Bressan. As it was—he swallowed, feeling the blood beginning to pound hotly in his face—it did not matter; he was still going to get command of the ship. He *must*. It was the only way of escape from the intolerable future toward which Bronwen, with her stronger will, was remorselessly impelling him. Only Ciccolanti, small and grim in his grubby whites, remained an obstacle between him and his dream of safety and release.

"Well?" Serafino's gaze was fixed upon Roger and disregarded the other passengers grouped behind him. Bressan's message had reached him while he was supervising a sullen Petelli and six scared and surly sailors as they repaired the big foredeck hatch with some thin deal planks and covered it with two undamaged awnings someone had found in a locker. Typically, the Flotta Soto had not seen fit to go to the expense of providing spare hatch timbers or tarpaulins. He had left Gino to see that the chocks were firmly knocked home, and had come up here to the boat deck prepared for trouble. And now he saw at once that there was going to be trouble—with Lannfranc, of course, as the instigator.

Since their first encounter at Port Said he had slowly begun to realise the jealousy that lay in the heart of this short, heavily built, handsome man. At first it had seemed to him quite incredible that anyone—but particularly an Englishman with a good pension and enough money to travel first-class across the world—could envy the life of an officer of the Flotta Soto. It had dourly amused him to picture Lannfranc's dismay if they were, in some magical way, to change places overnight and he awoke one morning to find himself on Don Ildefonso's meagre and uncertain payroll and with a large family to support back in Naples. If he were forced to live his life always at the sharp edge of poverty, never without the knowledge that dismissal would entail immediate, inescapable want; if he too limped from a maimed foot which often hurt and was always a dragging disadvantage in shipboard life. . . . For most of the voyage Lannfranc's angry envy had been an inexplicable but sardonic source of inward amusement to him, and it was only during his visit to the bridge last night that the Englishman's desire had become at least partly clear. Lannfranc itched to possess authority. He could not bear to watch decisions made and orders given by someone else. He was the sort of man who held an almost magical belief in his own ability to exercise command over his fellows and who would take up every new position with the words, "I must have things done *my* way."

Now, looking at that hot, excited face, the thrust-out jaw and the truculent grey eyes, Serafino understood well enough what was coming. Lannfranc was going to demand some sort of share in the direction of the measures which must be undertaken to save the ship and her company. At that knowledge his thin lips tightened into a hard line. Already badly under-officered, *San Roque's* cosmopolitan crew needed constant supervision if the best was to be got from them in this crisis. An addition to the bridge staff of a competent and experienced sea officer would be a true godsend, and if this officer also had the confidence of the passengers. . . . But not Lannfranc—not under any circumstances or on any conditions. Clearly, coldly, Serafino saw in Lannfranc an archaic enemy from the past. There had been another Lannfranc, aggressive, vengeful and ferocious, high in the sky above Naples sixteen years ago. . . . And now a stubborn obstinacy filled him, an iron determination that Lannfranc should not usurp a single one of his prerogatives as captain; should have no voice whatever in any future decisions, should never again set foot upon *San Roque's* bridge. His body tensed, Serafino stared back at that damply hot, ruddy face with a sombre bitterness which contrasted coldly with the Englishman's angry, mounting excitement.

Roger shifted his own glance from Serafino's face and gazed slowly, deliberately around him at the scattered wreckage on the deck, at the empty davits with their torn trailing ropes, at the great crumpled ruin of the funnel. "This is a bloody fine shambles, isn't it?" His voice was loudly scornful. "Now look here, Ciccolanti. You've got us into this and it would serve you right if we told you that you've bloody well got to get us out! But we're not doing that. What we *are* going to do is to help *you* get out of it." Roger's voice lost its hectoring tone and became roughly persuasive. "Look, we know all about you. We know that you are really only a second officer on a smaller ship than this one; we know that you were only acting chief because the last fellow resigned at a moment's notice, and they had to find someone else in a hurry. We know you've never had a command in your life before. It has been bad luck for you that things have turned out as they have—Onestinghel dying at Colombo and then this storm. We don't blame you too much for what has happened or the way you've dealt with it. Under normal circumstances and good weather conditions we wouldn't have cared who was commanding the ship; in a flat calm we'd have been happy enough to have had Gino on the bridge. But after what's happened we can't leave matters in the hands of someone who hasn't the experience or the knowledge to deal with them." Once more he stared condemningly around the canted deck. "You've had your chance—and this is the result. We're not prepared to leave you in charge any longer." He paused, but Ciccolanti made no response and after a moment he continued with growing anger. "The majority of the passengers are British and a lot

›f them have young children." He turned as if for corrobora-
ion to the crowd behind him, and there was a deep growl ›f assent. "They've got a right to make demands for their ›wn safety. There's no reason why they should sit here .nd let you drown them like a lot of mice in a cage, is here?" Again came the chorus of angry agreement and woman's voice shouted, "Little bastard, would, too, if 'e hought 'e could get away with it!"

Roger scowled quickly over his shoulder. When he spoke gain it was with an air of awkward, off-hand, rather sullen nodesty. "Now you know about me, too. So do the assengers. I'm nearly ten years older than you and I've een far longer at sea. I've held two different commands uring that time and I only laid down the last one a year go. I don't think there can be any doubt that my training 'as far more thorough than yours and my experience very nuch wider. I won't go into the differences between the Royal Navy and the Italian merchant marine, or the Panamanian shing fleet or whatever it is you really belong to. The act is that the passengers want me to take over from you." Once more, louder now, impatient and threatening, came he chorus of assent from behind him. "Now look, Cic-olanti—it's your life as well as theirs, isn't it? You don't 'ant to drown any more than they do. And you needn't hink people will make trouble for you later. Because nybody can see that you're not well at present." Roger rinned quickly. "We'll write a document if you like, stating hat as a fact—a breakdown through overstrain or something. 'll sign it and Bressan will too."

And then Serafino turned his head and looked at Bressan or the first time. "What do you know of all this?" He poke in Italian and Bressan's face coloured slowly. "I? Only hat you have just heard."

"And do you agree with what this man has said?"

Bressan's shoulders lifted helplessly. "A lot of it is true, n't it? You are not an experienced captain; he is. And 's obvious that when he says that a majority of the assengers want him to take over he's speaking the——"

"Do you *agree* with him?"

"I—I don't agree or disagree. I——"

But Roger had become impatient, and what was more he ensed the still greater impatience of the British migrants ehind him. "Well, Ciccolanti—come on. You've under-ood more or less all I've said, haven't you?"

Serafino, glancing round, noticed that Gil had come dow from the bridge and was watching the proceedings on th boat deck with interest; hands in pockets, he leant agains the bridge ladder and on his face was once more that peculiar uncertain mocking grin. Gil—Gil's father. What woul Don Ildefonso say if he knew what was happening at thi moment on the battered hulk that had so recently been th pride of his fleet? Probably he would want Lannfranc t take command because the man's past as a naval officer woul impress him and because of his well-known contempt for hi own employees. He would think Lannfranc more likel to safeguard the life of his precious son. Yes, if the Owne had been in a position to voice his opinion it would have bee in the Englishman's favour—and afterwards, of course, h would have thrown out the temporary master of *San Roqu* as a contemptible failure. But Don Ildefonso was in n position to make his voice heard; his hypothetical instruc tions could be safely disregarded. And for the first time i his life Serafino found himself thinking of Don Ildefons with complete indifference. For during the agonisingly lon hour while *San Roque* lay pinned on her side and awas in the troughs of the slowly quietening waves he had come t realise that Don Ildefonso was no longer the enemy with whor he had to contend nor dismissal the fate he had to fea Now he must fight the wind and the waves for his own lif and the life of his ship. Battered, dismasted, awash both for and aft and with her engines out of action, *San Roqu* became his ship at last and he himself ceased to be her care taker and became her captain.

Slowly he said, "Yes, I understand. But there are n things you can make to do more than I. I am not sick I and Signor Malestroit——" he made a quick movement c his hand towards the Third Officer standing beside him– "are—are making correctly all things that is possible to b done." He spoke with a dry calm which had its effec particularly on the first-class passengers who stood on Roger left slightly apart from the rest. Here, it was apparent, stoo no nervously exhausted and despairing Latin. Ciccolan might be incompetent—visible circumstances were undoubtedl in favour of Lannfranc's theory on that point—but he was i complete control of himself and, by his own reckoning, c the situation.

Inevitably it was Roger whose self-control now bega

to slip in the face of Ciccolanti's exasperating calm. Had everything he had said meant nothing to this grim-faced young man standing there in all the advantages of his authorised rank and the badges on his dirty white uniform? He was not used to his speeches being disregarded so nonchalantly; it left him at a loss. He had made all his arguments cogently, forcefully, and with every show of reason; Ciccolanti had parried them and turned them aside with one short and irrelevent statement. It wasn't good enough! He was being cheated out of something which he not only desperately wanted but which every instinct of race and class, training and upbringing, told him was justly his. And he had just made it absolutely plain why this was so. He heard the British migrants muttering loudly behind him and sensed that they were becoming exasperated both by Ciccolanti's obstinacy and his own seeming inability to deal with it. He drew a deep breath. "Well, I *don't* think so! None of us thinks you're doing any good or likely to do any!" His voice, loud and hectoring, sounded a note of exhausted patience. "Now look here, Ciccolanti! Are you going to do the only *sensible*—the only *reasonable*—thing you can do and let me take charge?"

"Take command of my ship?"

"It's *not* your ship! I mean, I know you've been appointed temporary master, but anyway—I mean that doesn't alter what's happened and—and—well, can't you *see* that you've got no chance!" Roger's voice struck a note of almost hysterical shrillness, his face was crimson and his mouth twisted into ugly fury as he struggled for an answer that fitted his purpose.

For the first time Serafino grinned widely. He had suddenly remembered something Japheth Wendlandt had once said to him while staring disgustedly at a party of rowdy British police officers in a bar at Port of Spain. "You only got to face up to the limey's and you'll win every time. They're so goddam used to people bowing and scraping to them that as soon as someone gets tough they're—what do you say—*kaputt!*"

Now he said deliberately, "I am captain of *San Roque*. I am not giving up that for you or other people. You understand always that."

In the immediate roar of rage that followed his words Serafino realised that he had been too abrupt—realised for the first time how much these people hated him. He saw

Lannfranc take a sudden step forward, jostled and pushed by the exasperated and menacing crowd behind him, and involuntarily stepped back himself. He glanced round with quick despair for Petelli and the deck crew, but there was no sign of them; they must still be working down on the foredeck where Gino had probably put them to clearing wreckage over the side. Once more he heard Lannfranc's furious voice: "You see! *You've got no choice!*"

The angry clamour of the mob of migrants was unmistakable in its implications of savage violence; his tongue flickered apprehensively across his lips and unsteadily he said, "You mean you make to mutiny?"

"I—what do you mean, *mutiny*?" Lannfranc's face lost its contorted anger and was shadowed momentarily by fear. "No one's talking about mutiny! It's—it's just——" He swallowed and tried to take a step backwards and was at once thrust roughly to one side by a huge hand.

"Ah—get outer my way!" Hogben had finally lost patience. Talk! That was all Lannfranc was doing or was going to do. Talk, talk, talk, nothing but arguing and talk. But there was only one way to deal with dagoes—and it wasn't by talking to them! Now he loomed over Serafino, his little eyes aflame with anger, his huge hands advanced before him like mechanical grabs. "All right, then! If that's how you wants it!" With one hand he seized Serafino by the throat and with the others he swept Malestroit to the deck as the Belgian struck viciously at his huge stomach. "Now!" With two quick jerks he ripped the epaulettes from Serafino's shoulders and flung them over the side. "Now you ain't captain no more—see! You ain't anythin' now. Nothin' at all!"

There was a swelling roar of satisfaction from the British migrants, Hogben had done it on his own. Lannfranc had become scared and backed down, adding still further to the perennial contempt in which they held his sort. But Hogben had gone ahead and done it. Now weeks of furtive hatred and bitter national and class inferiority were being avenged. For a moment they forgot their fear, the improperly understood peril of their situation and the past hours of sickness and exhaustion, in the spectacle of Hogben triumphant. For a moment in time he symbolised in himself all that they knew and valued—a whole industrial working-class ethos of anarchy and beer, a boasting, belching world of dingy corner pubs, foggy dog-tracks and squalid Saturday nights.

" Ron's done it! Good old Ron!" . . . " That's right, Ron, boy! Go on—give 'im some more!" . . . " Kick the dirty little tyke's teeth in!" . . . " Break 'is bleedin' neck for 'im!" Only Condron, quicker than the others, shouted, " Look out, Ron! Mind that other bastard!"

But he was too late. Gil had stepped quickly up behind Serafino, and as Hogben turned at his friend's urgent cry the heavy butt of Gil's pistol struck him a stunning blow in the face. For a second he tottered and then crashed to the deck, bringing Serafino down with him, crushing him with his twenty stone, spraying him with blood from an upper lip through which two front teeth protruded brokenly. In the momentary, bewildered hush, while Malestroit heaved Serafino, choking and gasping, from beneath Hogben's sprawled bulk, Gil reversed the gun in his hand and pointed it at Roger Lannfranc, who stood staring stupidly from face to face. " This is because of you! You are responsible! You started this trouble——"

" I——" But no one ever heard Roger's reply, for Paula Chelgrove's voice cut clearly through the sudden stillness. " I can't see what difference it makes *who* is captain! We've been told the ship is sinking. If it is, then someone ought to be organising the boats. I'm sure my brother——"

" The boats!" The words were echoed in a screech of approval by Mrs. Thorsby in the heart of the crowd. " We gotter take to the boats! Wimmin an' children first!"

" The boats! The boats!" It was a sudden shout of immense relief as the lifeboats, the shining white symbols of survival and rescue, were remembered. And now Hogben, propped against the rail and holding his battered bloody face, Gil with his gun, the whole taut, ugly episode of the last few minutes, all was forgotten in the sudden intense desire for the boats. It was partly the herd instinct for survival overcoming the fearful herd demand for a scapegoat, but included in it was an unvoiced but passionate wish to quit *San Roque* at all costs—to get away from this dangerous foreign ship with its untrustworthy officers and incompetent crew and its memories of anger and hatred and mounting fear. And forgotten beyond all else, utterly disregarded and unheeded, Roger Lannfranc glared miserably at the jostling crowd.

2

"The boats! The boats!" The words beat dully on Serafino's ears, muffled and muted under the singing and roaring of returning blood. He still felt the strangling grip of Hogben's iron hand on his throat and the crushing weight of Hogben's huge body on his bruised ribs. He leant weakly on the starboard rail, shaking his head dizzily while waves of sickness passed over him and pain stabbed up his right leg from his maimed foot. He felt battered and empty and exhausted, and in the back of his mind a small futile voice dully retraced a long line of causation about boats. "If only the Line had kept all its boats in good condition in the first place *San Raphael* would not have got into trouble at Fremantle in July. So *San Roque* would not have waited the extra two days in Naples for her new boats and Parodi's uncle would not have come down from Genoa in time and Parodi would have left on this voyage for Sydney, and you would have been still in Naples while *San Ramòn* completed her refit and . . ."

Then Gil was shouting at him, shaking him by the torn shoulder of his shirt. "Do something, for God's sake! You're still captain, thanks to me—but only just! Where has Petelli got to? He should be——"

From a great way off Serafino heard Malestroit's Belgian-accented voice. "The heroic Petelli? Our *Capitan d'armi*, Signor Sotomayor, is probably hiding in one of the lavatories. He is profoundly frightened of the English passengers; they scare him out of the few wits with which he was born."

"*Coño!*" Gil remarked, without apparent heat and, lifting his pistol, he fired twice up at the low grey sky. The two detonations sounded oddly flat and weak, their normal sharp crack muted muffled and deadened by the soggy, lifeless atmosphere. None the less they brought an instant hush to the hubbub of raised voice, and the clamour and shouting along the crowded boat deck suddenly stilled. The two shots close beside him jolted Serafino back into the grim reality of the present moment: a listing, lifeless ship adrift on a sin-black sea under a lowering sky; a herd of frightened, savage and probably uncontrollable human beings about to stampede for the few remaining boats.

Oddly light-headed now and still breathing with difficulty from a chest which felt crushed permanently out of shape, he climbed on to an upturned Carley float which had become wedged between a broken ventilator and the remains of the radio bearings aerial hurled down from the roof of the bridge. And now, as might have been expected, he saw that the mad idea first voiced by that gaunt old fool of an Englishwoman had infected them all. First-class passengers, migrants both English and Italian, crewmen and mess-boys, their combined will beat up at him like something so strong as to be almost tangible, almost solid—a will to get away in the boats.

Quickly, before the quietening effect of Gil's pistol shots was forgotten, he shouted hoarsely, " It is no good—the boats! Here, on the ship you have more safety! Listen——"

But at his words the spell broke. A high-pitched shout came from somewhere among the English passengers. " Listen to you? We *done* listenin' to you! You don't know nothin'!" And again a swelling roar of anger shot through with the sharp overtones of women's fear broke out among the sweating, jostling crowd on the canted deck.

" Quiet! 'Old on a minute!" Condron's voice cut harshly through the clamour. " 'Old *on,* I says!" Slowly now, for the second time, reluctantly and resentfully the noise stilled. Condron, his sloping forehead gleaming with sweat, his bony jaw bristly with orange stubble that seemed to take its hue from the kapok collar of his life-jacket, shouldered his way out of the throng and, keeping a watchful eye on Gil, carefully approached the Carley float and stared up at Serafino from red-rimmed eyes. When he spoke his voice was at once threatening and full of an exasperated, breathless demand for reason. " Look, mister, for Christalmighty's sake let's just *try* to be a bit sensible-like, eh? I knows you're a foreigner an' gets excited easy, but you gotter be sensible over this, see? 'Cos if you ain't, your pal here with the gun won't make no difference—we'll get you all right. An' then over the side you'll go, same as your shoulder-straps went. I give you my bleedin' word! You're lucky it's not bin done yet: f—ing mess-up you've made of everything so far!" He paused and thrust his hands deeply into his trouser pockets, hunched his shoulders and turned slightly so that he was addressing both Serafino and the crowd. " Second Officer says this boat's sinkin'. I heard 'im. An' 'e ought to know. No, no, not this minute, she ain't sinkin' —take another hour maybe. Right; what's to do, then? Take to the boats, of course! No!" He lifted a hand to still the shouts and angry demands that immediately arose. "No, we'll just 'ear why this young feller what's got us into this bleedin' shambles *don't* want us to get out." He jerked his head at Serafino. "Go on then—tell 'em."

Serafino breathed deeply, staring down at the upturned hostile faces, seeing many of his crew among them, their expressions as angry and fearful as those of the passengers: Meschia, the fat Chief Steward; Ruggiero, the quartermaster; Consolini; Ansaldo. He swallowed painfully, knowing that this, his first speech as Master might also be his last—perhaps the last of his life. Yet what he had to say must be said, for legally he was still responsible not only for the ship but for the lives of all aboard her. He licked his cracked lips.

"For this reason it is not good to use the boats." His voice was hoarse and muted by the deadly humidity to a dull, metallic flatness. "We are not outside this storm. We are *inside* of it! You think that it finishes—but that is not. We are in the centre—the *dead centre*! All round of us is the wind." He paused, trying desperately to find some way to make these people understand what he himself knew well, what every sailor knew—the set, invariable physical laws of the cyclonic system. The air rising over a warm patch of sea, the colder, heavier air rushing in below to replace it and forming a fierce wind. The first slow spiralling of the system caused by the turning globe; the condensation of the hot, sodden air far up in the sky falling in warm rain and releasing a fearful energy to spin the system with ever-increasing speed. Faster and faster and faster yet, the great winds roaring in their thunderous vortex around a centre into which their own centrifugal bias prevented them from forcing their way. . . . But simple as it seemed to him, he realised immediately that it would be quite impossible to explain it to these people whose comprehension had never risen above the small details of their daily lives. They would believe he was inventing something for reasons of his own. Then he thought of Bressan—perhaps if Bressan added his corroboration . . . "Listen! The Second Officer, Signor Bressan—he will say to you that what I say is true!"

"Will 'e? We'll see." Condron glanced quickly round and caught sight of Bressan standing apart from the crowd and talking quietly to an agitated Cavaliere Semprebon and a grimly silent Malpiero. "All right then, mister. What 'ave *you* got to say?"

Bressan did not move from his position against the rails, he only lifted his head slightly and gazed expressionlessly from his heavy-lidded eyes at the small figure on the Carley float. For he knew now—had known ever since Hogben's attack on Ciccolanti—that he had gone too far to retreat. As Gil Sotomayor had said, Lannfranc had started the trouble, and somehow—he hardly knew how or why—he himself had been inveigled into a tacit alliance with the Englishman. At least that was obviously the light in which his conduct appeared to both Ciccolanti and young Sotomayor. At any inquiry there might be later he would find himself denounced both by *San Roque's* master and the son of her owner. It would be of no use to plead exhaustion or illness, or to say that truly he had intended to do no more than to act as a go-between in an attempt to bring everyone together in the best interests of the ship and her company: no excuses would be accepted for his failure to uphold constituted authority against an attempted usurpation. It would be the final end of his sea-going career. And inwardly he knew that he had wanted to see Lannfranc take over, not only because of his own animosity towards Ciccolanti but because he considered Lannfranc would be a safer and more able captain in the present emergency. But that was out of the question now. Lannfranc had proved a broken reed and Gil's gun alone prevented Condron and Hogben and their friends from gaining control of the ship. Yet one pistol, however determinedly used, was not going to be a safeguard much longer, that was obvious. Unless Ciccolanti gave way quickly. . . . Bressan caught a glimpse of Hogben's bloody face above the crowd and shuddered; once the migrants took over there would be no mercy for Ciccolanti or Gil Sotomayor, nor for anyone who tried to help them.

"Well——?" Condron's voice was impatient and he jerked his thumb at Ciccolanti. "It's not only us as is askin' you—it's 'im, too."

Bressan licked his lips and lifted his eyes to that small, thin figure on the float, noting the torn shirt, the big gold-badged hat set at its usual, oddly rakish angle. Ciccolanti—Gino—Armando. He said coldly, "I cannot tell you that we are in the centre of this cyclone. We have no weather reports.

It is impossible to say where we are. We may, perhaps, be on the outside edge."

"But 'e says——"

"It is his opinion, that is all."

Condron shook his head in bewildered exasperation. "None of you knows nothin'—do yer? *Christallbloodymighty,* what a shower! Well, just try an' answer *this* one: Are we going to be better off on the ship or in them boats?"

But his friends had waited long enough. There was an impatient shout of "Boats! Of course we'll be safer in the boats! Cut out the jawin', Ted Condron!"

But Condron wanted assurance from at least one sailor. "Wait! Wait on a bit! Come on now, mister. Let's 'ave it straight, for Christ's sake!"

And now at last Bressan took the plunge. Very quickly, rather loudly, he said, "I do not think that Signor Ciccolanti is justified in refusing to allow the passengers—or as many of them as can do this—to leave the ship and go in the boats." For Bressan's mind had been working fast as he stumbled evasively over Condron's first questions and had evolved a perfectly logical answer to at least a part of the present situation. Without weather reports it was impossible to be certain whether they were in the centre of the storm or on its periphery. There were indications that Ciccolanti's insistence on the centre might be right, but . . . None of them had been in a cyclone before; none of them really *knew*. Also, it was impossible to tell which way the storm was moving; even if they were on the periphery they might easily be sucked back inside. *San Roque* could never stand a repetition of what she had gone through since her engines stopped, any sailor could see that. But what were the chances for open boats? In seas that crashed into each other and exploded into flying foam at sixty and seventy feet? In waves that fell with the weight of hundreds of tons of solid water? No one knew; no living man had returned to tell of such an experience. The boats were the newest and best in the world, they were unsinkable theoretically . . . But not, said a cold voice at the back of Bressan's mind, in practice. In practice nothing was unsinkable.

Still, if the storm returned *San Roque's* chances were nil while the chances for her boats were yet unproven. And Ciccolanti would not go in the boats, that much was certain. If the boats survived and *San Roque* foundered, he himself would be proved right, Ciccolanti wrong. He took one step forward from the rails and repeated, "I do not think he is justified." Then his own dark eyes met Ciccolanti's lighter, tawny ones, and in that moment a sudden clear ray of knowledge pierced the gloom of suspicion, jealousy and misunderstanding through which he had viewed this small embattled figure ever since Naples. And with a shock of desolating recognition he knew that Ciccolanti was the one for whom he had waited so long in vain, for whom he had searched with slowly fading hope throughout the long, long years—the one friend who would have understood him, accepted him unconditionally, valued him for what he was rather than what he seemed; Ciccolanti with his sardonic humour, his queer, hard grin, his stubborn patience, his odd aura of tired, slightly sullen innocence; Ciccolanti—and he had never known it—had wanted instead Gino's bright, ordinary happiness.

But it was far too late now. Those gold-flecked, light-brown eyes stared down at him with no hint of anything save cold, perplexed anger; the deep voice, hoarse and higher than usual, said, "But you *know* that is mad! You *know* the boats would not stand a chance!"

It was too late to change anything at all; there was no point in retracting, in going back, in trying to alter the roles they had to play. With a long, sighing breath Bressan said, "I do *not* know anything of the kind. I *do* know *San Roque* will founder if the storm strikes her again."

"No."

"Then you are the only one who thinks that. You are the captain, not I. But in your position I would try to get as many of the passengers as possible away in the boats."

They had been talking in Italian and now Condron exploded impatiently. "Come on! Come on! What's the answer?"

There was only one way out and Bressan took it. "Listen, Ciccolanti. They're going to take the boats whether you like it or not. It is best for everyone that it should be done properly. I believe I am right about the boats. I will go with them." He spoke with rapid urgency, sensing time running out, sensing the frustrated fury of the migrants rising to explosion point. "Call for volunteers from the crew to man them—or to stay on board if they all want to go. Try to get the passengers to draw lots or something for their own places. But for God's sake *give the order now!*"

The note of intense, of anguished, urgency in Bressan's

voice abruptly changed Serafino's mind at the last moment. Before the Second Officer's words he had decided that he would not—never under any circumstances or at whatever personal cost—agree in any way to the launching of the boats. As Captain, it was his duty to do everything to save the lives of the ship's company, not to allow—still less assist—them to endanger themselves further. Onestinghel would not have. . . . But Onestinghel was seventy-three, not twenty-six; they would have listened to Onestinghel and obeyed him, believing his age made him infallible. For himself it was different. Once more Onestinghel's words came back to him: "The English dislike youth." Yet that was no excuse for acceding to the suicidal demands of ignorant landsmen who did not even know that they were in a cyclone.

But Bressan was a sailor too; had, in fact, been longer at sea than himself. If Bressan not only urged the launching of the boats but believed in it sufficiently to want to go in them himself. . . .

"*Va bene.*" He stared briefly round him, rubbed his hand across his mouth, cracked and sore with the driven salt spray of the storm, and said tiredly, "All who can go in the boats—all right. Signor Bressan will be *commandante* of the boats. I say only this: it is better to be staying on the ship."

In the sudden pandemonium of shouting relief he turned, his shoulders sagging, and slid down from the float, feeling Gil's strong hand steadying him, seeing Gil's dark, hot face close to his own, hearing his furious voice. "Bressan! If ever I get back to Naples I'll make quite sure Bressan never——"

Serafino shook his head wearily and turned to the heavy-shouldered young Spaniard beside him. "Bressan's entitled to his opinion, isn't he? If he thinks——"

Gil stared at him with angry astonishment. "You're captain—not him!" He paused. "You don't think he's right about the boats, do you?"

"No. But if *you* do you'd better get yourself a place in one of them." Serafino glanced down at Onestinghel's big black automatic in Gil's hand. "You've got a gun after all." he said with bitter sarcasm and, turning away, climbed the ladder to the canted empty bridge, as disregarded now by everyone as Roger Lannfranc had been ten minutes ago.

XVIII

And now the listing deck became a scene of anarchic tumult. The last tattered shreds of recognised authority had been blown to the winds as soon as the Chief Officer, capitulating over the boats, had climbed down from his float, and there was no one left upon *San Roque* who could any longer give an order in the expectation of having it obeyed. The knowledge of this added a fierceness to the passionate instinct for survival which swept aside all notions of self-control both among the shouting, milling migrant passengers and the majority of the crew. With a hopeless sinking of his heart Bressan realised that there was no longer the slightest possibility either of calling for volunteers to stay aboard or of the orderly manning and launching of *San Roque's* six remaining lifeboats.

Shouting, demanding, pleading unavailingly, he was jostled and pushed from side to side, unheard and unnoticed by all. He saw Semprebon towering thinly out of the crowd, crying out something about provisions, throwing up his arms in despair; saw Petelli, his face crimson above his life-jacket, thrusting his way to the Number 10 davits with four deck-hands, and heard the heightened roar as the first boat swung low at the rails. Screaming and cursing in hoarse English and shrill Italian, the passengers flung themselves upon it in a struggling mass, to be held off for a moment by the winch handles of a gang of sweating deck-hands who had wanted the boat for themselves. Petelli's hoarse screech cut through the din, and to a chorus of frustrated rage the swaying boat lifted abruptly as the davits swung up again. "Now take it *easy*! For Chrissake take it *slow*!" Condron's voice bellowed agonised appeal, but as Number 10 lowered a second time a more purposeful rush forced back the sailors, and Bressan's shoulders slumped in despair as a flood of yelling humanity poured into the rocking, quivering boat.

Then suddenly it began to rain. Heavily, silently, warmly, rain poured from the low grey sky. With rapidly increasing strength it beat a growing tattoo on *San Roque's* deck, soaked the milling throng about Bressan and the davits and pocked the heaving black swell with a carpet of silver spray. Within seconds it was a torrential downpour, falling in nearly solid sheets and blotting out vision in a shimmering, quivering, rebounding screen of grey-silver spray. It added the final touch of physical degradation to the dishevelled, life-jacketed passengers, plastering their clothes soddenly to their legs and thighs, washing the women's hair across their faces in dripping strands, and smudging the last remaining traces of yesterday's make-up in greasy splodges over lips and chins.

But it brought abrupt cessation to the perilous struggle round the boats. Beaten down by that weight of vertically falling water, hardly able to see or breathe and only with immense difficulty retaining their balance on the slippery planking of the slanted deck, the crowd quietened, fell silent and edged away into corners or under the wings of the bridge for shelter from the open sluices of the sky.

2

In a little group by themselves the first-class passengers stood forlornly in the shelter of the port bridge wing, unwilling and shocked spectators of a play in which they no longer had a part. "If only," Bronwen said, staring tearfully through the hissing rain at the first drenched, crowded lifeboat still hanging in its davits, "if only they had listened to Roger!"

Angry, harassed and frightened, the rest turned upon her savagely. "If only your husband had possessed the sense to——"

"If Commander Lannfranc had *done* something, instead of just talking——"

"If he'd put up a better show with Ciccolanti, instead of——"

"If he'd used some proper initiative, rather than let that man Hogben——"

But the accusing, quarrelling voices striking at him obliquely passed nearly unnoticed over Roger, sunk in a despondency too deep to be the target of anyone's scorn. For it was all over now—his last, desperate bid for a come-back, a return to his old lost position of authority and command. He had failed, done nothing more than start an abortive mutiny, stirred up trouble which, assisted by the interference of Paula Chelgrove, had brought about the present chaos, thereby greatly enhancing the danger of an already perilous position. Bitterly he remembered the angry contempt in Gil Sotomayor's voice: "This is because of you! You are responsible. You started this trouble." And after that they had ignored him completely, all of them, just as if he was a—a mere passenger who had been a nuisance and now had been abruptly put in his place and could be left there. But he wasn't! Of course he wasn't! He was—he was Lieut-Commander Lannfranc, R.N., the captain of *Sting-ray,* the . . . But it wouldn't work; the picture, the old vision of himself seen from a distance of some six feet from where he stood and a height about fifteen inches above his own, refused to materialise. In a panic he flung over mental switches, desperately turning on memories, connecting and reconnecting recollected compliments, tuning in to old glimpses of himself through the admiring eyes of others. For a moment the periscope handles were there, but they dissolved as he grasped them, the control room was full of mist and he could hardly make out the dimming, shadowy figure of a stocky officer with a rakishly angled cap as the long serial film of the life and career of Lieut-Commander Lannfranc, R.N., faded, fused, and flickered for ever off the screen.

But Bronwen was tugging irresistibly at his arm. "Roger! Roger, you've got to do *something*! Are we going in the boats or are we staying on the ship? We'd better go in the boats, hadn't we? *Hadn't we?*"

Roger gave a quick shrug, and as the last remnants of the Technicolor might-have-been died for ever from his mind, he saw their present position in the wan light of reality. Gazing around at the messy clutter of the canted deck under the cataracting rain, feeling the soggy lifelessness of the ship beneath his feet, he remembered the ghastly roll just before six o'clock—they had nearly gone then. He shuddered; if the storm returned . . . But what, then, of the boats? Like the great majority of sailors, Roger had no more experience of lifeboats than has a landsman. Incredible journeys had been made in them; men had drifted for weeks in craft both smaller and far less seaworthy than the remaining pressed-steel boats in *San Roque's* davits. Yet again, if the storm returned, if they were, as Ciccolanti believed, in the calm dead centre of the cyclone. . . .

Ciccolanti—he was to blame for everything that had happened. A dull glow started to heat the cinders of Roger's exhausted anger. Ciccolanti had robbed him and thwarted him, robbed him of a bridge once more beneath his feet, thwarted him in his plan to escape once more to the sea. Ciccolanti wanted everyone to remain on board—of course!

He would have enough to explain to his Owner—assuming that he and *San Roque* survived it all—without the addition of a large-scale desertion of passengers in mid-ocean. Suddenly a picture appeared once more upon the private cinema screen in his mind, and Roger saw himself giving evidence before a maritime tribunal in Australia, a tribunal convened to convict Ciccolanti of gross negligence and incompetence. "And my opinion as an ex-naval officer was then, and remains to-day, that Chief Officer Ciccolanti was completely wrong in his estimation of the situation. . . ."

"Yes," he said, with a sudden return to the authority of his old manner, "we must go in the boats if we can." He glanced round at the faces—frightened, tired, querulous above the bulging orange collars. "Yes, the boats are the best bet now."

Bronwen nodded with relief. Roger had seemed so queer for the last few minutes—almost as if he had given up hope—that she had become increasingly frightened, which to her was a very odd sensation. Now she turned at once to Mrs. Crambatch, her mind holding doggedly to the main chance, not even in this extremity forgetting that there was still a future to plan for, remembering that while there was life there was hope of worldly success. "We'll be all right now." She spoke soothingly as if calming a frightened child. "Roger will see that we're quite safe. Probably in a few hours we'll be picked up and aboard another ship. Think of all you'll be able to tell them when you get back to Dunedin!"

Half an hour ago Mrs. Crambatch would have sobbed with relief and pleasure at these assurances of safety and would have gazed adoringly at Bronwen and from Bronwen to Roger. But as Roger opted for the boats, a sudden startling change came over Mrs. Crambatch. She no longer wept and trembled, and her pudgy, tear-stained face became flushed, her mouth thinned and her eyes behind her spectacles gleamed as they had in her cabin on the day she discovered the loss of her relic. "But Roger said we were safe on this ship. He didn't say anything about going in the boats. He said we'd all be right here."

"Only if he had been able to take over and make them see some sense. As it is, he feels we'd be safer to take to the boats—much safer."

"But I don't *want* to take to a boat!" Mrs. Crambatch's voice held an exasperated sharpness. "What about a ny things? I've got thousands of pounds' worth of very valuable things on board."

"But they're insured, surely?"

"That's not the point! They're irreplaceable—completely rreplaceable. And your husband *told* us we'd be safe on oard!"

Bronwen nodded unhappily. "Yes, yes, it's dreadful, agree. It seems a terrible shame to have to leave them, ut——"

"He *said* we'd be quite safe if he took charge. But he asn't taken charge, has he?"

"No, but——"

"And now he wants me to go in a boat and leave everyhing! I think it's absolutely disgraceful! He's a—a fraud! don't believe he's ever been a naval officer. I think he's ust an imposter! And you're as bad, young woman. Oh, es!" Mrs. Crambatch was trembling all over now, even er life-jacket quivered. "Don't think I didn't see what ou were after! I'm not that much of a fool. You and our precious husband who is so well qualified but can't nd a job in England, and who talks about taking over ne ship and saving everybody. Talks, *talks*—and does nothg in the end but tell us we must go in the boats! And hat's going to happen to all my things, I'd like to know, nd——"

"They'll be on the bottom in a few hours' time—and that's bout five thousand fathoms down, if it's of so much interest you," said Roger brutally. "And you'll be down there o, if you stay on board. And——" he glared from Bronen's weeping face to the old woman's quivering red one —I couldn't care bloody less if you are!"

For a moment Mrs. Crambatch stared at him with all the nbelieving, pop-eyed fury of the elderly and insulted rich. hen, as if dropping one handhold on safety and grasping another, she turned to Paula Chelgrove. "Miss Chelgrove! Vhat does your brother think? Do we *have* to go in those oats? Surely——"

"My brother has ceased to think since he came on deck." aula Chelgrove stared down from eyes as bleakly dull as n English winter "He never was any good at it and in times f crisis his wits become completely moribund." She glanced ith bitter loathing at the stooped figure of her brother anding beside her, staring vacantly at the deck between is feet, his hands trembling, his head shrugged sunkenly between his shoulders as if he half expected a shower of stones to be dislodged from the bridge above.

For Paula too had just had her moment of truth, acute and revealing, a flash of vivid recollection going back more than half a century. Two children, herself and Perry, walking home from a visit to friends towards the end of a long, sultry summer day. The stillness, the heat, the great thunderclouds looming up in black and purple behind them. "Come on, Perry—faster! We'll get caught!" And Perry, tired with the lazy, languid tiredness that no doctor seemed able to cure, idling, dawdling, refusing to hurry until the first great drops of rain spattered them and with a shattering crash the storm broke. And then he had stood where he was as if suddenly nailed to the spot, stood there in the middle of the lane, head shrugged between hunched shoulders, eyes vacant, mouth slack, unable it appeared, to see or hear or feel as the storm flashed and boomed around him. She had been forced to drag him to the hedge and hold him there, an inanimate lump, until the storm had passed and later, wet and sleepy and morosely complaining, he had not even remembered properly what had happened. And the same thing had occurred to-day, over fifty years later. The long indolent refusal to understand or cope with approaching danger, and then the sudden hunched petrifaction of fear as at last the full recognition of present peril pierced the lazy protective mists of that curiously slothful mind.

And of course that was how it had always been. She saw now, with a cold empty clarity, that it must have been like that in the war. The second court had been quite right in saying that he had been treated leniently, for he was useless —cowardly, slothful and quite useless. Yet inwardly she knew that she had always been half aware of this but had struggled successfully to conceal the knowledge from herself. A Chelgrove *couldn't* be like that, because if he was then nothing—the family and its position, the fact of *being* a Chelgrove, even—none of it made sense any more. She had done everything that she could for Perry; believed in him, fought for him, given him every chance. Her sudden demand to take to the boats had been made not because of any real belief in the necessity of doing so but solely because, with Lannfranc at last discredited, it would give Perry the chance to display his hereditary ability to lead and to show his real worth. He was shy, of course, and she had always respected his lack of self-assertion, considering it a gentle manly trait. But this time there had been no loud-voiced competition in his way—neither Lannfranc, nor Ciccolanti, nor Hogben. Perry would only have had to step forward, raise his voice, call for order—but he had not; of course, he had not.

"It's no use asking my brother anything at all." Paula paused, and then added grudgingly, "If young Lannfranc says the boats are safest, I suppose we'd better take his word for it."

"Well, if you want to come you'd better hurry!" Roger turned a glowering, harassed face upon them. "Because this rain's starting to let up and there'll probably be another rush in a minute." He pointed through the thinning downpour to where five soaked sailors were swinging another boat in at the rails. "Come on! That one—Number 7!" And, grasping Bronwen's arm and followed by the others, he dashed out from the shelter of the bridge wing and staggered and slithered down the oil-and-rain-soaked deck.

3

The rain, crashing down on the sloping deck, had expanded and distributed the patches of oil in all directions, emulsifying with them to form a surface so slick and slippery that it was almost impossible to move upon it without falling. This, coupled with the fierceness of the torrential downpour, had effectively stopped any further rush for the boats. It had also given a short time to Condron and his friends to organise their own near-monopoly of *San Roque's* remaining lifecraft. As the rain diminished with the abruptness of a tropical squall, it could be seen that beside four of the five further sets of davits there stood small groups of British migrants, armed with iron bars, knives and an occasional red fire-axe or shovel. The fifth boat alone was guarded by a set of young Italian workers who had caught on to what what happening rather late.

Now, as the rest of the passengers swarmed out once more and struggled, sliding and falling, down the greasy deck, a process of skilfully confusing discrimination, a tactic learned in innumerable strikes, lock-outs and unofficial stoppages, was put into action by the Englishmen. The fifth boat was soon filled, and every time an Italian tried to board one of the others he was headed off with an air of firm but harassed authority. "Not this one, chum. That's yours over there, see? All your mates is goin' in that one." . . . "*This* boat? What? Then 'e told you wrong. Try that one at the end. Looks full? Ah, but they're gettin' out in a minute—that boat's for your lot. Made a mistake they 'as, that's all." . . . "Gettin' out? Not bleedin' likely! Not outer *this* boat, mate. Only over-fifties in 'ere. What? 'Course they're younger, those are—they're for workin' the boat, see?" The weapons were not used; they were the unmentioned threat behind the words. Desperately, with growing panic, the remaining Italian migrants slid and stumbled from boat to boat. Furiously, uselessly, they appealed to Bressan or Petelli, but there was nothing anybody could do. With the exception of the deck crew and a few of the service staff, five of the boats were filled entirely with British and only the sixth held Italians.

At Number 7, the first boat in the line, the British first-class passengers had been allowed on with a marked lack of enthusiasm, but when the Malcolm-Bruces and Sessabandrians tried to follow them, Hogben pushed his way up from the stern attended by the three Ampel children—a bloody-faced giant surrounded by tight-faced dwarfs. "'Ere! We're not 'aving you lot! You just bleedin' well stay where you are, see?"

"But there is room! There are several seats left."

"They ain't left. They've been taken—engaged."

Dr. Sessabandrian put a thin hand on the gunwale and started to lift himself over. Hogben at once thrust a tiller bar into his chest and set him toppling back to the slippery deck. "Cut that out. Right out if you don't want your loaf busted open!" He turned to face the Malcolm-Bruces, still astonishingly dry and clean despite the events of the last hour, who stood looking up at him with mild, placating politeness, "I am sure that you could make room for our children, could you not? They would not, you can see, take up much space."

"There *ain't* no more room! I just tol' you! Now keep off. An' you kids——" Hogben turned to the three Ampels, each armed with the steel daggers they had bought at Port Said—"you keep 'em outer this. Stick 'em if they tries to get in."

"What about the ol' tart?" Rock Ampel pointed with his

dagger towards Countess Zapescu who, her fur coat bundled protectively in her arms, was attempting clumsily to climb in near the boat's prow. Hogben scowled at her briefly. "Well, she's white at any rate. I suppose she can . . . Hey! We're not 'avin' *that.* Not bleedin' likely!" For, stumbling in her high-heeled shoes as she stepped down from a thwart, the old woman had loosed her grasp on the fur coat and out of it, slowly, unwillingly and whining with irritation, had slid Brown.

Hogben pushed through the crowded seats towards the prow. "Now, missus, you put that dog back on the deck, see? We got plenty on board without that."

Countess Zapescu seized Brown and hugged him to her, then quickly she enveloped him once more in the fur coat as if his complete concealment might somehow diminish his undesirability in the eyes of the other passengers. She said rapidly, hopefully, "He will be most goodt. He is a *goodt* dog! To none will he cause distress or discommodation. He will sit always silent upon my legs—so!"

"No, 'e won't!" Hogben leant down and grabbed at the fur coat. "That dog's not stayin' in this boat, I tell you!"

From behind him Mrs. Ampel, her voice high with righteous indignation, said, "I should think not! Bringin' a dog in a lifeboat with all the kids' 'ealths to consider an' all! *Some people*——"

"No, no, no! He is *goodt* dog! Only his breath smells so very little. Nothing else—nothing at all. Do not touch!" The Countess stared around her frantically. "Where is one officer? Where——?"

"*I'm* in charge 'ere. We're finished with all them bleedin' dago officers—useless lot of bastards! You do as I say, see? Give 'im to me!"

"No."

"Then you get off too, see?"

"No. Oh Godt!" The Countess gazed distractedly round at the hostile faces of the other migrants which stared back threateningly. "Would you make that I drown?"

"You c'n choose. You c'n stay if you want—but *not* that dog."

"I—I have *paidt* for him. You have no right! You are not captain!"

Hogben seized her by the shoulders and pulled her to her feet. "Never says I was. But you do what I says just the same. Go on—get out!" Then he noticed Tino Cavagni, his face blushing crimson, rising from a seat in the stern. "You gettin' out too, lad?"

"*Si,*" muttered Tino. He had managed to get into the stern with two of Petelli's deck crew, and once there his tall, muscular build had effectually deterred the British migrants from ejecting him. Besides, he would be useful at the levers. But half a minute before he had become conscious of someone's eyes upon him and, looking up, he had seen Flora McKenrick in the prow, staring down at him, and the look in her eyes was one with which he was all too familiar. In that moment he had a sudden terrible vision—based, probably, on a film he had once seen—of the boat in a week's time—two weeks'—three—with everyone dead or in an exhausted coma, everyone except McKenrick. And she was getting up from her long patient wait in the prow and coming down the lifeless boat towards him. "Tino, you'll have to do what I want now. There's nobody to help you now, Tino—nobody at all." He had shuddered and the vision had gone, but McKenrick was still there, still staring. He had put up a hand to button his wide-open shirt, changed his mind, crossed himself instead and got up. After all, the worst that could happen if one stayed aboard the ship was only death by drowning.

Now Hogben pointed to the Countess and said, "Okay, then. Get 'er back on board with you." And coming forward, Tino assisted the old woman, trembling, weeping and clutching her muffled dog in her arms, to descend once more to the deck.

As soon as she had done so the ropes were loosened. Number 7 was the last boat to leave the side, and even as it began to drop Mr. Malcolm-Bruce, still polite, still with his fixed smile, only his black eyes full of anguished appeal, made one more plea to Colonel Chelgrove, sitting hunched in the prow. "Colonel, I implore you to take at least one of my children. I am sure that you cannot——"

But it was too late. Colonel Chelgrove, one-time commander of a battalion of the Queen's Rifles, the author of *Regimental Traditions of the British Army,* sat crouched on his seat, his mouth open and dribbling a little, his eyes, at once vacant and horrified, gazing at a point on the gunwale a few feet before him. For someone was sitting there, someone astonishingly clear and real, yet whom he realised well enough that only he could see; someone who swung short, booted legs and hitched up a big sword and grinned with bestial triumph from a wry-necked, congested face as the ropes whirred through the falls and the boat hit the water with a heavy splash.

4

High up, from a window of the useless, listing bridge, a small, hard-jawed, triangular face stared grimly down at the six boats lifting and falling on the heaving black water as they moved slowly away from the ship's side. They were full of movement as figures in the orange kapok life-jackets changed places and arranged themselves so as to give full room to the men pumping at the levers. Number 11 had Semprebon's tall figure at the prow, Malpiero's dark, saturnine face beside him; and there was Petelli, short, square, red-faced, at the helm of Number 8. Neither the Purser nor the Master at Arms had considered it safer to remain on the ship. Each of them must have at least twenty years of seagoing experience behind him and both had opted for the lifeboats. And there, in Number 9 just beginning to move away, was Bressan. Serafino stared down dispassionately and for a second Bressan seemed to smile and half raise a hand. The Second Officer too, and all the deck crew, more than half the passengers, and as many of the service staff as could manage to do so were leaving the ship, not so much because of what had happened or even her present condition but because they felt no faith at all in her captain, because they profoundly distrusted him and considered themselves better off on their own. They would never have done this if Onestinghel had still been in command; they had trusted Onestinghel. Bleakly Serafino realised that his failure lay, not in his handling of *San Roque* but in the management of her human cargo, and those six crowded boats moving slowly away across the dark water under the low, dull sky were the final proof of this. The orders and decisions of successful captains were never questioned; it was an accepted fact that mutinies occurred only on the ships of failures. He himself had given in rather than face a full-scale mutiny; had he not done so it would, he knew, have made little difference to the course of events. He, certainly—perhaps

Malestroit and Gil and even Gino as well—would have been thrown over the side, and the strongest section of the pas sengers would still have taken the boats and left the rest leaderless on the dead ship, to the horror of the returning storm. He knew that he had taken the only rational course there was nothing else that he could in all sanity have done and yet, watching those six white boats crawling slowly over the inky sea, he wished with an aching, illogical regret tha he had refused.

Down below the remaining passengers were lining the rails silent and hopeless. They would have gone if they could Everyone would have gone, leaving him alone, a solitary out cast upon a listing deck; alone with the silence, the slow heaving black sea and the lowering sky. There came the sound of footsteps on the bridge ladder and then Malestroit was beside him, looking at him curiously from red-rimmed slate-grey eyes. "Well?" The Belgian officer's voice wa awkward. He met Serafino's cold gaze and looked away towards the last boat, Number 7. And in the prow Hogben who must have caught sight of the two faces at the bridge window, suddenly stood up. He pointed to his bloodstained face and bellowed back at the ship, " Malicious woundin —that's what you done to me! Grievous bod'ly 'arm Serious crime, that is. You'll see!"

Malestroit gave a shout of half-hysterical laughter. "My God—again! Litigious to the last, those people!" Then he put a hand tentatively on Serafino's shoulder. "My friend they are quite capable of bringing a case against the wind— of suing the sea! But it was not your fault at all. And who can say? Even if you are right about the cyclone, they ma still succeed in saving themselves."

But Serafino stood, quite motionless, staring out stiffly a the last lifeboat as the men got the rhythm of the levers and she moved faster to join the others. For suddenly—it must hav been some trick of his tired brain or his eyes, sore with sleep lessness—he seemed to see a curious darkness round Hogben's head as the big man sat down; and the same thing, a tenuous hood-like shadow, about the heads of six others who sat nea him up in the prow. Then he blinked and it was gone. "No they will not save themselves," he said coldly. "I let them go, but they have no chance, really. No chance at all."

Malestroit stopped laughing and glanched at him oddly Then he said, "It was for them to obey you. Even when you could no longer make them do so you tried to warn them

You did all that you could for them except to let them take over the ship—and that you could not, in any case, do because you are captain."

XIX

He was still *San Roque's* captain. At Malestroit's words he turned with an effort from the window with its view of the six boats moving faster now across the dark sea, and at once felt the numbing, black despair begin to lift from his mind, as if a current of energy which had been temporarily cut off was once again flowing freely. Despite all that had happened, he was still the master of *San Roque*—nothing had changed that and nothing could. He cast a quick glance round the bridge, seeing the torn, scattered charts, the muddled signal flags and the broken glass on the bloodstained planking, and knowing that none of this made any difference at all to his position. For in this one respect the curious, age-old maritime laws that governed and encompassed ships at sea took no cognizance of *San Roque's* present condition or of anything that had occurred upon her. While she floated, those on board her stood upon Panamanian territory and owed allegiance to no one except her captain. The master of a ship might be old or young, good or bad, capable or incompetent, in maritime law it made no difference at all; while upon the high seas he was the sole ruler and arbiter of his little kingdom by ancient right and law and custom. It was not something, as Malestroit had rightly said, that he could give away and no one, not even his Owner, could take it from him until he reached port.

Turning to descend the bridge ladder, he was aware of an odd lightness, a feeling of new strength, as if in the middle of a long day's march a heavy burden had slid from his back. A little guiltily, for he should have known himself, he asked Malestroit, "The engineers—they are all still aboard?"

"Two or three went in the Italian boat, I think. The rest are all here."

But of course they would be, for like ship's engineers all the seas over, they distrusted the sea and everything non-mechanical that moved upon it. To them the engine-room was all that really counted; it was their private world and they would only willingly abandon it, thus placing themselves in the hands of the deck crew, if the great engines they cherished so lovingly were damaged beyond repair. And of course the engines were not damaged at all. Even though the funnel had gone, the fans which supplied the forced draught to the furnaces were still working, the furnaces themselves still firing, pressure for the turbines and the mass of auxiliary machinery still available—even up here one could feel the faint chugging of the pumps. *San Roque* was paralysed, but not dead—yet.

Yet if, as he believed, they were in the calm dead centre of the cyclone, they were trapped in the circle of the storm and the chances of survival for the powerless ship were small indeed. Broken, helpless ships had sometimes lived through such ordeals in the past, it was true; barques of early merchant adventurers, schooners trading among the scattered islands, junks caught in the terrible typhoons of the shallow China Sea. But they were wooden ships: *San Roque* was iron. And iron did not float.

Yet there must be something he could do for the hulk beneath his feet, even if it was only rectifying her list, clearing the wreckage from her decks and battening down every aperture through which the returning waves might flood. If only they had the power of movement. . . . But, deck officer that he was, his mind's compass needle swung inevitably to the decks. The first thing was to get the ship on an even keel once more, and while this was being done the huge, crumpled ruin of the funnel must be cleared over the side. There was no deck-hands left, but there were plenty of passengers and the work would be largely unskilled. Malestroit could organise it, dividing the stronger male passengers into groups and supervising them with the help of Gino. He gave the orders rapidly and then turned to go to the radio room. If only Brighenti could get the radio working again they could at least contact the outside world, call for assistance and find out, perhaps—his stomach contracted slightly at the thought—whether they were really in the centre of the cyclone or upon its outside edge.

As he turned to descend the companionway below the bridge, Gil stopped him and for a moment they stared into each other's faces with the curious mixture of amusement, distrust and resentment which seemed now an integral part of their difficult relationship. Then, with an almost angry, off-hand brusqueness, Gil asked, " Would you like me to help you at all? Isn't there something I can do?"

Serafino grinned reluctantly, uneasily aware that it was only because of Gil and his gun that he was still captain—perhaps that he was still alive. "Like Lannfranc? You would like to take over command, perhaps?"

Gil's eyes slid away in equal embarrassment. Neither knew on what terms they were now supposed to be. Awkwardly he said, "When he started I thought perhaps . . ."

"That I would give in?"

"I was not sure," Gil shrugged. "*He* was certain that you would."

"Then he must be even madder than I thought he was!"

"No, no—just English. You don't understand them. Onestinghel said you did not and he was right, as usual."

"Well, I don't have to now. All of them have gone. But if you wish for something to do, you would perhaps go down to the kitchens, see how many of the cooks are left and get some food ready. We may not have much longer before the wind returns."

Gil nodded, and Serafino left him and made his way quickly to the radio room, wondering how much use he could make of the Owner's son. Gil was not a passenger, after all, and even if he had no nautical qualifications his status—or his gun—was quite sufficient to make sure that his orders were obeyed by what remained of the crew and the passengers.

Serafino pushed open the door of the radio office and addressed Brighenti's bowed back, bent over his table before the battered front of the emergency transmitter. "How is it going? How much longer will it be?" But there was no response from the slumped figure in the chair, and Serafino saw that the radio operator was deep in an exhausted sleep, his puffy, unshaven face resting in his arms among a tangled mass of coils and valves.

For a long moment Serafino stood looking down at him, then he grasped an inert shoulder and shook it, at first gently, then with an impatient roughness. He *must* know how long it would be before the radio could function once more. Everything, everybody's life—and particularly the lives of those in the boats—depended on regaining radio contact with other shipping and the outside world. But it was no good. Neither shaking, tweaking his hair, nor pinching his ears could wake Brighenti. He had been working almost unceasingly for two nights and a day—and for the last fourteen hours in a radio room pitching and tossing like a howdah on a runaway elephant. Now he was inextricably buried in a sleep of drugged exhaustion into which he had probably fallen as soon as the ship's lessening motion had permitted him to cease clinging to his chair. Nothing could be expected of him until he had rested. Serafino glanced at his watch; he would allow him four—no, three hours. After that . . . But by then they might be back in the storm. He looked down bleakly at the motionless figure of the radio operator, shrugged and left the office.

So all hope of contacting the outside world must be temporarily abandoned. There would be no chance to give even a loose estimate of their probable position to other shipping or to send out demands for assistance for themselves and for those six white lifeboats packed with orange-jacketed humanity which, whatever had happened, were still legally his responsibility.

How silent it was, he thought, moving along these empty corridors on " A deck, from time to time fending himself off the starboard bulkhead with an outstretched palm. Past the best first-class cabins—a door was open and a green-carpeted floor was scattered with little dolls. Stooping, he picked one up and saw that it was a big wooden chessman in the form of a Roman soldier; he shrugged, dropping it, and went on. Down to " B " deck, down to " C "; the empty vestibule with papers scattered everywhere among the shards of coloured china and the earth from the broken palm pots; farther on, a litter of smashed crockery and knives and forks in the corridor outside one of the tourist-class dining-rooms. Passing the sick bay he heard a low, sobbing moan, and for one terrible moment he stood, breathless and still, in the tilted corridor, the blood draining from his face as he remembered an open scuttle, a bunk soaked with rain and spray behind a locked door. Had something come back out of the dark sea? Had . . . But he was not some bearded old Sicilian fisherman to conjure up sea-ghosts. Yet it was with a prickle of ice down his spine that he grasped the brass handle and thrust open the door. Like so many of his age and time, he possessed none of the nineteenth century's comfortably materialistic rationalism. Too many exotic fears were only too well justified in to-day's world for the adoption of a sceptical disbelief in any powers of darkness. But from the bunk on which, three days ago, Armando had lain sleepless and terrified, it was only Ettore, the bar-boy, who stared up at him from a white, tear-stained, pain-twisted face. " Signor Ciccolanti! I—I thought everyone had gone. There was a lot of noise and then everything got so quiet."

"No, it's all right. What's happened to you?"

"I fell down the service lift on "C" deck yesterday night—all the way down." There was a hint of pride in Ettore's weak voice.

"My God! You should be dead."

"There were some old crates at the bottom. But I broke my arm and some ribs. Tomei says they will mend all right. He's been giving me something for the pain, but it's time I had some more. And I want some water. Will you tell him, signore?"

Serafino had a sudden vision of Number 11, the boat commanded by Semprebon: somewhere towards the stern a bald head, a pair of steel spectacles above the life-jacket. His mouth thinned. "Tomei's not around at present. He . . . Anyway, I'll get them for you."

So now there was no one left to deal with further injuries. If Ettore was really the only person on board who had been seriously hurt in the storm, they were amazingly lucky; but as he went on towards the stern after giving the mess-boy his morphine pills and water, he realised with a sombre clarity that there would probably be more than broken limbs to deal with before long.

Petelli should be doing this, he reflected, as he moved quickly aft, checking, searching everywhere for signs of new danger. But Petelli was away in the boats with his deck crew and most of the idlers. But what else could one expect—what else could Don Ildefonso expect—from the scourings of the Naples waterfront whom the Flotta Soto habitually employed and for the wages that it paid them?

Serafino clambered up the ladder to the stern of "C" deck and gazed around him. This was where the disaster had started; those bent bolts protruding from the rust-stained planking had held the great cable pen before it had been smashed and the hawsers—which should have been securely lashed in coils but which had presumably been left lying loose—had been swept over the side.

Gingerly Serafino moved across the sloping deck and peered down into the dark sea which seemed so strangely, so ominously, close. There was nothing to be seen, of course; the list had buried the starboard screw at least a fathom and a half farther below the waterline than normal. In which case . . . in which case it must have lifted the post screw a fathom and a half higher than normal! Serafino swung round, his heart thudding with a wild hope, and, scrambling up the sloping deck, threw himself across the port rail to lean perilously far out and stare down. . . . The black swell heaved, then dropped away—and there it was, nearly a quarter of it exposed, a huge, dull-gleaming blade, a great muffled hub and another blade wavering down into the darkness. And over everything, between the blades and round the hub, snaking down into the translucent blackness was the taut, twisted, gigantic tangle of the stern hawser. Serafino drew in his breath sharply; the immensity, the fearful tension and complexity of that snarl-up of five-inch manila cable and tons of heavy forged bronze was awe-inspiring in its locked, motionless strength. But if only it could be raised, that solid mass of fibre and metal, by another six or seven feet, it would be possible to get down there with saws and axes and attempt to hack it free. It might well prove a useless effort, for it was possible that some of the cable had been chewed into its original threads and forced into the glands and stern bearings of the shaft, clogging them immovably; but almost anything was worth trying in order to have power again, to bring *San Roque* to moving life once more.

He would have to call a halt to the operations on the boat deck; he would have to flood all the forward starboard tanks and pump out the ballast from the port ones, thus increasing her list and lowering her head still farther. And if the cyclone struck them again or if they drifted out of the centre in that condition—then *San Roque's* first roll to starboard would also be her last. But he knew that he was going to give the order and accept the risks, even as he pulled himself up from the rail and started back at a limping run to the boat deck.

2

It took more than half an hour to get the ship into the desperately dangerous position from which work could start on the port screw; half an hour in which all and more than all the water pumped from the flooded bow was replaced; half an hour during which *San Roque's* prow sank lower and lower into the heaving, oily swell and her list to starboard steadily increased until it was hardly possible to climb the great slope to port except on hands and knees; half an hour in which the sweat that soaked the clothes of the remaining officers was due less to the lifeless humidity of the atmosphere than to the incessant, tearing anxiety at time running out, a deadly, foreboding fear of the approaching return of the storm.

They stood—Serafino, Malestroit, Aafjes, Zocco and Gino—hanging far over the stern rails of "C" deck until the increasing list made it impossible for them to watch the slowly emerging screw. From time to time they turned to stare apprehensively up at the lowering sky or the vague, diffused line of the close horizon, before uselessly, but by some strange force of habit, glancing at their wrists as if they really knew how much time they had and were gauging it. All the remaining passengers had been sent down to the starboard bow in order to lend their weight to the careening ship. It was little enough, hardly to be considered by comparison with the hundreds of tons of water now flooding into the bow, but nothing, however small or inconsiderable, could be neglected in this last gamble with fate.

At eight twenty-five, almost exactly two and a half hours since the stern cable had been torn overboard, Serafino judged that the port screw was sufficiently high out of the water for work to commence upon it. With the help of Zocco and two of the engine-room staff, Malestroit and Gino crawled over the side and were swung in bights of rope down to the water. The work had to be done fast, as fast and hard as two pairs of hands could hack and saw. Serafino gave them ten minutes and then had them both pulled up. They came over the side soaked with sea-water, pouring with sweat, and panting and trembling from the fierceness of their efforts. Gasping, Malestroit said, "It will work—if we have time. Saws are best. It is like cutting through hard wood. The axe—it blunts too quick. And the swell is making it more difficult. Sometimes one is almost submerged. But it will work, I think."

"Good," Serafino nodded, glanced round and saw Tino, who should have been down on the bow with the passengers, standing near Zocco and listening with interest. "All right, then. Cavagni, you can come down with me now—and after us it will be Signor Zocco and one of his greasers." Taking one of the ropes, he climbed through the rails, slid in an awkward scramble down the steep white plating of the hull, and swung in under the sweep of the stern.

And there it was, directly below him, huge now and with its great hub almost fully exposed above the water. Gripping the edge of one blade he lowered himself until he was standing on the thick mat of twisted rope that had so recently been a broad, coiled hawser in *San Roque's* stern pen. A second or two later Tino was beside him, and they knelt, seized the saws and thrust them down into the deep, frayed grooves left by the first two.

It was, as Malestroit had said, like cutting through wood, hard, fibrous, sticky wood which blunted the saws and clogged their teeth, while from time to time swells larger than average would flood up over the hub, immersing them, as they knelt sawing, to their waists or occasionally to their shoulders. After they had been working with a fast, harsh, exhausting rhythm for three or four minutes, Tino gave a grunt of satisfaction and, hanging his saw in the rope bight, bent and with both hands heaved at a piece of hawser he had cut loose. For a long moment nothing happened and Serafino, watching the muscles bulging on the mess-boy's strong arms, said, "You can't do it that way. It must be cut out bit by bit." Yet, surprisingly, the hawser yielded very slowly, a little at a time, until, with Tino straining every muscle, some eighteen inches lifted out of the mass before it stuck and a high swell rolling up submerged the kneeling mess-boy completely. But as it passed Tino emerged, spluttering, panting and grinning with triumph. He seized his saw once more and began to cut. "We'll get it all out soon, Signor Ciccolanti. Once we get one piece out the rest will be easier." And so it proved. By the time their ten minutes were up and they had been hauled back to the deck, a long strip of the compacted hawser had ben cut away from the hub.

Serafino did not go down again, but Tino seemed inexhaustible, returning regularly after every ten-minute break. When at last, after they had been working on the screw for nearly an hour and a quarter, he came up from his fourth trip, his hands were a mass of raw blisters and his legs almost too weak to support him, but he reported proudly that the screw was free.

"He is a horse, that boy," said Malestroit happily as he and Serafino climbed back to the boat deck as quickly as the great list would permit. "He has the muscles of a horse and, one fears one must admit, the intelligence of a horse—but a *good* horse."

Serafino nodded. Thinking of Cavagni's meagre wages, he said, " And he gets much the same treatment."

3

And now, with the pumps once again chunking and thudding rhythmically, it was possible to return to the work of clearing the wreckage of the funnel from the boat deck. But this proved a more difficult and complicated operation that had at first been thought. Since the funnel had crashed to the starboard side aft of the bridge, and since the ship was still listed perilously to starboard, it was natural to consider getting rid of it over the starboard side. If *San Roque* had been down by the stern instead of the bow this would have been comparatively easy. As it was, however, the starboard wing and superstructure of the bridge blocked the most obvious passage of the crumpled ruin of sheet metal and necessitated dragging it diagonally aft—which meant upwards—to the side.

While a gang of passengers armed with axes hacked and chopped at the wreck to free it as far as possible from the cables, pipes, stays and other encumbrances which it had automatically taken with it in its fall, the officers worked busily, attaching steel cables from two of the port boat winches.

Stopping to wipe the sweat from his eyes, Serafino, glancing at his watch, saw that the time was a quarter to ten. They had been over three hours in the centre, then. If, of course, this *was* the centre; he told himself with a small flicker of hope that he might be wrong. For if he was right they could expect little more respite from the storm. However slowly the system itself was moving, its farther side must be drawing inexorably nearer to them and they could expect to be back in that terrible vortex of thundering wind, sheeting spray and mountainous waves very soon now. If only they were permitted just a little longer—another half-hour, even. But that was unlikely; he never had luck of that sort. Nevertheless, in place of the rebellious, stubborn despair with which he was accustomed to battle with the peculiarly conceived personal enemy of his destiny, he felt a curious, cold elation; almost, it seemed to him, a presage of victory. For *San Roque* was almost alive again now, alive enough, at any rate, to stand a reasonable chance of defeating the next attack of the storm.

He watched Zocco tighten the last shackle on the long loop of steel cable and, straightening, lifted a hand in signal to Gino at the boat winch. Gino shifted the lever, the drum turned and the cable tightened. Everyone rested, wiping the sweat from their faces and watching the splayed-out mass of funnel as, very slowly, creaking and groaning, it moved a few feet across the deck and then stopped. The drum of the winch turned more and more slowly but the wreckage remained jammed. Serafino shrugged—they would have to try something else—and was turning to Gino at the winch when, with a sharp, metallic bang, the shackle closing the loop of rope parted. (It was, as Serafino found later, a flawed casting cracked almost half-way across.) But now the suddenly released rope hissed through the air with a noise like ripping cloth and flung Malestroit across the deck and against a broken davit with enough force to make him rebound from it like a rubber ball. Everybody stood motionless, a stilled into uncomprehending, horrified astonishment, staring at that crumpled figure in the stained white uniform which had been caught in such furious motion and lay now so still. Malestroit slowly raised an arm and then let it fall; from somewhere under his left knee there was a wet gleam, and a long, thin stream of blood ran out and slid down the deck. He seemed barely half conscious as Serafino and Zocco knelt beside him, surrounded by a dozen of the remaining Italian passengers; he stared up with a dazed wonderment and smiled slightly. Suddenly he looked very young—younger even than Gino.

The broken shackle had struck him across the left knee, pulping the joint into a wet and ragged mass of splintered bone and flesh. Had the cable wrapped itself round his leg it would have torn it off so quickly that it would have left him standing for a second on his remaining one, and then he would have bled to death immediately. But as it was, the great arteries behind the knee were not severed, and unless there were other injuries from the fearful force with which he had been hurled against the davit, his life was not in imminent danger. But it would be in danger soon enough, thought Serafino, as, three minutes later, he stood watching Malestroit being carried below while he wiped his bloodstained hands on his already filthy trousers. First aid, the applying of a tourniquet, the remembered measures against shock—everyone knew about those and could perform them; but Malestroit's leg must be taken off within a few hours—should be taken off now, by rights—if he were to have a chance of survival. It would have to be done and he himself would have to do it; there was no chance of evading the issue this time. But it must wait. They had already lost precious minutes and the wreck of the funnel still lay jammed across the deck. They could not expect to be given much more time.

They were given none. As Serafino turned once more to the funnel, the first squall of the returning storm hit them. Gino caught a glimpse of it travelling across the dark sea in a hissing path of silvery-grey water, and though it struck them with far less force than those which had battered *San Roque* five hours ago, it was an implacable warning that they had reached the other side of the cyclone's centre, for it blew from the opposite quadrant—the south-east.

4

So he had been right after all. But once more up on the bridge, alone with Gino, Serafino felt only angry disappointment rather than satisfaction at his correct reading of the cyclonic system. What were *San Roque's* chances now, with only one screw in action and a foredeck hatch of flimsy deal planks? And what of those boats? He shuddered and forced his mind away. It was better not to think of those at all.

The sea was rising rapidly and foam spat whitely from the crests of the growing waves. "Ring down 'Half ahead' on the port screw," he told Gino, and himself took the wheel. *San Roque* was still heavily down at the bow and listed at 34°, though the pumps would take care of that if only the foredeck hatch held. With any luck they would not be back in the main vortex of the cyclone for another hour or perhaps even longer, and by that time the list should be rectified. But with only half her normal power to hold her head-on to the weather, *San Roque* must be handled with dexterity and precision; if she swung even five degrees out of the gale-splitting line the wind could twist her round and throw her, once more broadside on and helpless, into the troughs. And then the telephone behind him rang and Gino, answering it, turned to him. "The engine-room. Signor Aafjes wants to speak to you. One of the mess-boys was in the vestibule and did the connecting. He wants to know if he should leave the line plugged in."

"*Va bene*. You take the wheel." Waiting until the cadet's hands were firmly grasping the spokes, Serafino looked at him appraisingly for the second time since they had entered the storm. Gino was filthy, filthier even than himself; he looked as if he had fallen down several flights of cellar steps. One trouser leg was torn open from thigh to midcalf and the flesh showing through it was scored and grazed and bruised a deep purple; his shirt was buttonless, and even the inevitable small gold cross that gleamed against his bare chest was bent out of shape, while his shock of black hair, never well brushed in normal times, was now a tangled, spikey mop. He was smiling, but with a strained, stiff smile on a face beginning to show all the signs of deep exhaustion. Gino badly needed sleep; without it he could not last much longer. He had been standing a full watch ever since Colombo, and in common with the other officers had been constantly on duty since they entered the storm. To be twenty-four hours without sleep was not too great a burden for a grown man, but it was a heavy strain on a boy. Yet Gino was now the only other working deck officer on board, and the chances of giving him any rest until *San Roque* was clear of the storm were negligible.

"Engine-room here," came Aafjes' unmistakably accented voice as Serafino lifted the phone. "I am wondering whether you would consider it worth while to let me try the starboard screw, Signor Ciccolanti? It seems to me just possible that, in cutting the port screw free, some of the ropes on the starboard screw might have become loosened. If I reversed the action it might possibly free it. I thought that I would ask you immediately in order that it might be done before we move farther into the storm."

Serafino felt his heart swell with a sudden glorious hope. To get full power again! That could mean that *San Roque's* present chances of survival would be doubled. She would be almost out of real danger then. "Yes, of course! At once! You didn't have to ask me in order to try a thing like that, Signor Aafjes."

"No, no. But there is one other thing, you see." The Chief Engineer's voice sounded apologetic. "It is possible that some of the rope might be flung once more into the port screw. I would not think it very likely, but the turbulence under the stern *could* do that. And of course we do not know how much rope may still be attached to the starboard screw since we were unable to examine it. There is, therefore, a risk."

In his heart Serafino felt the new hope dwindle and die. He could not take any risk, however small, of fouling the newly-freed port screw. Everything—every life on board—depended now on keeping that screw turning. "I see. Well then, you must not try it," he said slowly, heavily, and replaced the phone in its bracket. But—half-power, no deck officers except Gino, no helmsmen to keep *San Roque's* prow accurately into the gale, and a foredeck hatch of fragile planks which would be unlikely to stand half an hour of severe battering. No, he could not try to ride the storm again; in the ship's present condition that would be suicidal.

Then what could he do? Run before it as sailing ships did with bare masts a hundred years ago? But that was flatly against all the textbook laws for steam navigation—perhaps because it was considered to be quite unnecessary. After all, if a steamship had steam it need not run before a storm; and if it had no steam it could not; the textbooks had not envisaged a situation like *San Roque's* present one.

For nearly three minutes he grappled with the idea, holding on to the telephone bracket for support as the ship rolled and pitched in the rising seas. The textbooks said this, warned against that, and cautioned strongly against the other. The laws they laid down were accepted facts; one passed one's examinations by learning them and one was not supposed to question them, for they were the fruit of years of carefully sifted and selected experiences distilled into well-proven theories. They were compiled by "authorities"—people who knew. And, illogically, his weary mind formed a picture of these authorities for him—and they were all very old. Six or seven very old, very rich, very honoured men sat in comfortable chairs behind a shining table scattered with cigar boxes and silver inkstands in a great room furnished with all the sombre magnificence of a Palace of Justice. They were all looking at him with dislike and disapprobation. "We *know*," they said. "We wrote the books. You must do only what we say. If your actions are in accordance with the rules we have laid down, you may perhaps drown yourself and all aboard your ship. Never mind; you will die happy in the knowledge that you have followed accepted practice—and even if you feel you have reason to complain, you will hardly be in a position to do so. If, on the other hand, you flagrantly flout us, you may not drown or lose your ship but you *deserve* to do so and we hope you will—because we do not permit young, unknown men from poor homes to challenge us and make exceptions to our laws."

He smiled briefly and went to take back the wheel from the cadet. In future there would be no undisputed authorities in his life, and as if to prove it, he began, slowly and carefully and watched by an astonished Gino, to swing *San Roque* round in a full half-circle.

XX

Half an hour later Serafino, followed by Dr. Sessabandrian, made his way down to the surgery. *San Roque* was still in the uncertain squally area between the cyclone's centre and its circling vortex, but with the main wind force taking her on the stern and with her bow partly pumped out, the heavy, deadly sluggishness of her motion was giving place to a more normal pitch and roll. Her list too had decreased considerably, and the further ballasting to port which, carefully synchronised to the pumping of the bow, was still proceeding, would shortly have her on an even keel once more.

The improvement in the ship's condition had not been matched by that of the remaining Italian passengers. They had hoped that they were out of the storm and a mood of black despair had fallen upon them at the return of the plunging seas and the screaming, spray-laden squalls. It was true that they had recently believed that *San Roque* was sinking—three hours ago when they had cursed and begged to be allowed places in the boats—and she had not sunk; in fact, her engines could be felt vibrating once more. But it was not comfort enough, for they had seen with their own eyes what the storm could do; they had gazed in awed horror at *San Roque's* decks, had looked at sea and sky, and trembled and crossed themselves. Down below in their dishevelled but familiar quarters they could not forget these things, and, refusing the meal that Gil Sotomayor and the cooks had prepared for them, they lay or sat in mute despondecy except for the prayers of a large circle of kneeling women and the crying of the children.

Not all were affected in this way; it was mostly the old and the devout and the women. Some twenty or thirty of the younger men, largely those who had earlier volunteered to help clear the wreckage from the decks, had suggested with an air of half apologetic embarrassment that if the Chief Officer could use them in any way, they would do all they could to help him. They had looked at Serafino with hopeful longing, and he had known that above all else they wanted to trust him, to believe that he would somehow bring them and their families through whatever more was to come—and yet feared to do so because of all that had gone before. If he had spoken to them then, told them briefly and firmly of the ship's present condition, of what had been done to improve it and of what he now intended to do, he would have given them the faith in him which they so desperately wanted and received their wholehearted and obedient support in return. But he had not done so, would not do so. Instead, he had stared at them coldly and told them that he had nothing more for them to do and watched them turn back unhappily to their quarters. For these were the people who, three hours ago would not have lifted a finger to save him if Hogben and Condron had carried out their threat of throwing him over the side. By withholding their support—indeed, by tacitly agreeing with the mutineers—they had done more than imperil his life : they had demonstrated their lack of faith in his capacity as master of the ship. He would not forgive them, any more than he would forgive Bressan, Petelli and the deserters in the boats.

Gil, who had been with him at the time, had seemed surprised. "But they are only asking to help you—and it would be good for them to be allowed to do so."

"I do not need their help. When I needed it they did not give it. Now it is too late."

And Gil had looked at him oddly, had shrugged and said no more.

The help which he had really wanted had come from a surprising quarter—from Dr. Sessabandrian. With Gil, who appeared to have fallen effortlessly into his new role of ship's officer, he had gone down to the first-class saloon where the few remaining first-class passengers were gathered in a corner watching the children eat. There had been no food served since the previous midnight, and though the adults were too upset and exhausted to feel hungry, the children were ravenous. They had eaten all the spaghetti with meat and tomato sauce which Tino Cavagni had brought up to them, and were consuming slice after slice of some stale cake which had been prepared before the storm for the tourist passengers' tea. Watching them, Serafino had, for the first time for days, felt an inclination to laugh. The table only needed a little decoration to have the appearance of a successful juvenile birthday party. The contentment, the happy expectancy, on the children's faces was so at variance with the haggard expressions of the adults—except for Tino, who in any case was not really an adult, and who was beaming with pleasure as he handed plates and filled slopping cups with weak tea—that for a moment the grim tension within him began to relax. He caught the eye of Ian Malcolm-Bruce and smiled stiffly. The Chinese boy, still as neat and clean as if he was back in his father's great house in Singapore, stared back for a moment from his narrow black eyes and then giggled undecidedly. This appeared to cause one of the little Sessabandrians, a skinny black monkey with an outsize napkin tied round his neck, to choke into his cup and elicited an automatic reproof from his father. "Mind your manners, Edwin! And sit up straight, please! You will remember that you are at a table with others. Also, I think you have had sufficient. With more you may become ill. Cease eating, therefore, at once." And while Fiona Malcolm-Bruce, who had adopted the position of nursemaid to the little Sessabandrians ever since Colombo, started to untie the big napkin, the doctor had turned to Serafino. "And how is Mr. Malestroit at present?"

Serafino had glanced at him in surprise; he had not imagined that Dr. Sessabandrian had bothered to learn the names of anyone on board. "I do not know."

"You do not *know*? But that is very wrong, I think. Mr. Malestroit was most badly injured and you do not *know* how he is!"

"I am now to go and see." Serafino's voice had been brusque, but the Sinhalese had taken no notice. "Well, I consider that I had best come with you. I would wish to do what I can for this poor man."

"But . . ." Serafino had stared at him, perplexedly. "You say to me that you are not a—a medical doctor?"

"Nor——" Dr. Sessabandrian had replied with his effortless ability to have the last and sharpest word—"are you."

Malestroit lay moaning and shuddering on the examination couch in the surgery, held there against the rolling of the ship by two canvas straps. Renzo, one of the few remaining mess-boys, who sat beside him, trying to steady him still further, looked up as the Chief Officer entered. "He is very bad, signore. I did what you told me and now I am trying to keep him as comfortable as . . ." He broke off unhappily as Serafino bent over the bloodstained figure on the couch.

Malestroit's broad, strongly featured Belgian face was grey and taut and shrunken, and pouring with sweat. His bloodshot eyes, the pupils reduced by the morphine he had been given to tiny black pinpoints, stared up without recognition, and another long, breathless, humming groan came from his thick, bloodless lips.

Serafino lifted the towel which had been laid over the smashed knee and gazed with revulsion at the coagulated ruin of blood and twisted, torn ligaments and splintered bone. The patella had been ripped off, and now hung by a piece of purple skin, displaying a part of the crushed joint beneath. Renzo's face went a pallid olive green, he turned quickly away and Dr. Sessabandrian took his place. "Very bad. Very bad indeed," he said condemningly. "You will remove the leg?"

"Yes."

"You are right, I think. Very well, then. We must prepare."

There was no doubt that whatever his limitations might be in other directions, Dr. Sessabandrian was a man of quick natural intelligence. With Serafino, he went rapidly through the cluttered, untidy drawers of the surgery, selecting instruments and equipment of a sort which looked as if they might be useful and placing them in the sterilizer. The surgery was small, and when from time to time Renzo got in the way he received sharp and spiteful jabs from the doctor's pointed forefinger, which much practice on his children had developed nto a formidable weapon.

In twenty minutes they were ready and together with Renzo, now reduced to a witless but cringing obedience, they started very gently to lift Malestroit from the couch to the small white operating table. But as soon as his leg was touched he screamed with such an animal howl of agony that they fell back, the faces of the two Europeans paling under their an.

"No good," Serafino muttered when at last the soaring scream had died down to a moaning sob. "So now we are to give him the *etere* on that place first thing. Afterwards he goes on to the table."

Clipping the gauze pad into the small, metal-barred mask, Serafino placed it carefully over Malestroit's mouth and nose, took the brown glass bottle from Renzo's trembling hand and began very gently to dribble its contents over the absorbent cloth. And as the heavy, acrid stench of ether filled his own nostrils and throat with the remembered choking, sterile coldness, he was back once again in the rubble of the bombed school at Naples, sixteen years ago in time, and the begrimed and sweating doctor was kneeling in the stones beside him and he was choking and staring over the top of the mask through the veils of hanging dust at the blue sky, serene and infinitely distant above him.

Three minutes later they lifted the silent body on to the table, the ruined leg supported shudderingly by Renzo, who immediately afterwards was violently sick. Both Serafino and Dr. Sessabandrian turned upon him angrily and the latter took the opportunity to slap his face, an opportunity for which, Serafino felt sure, he had been waiting impatiently for some time. "This boy is hysterical, I think. He is of no use to us; he merely gets in the way. You should send him away before he seriously impedes us."

"Get out, Renzo. Stay outside. If I want you I'll call for you." Serafino, aware that his own stomach was heaving, his own hands slippery with sweat, watched enviously as the trembling mess-boy left the room. So it had come at last. He had refused the first time when it had ben easier, when he had had a calm sea, a sound ship, Tomei and the aid of "Medrad"; and now, with none of those advantages, he was back again looking at those same surgical instruments which Tomei would have laid out for him eleven days ago—and with no possibility of refusal open to him. For it was Malestroit this time, and that made it all quite different. And in a half-comprehending way he knew, somewhere in the back of his mind, why this was so, why it mattered so much more that he should do everything he could for Malestroit than it had mattered in the case of the late captain. It was not so much a question of their respective ages as of the vast gulf of time that separated them as people—he and Malestroit on one side, Onestinghel far away on the other. To-day everything moved so fast, changed so rapidly, and history was made at such a speed, that inevitably the generations became separated from each other as never before, holding as few values, ideas, standards and beliefs in common as if they were parted by a hundred and fifty years of ordinary evolution. Because of this, the elderly lacked true reality in the eyes of the young; they appeared as phantom figures from a curious past when everything had been quite different—not only materially, but spiritually and morally as well. Onestinghel had known this himself. "I am so old, compared to you, that often I must seem to represent quite a different species." And of course he did, for he was a being from several days before yesterday, and even yesterday was a dead world. But Malestroit belonged to to-day, and because of this he was real in a way that Onestinghel was not. He belonged indivisibly to Serafino's world, sharing its values and tastes and reactions, being one with it and with him. And now this life lay in his hands, and everything he felt and knew and hoped for must somehow help and guide the short-bladed, long-hafted scalpel in his sweat-slippery palm.

It took over an hour. It included continual pauses, consultations and arguments with Dr. Sessabandrian. Twice Malestroit started to come out of the ether and both times he was urgently put back to sleep, more by asphyxiation than anaesthesia, until the surgery was so full of fumes that Serafino began to wonder if he himself was not in a partial coma.

Instruments were thrown to the floor by the rolling and pitching of the ship—the best of the two scalpels was broken in this way—and had to be resterilised. The steriliser itself boiled over and Renzo, called in to deal with it, took one look at the half amputated leg on the table and collapsed in a heap on the floor. Dr. Sessabandrian kicked him partly under the examination couch, where he lay groaning and vomiting for the rest of the operation. In a sliding, creaking, rolling hell of steam and ether fumes Serafino at last dislocated the crushed joint and started to probe for the great artery. A sharp spurt of dark crimson indicated that he had found it, and, dry-mouthed, with breath suspended, he clamped it, loosened it and held it while Dr. Sessabandrian's agile, blood-slippery brown fingers turned it in upon itself and tied it. There was no real danger of hæmorrhage at present, with the thick tourniquet sunk bluely into Malestroit's thigh, but later, when it was removed, the full pressure of blood driven by the young Belgian's strong heart would pound down that abruptly curtailed tube—and God alone knew what would happen then.

The great tendrons presented a further problem. Did they

contract as they atrophied useless in the thigh? Serafino thought so, the doctor did not. They compromised and left an extra half-inch protruding from what was becoming slowly but recognisably an untidy stump. Another great vein, a smaller one, some muscle tissue which bled with disconcerting freedom, and then the worst seemed over. From the inside of the knee where the skin had been largely undamaged Serafino was able to cut a large flap, and this they brought across the completely severed stump and stitched to the edges of those parts it reached. They sterilised with spirit as much of the shortened leg as possible, and then, with anxiously held breath, loosened the tourniquet. Beads of blood appeared at once between the clumsy stitches at the blue edges of the wound, but they were small and once wiped off, did not return. Very slowly and with long pauses they continued to loosen the tourniquet, and at last, when it was apparent that there was to be no hæmorrhage they padded and bandaged the stump, shot a heavy dose of penicillin into the thigh, and lifted Malestroit—a curiously deformed and misshapen Malestroit—back to the couch.

He should have been on the bridge. All the time he was bending over the operating table a picture of the bridge had imposed itself, ghost-like but insistent, between him and the work he was doing. And though he had resisted stubbornly, tried passionately to concentrate on the half-dozen inches of living flesh and bone before him that vision had returned implacably, continuously, as every increasing pitch and lurch of the deck beneath his feet told of the inevitable return of the cyclonic gale. He had no real right to be down here, shut away in the private world of the surgery, fighting for one man's life, when the lives of so many others demanded his presence on the bridge. As soon as Malestroit had been lowered to the couch and strapped there, he wiped his bloody hands on a towel and went quickly to the door. Then he remembered Dr. Sessabandrian and turned back awkwardly. " Signor—doctor. It is very good—what you have made to do for us. I——"

" No, no—nothing at all." And for the first time since he had known him, Serafino saw an odd look of embarrassment on the dark, narrow, bad-tempered face. Dr. Sessabandrian even tried to smile slightly. He was not used to doing so and it was a peculiar and uncanny grimace. " You did all that was important yourself." He stood at the washbasin, holding to its edge for support with one hand while he ran the water with the other. "For a young man of twenty-six you are not unaccomplished—you know that?"

Once more Serafino was surprised at how much the Sinhalese had found out, but Dr. Sessabandrian went on talking in his odd, sneering voice as the water flowed into the basin and slopped from side to side. "All Europeans seem always to think that persons of colour—of different races—should respect them. How wrong they are! Yet very rarely—very, *very* rarely—one may find a member of the Caucasian race who makes one feel that they are not entirely lacking in virtue."

Without glancing up, the doctor frowned down at the water and Serafino, struggling to translate into Italian, suddenly realised that he had just been paid the greatest compliment that Dr. Sessabandrian had ever paid any European throughout his whole angry life.

2

Back on the bridge once more he found Gino still at the wheel with Gil standing gripping the rail beside him. He gave them a brief glance and then lurched over to the barometer. It was down to 28.53 and a small half-hope that he had been cherishing, a hope that this part of the cyclonic system might prove less furious than that throughout which *San Roque* had already fought her way, died stillborn. They were back in the vortex now, and the uneven shriek of the wind had given place once more to the solid, roaring thunder that at last muted the ears to a deafened silence. The sea was no longer a sullen, oily black as it had been in the centre, but so covered in foam and spray as to appear almost entirely white. Mountainous waves of grey-white snow, with spray ripping in sheets from their crests, tore past *San Roque* on either side like uncertain icebergs. No longer down by the head and with her list either corrected entirely or unnoticeable in the terrific sea, the ship swept on with the storm. And now there was a weird difference in her motion; the short, shaking lift, the groaning stagger and the plunge of last night had given place to a long, rolling, sliding swoop—a vertiginous glissading movement which Serafino imagined must be the same thing, on a gigantic scale, as a surf-rider experienced when shooting down the front of a breaker. Though they were travelling with the storm, they were not yawning or broaching as he had feared they might and the rudder still retained its grip on the water. Yet now and then one felt rather than heard a heavy thud and the deck shivered beneath one's feet, but one saw nothing for it was upon the stern this time that the great blows fell. And the stern, unlike the bow, was not built to withstand a battering of great force for any length of time.

Serafino saw with satisfaction that Gino had rung for full speed on the port screw—it must have been the first independent engine order that he had ever given—so that they were doing all that could be done to keep the stern out of trouble. He moved handhold by handhold over to the wheel and, nudging the cadet to draw his attention, shouted, "All right I'll take over now! You go and get some rest." For a moment he did not think Gino had heard him, and then the boy turned his head and Serafino saw that exhaustion was giving place to fear. Gino's face was grim, the lines about his young mouth were hard and tense, and the dark eyes, circled with weariness, held an uncertain gleam that could easily become a glare of panic in any further emergency. He was holding his fear clutched into him and struggling to keep it under control with all his will-power, but he might not succeed much longer. And it was worse, apparently, than it seemed, for he did not want to leave the wheel; he wanted to stay still, the struggle within him left no strength for purely physical movement. Slowly, carefully, Serafino prised the gripping fingers away from the spokes. For a moment it seemed that Gino would resist—but then he let go abruptly and, anchoring himself at once to the rail Serafino had vacated, stared stiff and unblinking out at the storm.

It had been just two o'clock when Serafino took over the helm. They had been in the cyclone nearly twenty-four hours and they could probably reckon on at least another twenty-four ahead of them. For though *San Roque* had ploughed through the other side of the system almost to the centre in something less than half that time, she had been heading into it rather than running before it. Under the new tactic Serafino had adopted there was no theoretical reason why the ship should not be driven round and round in the huge circular maelstrom indefinitely and without ever emerging again, but in practice the strong centrifugal bias would almost certain eject her at a tangent from the circumference sooner or later—if she had not foundered first.

There was nothing more anyone could do and they stayed there, the three figures on the bridge, gripped motionlessly to the wheel and the rails and staring out with stiff, set faces at the roaring world of wind and sheeting spray and gigantic tossing seas.

At four-thirty the door behind the chart table crashed open and Tino Cavagni staggered across the swooping bridge. He took one scared look at the enormous waves and shouted, "The radio's working again, signore! Signor Brighenti says he has got the emergency set in action."

For a moment Serafino, remembering that slumped, exhausted figure with its head pillowed in the jumbled metallic entrails of the transmitter, stared at him incredulously. But it must be true—Brighenti must have gone back to work and done it somehow, at last. He glanced quickly at Gino; saw the same stiff face, the same half-closed eyes which for a second slid in his direction while the mouth twitched in a small, weak smile. That was no good; one could not entrust the wheel to someone in that state. He jerked his head at Gil. "Will you take her? Keep her like this—see? It doesn't matter if she swings a bit left—but not right. You've got to keep your eyes on the compass all the time."

Gil nodded, taking the wheel with as much nonchalant confidence as if he had been a trained quartermaster; and as the strong, heavy-shouldered figure stepped into his place on the raised wooden grid, Serafino turned quickly to the chart table and pulled a pad of radio forms from a drawer. Now at last, after nearly forty-eight hours of silence, *San Roque* could talk once more to the outside world; she could explain her danger, ask for help and, above all, try to get assistance for six white boats full of frightened people adrift somewhere behind her in the storm.

And that was not all. Far away on the other side of the world a big man would be sitting at his desk in his office in Naples, waiting desperately for news of his ship and his son. For Don Ildefonso would know all about the cyclone by now—it would have been charted and reported by other ships in its vicinity, and Naples, with their knowledge of *San Roque's* position at the time her radio was silenced, would have little doubt that she was in it.

Serafino raised his eyes to the broad back of Gil where he stood gripping the wheel. He would like to tell the Owner just how well both his ship and his son were doing. The grudging admiration he had felt for Gil since this morning had increased continually during the last hours on the bridge while Gil had stood beside him, gazing steadfastly at the terrible seas with no sign of the fear which, as a landsman, he must surely be feeling acutely. But of course he was a Spaniard, and a gaunt, savage courage was inbred in men of his nation; it was their most outstanding, in fact their sole, virtue. None the less, Don Ildefonso must wait. The first call must be one of help for those boats. The radio might not stay in action; this might be only a short and very temporary respite from the deaf-dumb-blindness which had isolated them so long. Bending over the pad, he scribbled, "*To all shipping. Immediate assistance required for six, repeat six, ship's boats fully manned and adrift. . .*"

He estimated their position as closely as he could, knowing well of what little value such a vague assessment would be. Only by the greatest good fortune would the boats be found by another vessel steaming to their rescue on the wildly marginal bearings which were all he could give. Of course, if the boats had met such seas as those through which *San Roque* was swooping and plunging there was no real point in searching for them anyway; but, silently cursing Bressan, he thrust the thought to the back of his mind and scribbled directions to Brighenti at the bottom of the form. "Send at once *and keep on sending.*"

3

The radio functioned for four hours. From half-past four until twenty to nine Brighenti, his legs grappling him to his seat in the reeling radio room, tapped out message after message, and as the tropic night closed down, the world the enviable, calm, safe, hardly imaginable world beyond the thundering circle of the cyclone, learnt for the first time what had happened to *San Roque*.

And messages came in, offers of assistance, information about weather conditions upon every side of the cyclone, information about the cyclone itself, and always demand after demand for *San Roque's* true position. For the ship was tiny, a minute particle of floating matter in comparison with the vast area of the storm in which she was embedded. With visibility reduced to less than forty yards, with fifty foot-high waves topped by another thirty feet of atomised spray rendering radar screens about as useful as a gypsy crystal ball, there was no hope of finding *San Roque* unless she could pin-point her position accurately which with no sun or star to fix upon and with her radio bearings aerial gone, she was quite unable to do. For other ships to plunge voluntarily into the cyclone would in any case be dangerous and undoubtedly damaging, and though there might be captains and crews who would risk their ships and their own lives if there was a real prospect of finding *San Roque* or her boats, they would not make the attempt without accurate directional bearings.

Serafino knew this well enough and so, almost certainly, did Brighenti; but it remained a secret from the rest of those on board to whom, as Serafino guessed, Tino had relayed the news that the radio was once more functioning and that calls for assistance were going out. And as night fell and the barometer sank still lower and *San Roque* continued her twisting, swooping race with the mountainous seas, the passengers would be in need of any sort of comfort, however meagre, that could be given them.

At twenty to nine, when the emergency set failed, Naples had already been put in full possession of the facts. Back there in Naples it was not yet three o'clock—the mid-siesta hour of a hot, late summer afternoon. But to-day they would not be having much of a siesta in the offices of the Flotta Soto on the Via De Pretis, thought Serafino with a certain harsh satisfaction, as, leaving Gil at the wheel, he climbed down, handhold by handhold, from the bridge. Once below decks he made a brief tour of the ship, taking Tino with him to help with jammed doors and hatches and to secure those which had broken loose and were flailing themselves to bits on their hinges. Below decks, *San Roque* re-echoed with the crash of swinging doors and the tinkle of smashed glass and crockery reducing itself to ever smaller fragments.

From the empty vestibule he talked to Aafjes on the phone, operating the switchboard himself. The Chief Engineer's calm, guttural voice explained that everything was still all right in the engine-room. The attitude of Aafjes towards the Chief Officer, an attitude which until the storm had been one of mildly amused indifference, had undergone a great change since the freeing of the port screw. The decision to take the appalling gamble of unbalancing the ship still further in the dead centre of an unpredictable storm had impressed him deeply, and the fact that the gamble had succeeded had done so still more. It had always been a contention of Aafjes that most captains were slightly mad and became madder as time went on. Ciccolanti had demonstrated a more than adequate degree of madness this morning; he was, whatever Semprebon had said to the contrary, of the stuff from which captains were fashioned. "We would like food sent down to us when this can be managed, signore," he remarked at the end of his report.

"But cannot your men eat when they come off watch?" Serafino asked, puzzled.

"Both watches are down here."

"Surely you don't need both watches to keep one turbine in action?"

"No. But they prefer to be on duty."

Serafino shrugged. It was typical of engine-room staff to feel safer in their engine-room, though in fact if the ship foundered they would be trapped down there without any chance of escape at all. But then he himself had always considered engineers to be rather curious people. "Very well. I will see what can be done."

Moving about the ship was becoming more difficult and painful as the storm increased in strength; one staggered at every step and one's body was continually thrown against projecting pieces of ironwork until it seemed a single huge aching bruise. Serafino hurried through the rest of his tour as quickly as possible, his mind set upon returning to the bridge.

Empty corridors; crashing doors. In the first-class saloon the broken piano still gave out its high quick arpeggio when the ship rolled particularly steeply. Countess Zapescu, a bundle of dishevelled black, sat clutching a whining Brown tightly to her; on the floor, against the sides of fixed chairs to which they held firmly, were the children, the two little Sessabandrians wrapped for some occult reason in the Countess's ancient fur coat. They were listening with determined attention to Fiona Malcolm-Bruce reading to them from a big, brightly coloured book. Serafino said, "We have been in radio contact with ships. Soon there will be help. From now it is not long this continues. We are in good safety soon."

No one looked up; the children in particular ignoring him as if he did not exist, while the Chinese girl read on steadily in her lilting, accented English. And his own knowledge of children, based upon his two younger brothers and his sister told him that this was a deliberate strategy, a defensive reaction against fear far more sensible and effective than those produced by most adults. In repudiating him they were excluding also the ship and the storm, so that they might remain shut away in the warm, safe world of the coloured story-book.

In the quarters of the remaining tourist passengers the scene was one of almost complete prostration. The fear and apprehensive anger that had filled these people throughout the previous night had given place, inevitably, to sheer exhaustion. Many had jammed or tied themselves in their bunks, and now they lolled and rolled lifelessly with the ship's motion, uncaring, unthinking, and hardly more than semi-conscious. Something must have gone wrong with the plumbing, or perhaps the lavatories had become blocked with the incessant sea-sickness of so many people, for the long dormitories on "C" deck stank as foully as the ancient prison ships which had once borne convicts to exile in these latitudes.

Serafino repeated his message to the few small groups who seemed in a condition to understand it. "We've been in radio contact with other shipping. Help is coming as fast as possible. The sea will probably die down before morning." But his words were unnecessary; they looked at him out of lustreless, disbelieving eyes and said nothing. But the expressions on their faces spoke for them, said all the things which, largely illiterate and wholly inarticulate as they were, they could not say themselves.

For they had been strained past breaking point; they had broken and were numb. Months—perhaps years—ago the idea of emigration had come to them and someone had gone first to find out and then there had been letters, occasional remittances of foreign money and a continual growth of hope. They had talked it over endlessly during the long village evenings, had gone at last to the office in the market town and put down the money. And in due course, after months more of waiting, after the difficulties and suspicions of dealing with countless unintelligible documents, the time of packing and farewells had come and the village had fallen behind them, the last known fields had disappeared round a bend in the road, and all was suddenly quite new and astonishingly intimidating.

The confusion of roaring, stifling Naples, the first sight of this ship, so white and calm and safe; the long voyage, the growing fear of the British migrants, the growing doubt of the new adventure and the growing homesickness as Italy receded farther and farther across the world. And then suddenly, striking so fast that even now they could not fully understand it, the living nightmare of the last twenty-four hours. A great many of them still hardly knew what had happened this morning; very few knew the real reason for the disaster which had struck the seemingly so secure ship; none knew anything of the cyclonic system, and all had given up hope of survival. The whole thing had been a terrible mistake. They should never have left home—the village the small church, the well-known fields—for by doing so they had displeased God and now he would destroy them.

Seeing that his announcement met with total indifference Serafino turned, shrugging, to Tino. "*Alora*—I can do no good here. Let's go." And leaving the tourist decks, he felt a relief that was not entirely due to passing out of the sour stench of the dormitories but also to the knowledge that the condition of all the passengers aboard incapacitated them from any further riots or stampedes such as those which this morning had preceded the launching of the boats. And at the bottom of his mind he felt a new contempt for these people—for them as opposed to himself or Gil, for instance—which had never been there before.

He called briefly at the sick bay before going back to the bridge. Malestroit had been moved in there and now lay in the bunk opposite Ettore, while Renzo sat in a chair between them steadying each with an outstretched arm against the chaotic motion of the ship. Malestroit was deep in a drug-induced sleep, his flushed face swollen and puffy and glistening with sweat under the glare of the bare electric globe behind its wire grill. Serafino leant over Renzo and, steadying himself against the iron bunk, lifted Malestroit's right wrist and fumbled to find the pulse. The beat seemed very fast, the flesh burning hot. That could mean the commencement of septicaemia. They had done all they could, he and Sessabandrian, to keep the operation as sterile as possible, but neither could work in rubber gloves: Serafino had tried and failed while Sessabandrian had torn his off furiously when his slippery fingers dropped a clamp into the wound. Well a few hours would tell them the worst, and anyway there was nothing to be done now; there had been only one phial of penicillin in *San Roque's* surgery and they had used that.

Serafino laid down Malestroit's hot, limp wrist and turned to Ettore. "How are you?" But there was no answer and he saw that Ettore was barely conscious, his small, grey ıonkey face contorted and sobbing with pain. The plunging f the ship was jarring his broken bones mercilessly, and ven through the cloudy mists of morphine the agony of those rating edges tore at him with red-hot pincers.

It was a greater relief to get out of the sick-bay than it had een even to leave the miasmatic stench of the dormitories.

4

ack on the bridge the barometer was down once more; it as registering 27.94. Serafino stared at it, appalled; he had ever set eyes on such a low reading throughhoout his ten ears at sea, nor could he imagine what such a drop in ressure could indicate—surely the cyclone could not get ıy worse? But it seemed that it could, for though it was uite impossible to see anything outside the bridge and qually impossible to hear anything inside, *San Roque's* vooping motion was growing wilder, she lay over farther hen she rolled and winced and shuddered more often from ıe blows that crashed upon her stern. The storm continued › increase steadily until two in the morning. At two twenty-ve *San Roque,* yawing violently, was struck squarely on ıe starboard beam by a gigantic sea. The force of the blow ammed through the reeling ship like a salvo of shells; hurled Serafino from the wheel and sent him tumbling with il down into the port wing scuppers, while *San Roque* eeled over in a roll which must have outdone even the rrible one of the previous morning. No one ever knew how ır she rolled or why she recovered, for no one saw the inometer. Gino was nearest to it, he was lying spreadeagled n his stomach upon the chart table, gripping adhesively › the edges with hands and feet, but he had been like that ›r a couple of hours without opening his eyes and he did ot open them now, as he slid slowly, head-first, to the eck. Gil and Serafino were grappled together in the port ing scuppers, clinging as tightly and as frantically as ever ıey had during their fights. As *San Roque* lay on her beam ıds, hanging poised between life and death, Gil got an m free and crossed himself, and for the first and only time erafino saw a quick flame of fear in the dark, slightly p-tilted Spanish eyes.

Three seconds later they were up once more in a twisting, vooping ascent that put the ship miraculously back on an even keel. But as they both clambered dazedly to thei feet, Serafino's instinctive sailor's sixth sense told him tha something was wrong; something had given way somewhere He signed to Gil to take the wheel and glanced quickly roun the bridge, but there was nothing to help him deduce wha was wrong. Over the floor Gino, eyes still tight shut crawled on hands and knees to the companionway leading t the captain's quarters and disappeared down it. Serafin made no effort to stop him. Gino had done very well fo a boy of his age up to the previous afternoon, and no on had the right to expect more of him. To-morrow he woul be all right—if to-morrow ever came for any of them

Struggling out on to the starboard bridge wing the gal blew his eye shut and ripped his already torn shirt int tatters. And they were going *with* the wind and under th full power of one engine! As he crawled breathlessly back int shelter, he wondered what their speed could possibly b with a hurricane like this one thrusting them on. Yet th storm was travelling faster than they now; the rudder wa largely useless and the ship was perpetually yawing an showing every inclination to broach-to. It only needed a uneven gust in the gale combined with a trick of the wave to have *San Roque* wallowing helplessly broadside in th troughs once more. The only wonder was that it had no happened yet.

5

Gino had retired mentally about as far as he could durin the past ten hours, through the real retreat had only take place in the last two. Before that, he had been going bac —going inwards into himself—only very slowly and reluc tantly, step by unwilling step. It had all started when he ha been put at the wheel during the return of the storm When Ciccolanti had actually left him there at the helm in charge of *San Roque,* he had at first been intensely please —not proud or flattered, because he was well aware tha Ciccolanti had nobody else to entrust with the helm, bu pleased, none the less: it was interesting to have the shi really in his hands.

Because he had been standing deck watches ever since the left Colombo, he had been in nominal control of the shi for several hours each day, but it had been much too nomina

) be interesting, for Petelli had generally been with him and e had known that in an emergency both the helmsman and ie telegraphist would have turned for orders to the *Capitan 'armi* rather than to himself—would, in fact, have disregarded im.

Now it was different, he really *was* in charge of *San Roque.* ut it would have been pleasanter to have commanded her calmer weather; in rising seas it was not really a suitable osition for someone as inexperienced as himself. He had iddenly realised that if he made a wrong move he could quite isily bring about his own death. It was a sobering thought, id as the waves had started to buffet *San Roque* on her ern and port quarter, he had begun to wince at the blows as iough they were delivered upon his own body. And, of ourse, in a way they were; anything that hurt the ship hurt m by further endangering his life.

It had been lonely on the bridge. Gil Sotomayor had mained silently with him for a little and had then gone own to the Captain's quarters for about twenty minutes efore returning. Those twenty minutes had been the longest ino had ever spent in his life. The storm was rapidly creasing once more; the waves rearing up, huge and ightful, tore on abreast of the still listing ship, and when *n Roque* mounted a huge sea and skidded down its back a sheet of foam Gino had felt physically sick with fear. a quick panic he had rung down for full speed, but ough he had acted perfectly correctly, the consequences had iturally been a heightening and speeding-up of the swooping, ller-coaster motion.

Isolated up here by himself, dry-mouthed and trembling, had realised for the first time how horrible the sea looked, rrible and menacing and unspeakably evil: he had not been le to imagine why he had ever liked it. During the first irt of the storm he had been quite happy—frightened casionally, as at the terrible roll at dawn, but with an cited and not altogether unpleasurable fear—for his life d been in other hands then, in the hands of the Chief fficer, with Bressan and Malestroit and Petelli to help him. ow that it rested bleakly in his own, his fear was not at all easant; it was black and cold and altogether horrible.

He began to try to keep his eyes steadily on the compass, ly lifting them from time to time to stare past the boards the broken window at the plunging bow. The compass as small and calm and exact. How safe it looked behind its thick glass. If one was a beetle or a spider and was shut away in sealed security under that glass, how safe one would feel. Or better still, if one was something inanimate that could not feel at all, like the spokes under his hands. He had gripped them hard, trying to feel part of them, solid, uncaring and indifferent to all outside events.

And later, when Ciccolanti had come back, he had shifted his grip to the wooden rail with an angry, painful effort, for he needed all his time and concentration to hold back those dark clouds of panic which threatened every minute to descend upon him and envelop him in their deadly, choking fog. His body too was somehow ceasing to be *him*, as it had been for the last seventeen years, and becoming merely an extension of himself—the real self, the genuine Gino being within. He felt a little better like that, and only hoped that people would leave him alone and not call him fully back into the castle of his body, within which he had retracted like a snail within its shell. But as time passed he began to fear that they might do this—people always did disturb one in his experience. He was shut up in his body quite securely, but it would be better if he took it away and put it down somewhere where it would not attract too much notice.

It was then that he had found himself lying on the chart table. That was much better. It was hard and solid and he could fix his body firmly there and retire and wait. He retired into his head, became very small and compact and wandered about in the back of his mind, closing doors and clamping hatches. When he found that he was on the floor it was not at first easy, so small was he and so far away, to start the engine of his body and get it moving; he felt as if he was perched in the driving cabin of some colossal earth-moving machine. He decided to take it downstairs and garage it in a more permanent position before retiring once more to the tiny attic somewhere safe at the centre of his head.

6

At four o'clock Countess Zapescu decided that she must try to get to her cabin unaided. It was no use hoping that anyone would come back to the saloon now, and anyway she wanted to feed Brown. She still felt sick and dizzy and unreal —at sixty-nine one should not be pitched from one's chair nd thrown, with four screaming children and a mass of roken furniture, from one side of a room to the other —as well as bitterly resentful. It was true that, with the ustralian schoolmistress gone, she was now the only adult irst-class passenger who did not suffer from sea-sickness, nd because of this she had tacitly agreed to keep an eye on he children whose parents could no longer stand the motion f the ship. It was true, also, that they had not specifically equested this service of her, but when Mr. Malcolm-Bruce ad staggered to his cabin six hours ago and had shortly been ollowed by a putty-faced Dr. Sessabandrian, it was obvious hat they intended to leave her in charge of their children indefinitely.

And then—when suddenly the ship had seemed to turn ight over, when everything which had been flung to starboard yesterday morning was hurled to port, when the aloon had been full of somersaulting furniture and tumbling odies and she had been thrown from her chair and Brown rom her arms—what had happened? Both the Malcolm-Bruces and Dr. Sessabandrian, all miraculously recovered rom their sickness, had rushed in, shouting and yelling for heir children like mad things. Had they taken any notice f her, lying battered and groaning under a broken table nd half the piano? Not the slightest! It had been "Ian! iona! Are you all right? My God! Are you hurt? re you quite all right?" . . . "Edwin! You and your rother—where *is* your brother? Ah, there! Yes! You re not damaged in any way? You are certain of this? here, there! Do not weep, then. It is all right now. I, our father, promise it!"

But of course the children had not been damaged. They had een frightened, naturally, but their light, rubbery little bodies ad merely been bounced across the floor as harmlessly s in any of the fun-fair machines on the Prater. It was *she* ho had been hurt, most painfully hurt all over—she and oor Brown, one of whose paws had been crushed by a hair leg and who was screaming with pain. Yet had hose people come to her help? Not for many minutes; ot until they had felt their children all over and kissed hem and hugged them and wiped their eyes. Then, and nly then, had they lifted the piano and helped her up nd found a broken chair for her to sit in. And soon after hat they had gone to their cabins with their children and ithout waiting to help her find her bag or her fur coat or doing anything for Brown. Well, there it was. That wa what happened to you when you were old and ugly and poo

For more than an hour she had sat, waiting for someone t come back and help her to her cabin, moaning softly an holding Brown's little paw in a handkerchief until slowl the old dog's whimpering had died down to a gentle whir and he had ceased to shiver in her arms. It was then that sh remembered the big can of jellied tongue which the mes boy, Tino, had given her yesterday. For when she ha bought her passage and Brown's the Line had undertake to feed them both, and though, since the storm, she herse had not felt like eating, she had determined that Brown wa not to be cheated out of his food. She had demanded som thing for him and the boy had gone away and come bac beaming with the canned tongue.

She had been delighted. Brown had never had such luxury in his life and never would again—he must ha every scrap; and for fear of the ravenous children, sh had hidden the can in her cabin. Brown was old no and even if this wretched ship did not sink, he could not, the course of nature, be expected to live much longe But his life had been a happy one. She had been very po throughout it all and she had not been able to give hi the same delicacies as his mother, Picture, or any of h earlier dogs had enjoyed, but as he had not known abo them, presumably he had not minded.

For twelve years he had been all she cared about, trotti after her from boarding-house to pension to cheap re dential hotel, eating what he was given—scraps of th lodgers' dinner here, left-overs from the kitchen ther cold potatoes, fish heads, cabbage stalks and cheese rinds. H had flourished on it from puppyhood, but it had alwa been a sorrow to her to know that she could not afford th proper meals of beef and liver upon which richer owne could feed their dogs. For years Brown's happiness had be the most important thing in a life which, but for him, wou have been nearly meaningless. And as he grew older an lost the desire for walks and barking scuffles after imagina rabbits in the Parc Rousseau, food became the only thi which gave him true pleasure—food and wheezing blissful before a gas-fire in winter or lying upside down in a pat of sunlight by the window during summer.

And now what could be a better consolation for what ha happened to him than a second large dinner? But she wou have to make her own way to her cabin without help. The Countess collected her things, put her bag, which contained her passport, into one of the large pockets of her coat, wrapped Brown in the coat itself and tried to stand. But either she was still too weak after her fall or the ship's motion made standing impossible, for she fell back at once into her chair. Very well then, she would go on all-fours —fortunately her cabin was the first one outside the saloon door so that it was only a question of crawling across the carpet and dragging Brown with her. The thought of the tongue and of Brown's delight spurred her on, and within three minutes she was at her cabin doorway.

And there, face down on the bunk, she found Gino. He lay gripping the wooden sides and trembling in long, shivering spasms which shook his entire frame as though with extreme cold. For a long moment the old woman, balancing herself on hands and knees in the frame of the doorway, stared at him with a surprise which gradually turned to dread. Had he come down here to eat Brown't food? She lunged forward and pulled open the locker under the washbasin, but everything was as she had last left it; the big can of meat untouched beside Brown's plate and the knife she used for cutting up his food. She took them out and the old dog gave a short, wheezing bark of anticipatory pleasure. Once Brown was eating contentedly, she turned once more to the figure on the bunk. What was wrong with the boy? She asked, in the guttural Italian that she was quite capable of speaking when she wished, "What is it, *giovanotto*? Are you ill?" But there was no response; no sign that he had even heard. And then a picture from long ago slid into the spotlight of her memory. A grey autumn afternoon; a young man in the field uniform of the Imperial Austrian Artillery lying face down on a sofa in one of the tall, many-windowed rooms of the Reichenbachs' big town house; Dorothea's tearful face turned to the doorway. "Don't come in. You can't do anything. He's been like this all day!" It had been her youngest brother, Eugen, lying there. He had only been at the front two months, but it had been too much for him and the very thought of going back had thrown him into just this state of paralysed fear.

Absently the Countess pulled herself up into the armchair beside the bunk and, putting out a claw-like hand, touched the bronzed skin below the short sleeve of the dirty shirt. Gino shivered convulsively and shrank away, but she went on stroking his arm, pleased somehow to have him here, pleased with that odd, half-malicious, half-pitying pleasure which the old feel for the young when they are ill or hurt. She had not touched a human being like this for more years than she could remember; probably not since poor Franz was a child—so long ago, so long ago. Her thin, withered old fingers moved lightly across the boy's smooth, firm flesh, while her mind, drifting away from the creaking, lurching cabin, slid back into the past, and slowly the long, spasmodic shivering ceased, the taut muscles relaxed and Gino slept.

XXI

Dawn—a second dawn in which a thundering blackness gave way to a roaring, almost equally opaque whiteness. They had been in this storm for ever and the time before the storm was only a dream, a tiny circle of light at the end of an inverted telescope, impossibly remote and irrelevant. And the future? With a light-headedness born of forty-eight exhausting hours without sleep, Serafino had a nightmare vision of eternity as an endless pitching and plunging onwards towards a hopelessly impossible goal in a hell of screaming wind and sheeting spray. For at last the dark doubts and forebodings which had taken firm lodgement within him since his tenth year, shadowing his life, setting him apart, a scapegoat for the guilt of a sadistic God, were becoming true—as he had always known that they would.

He shook his head, which felt swollen and hollow, a booming cave within which circular winds roared drowning his thoughts, and glanced at Gil standing beside him, soaked like himself by the thin sprays of brine which hissed between the edges of the boarded window. Gil's face was bruised and puffy, his heavy jaws black with stubble, his eyes narrowed and bloodshot. They had been together on this bridge for the last twelve hours, and since the terrible roll at half-past two they had not shifted from their respective places but stayed, gripping wheel or rail, swaying with aching muscles to every plunge and roll of the lurching bridge.

San Roque's motion was slower now, she staggered more often on the crests, plunged more deeply, rose more wearily. As the grey-white light increased, Serafino tried once more to get a sight of the ship from the port wing. Gil took the wheel mechanically at his nod, and he staggered slowly out to the projecting, uncovered end of the bridge. So strong had the wind become that it threw him over the forward rail, bending him almost double until he had to fight with all his strength to stand upright once more. Then, holding on to the port alidade for support, he saw with a leaden sinking of his heart that the foredeck hatch cover had gone—doubled awning-canvas, planks, chocks, ropes, all had disappeared without trace, leaving only the bare iron combing, an empty frame round a hollow square of blackness. Though they were still driving on before the storm, the waves were breaking at angles which every few seconds brought sheets of solid spray diagonally across the foredeck. It was impossible to guess what weight of water went down the open hatch each time this happened—probably not very much, for the velocity of its flight was too great to allow of a heavy fall—but it was happening all the time and faster than the pumps would be able to deal with it. Minute by minute *San Roque* was very slowly but surely filling by the head once more.

And this time there was nothing to be done. There was no possibility of closing the hatch because there were neither the materials to do so nor the men to use them—and in any case it would have been suicidal to venture down on to that exposed foredeck in the present state of the storm. He turned and started to struggle back into shelter, but before he did so he cast one rapid glance astern. The wind blew his eyes shut almost immediately he turned his head, but in that second he saw that the ruin of the funnel had gone; it must have occurred at the time of the great roll last night when he had known with a sudden instinctive certainty that something had given way somewhere.

An hour later Aafjes rang the bridge to say that water was coming into the engine-room—he thought from somewhere in the stern. It was not rising fast but was increasing steadily, and though all the pumps were working at full power, they did not seem to be making much impression. Serafino's guess that the pumps were already overburdened by the amount of water flooding through the foredeck hatch was thus confirmed, but he made no mention of it to Aafjes. Instead he asked, "All the auxiliary pumps are working, I suppose?"

"Of course, Signor Ciccolanti." Aafjes sounded slightly offended and Serafino's cracked lips twisted into a painful smile. "Well then, there is nothing more we can do. Let me know how it is in half an hour." For everything depended on time now, and on less of it than he had thought. Driving on before the storm and with her pumps working to capacity, it would have taken *San Roque* many hours to fill by the head through the fore-deck hatch. But if the water flooding into the engine-room from the stern continued to rise, as it must in the circumstances, it would not be long before it reached the level of the fire-room doors and extinguished the oil furnaces. Then the needles on all the pressure gauges would fall back, the pumps would chug to a stop, the starboard turbine whine down to silence, *San Roque* would stagger, fall off into the troughs of the great waves—and that would be the end.

And now the knowledge that he could do no more, that everything was out of his hands, came as a dark, sombre relief. In a few hours everything would be solved one way or the other without his intervention. In a few hours. . . . Then Gil's hand was gripping his arm and Gil's voice, higher and sharper than he had ever heard it, shouted, "Look!" Following Gil's pointing finger, he stared out across the starboard wing and caught a fleeting glimpse of something tumbling on a huge sea, something that lifted a white whale-back from the sheeting spray and on one end of which he saw an inverted "No. 7." Then it tumbled over once more and was lost in a mass of foam.

So it had happened, as it was bound to do. No boats, however new or seaworthy, could survive a cyclone. Unsinkable in theory, they were also unsinkable in practice; the long buoyancy tanks under the thwarts would keep them afloat but would not prevent them capsizing and rolling over and over interminably. Had Number 7 followed them and caught up with them? Or had it been flung erratically through the great swaying circle of the vortex from some other part of the storm? Either notion seemed impossible and he shook his head dizzily. The complexities of this cyclone were too much for him. And who knew but that somewhere behind *San Roque*, somewhere back in the great tossing wastes of the storm, five other white boats might be tumbling and rolling emptily in the waves, driving on after the ship as if impelled by some ghoulish affection or by the spirits of the drowned.

2

An hour—two hours. Water was gaining more rapidly below, and at his last report Aafjes' voice had lost its habitual calm and sounded a note of hollow despair; it could not be long now before the first furnace blew back and went out.

The eight-day chronometer clamped in its brass case to the bulkhead behind the chart table was still unharmed when so much else on the bridge had been broken. Decorously, exactly, it counted off the minutes, and would go on doing so when the pitching roll among the mists of whistling spray gave place to a low, slanting glide into the ever-darkening green depths, until at last the growing pressure halted the hair-springs, and time, which had no meaning in the profound perpetual night of the ocean bed, ceased for ever.

When that happened he would be up here with Gil as he had been for—how long? An eternity it seemed now. Would they, in those last dreadful seconds, grapple themselves to each other in the ultimate agony of death as they had done in life? Yet he would have preferred to die by himself. The oddly un-Italian solitariness of a nature which, even in overcrowded Naples, maintained a certain aloof isolation made him wish to finish his life as he had lived it—in a stubborn singleness of spirit, and alone. For death was not, perhaps, so dreadful, after all; at its approach he felt the heavy burdens of the past begin to slide from his shoulders. He had lived his short life out, done his work, and now he would have rest—if there was rest. And if his life had been one of struggle it had at least given him the sea.

There were no traditions of seafaring in his family, nor had there been any early predilection on his part. His father had come home one evening and explained that there was an opening in a small freighter Line for a cadet—and next day he had applied and, in due course, been accepted. He had gone to sea soberly, seriously, at sixteen, in just the same matter-of-fact way in which he would have entered a factory as an apprentice or an office as a junior clerk—and he had found a totally new world, an ordered, rather complex, very un-Neapolitan world in which winds and stars, ocean currents, magnetic bearings and other satisfactorily elemental things took their large and proper place.

The sea life had suited the streak of slightly bitter monasticism in his character, and it had done more than that:

it had successfully insulated him from Naples. Without it, he would have become a Neapolitan like the rest of his family; he could never have withstood the fierce and constant pressures of that most unique and intense of Mediterranean cities. He would have been trapped—not merely for a few days between voyages, but for ever—in the blind groove of earning and spending with all its frustrating complexities of debts and time-payments, insurance and taxation. Probably, too, he would have been married by now: the entire life-pattern of south Italy swung like a mad compass needle around sex, while the rigid morals of the south equated it with marriage—and supporting a wife and two or three children in some poor apartment in another Vic' Re Galantuomo. Caught, caged, held in the city; by day the overalls of the factory worker or the cheap suit of the clerk; by night the hot, panting routine of the ornate double bed where the weary process recommenced—cycle after cycle of cornered, claustrophobic lives.

But it had not been like that. He had never become a Neapolitan and had foiled the city's attempts to grasp him. Yet though he had realised, even after his first voyage as a cadet, that he was happier on board ship than he had ever been before, it was only now that he fully understood how much his sailor's life had meant to him. And suddenly he knew that he regretted nothing of what had happened and that he was not even really frightened of what was to come. Drowning was the end to which he was properly destined: his bones would never lie in churchyard or ossuary, but in the vast, swaying vault of the great oceans, above which his soul would float endlessly, effortlessly, on the sleeping wings of the wandering albatross.

And that faceless, silent enemy of all his days whom he had known as God until he was ten and afterwards as Fate—that invisible, all-powerful tormentor whom he thought of as always waiting for him in dark corners, always hidden just over the calm edge of the horizon—that foe was now powerless to hurt him further. At this knowledge the heaviest of all the loads he had borne so long slipped from him, and he was free at last. Standing gripped to the wheel, soaked with spray, filthy with oil and dirt and Malestroit's blood, with every weary muscle aching throughout his exhausted body, he began to laugh. His dirty face broke into a slow grin, his cracked, dry lips splitting and bleeding, and he laughed silently in the way Onestinghel had been used to laugh.

And then, with a long roaring whistle, a distant howling vhich rose rapidly to a shrieking crescendo, a great gust hit he ship, heeling her over until the water ran up the foredeck, ıp to the iron combing of the open hatch and over into he great square hole like a green waterfall. *San Roque* huddered and rose again, and as she did so Serafino left he wheel once more to Gil and stumbled out on to the star- oard wing to glare red-eyed through the driving spray, and ıe was no longer laughing. For that gust had hit them on the ort bow, while for the last twenty-four hours the gale had hundered down on them unchangingly from the starboard uarter. It could mean—it *must* mean—that at last they were oming out into the area of uncertain, chaotic bursts of wind n the periphery of the cyclone. He staggered back into the ridge and over to the barometer. It had risen to 28.82 nd was still rising. They were coming out.

3

nd now hope, awakening as painfully as the resensitising of numbed limb, dragged him back from the cloudy, exalted esignation in which the last hour had been spent. He must ight for his life now; he must anticipate these gusts as far s he was able and swing the ship's bow to meet them. Iere came another—this time from starboard. He could ear the high, screaming note and see the tunnel in the pray. Pushing Gil aside, he swung the wheel; but he was oo late and the squall struck *San Roque* directly upon the tarboard beam, heeling her over to 40° and flooding another reat wave down the open hatch. He must become quicker han that or they would not last forty minutes; they would o down at the edge of the cyclone within a few miles—an our or so—of safety.

At such a thought the prospect of death which he had egarded only a few minutes before with something more than esignation, with something very like pleasure, filled him vith fierce revulsion. The instinctive desire to live flooded ack, doubly strong for its hour of banishment, and every ıuscle in his overstrained body seemed hotly renewed with trength, every nerve vibrant with feeling. No longer was ıe sea anything but his mortal enemy, the albatross nothing ut a bleak symbol of despair blown for ever round the lobe over the wastes of tossing waters. Instead, it was the ship beneath his feet, the ship for which he now felt a passionate possessive affection, that seemed to lend him something of its own will to survival. He had been sent to *San Roque* as a temporary replacement; sent reluctantly by an employer who thought him too young. With still more reluctance he had been appointed temporary master on the death of her captain and reluctantly he had taken command. But, once taken, he had held it, and not even a mutiny and the desertion of half of his crew and passengers had been able to prise it from his grasp. And now his whole being was concentrated into one furious resolve: not to allow the ship to founder at this ultimate hour and after all that she had been through. It seemed to him that the very intensity of his will would buoy her up and bring her out of this last agony alive. *San Roque, Protector of Earthquakes keep us afloat. Still the sea, shepherd-saint of Tuscany, so that this ship named for you may limp home at last* He had not prayed for so many years that the saints, those familiar and esoteric confidential friends of all Italian childhood, must have forgotten him long ago—but perhaps they never forgot anyone.

For half an hour he struggled at the wheel with Gil beside him. But *San Roque* was heavy now with the weight of shipped water and she answered only slowly and sluggishly to the helm. After thirty minutes Serafino realised that all they were doing was insufficient in itself to save the ship. For they were close to the cyclone's edge and the gusts came at them with the force of dynamite charges and from all directions, while at least one in every four or five heeled them over far enough to send a great wave, ton after ton of solid green water, roaring down that open square deck below them. And every time *San Roque* rose, she rose more slowly, every sea that flooded into her lowered her still more deeply in the water and made her more vulnerable to the next. At three forty-five the telephone on the bridge buzzed shrilly and Aafjes reported that the rising water in the fire-room had just extinguished the first furnace. They had clamped the fire-room door and rigged some sort of auxiliary hand pump but it was not keeping pace.

" Well, for God's sake use something else!" Serafino's voice was a hoarse scream. " We're coming out, Aafjes! You've got to keep up pressure on that turbine—you've *got* to! I don't care *how* you keep the water down—even if your men have to drink it or carry it upstairs in buckets and thro it out of the scuttles! If you give me engine power for another couple of hours we'll be all right. If not, we'll go down in twenty minutes!"

He slammed down the phone and turned back to the bridge windows, thrusting a hand distractedly through his matted hair. That hatch *must* be closed. He looked down at the staggering foredeck, swept bare of every object save the twisted base plates of the two hydrocranes. It might just be possible to work down there now, for short periods between the gusts. There would be every chance of being swept overboard, but with a couple of lifelines rigged fore and aft, a gang of resolute and experienced deck hands might manage to cover the hatch with strong timbers and a heavy tarpaulin and batten it tightly with chocks. He had a quick vision of the hatch secured firmly with stout beams under stiff new canvas, and the knowledge that he did not possess these things, let alone the men to use them, was a knife twisted in his heart, a pain of the sort he had known only once before in his life—the time he held *San Roque* " in irons " in Colombo roads.

But there must be something, somewhere on the ship. Wood.

Most of *San Roque's* decks were iron and all the floors in her passenger accommodation were covered with thick, durable rubber composition, but somewhere, surely, there was wood. Yes—down in " E " deck, where the service staff had their quarters, the corridor floors were of plain wooden planking. Those planks might be prised up and cut to the length of the hatch. Then covering, for without some heavy, woven material to hold them in place the planks would be useless. Well . . . there was the first-class saloon carpet, that was the biggest piece of fabric in the ship. It would become waterlogged immediately; water would drip through it in rivulets and it would not last long—but it would not have to. Chocks? Any of the thicker table-tops would make them. Men, then—to do the work. It would have to be the engine-room personnel. The great division, the traditional separation between the deck and the engine-room was ingrained in Serafino's mind that for a moment he wondered whether the engineers would consent to the astonishing suggestion that they should actually work on deck—but of course they would, for they would be saving their own lives.

It was at this point that Gino clambered up the stairs and came on to the bridge. He had slept for over ten hours, face down on the Countess's bunk, and had awakened to the sight of the Countess asleep in the chair beside him with Brown cradled, distended and snoring, in her arms.

He had jumped up in the acutest embarrassment. What in God's name was he doing here, asleep in a passenger's cabin? He could remember nothing of how he had got there or why. The ship was still in the storm, her motion was unpleasantly heavy and sluggish, and even his short two years at sea were enough to indicate the reason. He must go back to the bridge at once. He was about to slide out of the cabin without disturbing the old woman or her dog when he noticed a large can of meat standing in the circular metal clip that was meant for the water carafe. At the sight his stomach tightened; he could not remember when he had last eaten but it seemed days ago. There was only about a quarter of the original contents left in the can, but he quickly scooped it all out and, bolting it in great mouthfuls, made for the bridge.

At the sight of Gino coming out on to the bridge, munching and smiling a little guiltily, Serafino felt a glow of pleasure. Now there would be two deck officers to deal with the collection of materials and the attempts to cover the hatch. He left the wheel to Gil, grasped the cadet's shoulders and thrust him before an unbroken bridge window as *San Roque* heeled before a blast of wind and another few tons of water poured into her hold. "Look—see that?"

"The *boccaporto?*" said Gino stupidly, his brain not yet quite clear of the mists of sleep.

"It's got to be covered. I'm going to get the engineers on to it, but we'll have to supervise them—you and I. Now listen. . . ."

4

It took nearly two hours when it should have been possible to do it in half that time. But there were continual and exasperating snags to be overcome. The planks in the "E" deck corridors were not nailed to their joists, as might have been expected in a cut-price ship of the Flotta Soto, but screwed down carefully and tightly with brass screws, each of which had to be separately extracted by hand, while the two great rolls had so bent and wrenched the clips that had held the first-class saloon furniture to the floor that the legs of several chairs and tables had to be cut away with hacksaws before the carpet could be taken up. But at last, sweating, shouting, running from deck to deck, their bruised bodies continually thrown against doors and bulkheads, Serafino, the cadet and six boiler-suited engineers collected the materials together and carried them forward.

Even so, the covering of the hatch itself could hardly have been accomplished if the gale had not already been moderating or if *San Roque* had not take so much water that her reaction to even the most explosive gust was a heavy, slow, groaning heave rather than the steep, heeling roll of the earlier part of the storm. But it was hard and very dangerous work. Despite the lifelines, there was an ever-present possibility that the dripping, overalled men, clinging and clambering round the combing, might be swept helplessly overboard by the walls of water which every few minutes raced across the foredeck.

Yet in the end it was done, and at the cost of only one broken limb—that of an engineer flung down the hold into the swirl and plunge of water below and three-quarters drowned by the wave that crashed down with him. Then the newly-cut chocks were driven in, and the next wave to break across the foredeck hit the carpet-covered hatch with a dull boom and poured in floods of foam over the starboard gunwale. Climbing, sodden and weak with exhaustion, back to the bridge, Serafino was greeted by Gil with that peculiar grin which held both mockery and knowledge, a complicity of understanding at once intimate and sardonic. "Look!" Far out across the heaving sea, still full of racing, white-capped waves but clear at last of driven spray, it was possible to see the long line of the horizon. A break in the storm had opened up a livid gash in the iron-grey clouds, from which a fan of gold light radiated across the sky and glittered on the great backs of the waves. Hope breaking through despair; life gleaming, beckoning, through the darkness of death. They were out of the storm at last.

"*Estamos salvados,*" said Gil, and his voice held the same dry yet subtly friendly mockery as the expression on his grimy face. Then he turned back to Gino at the wheel and left Serafino by himself to stand staring out silently as the cloud rift expanded and the golden light, increasing and deepening, crossed the wide wastes of water, turned their tossing crests of spray to dancing rainbows, and at last with soft fingers touched his face.

5

Serafino stayed on the bridge another two hours, most of the time slumped in the swivel chair beside the chart table. He remembered just enough of nautical good manners to phone down to the engine-room and thank Aafjes for the loan of his men and praise their work, then he remained mute and moving only with the decreasing motion of the ship, his dirty, scratched hands resting before him on the table-top. It was only when Gino came behind the table to get his sextant that he looked up. "Can you get a sight, then?" Gino looked at him with eyes at once apologetic and a little fearful. He realised now that he had spent the most critical hours of the storm asleep below decks, and though he could not think why this had been so, he was well aware that he had not behaved entirely as he would have wished. It would have been pleasant to have this denied, but, fearing to have it confirmed, he dared not ask about it. Instead: "There's quite a big patch of clear sky now," he said awkwardly. "I think I can get a fix on a star."

"I'd better do it." Serafino began to rise wearily from the chair, noting for the first time in hours the pain in his lame foot.

"No, no, signore, let me—please let me!" There was such urgency in the cadet's voice that Serafino sank back once more. "All right. Only be careful. I want it exact."

But even so, when Gino had worked out his fix, Serafino went on to the bridge wing and took another. He could not believe that Gino was correct, the storm could not have taken them so far out of their course—it was impossible. But it was not. His fix and Gino's were identical. The storm had taken them over six hundred miles off their course. For the last twenty-four hours they had been driving at their fullest speed before the storm, and how fast the storm itself was moving no one would ever know. Even so . . . He shrugged and leant over the chart that Gino had spread on the table.

And then Tino was on the bridge, looming broadly through the dusk. "The radio is working again, signore. Signor Brighenti says it should stay working now. There's a call coming through from Naples——"

"All right. No—don't go. Wait a minute." With Gino

leaning over his shoulder, illuminating the chart with a flash-light, Serafino slowly moved set-square and dividers, laying off a course for the Australian coast. Then he pulled a radio form from the drawer beside him and laboriously, his hand-writing an almost illegible scrawl, wrote: "*Sotflot Naples. Ship clear of cyclone. Damage mainly superficial. Estimate position*——" Gino pushed the slip of paper before him and slowly, painstakingly, he traced the figures and continued: "*Am proceeding Broome to effect clearance starboard screw and disembark remaining passengers. Request Sydney agent flies Broome immediate. Estimate*——" once more he paused, groping wearily for figures of speed and time—"*make port within thirteen hours. Ciccolanti.*"

XXII

From the still darkness of exhausted sleep he slid reluctantly into a long, swaying, uneven dream, as fitful and flickering as the great seaweeds that seemed to loom darkly around him. For *San Roque* had foundered and lay on her side in the dim stillness of the ocean bed. There had been a moment as the bows slid beneath the furious sea, when sunlight breaking through the flying spray had turned it to an arch of dancing rainbows and he had known with an exultant, unearthly joy that happiness of an incandescent brightness was to be his for ever as soon as he had plunged beneath the huge, sunshot green wave that roared up the deck towards him. He had run to meet it, had hurled himself into its sparkling jade coolness—and at once that assurance of vivid delight and of something still brighter beyond delight had disappeared, and he was sliding into soft, twilit darkness, holding a fading promise.

He wanted desperately to leave his body; if he could but do that he knew he would flash upwards again like a released bubble into the glowing, golden day. But he could not, and darkly, sadly, on the ocean bed he descended from the canted bridge and walked away.

Then the opaque dimness was rain: it was raining gloomily, greyly, in the Vic' Re Galantuomo and the old beggar at the corner thrust out a crutch to trip him and the communist cobbler at No. 2 stared venomously at him, spitting as he passed; even Dr. Gallifuoco turned his back silently, picked up his chicken and went indoors. He came to his own house and tried the door, but it was locked. He pushed at it and very slowly, exerting all his strength, thrust it open—and sun flooded out and the flashing rainbows danced in spray at the end of the passage. But before he could move towards them something pulled him sideways, and he was standing in front of Don Ildefonso and that contemptuous, growling, foreign-accented voice was saying, "If you knew what I think of my junior officers! I take them because no one else wants them—and therefore they're cheap." But the spray rainbows were dancing exultantly in his memory and Don Ildefonso was a windy shadow who could be banished by them at will. He tried to summon them, and the Owner's haughty, bull-like face grew grey and contorted into a mask of sweating pain and became Onestinghel's face and said wearily, impatiently, "Yes, yes—send Tomei to me. You are in command now. Go to the bridge."

He was lying trapped among the rubble of the bombed school, and he was very young again and very vulnerable and worried about his clean shirt. Great stone figures loomed above him in the swirling dust which blotted out the last piece of blue sky in which a fading flicker of rainbow light danced. The figures were talking to him, blaming him for the death of Onestinghel and Bressan and the boy Armando; blaming him in very quiet, reasonable voices which left no doubt in his mind that he was desperately guilty and would never be forgiven. On and on went the soft voices, calmly logical and coldly convincing and utterly damning. He was crying bitterly in the gathering darkness, and the figures were no longer stone but shadowy people moving through the shadows around him—Lannfranc and his wife, Mrs. Cram-batch, the old English colonel and his sister, Miss McKenrick, Hogben. They did not touch him or look at him, though he called to them, his voice tiny in the immensity of the gloom, but each one took from his shoulders a black, amorphous shadow, and laid it upon him, drowning him in a darkness of choking, sterile, ice-cold ether.

He was engulfed in black sorrow and darkness and shame. Everything he had ever done had been wrong and the darkness knew it and abominated it. The darkness jeered at his poverty and at his lame leg and told him that there was nothing more save an endless misery, from which there could never be hope of release. And he knew that this was completely just, and in an agony of guilt and self-abasement he tried to worm his way under the heavy slime of the ocean floor. In that slime, amid bones and filthy, flaccid dead things, Armando's eyeless face approached his own and the mouth snarled open, displaying long, thin, glassy teeth —fish's teeth—between the rotting lips. He screamed and struggled to escape, knowing that he could not, that this was the bottom hell and that he was embedded in it for ever. And as the fish's teeth sank, like poisoned, ice-cold needles, into his shoulder, he awoke.

He lay in bed and his cabin was filled with the soft light of dawn. Gil was sitting on the bunk beside him and Gil's hand was on his shoulder. "Well, well! I came to see how you were. I would have let you sleep longer only you did not look as though you were enjoying yourself."

Serafino groaned and shook his head, heavy with the evil darkness of his dream. He tried to rise, but Gil pushed him back with a hand on his chest. "Wait a minute. Don't you want to hear how we've been getting on without you?"

"What's the time?" It was an effort to speak; his jaws ached and his voice sounded dull and husky.

"A quarter past five." Gil pulled a cigarette case from his pocket. "I and Gino have been taking it in turns upstairs. He's a good boy, Gino." He spoke matter-of-factly, but under his calm voice Serafino sensed a jubilant excitement. "Yes. We sighted the Australian coast half an hour ago. We—wait a moment!" For Serafino had pulled himself up on his pillow and swung his legs out of the bunk.

"I've got to get up to the bridge. We must be quite close by now." The dream was fading rapidly, reality flooding back, and with it happiness and a pleased excitement. He knew very dimly in the back of his mind that somewhere in his dream there had been another, far greater, happiness that had seemed within his reach—how or why he did not know. Still, to be alive and safe was good enough to-day. He was on the floor now, rummaging in a locker for his last clean shirt and trousers. "We might run on a shoal or something. Gino's chart-reading can't be trusted yet. He had no business to have left me asleep like this."

Gil was laughing delightedly, filled with the same joyful, irresponsible relief that was now flooding Serafino. "He told me so. It's my fault. I wanted to be the one to wake you up. I've got something for you—look!"

But Serafino was struggling into his shirt. "In a minut Wait till we're on the bridge." But Gil thrust a radio forr into his hand and, pausing for a second, he gazed down at i It was very short—hardly more than half a dozen word "*To Captain Ciccolanti, San Roque. Warmest congratul tions. Sotomayor.*"

He read it three times, at first incredulously, then wit awed delight. Then he lifted his eyes to Gil. "When—whe did this come?"

Gil's hot, dark, Spanish face was alight with triumphar pleasure. "Two hours ago. We've been in radio conta most of the night. There's a lot of other stuff for yo on the bridge and more coming through. We seem to hav caused a lot of interest in the last few days and I thin we'll be having quite a reception—from the Press, at an rate. But I thought you'd like that one first."

Serafino nodded wordlessly. For no reason that he coul find he felt suddenly embarrassed. The relationship betwee himself and Gil had altered again. Instead of the dismiss he had come over the last few days to take for grante he was being retained and given the highest promotion, an therefore Gil was still the son of his employer—more tha that, of his benefactor. "Your father . . ." he bega awkwardly, but Gil cut him short. "My father has had considerable shock. He has spent a very unpleasant tw days wondering whether he was going to lose his best sh and his only son. What is more, if *San Roque* had foundere I think it would have finished the Flotta Soto for goo Coming on top of the affair of *San Raphael's* boats—I d not think it would have been possible for him to have carrie on. Now that you are his senior captain, I do not mind tellir you that I am not sorry that it has been like that." G lay back on the disordered bunk, smiling and letting th smoke of his cigarette dribble slowly from his nostri "He pushes people around too much, my father. Everyo is frightened of him, of course, and that would be all rig if everyone did not hate him because of it. I think that rather a high price to pay for always getting one's own way He shrugged. "If it had not been for what has happened us, I imagine my father would soon have believed that th very waves obeyed him through fear. They have just demo strated very clearly that they do not. However——" h dark eyes, narrowed against the cigarette smoke, gleamed u at Serafino "—this storm has been of use to both you and me, so——"

"You? How——?"

Gil laughed. "How do you think? I am recalled. I am to fly back to Naples on the first plane I can catch. The Australian exile is terminated before it is begun." He paused, and when he spoke again his voice held a slightly brusque uncertainty. "I told him that I would not do that. He sent me out here—now he can wait until I am ready to return. I said that I would wait until *San Roque* was refitted and come back on her return journey—if her captain agrees." He ground his cigarette carefully in an ashtray, the quick, uncertain grin hovering round the corners of his mouth.

Serafino said slowly, "Her captain would have asked you in any case." It was not true; he would rather that Gil flew back to Naples and left him in complete and undisputed control of his ship, but it must be said, and he knew darkly that in future much that was untrue must be said. He had risen to a position in which diplomatic expediency had an important place—as important, or more so, than skill and technical knowledge and professional ability. But he saw that Gil believed him. Gil's dark eyes shone momentarily with a deep, genuine pleasure and in that moment one door closed in Serafino's mind and another opened.

He smiled at Gil, but behind the smile was a touch of contemptuous envy which he himself hardly noticed, aware only that once again Gil was an important factor in his life, a factor to be taken into account continually if the golden road to success and wealth and power that had suddenly opened out before him was to be successfully trodden. Still smiling, he vowed inwardly that nothing, nothing at all, should be allowed to come between him and the bright promise of that future—nothing and nobody. For the long, bitter fight was over; he had vanquished his fate and was free of it for all time. He was his own master at last.

But Gil was talking again. "Our friend Malestroit is much better this morning. I have just had a look at him. He wants to see you——"

"Yes. Later, if there is time."

"But the other one—the mess-boy—died before dawn."

"Ettore?"

"Yes. You remember that roll—the time the funnel went over the side?" Gil shuddered; he would never forget it himself. "It threw him out of his bunk, and what with all his broken bones . . . He lasted all yesterday and most of last night, but he was unconscious all the time. Anyway, that little black man, Sessabandrian, was with them both all night. He's very upset about Ettore. When I went into the sick-bay I think he had been crying."

2

The sky was aflame with green and silver dawn, the sea a flat, windless plain of liquid glass through which *San Roque* slowly cut her wide furrow. Coming out on to the bridge, Serafino found most of the Malcolm-Bruce family accompanied, as always, by the two small Sessabandrians. Under Gino's supervision Ian Malcolm-Bruce was steering the ship. Suppressing a quick spurt of annoyance, Serafino listened politely to the Chinese millionaire's congratulations and thanks. Ten years of sea training had made it an automatic habit to check the barometer, the ship's course and speed and the log immediately he set foot on the bridge, but he knew now that there were other things of more importance to success than unthinking routine, so he controlled his impatience and accepted the profuse floods of praise and gratitude with the dignified deference due to a man of great wealth who might one day be of assistance to him. He asked after Mrs. Malcolm-Bruce, complimented both parents upon their children, and eased the lot off the bridge with an easy geniality which he had never known he possessed and which would have surprised Onestinghel as much as it would have pleased him. Last to go down the ladder, Mr. Malcolm-Bruce turned and, taking a white envelope from his pocket, pressed it gently into Serafino's hand. " A very small token of my esteem. I hope you will accept it in the spirit in which it is meant." Opening it a minute later on the chart table, Serafino found it contained a cheque for four thousand Australian pounds.

As the ship slowly approached the long, low coastline and the small, white pearling port of Broome came into view, he took the wheel from Gino and sent the boy below to change his clothes. Gino protested mildly; he wanted to appear in all the heroic dirt and glory of his storm-beaten rags. But there was an unusual air of authority about *San Roque's* ıew captain which Gino had not noticed before, so he went .nd did as he was told.

Then Gil, clean and in fresh whites, was back on the ›ridge. " There's something you forgot." He stepped behind he small, erect figure at the wheel and Serafino, feeling two ıard, flat surfaces laid on his shoulders, glanced sideways .nd saw Gil's fingers screwing down the buttons of gleaming, our-barred captain's epaulettes. " Onestinghel's?" he asked, nd a small cold shudder ran through him.

" Yes. He'd have wanted you to have them. He liked 'ou, you know. Keep still a minute."

And Serafino remained still and his shoulders, which had agged for a second, squared again under Gil's hands. They vere dead, so many of them—Onestinghel, Bressan, that boy Armando, Lannfranc, Semprebon, Hogben and all those vho had gone in the boats. Some had been his enemies, had .ated him, distrusted him and even tried to kill him. But ›ne and all they were gone now, and existed only as part ›f his own past, in the same way that his father existed or is dead schoolmates in the broken rubble of sixteen years go. It did not matter; death was not so very important, he .ad learnt that, and those who died dwindled rapidly in the nemories of the living—for they were the past, and only the ›resent and the future with their never-ending vista of posibilities were important.

3

.n hour later Gino, a slender figure in clean whites up in the ›row, raised his hand; two boiler-suited greasers from the ngine-room flung over the handles of their winches and *'an Roque's* bow anchor chains roared through their hawseipes. The long journey was over. From the tropical, palm-inged shore of the old pearling port motor-boats and launches .ying the Southern Cross at their sterns cut quick white ırrows through the glittering water towards the battered, ismasted and funnelless ship which had ridden out a full-scale yclone. Then they were climbing up the rope ladders which eplaced the gangway, ripped off almost unnoticed during the rst part of the storm: the port authorities, ship's agents, ustoms men, and a doctor and three orderlies from the ospital; while below them journalists and photographers, waiting their turn, stood up in the rocking boats to photograph the ship from a dozen different angles.

Once aboard, the harbourmaster and his men glanced round them with shocked wonderment at the twisted rails, the empty, battered davits, and the decks swept clear of all but the heaviest machinery. For the most part they were ex-sailors themselves, and the ship's condition made more obvious to them than to the reporters, now following them up the ladders, the size of the ordeal through which she had passed. Around them a crowd of laughing, weeping foreigners grasped their hands, shouting, gesticulating, pouring out a flood of incomprehensible greetings, demands and questions. With difficulty they pressed through the throng to the foot of the bridge ladder, down which a short, gaunt young man descended to greet them. He saluted briefly and in turn they wrung his hand with all the ardent Australian admiration for physical courage and endurance. "Congratulations, Captain—Captain——?"

"Ciccolanti."

"You've brought your ship through one of the worst cyclones recorded in years, Captain. Did you know that? A great feat of seamanship—you must be a very fine sailor, sir. I am sure that if there is anything we can do——"

"Captain Ciccolanti? I'm Bembrose, sir, from the Sydney office. We've been notified by Naples to take over your passengers and fly them south. With your permission I'll explain matters to them——"

"Captain, I want to make it clear that all the port facilities are at your disposal. There will be no difficulty about your starboard screw; we've got plenty of divers who'll help out—only too pleased to. And if——"

"Excuse me a second, Harbourmaster. Captain, I've had a quick look round your sick-bay. I think we ought to get the thigh fracture and the amputation case ashore. They're both going to be all right, of course, but I must make a careful clinical examination as soon as——"

". . . new crew from Naples in *San Raphael* . . ."

". . . refit in Sydney, I imagine, and that's bound to take time . . ."

". . . manifest and ship's documents—but only when you're quite ready . . ."

". . . or water and supplies . . ."

". . . Naples . . ."

And now the newspapermen were crowding round, brandishing cameras and notebooks, sweating profusely in the blazing tropical sunshine, mopping their crimson faces and waiting impatiently for their turn.

"Captain Ciccolanti, I represent the *Sydney Morning Herald,* Australia's oldest newspaper, as you probably know. On behalf of . . ."

"Captain—one moment, please!"

"Look—hold it like that, Skipper! Fine! And if you'd just shake hands with the harbourmaster again. Thanks. And we'll just have *one* more, if you don't mind. Still a moment! Thank *you*!"

"*Pix,* Australia's illustrated weekly. I'd like——"

"Captain Ciccolanti, I'm from the Melbourne *Age*. If you'd just make a short statement now, and then later, when you come ashore, perhaps——"

"*Time—Life. Time—Life.* Make way, *please*!"

Dazzled, confused by the rapid flow of questions, the continual interruptions, the demands to shake hands with officials, to be photographed by himself, with Gil and Gino, with the Malcolm-Bruces or before a crowd of Italian migrants, Serafino none the less moved carefully, accommodatingly, through all the motions and actions that were required of them. Struggling with his poor English, he made the statements for which he was asked, and when he spoke a sudden quiet fell over the crowded deck. It alarmed him, that respectful silence, but only momentarily, for as he turned to glance up at the bridge where he had fought the long battle with the sea and the wind, the sun caught the new epaulette on his shoulder in a flash of light, reminding him that he was a captain now and that it was only proper that there should be silence on his ship when he spoke. And yet how far away the events of which he told them seemed to be—how remote. And beyond them—remoter still—a tiny speck in the distance, the Vic' Re Galantuomo was almost out of sight. Could the captain who stood here, the hero of the hour, the shipmaster upon his own dear deck, really have set off from that hot slum alley, an unknown officer, less than a month ago? He grinned at the thought, his old, wide, humourless grin—and once more the cameras clicked and whirred.

4

Both Gino and Gil were questioned and photographed, if not with the respect and attention displayed towards the captain, at least with a lively interest. Gil had had this experience before, and recently in the most humiliating and adverse circumstances. He was prejudiced against the Press and his replies were brief and often a little surly. But Gino was as passionately pleased and proud as only his youth made possible. The photographers and reporters treated him with a jocular friendliness more suited to his age and rank than the respectful admiration with which they questioned the captain. How old was he? Seventeen? That cyclone was a pretty big experience for a seventeen-year-old, wasn't it? Had he been frightened? Of course he had, but never mind—who wouldn't have been? Had he got a girl of his own back in Italy? No? Perhaps he'd find an Australian girl—there would be plenty who would be keen enough to meet him. Did he still like the sea? Good-oh! Well, he'd certainly seen the worst it could do. Now, after he'd had another picture taken, how would he like to tell them how it felt to go through one's first big storm? They would help him with his English.

But suddenly a wail of despair cut through the genial flow of questions and the shouts and laughter of the crowded foredeck. Gino raised himself on his toes to peer over the crowd, and then, pushing the journalists aside with hurried excuses, he slid and elbowed his way through the throng to find a distraught Countess Zapescu trying to seize Brown from the arms of two customs officers. "No, no, no!" she was shouting, the tears pouring down her lined, pouched face. "Give back to me! And do not holdt the little foot so—it is hurt! He is not to go, not without I am with him—no, no!"

"*Che cosa fanno?*" Gino was beside her. "Why they take Brown?"

Backing towards the rail, a big, florid, sweating customs officer tried, with an exasperated attempt at kindliness, to explain. "It's regulations, see? This lady's landing here and quarantine regulations say no dogs allowed to land. *I* can't help it. I'm sorry for her—very sorry. I've *told* her so a dozen times. But we *got* to take the dog. If you would explain it to her, young feller, as how it's Australian quarantine regulations. . . ."

Gino said quickly, "I do not think she is understanding. oon you give the dog back—yes? One month—two months —then she receive it one more time?"

"Well——" Embarrassed, the big Australian shook his ead unhappily. "Well no, it's not like that exactly. You ee, it hasn't done its time in Britain—understand? No, of ourse you don't. Wait on a minute." He evaded the Couness's outstretched arms and handed the mildly protesting Brown to his still taller colleague. "There—take the dog, ack. Best put it down below in the boat—in the box aft. Now I'll try an' explain." Mopping his face with a big haki handkerchief he turned patiently again to Gino. "It's ike this, mate. No dog's allowed in Aussie unless he's lone six months' quarantine in Britain first—cop that? Afterwards he has to do another three here—and then he's assed free. You see, we *got* to take special precautions ere owing to wild dogs—dingoes we call them. If *they* once ot infected——"

"Yes, yes. But this dog, it has not been to Britain. We take n board at Napoli. So what——?"

The customs officer shook his head regretfully but his oice was firm. "Sorry, mate, real sorry. We can't do nything else, though."

"You mean——" Gino gazed at him horrified—"you *kill* ?" and received a brief, uncomfortable nod of assent. No, no—not kill!" He grasped the man's arm urgently. uddenly it had become the most important thing in the vorld that Brown should not die. "You do not understand! his lady—she has nothing—only this dog. You cannot . . ." ut they could, he knew they could. From the launch below ame Brown's short, querulous bark, and, his eyes wide with anic apprehension of the old woman's terrible grief, Gino tammered, "Wait! Wait—not yet. I will bring the Capain——" And he thrust back quickly through the jostling rowd to the ring of reporters round Ciccolanti's small, miling figure.

"Signore! Signore—one moment!" He broke with diffiulty through the tight circle of journalists and Serafino turned nd glanced at him irritably. "What is it, Gino? I am busy ith these people. I will attend to everything else later. ut now——"

"It's the dog!" Gino's glance flickered quickly over the nnoyed faces of the interrupted reporters; they were busy nen always in a hurry, they did not like waiting. "It's

Brown. They are taking him away to kill him!" With stam-mering urgency he explained what had happened and saw the Captain's wide golden brows draw together in a frown.

"I see. But, Gino, I can't do anything. It is this country's regulations; you cannot go against those."

"But there *must* be something, Signor Ciccolanti! You don't know what that dog means to her! It will *kill* her, if they destroy it! You could do *something*. I know you could!"

But Serafino had put up with enough. He had been enjoying the admiring comments of the journalists which had grown ever more ardent as he had come to the climax of his story. No one had ever before lavished such praise and respect upon him; it made him feel—he did not know exactly what, but quite different from anything he had felt before. And now young Gino had to come pushing in like that to spoil it. He frowned angrily at the distraught boy, and when he spoke his deep voice held an unaccustomed edge of brusque authority. "Now, for God's sake, control yourself. These people will think that you are hysterical if you go on like that. I have told you there is nothing I can do—that is all there is to it." He turned back to the reporters and they edged in closer towards him, using a hardly discernible expertise, learnt in long years of professional experience, to elbow and nudge the cadet behind them.

And as the ring of bulky backs shut him from the small thin figure with the big, gleaming epaulettes on its shoulders Gino stared at his new captain with a bewildered puzzlement and then, turning away, he blushed deeply as if he had publicly accosted someone whom he believed to be a friend and found that, after all, it was only a stranger.

THE END